(Left to Right- Shri Feroz Abbas Khan, Director, Mughal-e-Azam; Shri Moulik Kotak, Owner-Chitralekha Group; the author- Niraj Srivastava; Shri Amitabh Bachchan, The Iconic Legend and Shri Ashok Kacker, Senior bureaucrat).

Darbar-e-Musannis

The author hails from an illustrious family of doctors (three generations of Ophthalmologists!), but decided to deviate into Management. Insanely passionate about cars and books, he has a formidable personal library of over 15,000 titles. Being a direct descendant of Diwan Rai Gurbuksh Singh, Diwan to the erstwhile Maharaja Chet Singh of Benares, the author revels in the regal and ceremonial melodrama of ancient royal courts.

Niraj has a Master's in Business Administration from MONIRBA, University of Allahabad, as well as a Doctorate in Management from the University of Canterbury. He is also a member of the Royal Society Of Literature, England.

Niraj's debut novel has been celebrated worldwide – He was the Winner at the 5th Annual Beverly Hills Book Awards, USA, and Runner Up at the London Book Festival 2016. Gifted with a vibrant imagination and an unshaken belief in the limitless possibilities of words and colours, he creates warships out of floating pencils and spaceships out of an emperor's turban.

An all India University boxer, accomplished bathroom singer and intrepid yodeler, having business interests in real estate and education, he has recently shifted to Gurgaon and lives with his mother, wife Smita, and children – Devesh and Riticka.

This is his debut novel, where Niraj has given new twists and uncannily plausible turns to the history of the Magnificent Mughals. The ancient walls have indeed spoken to him !

DAGGERS OF TREASON

NIRAJ SRIVASTAVA

Praises

Daggers Of Treason

"This book brings out the grandeur and mystery of the mighty Mughals. An engaging read, this first volume excites the reader's craving for more. The colour, pageantry, intrigue, perversity and evil coalitions, **hidden in forgotten manuscripts of libraries are cleverly intertwined with plausible fiction. A captivating read for history lovers."**

Prof. Rajendra Srivastava, Dean and Novartis Professor of Marketing Strategy and Innovation: Indian School of Business, Hyderabad.

"Daggers Of Treason is an explosive account covering the last years of Akbar's rule, **with the lingering mystery of Anarkali and the treacherous shadows of a royal court. Gripping, turbulent and thrilling, this is historical fiction at its best! A must read!"**

Pramath Raj Sinha, Founder & Managing Director, 9.9 Media and Founding Dean, ISB, Hyderabad.

"Here is an author who delves in the historic and grandiose past of the Mughal era simultaneously teasing our sensory taste buds and stereotyped perceptions of a period when Mughals had laid siege. **With what I have read, I guarantee you that you would not have come across a more well researched book which creatively dives into the whirlpool of the Mughal era shattering historical facts that we took for granted. And, if you thought you knew it all, a definite read is in for you. A historic fiction worth reading again and again!"**

Shail Raghuvanshi, Writer, editor, reviewer. (For newspaper, radio and television).

"This is going to be an epic series (in the true sense of the word!)" Lesley Jones, Freelance editor with major publications, United Kingdom.

Based on the Mughal era in India, **deeply researched, weaving facts and fiction seamlessly and so realistically created** Glimpses of Mughal grandeur, intrigue and seeds of future fratricide/bloodshed. A true-blue historical thriller, where words conjure up images of the most magnificent of the royal courts. **Enthralling, with the mystery of Anarkali and her son. Lost in the shrouds of Time! An extremely interesting and an unputdownable' book.**

Col. Lalit Rai, Vir Chakra, Kargil war hero.

"I have read Daggers Of Treason and found it **very interesting, descriptive and mesmerizing!** The narrative is enticing and gripping and transports you to the Mughal era. **I feel it has great potential in the making of a very interestin and informative historical film."**

Zaheeda, heroine with Dev Anand in epic films 'The Gambler and 'Prem Pujari'.

"Beautiful! I am spellbound; Totally bereft of words...."

Ms. Roshni Rawail, Educator; from an illustrious family of film producers, Mumbai.

"An excellent example of history as fiction for the lay reader. The author's research results in a book that glitters, a fine chandelier illuminating what once was."

Suneel Sinha, New Delhi, Senior Journalist.

"I was enchanted by these poignant and mystical plausible twists of 'Daggers Of Treason'. **The chronicle has genuine historical fervor and charm.** The malleable elegance of 'A Ship Of Many Oars' continues and bolsters Niraj as a brilliant storyteller."

Col. Vikram Shekhawat, Sena Medal. Kargil war hero.

"Once again, the master storyteller, **Dr. Niraj Srivastava, takes us through a journey in time. We arrive five centuries ago, paths through graveyards leading into palaces, commoners, nautch girls, fakirs and princes interwoven as the sinews of the story pulsates with passion and treason.** When a young boy Firdaus addresses the Fakir or the wandering monk as Jahanpanah or the Emperor, one is subtly invited to see an emperor in every Fakir one meets in the streets! In these pages, one may discover oneself amidst the conflicts and dissonance that often comprises life. **Or, one may simply enjoy an intriguing story, brilliantly narrated."**

Pawan Kumar Mishra, International Vedic Astrologer, transpersonal coach and author of *The Living Hanuman.*

"A riveting historical thriller that will keep you on the edge of your seat and stun you with its well documented revelations!"

Suhail Mathur, Bestselling Author & Literary Agent.

"Remarkable (and fascinating at times) history of the Mughals. Brilliant and compulsively readable book. Captivating narrative where the author makes the historical characters come alive."

'Joy' Singh Bana, Jai Vilas, Jaipur.

All illustrations inside are made by Smita Niraj Srivastava

ISBN : 978-81-936662-0-3

Imperial Ink Publishers, Allahabad.

All illustrations are of the artist's imagination.

Marketed and Distributed by Invincible Publishers

Printed in India by Excel Printers Pvt. Ltd

Registered Address: 201A, SAS Tower, Sector 38, Gurgaon-122003

THE CURSE OF THE MUGHAL SERIES

DAGGERS OF TREASON

NIRAJ SRIVASTAVA

Imperial Ink Publishers, Allahabad.

Intesab Wa Tashakkur

Baraiye

Pidar wa Madar

wa Jauzah

wa Pisar wa Deukhtar!

Dedicated with eternal love and gratitude

To

My Father and Mother,

(Late Dr. Devendra Srivastava & Mrs. Pratima Srivastava)

My Wife – Smita

My son Devesh, and my daughter, Riticka

DRAMATIS PERSONAE

From the lost pages of History

<u>**Emperors :**</u>

Jalal Ud Din Mohammed Akbar – 3rd Mughal Emperor; father of Prince Salim (Jahangir). The first of the Grand Moghuls.

Nur Ud Din Mohammed Jahangir Padshah Ghazi – 4th Mughal Emperor. Salim Jahangir. Eldest son of Akbar. Father of Princes Khusrau, Pervez, Khurram, Jahandar and Shehreyar.

Shahab Ud Din Mohammed Shahjahan Padshah Ghazi – Succeeded Emperor Jahangir. Favourite grandson of Emperor Akbar, famously christened 'Khurram' or 'Joy' by him. Builder of the Taj Mahal. Known as the Magnificent Mughal. Father of Princes Dara Shukoh, Shah Shuja, Aurangzeb and prince Murad.

<u>**Royal family :**</u>

Hamida Banu Begum aka Mariam Makani – Queen and Chief Consort of Emperor Humayun; Mother of Emperor Akbar.

Heer Kunwari aka Mariam Uz Zamani – Emperor Akbar's Chief Rajput wife. Mother of emperor Jahangir. Daughter of Rajah Bharmal of Amber. Erroneously referred to as Jodha Bai.

Salima Sultana Begum – Akbar's cousin and later, wife. Widow of Bairam Khan, and step mother of Abdur Rahim Khane Khana.

Queen Manbhawati Bai aka Shah Begum aka Man Bai – First rajput queen of Emperor Jahangir. Daughter of Kachhawas of Amber. Mother of prince Khusrau.

Manmati Bai aka Jagat Gosain aka Taj Bibi Bilqis Makani– rajput queen of emperor Jahangir. Daughter of Raja Udai Singh (Mota Raja) of Jodhpur. Commonly referred to as Jodh Bai - Sister from Jodhpur. Mother of prince Khurram (Shahjahan).

Prince Murad – Second son of Emperor Akbar. Died in 1599 of acute alcoholism.

Prince Daniyal – Third and youngest son of Emperor Akbar. Died near Burhanpur, Deccan, in 1604.

Prince Khusrau – Eldest son of prince Salim and queen Manbhawati Bai.

Anarkali alias Zehrunnisa Begum *urf* Nadira – Kashmeri dancer; concubine in prince Salim's harem. Mysterious and enigmatic historical figure, lost in the shrouds of Time.

Royal Courtiers and Generals :

Mirza Raja Man Singh–Rajah Of Amber (Jaipur). Trusted general of emperor Akbar. One of the nine ' Navratnas'. Brother of prince Salim's rajput wife, Man Bai, and maternal uncle to Prince Khusrau.

Sheikh Abu'l Fazl Ibn Mubarak -Allami- Closest confidant of emperor Akbar, Vizier of the Realm, noted historian and one of the Navratnas. Killed in 1602 by the Bundelas.

Zamana Beg aka Mahabat Khan – Born Sagar Singh, son of Raja Uday Singh of Mewar. Close cohort and trusted general of prince Salim.

Sharief Khan – Close confidant and Vizier in prince Salim's parallel kingdom of Illahabas.

Khubu Chishti – Grandson of Hazrat Salim Chishti. Foster brother and trusted general of prince Salim.

Mirza Aziz Koka Khan e Azam – Foster brother of emperor Akbar and father in law of prince Khusrau.

Mir Zia Ul Mulk Qazwini - Close to prince Salim. Was instrumental in saving prince Salim from the plot to arrest and assassinate him.

Sayyeds of Barha - Dynastic followers of the Mughals. Brave and celebrated warriors. They had the privilege of heading the Mughal army's vanguard (*Harawals*).

Shamsuddin Atgha - Husband of Akbar's foster mother Jiji Anaga. Governor of Lahore.

Haji Jamal Baluch–Best Huntsman of the Realm.

Chitt Ranjan–Hunting Cheetah. Ennobled by Akbar and entitled to drums, liveried servants and all the privileges of a Court Noble.

THE CURSE OF THE MUGHAL SERIES

DAGGERS OF TREASON

CONTENTS

Allah hafiz !

Hazaarah Shukar!

(A Thousand Thanks!)

It sounds ridiculous – but I am stuck for words!

After having written more than ninety thousand words for this book, I am at a loss to find the right words which may adequately convey my gratitude to all concerned. Believe me, fiction is easier to write than a few words from the heart!

Let me begin my journey from the Agra Fort... Thank you, ancestral abode of the Mughals, for welcoming millions like me into the warm embrace of your ancient arms. Thank you for letting your walls, stones, and peeled frescoes speak to me as a mentor teaches his favourite student. I hope I bring credit to your illustrious name. In the same context, I must thank Shri Aamir who is more of a Persian scholar than merely a tourist guide of Agra. He conveys more than the tourist guides ever can, and walks that extra step to procure hidden information for anyone who needs it. Many thanks, Aamir Saheb!

Though I beg a thousand pardons from *Firdaus Makani* Zahiruddin Mohammed Babur and *Jannat Ashiyani* Nasiruddin Mohammed Humayun for not paying courtesies at their *Darbar e Jannat,* I must record my glorious good fortune in being revealed the truly marvellous, exalted and most propitious forms of *Arsh Ashiyani* Jalal Ud Din Mohammed Akbar, *Jannat Makani* Nuruddin MohammedJahangir, and the Most Magnificent *Sahib-i-Qiran-i-Sani* Shahabuddin Mohammed Shahjahan as they peered over my shoulder to see if I had the story right! A *chaar taslim* is also due to the restless spirit of Fatima Bano Begum, as she flitted in and out of the most improbable corners, rafters and crevices of Agra Fort, beckoning me to new angles of ageless lores.

To all the Timurids, *Hazaarah Shukar*!

Many libraries have I scoured for source materials on the Mughals, but the Koh-i-noor amongst them is the Khuda Baksh Oriental Public Library of Patna. This Library of National Importance has two Persian and two Arabic manuscripts which have been declared as 'National Treasure' by the Indian Government. It has the largest collection of Mughal and Persian documents in the world, and welcomes research scholars like favoured sons coming home! I am honoured that my debut book *A Ship Of Many Oars* has been accepted by this most honourable institution and carries the ascension number: ACC #211433. Though all the staff members are very supportive, special mention must be made of Shri Masood Hasan Saheb, Shri Hasibur Rehman Saheb, and Shri Mohammed Shahjahan Qasmi Saheb who are really 'angels' in this hallowed abode of knowledge. My search for hidden treasures of Mughal books and manuscripts would not have revealed their mystical content, had it not been for the tremendous support and encouragement of these three angels. Many thanks!

Shahjahan Saheb at Khuda Baksh Library was my points man for all the Persian transliterations. Many thanks, once again.

A special word of thanks to my editor, Lesley Jones of the United Kingdom, who despite being an acclaimed editor with several major UK publishing houses, found time to edit my manuscript and 'vaporise' my errors. Her words: 'This is going to be an epic series (in the true sense of the word)' spurred me to write and revise until I was nearly dead. Many thanks, Lesley!

Hazaarah Shukar to Shri Ajay Setia and his Team at Invincible Publishing for stepping forth to market and distribute this book, worldwide. I am also indebted to you for your many markers on book promotion...We have many miles to cover together!

To all my friends and relatives who had to suffer my Facebook assaults of book updates, *hazaarah shukar* for tolerating me. To my sister in law, Vandana, many thanks for sample reading my chapters and for your incisive comments as well as words of encouragement. To my brother-in-law, Sundeep Gupta, many thanks for your early words of encouragement and praise. Coming from an adept like you, it was high praise indeed. I hope to return the favour some day!

To my son, Devesh, many thanks for concentrating on your medical studies and not having me worry about your academic progress. Your 'two-liners' of encouragement and praise after every chapter brought a smile to my face time and again.

To my daughter, Riticka, many thanks for trying your awesome marketing skills in selling the book back to me. You almost convinced me to buy a copy! Your Whatsapp of 'Niceeee' after every sample was much cherished.

Many thanks to my mother, and my sister, Nupur, for being more worried about my health than the health of my book!

For my wife, Smita, many thanks for being my bulwark in choppy seas, and for giving me wings to fly and soar, and do my heart's bidding. I wish I had listened to you many years before, when you always nudged me to write! Many thanks once again, Smita, for your unstinting love and support and for putting up with an ill-tempered recluse, and a stack of heavy, dusty books!

For all the illustrations in this volume, you sat inside my brain (which confirms that it is pretty big!) and etched every line, bend, and shade as I had envisaged. *Hazaarah Shukar*!

You were my first reader and biggest supporter, for which I shall forever remain by your side.

This work would not have been possible without the blessings and guidance of Shree Batuk Bhairav, at Whose Feet I repose my trust. Each twist, turn and denouement has been guided with His eternal Grace. Many thanks, Bhairavjee!

Allahabad

20th June, 2016

nirajsrivastava.author@gmail.com

nirajsrivastava.in

BAYAAN – i - MIR TOZAK

(The Words of the Master Of Ceremonies)

Illahabas,

12th June, 2016

Sunday, 7 Ramadan, 1437 A.H.

I am the self appointed Mir Tozak for this series on the Royal House of Mughals.

I beg your pardon – Firdaus Makani Zahiruddin Mohammed Babur will have me skinned alive and sewn inside the carcass of a mule! How could I forget his pathological hatred for the word ' Mughal' ? Please remember them as The Royal House of Timurids, for my sake !

For more than a year now, I have immersed myself into the life and times of the Magnificent Mughals–reading, researching, travelling, listening, dreaming and doing all that which is required to bring the drama and the majesty of this proud and imperial dynasty into your hands.

When I had decided to narrate this story on Sahib-i-Qiran-i-Sani Mughal Padshah Shahjahan (Prince Khurram), it was meant to be a single volume beginning with His Majesty's rise to power and his eventual decay as a prisoner in the Shah Burj of Agra Fort. However, with my proximity to the royal court and its treacherous, scheming ways, with my covert sightings from behind brocaded curtains and darkened corners, and from the vast amount of hidden facts in the forgotten ancient books and wagging tongues of historians, courtiers, friends and enemies now fossilized in the crypts of Time, this proposed single volume has grown into a four volume series titled ' The Curse Of The Mughals'.

Many of the characters you will recognize, and many you will not. Some of them will recognize you too, as your paths may have crossed in some previous life. But, bear this in mind, my friends, ninety percent of the people and almost a hundred percent of the locations are correct. They did live and die in those climes.

And I am willing to bet a hundred gold mohurs against your measly forty dams about the veracity of my words herein !

If you ask me after sunset when the moon rides high and my spirits assuaged by the perfect red wine from Samarkand, then I would have to truthfully tell you that I am not clear myself as to where fiction overtook facts, or facts became fiction! I rode 'musth' elephants with Emperor Echebar (or was it Akbar ?), enveloped the softness of Anarkali in my arms, practiced Turqi with Begum Ruqaiah Sultana, swarmed into the treacherous Bundelas with the learned Sheikh at Antari and towards the end, watched a hapless emperor bequeath his empire to a worthless son.

I was all of them and more.

In the manner of the Mongols who gave the maternal lineage to Babur, I became a nomad myself, travelling by road from the imperial capital of Agra to the Deccanese swamp of Burhanpur, Aurangabad and beyond. I travelled with my harem, as my Chief (and only) Consort travelled with me.

I crisscrossed the breadth of the Mughal empire, from Aurangabad in the west to Illahabas (now Allahabad) in the centre, to the Suba of Bengal and Bihar in the east, over potholed rutted roads. And I imbibed the spirit of the Mughals.

Burdened with my imperial duties and the numerous responsibilities of a Court almost always at war, I have been further confused by the constant transitions from the Hijra to the Illahi, Julian and Gregorian calendars. I wish I could take the perpetrators of this historical dates labyrinth down into the dark dungeons of Akbari Mahal and string them up with red chilly paste on their shaven armpits and groin.

Remember, I am the Mir Tozak, and not the Wakia Navees, hence my words will tell the story in its undisguised form, unadorned and uncut. The Wakia Navees will only record what is acceptable to the Majesty of the Court.

My fellow readers, this first volume is just the beginning of an exciting kaleidoscope of events which will enthrall you in its majesty, and lead you onto exploring myths, established history and traveller's gossip.

Take the time, dear reader, to hear me sometime, as I call the Court to order in the Diwan e Aam.

Tread carefully, my friends... this is the real story, as it transpired. Keep your 'bishtis' near you, for many a bag of water will be required to douse the flames which my story shall ignite!

Ba-adab, Ba-Mulaizah, Hoshiyaar...

The story is about to erupt.

Mir Tozak,

Niraj Srivastava

Zat 1200/ Sowars 300

Illahabas

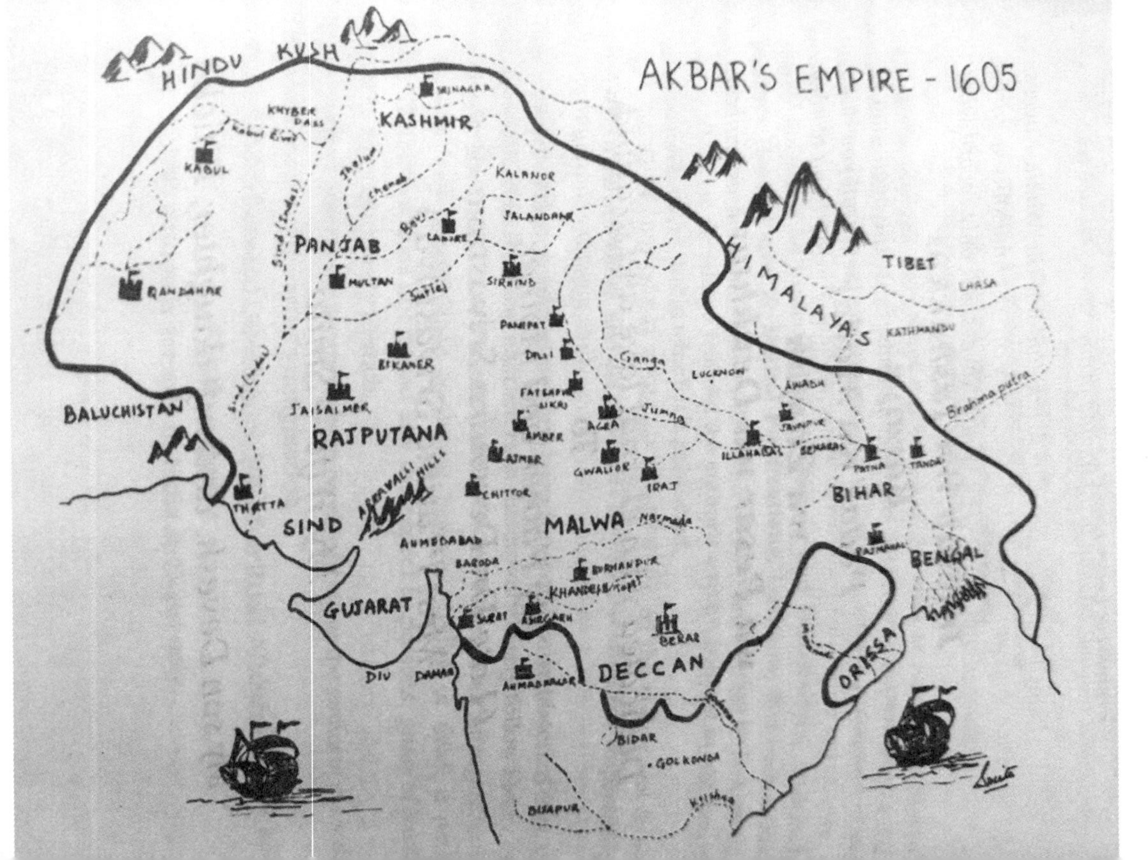
AKBAR'S EMPIRE - 1605
HINDU KUSH
KASHMIR
KABUL
KANDAHAR
PANJAB
MULTAN
LAHORE
KALANOR
JALANDAR
SIRHIND
HIMALAYAS
TIBET
LHASA
KATHMANDU
BALUCHISTAN
BIKANER
JAISALMER
RAJPUTANA
PANIPAT
DELHI
AGRA
AMBER
AJMER
GWALIOR
IRAJ
CHITTOR
LUCKNOW
AWADH
JAUNPUR
ILLAHABAD
BENARAS
PATNA
TANDA
BIHAR
BENGAL
THATTA
SIND
AHMEDABAD
MALWA
Narmada
BARODA
BURHANPUR
KHANDESH
GUJARAT
SURAT
ASIRGARH
BERAR
DECCAN
DIU
DAMAN
AHMADNAGAR
ORISSA
BIDAR
GOLKONDA
BIJAPUR
Ganga
Jumna
Brahma putra

Family Tree

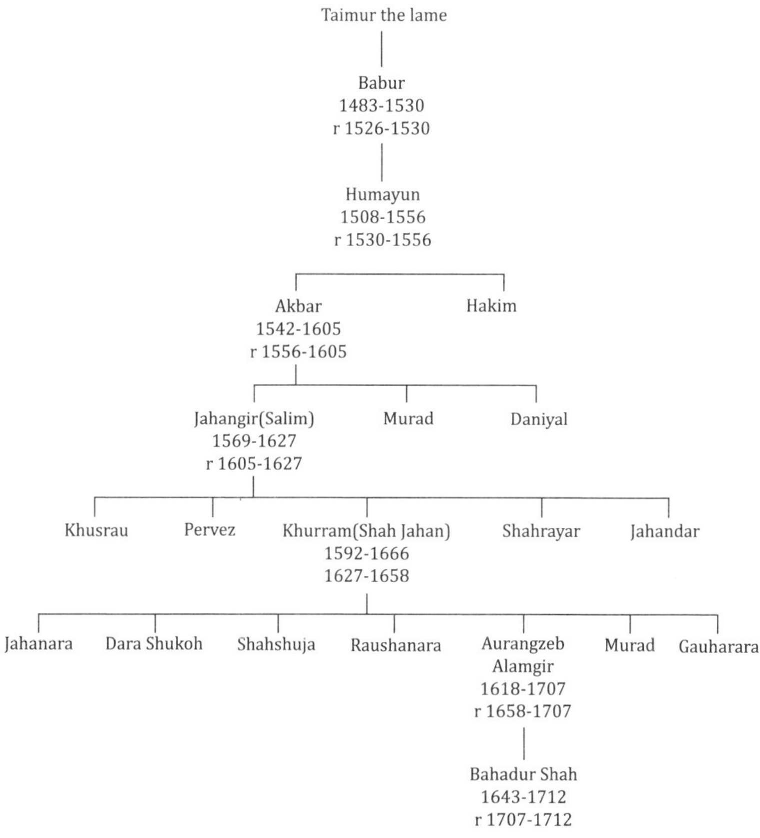

Taimur the lame
Babur
1483-1530
r 1526-1530
Humayun
1508-1556
r 1530-1556
Akbar
1542-1605
r 1556-1605
Hakim
Jahangir(Salim)
1569-1627
r 1605-1627
Murad
Daniyal
Khusrau
Pervez
Khurram(Shah Jahan)
1592-1666
1627-1658
Shahrayar
Jahandar
Jahanara
Dara Shukoh
Shahshuja
Raushanara
Aurangzeb
Alamgir
1618-1707
r 1658-1707
Murad
Gauharara
Bahadur Shah
1643-1712
r 1707-1712

ASI PROTECTED CEMETERY NEAR CHUNAR FORT. IN EXISTENCE. STORY BEGAN FROM HERE.

(PROLOGUE)

TALASH-E-IBTEYDA

(The Search Begins)

Chunar,

Uttar Pradesh,

18th September 2014

From a few miles outside the suburbs of Chunar, the outline of the Chunar Fort can clearly be seen on my left as I drive up the twisted, knotted tar road, which grandiosely proclaims itself as the NH 7 and runs through clear fields of mustard on either side.

Chunar Fort, cresting a hill on the Vindhya Range, looks desolate and forlorn in the harsh autumn sun of September. Stark, muddy and befuddled with ancient worry lines creasing its brow, the two-thousand-year-old fort seems ready to jump into the gently curving Ganges flowing beneath.

The small shrubs of *madar* and *nagphani* grow along the hillside, with *karonda* berries giving them colourful company in an otherwise dreary countryside. Tamarind trees, perched precariously, are an anomaly in the sparse forest of sal, teak, and *mahua* trees, and give some comfort to the young goatherds from the scorching sun and the burning rock-strewn escarpment of the small hill holding aloft the fort.

As the car turns left, the driver opens his door, and delivers a thick stream of *paan guthka* mix onto the unsuspecting craters in the road. A few gestures and pointed fingers, and we have our new set of directions.

The twisted, dusty road heads out to a semi-paved street, which, after a mile or so, divides into a fork. The right arm sweeps up towards the fortifications of the Chunar Fort and the left arm leads us to the cemetery. The blue-coloured board of the Archaeological Survey of India warns us that we are within two hundred metres of a protected site.

My research on the Great Indian Mutiny of 1857 brings me to this cemetery, as here lie interred the bodies of several British troops and officers of the British and Indian Invalid Battalion, who were entrusted, as a part of their light duties, to keep the fort secure. I stand at the gate and look upon the two score or more of graves.

Most of the graves are simple and unmarked. A few are raised, and carry a rank and name engraved on the headstone. Overgrown grass and weeds keep a tight embrace on the graves, as if reluctant to share the secret of the buried souls, and their hidden stories.

A few graves are more tomb-like, with elaborate headstones, ornate structure, and names clearly engraved. A couple of them are like mini mausoleums, with rising pillars and crucifixes, and small circular verandas encircling them. The names of Colonel South, Mrs Gladys South, and a Mrs Pearson adorn these tombs and stare fixedly at me.

I shiver and turn away.

I wander amongst the graves, noting down names and years, silently praying for a familiar, known name, which can justify my laborious search into the tattered shreds of facts and fiction which so envelop the Great Indian Mutiny.

I espy a gold-coloured chain linking four small posts around a grave. The grave is slightly raised on a shallow stage with elaborate lettering on the gravestone. As I study the grave from a distance it seems to be different from the others; while the others are laid in almost military order with their gravestones facing east, this particular monument has its headstone in the north. Intrigued, I decide to take a closer look.

The grave is larger than the others, and rests higher because of its raised platform. In the centre, the etched silhouette of an antique pen case is evident and unmistakeably points to the final resting place of a man of some repute. I wish to step closer, but the chain link holds me back. In deference to the buried personage, I step back.

I critically examine the surroundings for some evidence or correlation, and am sure that this grave has been recently tended, as several inches along the sides have been carefully scraped clean of weeds and grass. I turn towards the headstone, and stare in surprise – for the lettering is in unmistakable Urdu or Persian.

In my amazement, I cross over the chains linking the post, and peer closely at the letters.

'Step back, Sahib,' commands a voice over my shoulder. I freeze and turn to see a middle-aged, dark complexioned man in a scruffy shirt and trousers staring intently at me.

'Hello... I am a research scholar from the University of Allahabad, and am here for some information,' I qualify, as I step back.

'What is it you seek, Sahib? Rarely does anyone come here... As you can see, there is nothing much of importance here.'

'What is your name, friend?'

'Munnawar Sen, and I am the caretaker of this graveyard,' was the slightly hostile reply. It was as if I had challenged his fiefdom.

'Well, Munnawar Sheikh, I am glad to have met you...'

'I am Munnawar Sen, not Sheikh,' was the tightly rolled reply to my interrupted overtures of friendship.

Well, well, I thought; a nice bend in the woods! Firstly, a Moslem grave in a Christian cemetery; and now, a traditional Moslem name with an equally traditional Hindu surname.

This person could be a treasure trove of information. I step close to him, and with a gentle touch on his arms lead him a few paces away. I turn towards him and quietly ask 'Munnawar, I was told by the SDM Saheb at Mirzapur that a person called Brij Lal is the caretaker here.'

'What of Brij Lal, Sahib? He comes here maybe twice a month for a few hours and then goes back to his duty at the Engineer Saheb's house by the burning grounds. I am the self-appointed caretaker of this cemetery.'

'I can see that, Munnawar. Can you please tell me more about this cemetery?'

'What is there to see here, Sahib?' He spreads his arm and, squinting against the sun, points towards the fort looming in the distance. 'You should go to the fort there, Sahib. It is full of interesting stories and places. There is a museum also inside.'

'Interesting stories?' I am always on the lookout for a tale to embellish my evenings.

'Yes. Stories of love, of plunder, and hidden treasure. Of spirits who will call you by your name and lead you to your doom into the bottomless well, by the side of the stables.'

I can feel goosebumps on my neck, and quickly steer him back to the present. 'Munnawar, you must know all that is important in this graveyard. You see, I am a history research scholar, and am extremely curious to know about this Moslem grave in a Christian burial place,' I explain, pointing towards the freshly tended grave surrounded by the golden chain links.

Munnawar looks at me, and sighs. 'Sahib, this was a Moslem burial place from the time of the Moghuls. The Englishmen came much later... during the siege and plunder of the Sepoy Mutiny in 1850.'

'1857.' I cannot stop myself from correcting him. 'Who lies there?' I ask, indicating the grave with the epitaph in Urdu or Persian.

'An enlightened *fakir*. See, we have been tending the graves here since the Moghul period... Almost four hundred years. The railings and boundaries were raised only about twenty or thirty years back by the government. Before that, there was just a low brick wall to demarcate the *kabristan*.'

'But who would come here?' I ask myself, out loud.

'Jackals and hyenas. They are friends with the spirits entombed here. On moonless nights nobody comes here. Not even me. From far away you can hear the chatter of voices in a foreign language, much like gibberish, and hear the shrill laughter of women suddenly changing into the wailing and lamenting of a hundred tormented souls. Even the jackals watch from the fringes, and always in a cluster, never alone.'

'Is this true, Munnawar?' I ask with incredulity.

'Yes, Sahib. In certain years, on the ninth of September to be exact, there are sounds of a great number of horse riders and war drums coming towards this cemetery. It is as if a large body of men are on the move.'

My spine is tingling, but my brain negates as I say, 'What utter nonsense, Munnawar. Stories good enough to relate over the village bonfire, I am sure.'

'Sahib, it is difficult to believe, I know. But ask Jaggan Lal, the earlier *Pradhan* of our village. Many years ago, on a rainy night in September, Jaggan Lal was sleeping in his field as he had cut channels from the minor canal to irrigate his lands. Hearing the leisurely trot of hooves in the silent night, he got up to see a headless warrior mounted on a horse with a beautiful lady sitting in front. The lady was veiled, but soft sobs could be heard. Jaggan fainted, and when he was found the next morning, he was running a very high fever, and had lost his speech.'

Well, I am not too far from losing my speech, either, I thought.

Munnawar continued with eyes squinting in the sun. 'Jaggan could only explain with signs and gestures. He took the villagers to the spot where he signalled the riders had passed, and yes, there were fresh hoof markings in the soft, irrigated mud. The size of the hooves and depth of indentations suggested a robust horse.'

My nerves are in a free spin as I fearfully look around at the silent graveyard. Even the shrubs and the trees seem to be standing in silent vigil. I shake my head, and, wiping the perspiration on my forehead with the back of my palms, I move again towards the raised grave. Munnawar follows.

I study the calligraphy on the epitaph, spread over several lines, but can only guess at the language – Urdu or Persian. The intricate flow of the lines in hyper and sub, supplemented with dots, gives no clue to my untrained eye. I decide to take a few pictures of the headstone, and, with Munnawar's silent approval, click some long and close shots.

I look at the sun and decide that the headstone is in the north, as the sun, past noon, is on its southern leg opposite to the burial mound. 'Munnawar, why is this grave placed like this? All the others are laid out facing east?'

'That is because the Moslems are buried with their faces turned west, towards Mecca. When the head is laid on the north, it is easy to gently turn the face west.'

'What else do you know about this grave?' My curiosity is not to be sated.

'Nothing much. Except that a Hindu comes here, twice every year, to say prayers and to make offerings. See, he was here a few days back.'

I look closely, and towards the foot of the grave are dried petals of roses and small marigold flowers, now curled into yellow popcorn. An army of small, red ants is heaving, pushing and pulling a small fragment of a discoloured sweetmeat. It seemed like a fossilized *Petha* to me. The placement of flowers at the foot is a purely Hindu ritual, I muse. The Moslems always place the garlands and the flowers near the head and the upper body.

Today is the eighteenth of September... had he come in the last ten days? I stagger off into the shade of a small black plum tree and ask, 'Does he come here in September?'

'Yes, in early January and September. You missed him by merely four or five days.'

'Can you tell me where he lives? Or which village?' my words are tumbling out of their own accord.

'His name is Ramnik Bhai, and he stays in Ahraura, a few miles from here. I know his house. Maybe I could take you there some time. That is, if you really want to waste your time and money,' chuckled Munnawar.

Ah-ha! So Munnawar Sen actually can smile!

'You see, Munnawar, I have come a long way, and might not come again. Your spooky stories have rather piqued my enthusiasm – could we meet him today?'

'We could try. It is on your way back... But, come... I shall take you there.' Mopping his brow with his *gamchha*, Munnawar strides towards the car.

A fifteen-minute drive through Dargah Sharif Road and a country lane brings us to a small settlement of about a hundred houses. What immediately strikes me is the enormous number of wells. It seems that each house has its own well! We come to a stop in front of a large cottage with thatched roofs, set inside a low brick wall.

Munnawar saunters to the gate, and, cupping his mouth, shouts, 'Ramnik Bhai!' In response, a terrified goat bleats and pulls at the string charpoy to which it is tethered.

'He is not at home. Shall be back by late evening,' replies a feminine voice. Possibly his wife, I surmise.

I offer to drive Munnawar back to the cemetery, but he refuses.

Suffused with curiosity, and laden with my pictures of the mysterious grave, I am driven back to Allahabad.

*

Ahraura,

District of Chunar

23rd September, 2014

I look into my glass of milky tea and wait for Ram Dhure to speak. Well over ninety years old, he still sports a decently luxuriant moustache, and is prone to twirling the ends into a silver curl. His eyes, clouded with distant memories of the forgotten past, reflect no emotion.

Ram Dhure leans forward on the charpoy and motions his youngest son, Ramnik Bhai, to fetch a photograph from inside. Ramnik returns with an image set in a much-marked wooden frame. Ram Dhure looks intently at it for a long time and then silently passes it on to me.

It is not a photograph, but a wrinkled painting on cloth. I hold it gingerly and gaze at the painting of an aged Moslem ascetic wearing an oversized turban with a red feather sticking out from it. The face is lined and bearded, but the eyes are hypnotic.

'This cloth has been with us for generations... For more than three hundred years.'

Cloth? I look up, surprised. The antique value of this painting would be several thousand dollars. I peer more closely at the fabric and can feel its coarseness and brittle creases. To have survived three centuries with enormous neglect and negligible care speaks volumes about the quality of the fabric of those days.

I address Ram Dhure. 'It definitely is an old painting, and well preserved for its age. Three hundred years is a long time.'

'This painting was done when Aurangzeb Shah lived.'

'You mean Emperor Aurangzeb. Right?'

Ram Dhure spits a gob of tobacco towards the tethered goat, and replies, 'Yes. Yes. The same. Badshah Aurangzeb.'

Holding the frame aloft, I say, 'Well, sir, if what you say is correct, then this painting is more than three hundred and fifty years old and worth a fortune. Several thousand dollars.'

'How much in rupees, Sahib?' queries Ramnik Lal.

'Could be twenty, twenty-five lacs.' I give a measured estimate and watch the eyes of the father and son duo light up. I shift closer to the old man, and ask, 'Ramji, do you know who is depicted in this painting?'

'Sahib, my grandfather told me that this sadhu was a Moslem *faqir* by the name of Allah Baksh, and he came here from the mountains beyond Kashmir. It was said that he could speak in many languages and could ride a horse like a cavalry officer.' Ram Dhure was looking pensively at the painting.

I look again at the painted cloth and can make out the figure of a bearded man sitting on a huge boulder with his face turned towards the artist. Even in the crinkled fabric, I can make out the broad forehead and aquiline nose in a wizened face. The lips are thin and unsmiling, and make no effort to meet the large mole slightly above the left nostril. The eyes are commanding, and gaze resolutely at the painter. The white beard is long and full, trimmed neatly in a curve. The face is regal, but the accoutrements ascetic.

Most imposing is the heavy turban wound around his head, with its red feather sticking cheerfully out at an angle. Long hair in silver grey escapes from below the turban and collects at the nape of his neck. The head is not bent with age, nor with the weight of the high turban, but sits erect. Next to him, on the ground, lies a thick wooden staff with a greenish scarf tied at its head.

'What do you know of him, Ram Dhure? Have you seen him? Maybe in your childhood?'

'Sahib, you have not been paying attention. I am *not* three hundred years old.'

Suitably chastised, I mumble an apology. There are too many questions forming in my mind, and the answers are by no means enlightening. I decide to become the research scholar and take out my pen and diary.

'There are too many unanswered questions for my liking, Ramji. I will try to keep this short and focused now... so, please tell me all that you know about this *faqir.* From the beginning, if you don't mind.'

Ram Dhure settles back on his charpoy and eases a twisted packet of tobacco from his *kurta* pocket. A few seconds later, his thumb is busy twirling the tobacco flakes on the open palm of his hand.

Squinting his eyes in concentration, he falteringly starts. 'Sahib, this story has been passed down in our family through generations. Nobody knows for sure, but our forefathers became the disciples of Hazrat Allah Baksh many centuries ago. And Hazrat Allah Baksh also adopted our family as his own.

'We do not know how exactly my forefather, Tepia Gond, met the Baba, but my grandfather and the village elders are fond of mentioning this incident: one night, as my ancestor Tepia Gond was walking by the Ganges in search of his lost goat, he came across an elderly Moslem who was sitting by the river and staring intently into the water. Since it was close to three o'clock in the morning, the favourite hour of the *djinns* and *prêt atmas*, Tepia Gond stood a good distance away, and watched.' My pen was now racing furiously across the paper.

'Tepia heard the figure sigh and softly call, "Janni, Janni," to the dark, swirling waters of the Ganges. The old man leaned forward, as if expecting the river to answer him. When silence was the only answer, the man slowly seemed to sink into the wet sands. My forefather, Tepia, could bear the despair of this lost soul no longer, and hastened to him. At the sound of Tepia's approaching feet, the Baba turned around and fixed his eyes on him. Legend says that Tepia froze at the mesmeric glint in the Baba's eyes. It was as if the half-travelled moon with its icy sheen had emerged out of Baba's eyes.

'For several minutes, Tepia just stood rooted to the spot. Then slowly, the icy glint from the Baba's eyes diminished and my forefather was able to move again. He advanced towards the Baba and, upon nearing, made the necessary salutations with folded hands. It is said that for several hours, till the sun rose, they both sat in silence by the river bank. The Baba, however, did not allow him to sit by his side – he was made to sit a few feet behind. In fact, the villagers say nobody was ever permitted to sit in front of, or by the side of, Baba Allah Baksh.'

'Well, his actions were unlike a *faqir*...more like a feudal lord!' I exclaim.

Ram Dhure incinerates me with his contemptuous stare, as he says, 'It is easy to sit along with kings and regents. It is difficult, and wishful thinking, to consider yourself in the same league as a *sadhu* or a *faqir*, and to entertain ideas about sitting in their presence, for they are the beloved of the Gods, and much above our station in life.' My sensibilities, numbed by urban frivolities over so many years, are in for a rude reality check.

'As the sun rose, Tepia just picked up the small bundle of belongings of the Baba and stood with folded hands. The Baba, without a word, followed Tepia home. It is said that Baba did not speak for several days and was content to just sit by the river. On many nights, Tepia had to fetch him from the river banks and coax him to eat a few a *rotis* with milk.'

'Did he stay in this same house?' I ask, looking around and trying to imagine what it must have been like three hundred years ago. Were the buffaloes just as skinny then?

Ram Dhure stands up and points towards the river Ganges flowing couple of kilometres to the west. 'We stayed near the river then, a hamlet of about a dozen houses. Baba stayed there... Although he was welcome inside our house to eat and sleep, he preferred to stay in a small thatched hut which was built specially for him. At times, however, he came inside our house and ate with us.'

I am trying to reconcile all this information with the startling discovery made a few days ago at the cemetery from the inscriptions of the epitaph. It is becoming increasingly difficult for me to relate the simplicity of the present scenario with the historical significance of the past.

'Sahib, most of the houses that you see in this village are of the *murids* of Hazrat Allah Baksh... You remember Munnawar Sen from the cemetery? His ancestors were our neighbours then, and, after embracing Islam, became *murids* of Hazrat. For generations, they have been custodians of the graveyard.'

'So, till the mutiny of 1857, Baba's grave was the only grave there?'

'No, no. It is a very old cemetery. When Babur first invaded Chunar Fort, his fallen soldiers were buried there. Thereafter, Hazrat had also expressed his wish to his *khalifa*, Tepia Gond, to be buried there. He said he wanted to be with his own. And, so he was.'

'Ram Dhure, are you sure that the person we speak of, Hazrat Allah Baksh, is the same person who is buried at the cemetery here?'

I can see a shadow of annoyance pass over his face, as he takes his own time to form the answer. 'Baba Hazrat Allah Baksh, as per my forefathers, was a much travelled and revered mystic. He had many followers, and his burial was witnessed by half the village. Wait, I will show you a few of his things which he left to my ancestor Tepia Gond as a blessing.'

'Blessing?'

'Yes... blessing. It has been narrated to us through generations and it shows the love that Baba had for my forefather. Baba always told his *murids* that Tepia Gond was his actual *khalifa* and ours, his adopted family. Ramnik, please get the green bundle of Baba's *rehmat* kept in my wooden trunk.'

As we wait for Ramnik to fetch the desired article, I look at the gaunt figure of Ram Dhure and marvel at the providential destiny of his being part of a history as monumental as this. I just had to ask, 'Is there something more that you would like to tell? Something... anything that comes to mind?'

'Well, villagers have always maintained, and it is corroborated by my ancestors, that Hazrat never slept on the ground. He would arrange a stone slab supported on rocks, or sleep on wooden trunks, but never on a floor. He is rumoured to have been quite a *mastan*, as he was fond of riding on buffaloes, and could also be found sitting atop haystacks. In fact, he preferred to address his *murids* and others who came to see him, sitting atop the haystacks!'

Oh, wonderful, I think. The mendicant turns out to be a delinquent *faqir*!

'Another thing, Sahib. Baba was not afraid of tigers, cheetahs or elephants. Our ancestors saw him chase cheetahs and tigers that strayed too close to the hamlet, by twirling his wooden staff and growling in a peculiar way at them. With elephants he was friends! It is said that elephants in his presence would raise their trunks in salute and would vigorously shake their great heads. He would walk around them, as if inspecting, and the elephants, though trumpeting, would also succumb meekly to his touch. He was prone to speaking softly, but with a guttural nuance. The funny thing is, Sahib, that Hazrat was enormously scared of deer! He would not let deer come to our settlement and would create a mighty ruckus if he ever saw one. He would also bless those who could hunt and kill deer with small gifts of amulets, fruits, and prayers.'

Ramnik walks up to us, and reverently sets on the charpoy a small bundle wrapped in red cloth and tied with a golden thread. Ram Dhure picks it up and puts it to his forehead before untying the string. He spreads the cloth and smooths the edges with his hands. I lean over for a closer look.

At first glance, the bundle seems to contain just the very ordinary possessions of a roving mendicant: a weathered copy of the Holy Quran with faded letters in gold on a red cover; a small thimble-like ring, which I know from my studies of medieval history to be an 'archer's ring'; a green satin scarf with faded gold motif ; a string of pearls yellowing with age; a scroll on plain white satin, dimmed with age, the intricate designs of a huge building with scribbles on the side; and a small packet wrapped in green cloth.

Rolled into one corner of the bundle are two other items – a thick black manuscript with silken cover, and another folded piece of red silk.

I turn and ask Ram Dhure, 'May I look at them, please?' He nods his assent and I pick up the Holy Quran first. It is weathered, no doubt, and the pages fragile, but the cover is beautifully made in red velvet with faded gold lettering. The pages inside carry black calligraphy, and the lines and words are not perfectly synchronized – which denotes a handwritten copy. I unfold the green satin scarf and it turns out to be almost eighteen inches long and ten inches wide. The faded picture of a couchant lion and the rising sun is clearly evident.

I pick up the archer's ring and scrutinize it carefully. It is made of white stone, highly polished and smooth to the touch. As I hold it up to the sky, I can see the golden inscriptions, minutely inlaid on the inside of the ring. I can feel a chill go up my spine.

I flick through the black, silk-covered manuscript and it seems to be covered entirely in Persian scribbles, with a few sketches. I unwrap the red silk and pull out a folded cloth, which seems heavy and creased with dried paints and varnishes. As I stretch it on the charpoy,a commonplace family portrait of a father with his two sons stares at me. Towards the back stands a beautiful woman in a turquoise dress. They look like royalty with their rich trappings.

With bated breath, I slowly untie the small green packet – inside is a heavy gold ring covered with a beautifully embroidered blue square cloth, possibly a lady's handkerchief. I pick up the gold ring first. It is heavy and not very intricately crafted – the face of a snarling tiger stares at me. The lady's handkerchief almost beckons me to pick it up. The pull is mystical, and I succumb. The blue cloth is intricately embroidered with *zardozi*, or gold thread embroidery, and is silken to the touch. The glitter of the *zari* threads has not diminished even after centuries. I smell the handkerchief – do I smell the fragrance of rose attar from a long forgotten queen?

I am perspiring with tension, and I pick up the archer's ring again. I gather the courage to ask, 'Ramji, will you please sell this to me?'

He looks shocked, as if he never expected this from me. 'No. I will never sell anything from this. It is Baba's *rehmat* and not for sale.'

We look at each other, both determined to have our way. I do not have to act – my yearning for this ring is so strong that tears come unbridled to my eyes. I sit down quietly on the charpoy again, and tears roll down my cheeks.

Ramji is nonplussed, and seems forced to ask me, 'What is it to you, Sahib? It is not of any value. If you had asked for the big, gold ring, I would have understood. This is just a ring for the *sitar* players. Why do you cry so?'

How can I tell him about the enigmatic, historic significance of this ring? I have no wish to lie to him, therefore I give him the best answer I can, under the circumstances. 'Sir, this ring can be vital to my research. You know I came here for my research project which is a part of my PhD. If I can complete it successfully, I shall become a doctor...'

A questioning frown crosses Ramji's face.

'No, No, Ramji... please don't be confused. Not a medical doctor, but a doctor of history.'

Dadu looks at me with baleful eyes and then calls up a gob of fresh phlegm from the interior of his chest. A quick twist of his head in synchronization with his cough, and the phlegm is deposited on the leaf of *sadabahar* bush, from where it hangs like a maudlin Christmas decoration.

'Suppose I give it to you, what will I get?'

'*Dadu*, I am a student, and don't have much. But I shall be happy to give you all the cash that I have... See, I have three thousand six hundred rupees with me. Please, take it.' I hurriedly hand over the cash.

Dadu is now in his element, and looks with amusement at my proffered cash. Before he can refuse or make excuses, I take off my watch, a gift from my father, and put it on the charpoy.

'See, it is a Rolex, very expensive. You can keep it.' I have nothing more to offer.

Ramnik reaches out and tries the watch on his wrist, as I avert my eyes. Speak of a kangaroo with a crown!

Two generations have been bribed, but I still wait with trepidation. Finally, the venerable *Dadu* nods his assent. I almost whoop with joy and am literally ready to hoist him on my shoulders. I quickly take a few pictures on my cell phone of the other articles, and, after carefully packing the archer's ring in a torn piece of paper, I am ready to leave.

I mourn the loss of my father's gift to me, and in reckless retribution, ask, 'Ramji Sahib, I am taking this black diary. It is not of any use to you, and I can practice my Urdu from it.'

Ramji Dhure squints against the sun, but the feel of hundred rupee notes in his hands works in my favour. He stuffs the currency notes in his pocket, and curtly asks me to leave. He probably fears that I may ask for some more items!

'Ramji, *Dadu,* I shall never forget your help, and shall prominently mention it when I publish my thesis. You have my word.'

And so I have.

Who will believe my incredible story of the Second Empire, unless I show them the evidence beyond refute?

(CHAPTER 1)

ZAHUR E KEHKESHANE AAFTAB

(Birth of a Million Splendid Suns)

Shah Burj,

Agra Fort,

14th September, 1660

One hour past midnight

Observations by the spirit of Fatima Banu Begum, dead child of Akbar:

'I was my father's first born, and he loved me so!' I loved my father too, more than the chronicles will ever record, and though my elder dead brothers, Hassan and Hussain reside in the deserted halls of Fatehpur Sikri, I continue to haunt the corners, shadows, and the subterranean chambers of Agra Fort.

I cannot bear to see Khurram, my father's favoured grandson, lying in a demented stupor, imprisoned, bruised, with two front teeth broken and bearing heavy pain in the right shoulder. All because of that wretch Aurangzeb. What business had he to serve his brother Dara's head on a silver tureen to an already heartbroken and mortified emperor, now lodged as a war criminal in his own fort? Crying for a pair of shoes and a pitcher of water?

I must relieve his tormented soul with words of joy and magnificence.

Maybe my father's spirit shall venture out this night from Sikandra at Bihishtabad and join me in comforting his beloved grandson. How can he forget Khurram's steadfast devotion to him at his deathbed almost fifty-five winters ago?

I shall not wait, but ease Khurram's pain! True are these words of joy and pain...

*

The Imperial Palace,

Shahi Qila, Lahore

5th January, 1592

Just before midnight

There is a flurry of activity near the emperor's bedchamber, and the senior eunuch of Prince Salim's harem, Qaid Akram, is stopped by the imperial guards.

'Delay me not, for I have brought news which shall be music to the *Padshah Ghazi*'s ears!' he intones with a wave of his hands.

The imperial guards have been forewarned by Saeed Alam, *khojasera* of the emperor's harem, about the possibility of some late night news, so a guard enters the anteroom of the royal chamber and wakes up Saeed Alam, who is asleep on the floor.

Saeed Alam's face breaks into a huge smile as he sees the happy face of his counterpart from the prince's harem, and a slight nod by Qaid Akram confirms the good portents.

The chief eunuch runs softly into the royal bedchamber, and, falling on his knees, excitedly announces in a voice loud enough to carry past the silk curtains, '*Padshah e Hind, Zindabad*'(Long live the emperor!) 'Forgive the intrusion, *Alampanah*,but there are good tidings from the *zenanakhana*!'

Emperor Jalal Ud Din Mohammed Akbar, who has been reclining on his gold and silver bed, surrounded by small, sequined bolsters, rises and walks past the now prostrate attendant.

As he steps into the adjoining rectangular chamber, the imperial guards bow their heads and draw their spears close to their person. Qaid Akram, quailing at the presence of the Great Moghul in such close proximity, throws himself on the floor.

'Rise.'

'Lord of the Universe, King of Kings, Protector of the Poor, Majesty of the Sun, may you live a thousand years! Prince Salim has been blessed with a son! May he live a thousand years!' The voice of Qaid Akram is uncharacteristically high, as he lies prostrate on the floor.

The emperor's senior eunuch, not to be displaced in this highly auspicious moment, flings himself at the feet of the emperor, crying, '*Padshah, Mubarak*! *Padshah Salamat*!'

Emperor Akbar, with a brief smile, takes off his priceless Persian pearl necklace and drops it into the folded palms of Qaid Akram.

The Emperor turns and instructs Saeed Alam, 'Let the drums roll, and illuminate the palace!'

As the eunuch rushes to carry out the orders, Akbar claps his hand and two attendants standing behind the golden brocade curtains step out. A glance from the emperor galvanizes them, and they rush to gather his imperial robes. Akbar gestures to them for his sword and turban as well.

When Akbar has been fully dressed and is wearing his imperial turban of green and gold, with a *serpench* of diamonds surrounded by rubies and emeralds, and with the scabbard of his personal sword in hand, he steps out on to the balcony overlooking the central lawn. As he casts his eyes over the royal palaces, he sees a multitude of faces turned his way.

Emperor Jalal Ud Din Mohammed Akbar, Ruler of Hindustan and Shadow of God on Earth, stands resolute against the arches of his royal chambers, illumined by the glow of lamps now appearing over the palaces. None had the temerity to gaze at the emperor for long, yet none could take their eyes away from the dignity of the monarch.

Akbar, his arms and chest swelling with pride and joy, draws his diamond and jewel-encrusted sword from its gold-green scabbard with a flourish, and holds it aloft.

The gruff voice of the emperor rings through the silence commanded by his royal presence, as he thunders '*Haq; Aqeeda*!'His blade points towards the heavens.

Immediately, the palace and the fort reverberate with ecstatic cries of '*Allahu Akbar*,'and '*Padshah Zindabad*' as the courtiers on night watch, imperial guards, attendants, and the ladies of the harem celebrate. Quli Murad Beg, a Persian noble with some strains of Chagatai blood, starts beating his sword on his shield – an old Turkish Mongol martial custom. Instantly, the beat is taken up by the almost thousand strong night watch of imperial guards, as they beat their spears, swords, and scimitars on their shields.

The royal drummers seated in the *naubat khana* of the main gate, alerted by runners bearing the emperor's order and the sounds of rejoicing, raise the tempo of their beats. Soon enough, the sounds of the auspicious *shehnai* and *shankh*can be heard all across the fort.

A smiling Akbar turns back towards his royal chambers and glances to his left towards Prince Salim's royal quarters. Prince Salim is at the balustrade of his balcony, his head bowed in the emperor's direction. Akbar stops and raises his sword again in a blessing to the royal prince.

The prince drops to his knees and genuflects.

*

The Royal Harem,

Shahi Qila, Lahore

Same night, past midnight

The rejoicings have not stopped since *Padshah Ghazi* Emperor Akbar raised his sword with the cry of 'For Faith is True' and unleashed the joy of a kingdom. The importance of this birth and its ensuing celebrations can be deduced by the royal presence of the emperor, unannounced and in the dead of night. In his joy and the spring of hope, the emperor had stepped out without even a silken shawl, in the biting cold of a freezing January night. Akbar, a stickler for royal protocol and aware of his own august persona, considered divine, had never shown such evident and spontaneous joy – not even when his son and heir, Prince Salim, was born.

Small groups have formed in the *zenanakhana*, as the royal attendants and eunuchs bring out *dholaks, veenas and shehnais* to sing the celebratory songs of Persia, Afghanistan, Rajputana, and the Timurids.

The queen, Princess Manmati from the Royal House of Jodhpur, lies exhausted after a three-hour labour. She watches with a faint smile as the newborn prince is bathed and then covered in silken wraps.

The chief nurse, Motibai, carefully puts the new born prince in the cradle of the queen's arms as she lies in semi-stupor. The little prince, with some primeval instinct transcending time, turns his hungry lips to his mother's breast. The queen smiles and turns on her side to nurse him.

Prince Salim has been sitting outside the royal chamber of the queen for more than three hours now. Moghul practice forbids the prince from seeing his son during night hours – he will have to wait until sunrise for a glimpse of his son. Just a few more hours to sunrise, he comforts himself, as he leans back on the bolstered *diwan*.

'Your Majesty, the queen and the prince are comfortably sleeping,' announces the eunuch, as he settles some more bolsters around Prince Salim.

*

Royal Chambers

Shahi Qila, Lahore

Same night, past midnight

The senior queen, Ruqaiah Begum, is sitting with Emperor Akbar, and softly smooths the golden bed sheet, as she listens attentively to the emperor's voice.

'Begum, you must call the astrologer Gobind, and reward him for his predictions. Ask him to draw a birth chart also for the young prince. *Insha~Allah* he shall rule the world!'

Begum Ruqaiah gently dips her head in acknowledgement, with a soft '*Insha~Allah*.'

Akbar gently covers the palm of the queen with his own hands, and thinks about that fateful day, hardly a fortnight ago:

As Emperor Akbar was heralded into the Royal harem for his midday meal, cries of 'Ba-adab, Ba-Mulaizah, Hoshiar... Jahanpanah Jalal Ud Din Mohammed Akbar tashreef farma rahe hain' preceded him.

Akbar passed by his queen Ruqaiah Begum's suite, and a soft 'Majesty' was whispered. Akbar turned with a brusque 'Yes?' Only a fool, or his queen, would have the temerity to address him without following royal protocol.

'Your Majesty, the astrologer Gobind is here, and has many good words to say about the child due to be born to Princess Manmati.'

Akbar turned, and with Queen Ruqaiah Begum following, strode into the chamber where the hakims, vaids, astrologers, and storytellers sat behind the marble purdah and conversed with the royal ladies. The eunuchs and female attendants bowed and withdrew.

'Speak' said the emperor imperiously, and Gobind Pundit dissolved into a verbal mess, but he managed to convey the astonishing good fortune and divine blessings being perceived for this birth. It was as if the heavens themselves were proclaiming the advent of a glorious age. 'The realm shall grow and will be forever remembered by the actions and deeds of this imperial child,' he said.

'You shall be weighed in gold, if all that you say is correct. Here, take this.' And Akbar dismissed him from his presence, indicating that his chief steward should bestow on him a gold mohur through the Begum's hands.

Akbar, looking at the silvery light outside, a precursor to the red glow of the dawn, sighs, and, clasping the queen's hands even more tightly, exclaims, 'Begum, tonight I feel a sense of joy, and impending good fortune, which I have not experienced for several years. My heart is bursting with pride and happiness at the birth of the little prince, and I have a good mind to take him under my own protection.'

'You *are* the Protector of the Realm, Your Majesty.'

'I know, Begum. But I will take him into my own palace, and you shall adopt him as your own son – heed the advice of your learned astrologer.'

'I shall feel honoured, Your Majesty. And my arms will no longer be bereft of a child to hold, which Allah in His Wisdom denied me.'

'Allahu Akbar!'

*

Outside the Shahi Qila

Lahore

Same night, past midnight

The sounds of rejoicing and celebrations coming from the fort tear through the cold, chilling fog and travel from house to house, seeking to rouse the sleeping citizens and their burdened hearts. This winter has been very severe, even by standards of the north-western cities of the kingdom. Most of the mountain passes to the north and west, leading to the inhospitable mountainous terrain of the Salt Range, are covered in snow. The otherwise traversable passes of the Lower Himalayan Range, to the north-east, are snow bound and closed. Over the past forty days, several merchant caravans and small troop encampments have been feared lost in the terrifying cold and snow.

The high-spirited beat of the drums assures the populace that all is well. The good fortune befalling the royals is evidenced by the sparkling earthen lamps which are sprouting all over the ramparts and balustrades of the fort. Palace attendants can be seen running around on the battlements with burning torches, lighting up the alcove lamps. A train of a dozen female attendants can be seen hurrying across the open area from the Constabulary to the Imperial Chambers with trays of gold, laden with *diyas*. They would illuminate every nook and cranny of the vast fort, waiting for dawn, when the rising sun will serenade the newborn prince with its ravishing rays, and the promise of a future as resplendent.

The fortune of the emperor is the fortune of the realm...

The houses and mansions in the city are becoming alive with lighted lamps of gold, silver, metal, and clay, coming together to create a forest of shimmering jewels. Even in the shadows and chill of a bleakly algid night, the warmth dispersed by the glow of these little lamps is enough to defeat the despair of the winter gloom. Men and women are gathering in front of their houses, and on the roads, on the roofs, and in the bye lanes; the dogs and horses, sensitive to nature as well as the supernatural, are alert and watchful – as if they too understand the waves of joy and forthcoming plenitude.

Cries of *'Shahenshah Salamat'*and *'Hukumat Salamat'* spread through the silent corridors and reach the royal apartments. The Great Moghul, unable to sleep, paces the length of his bedchamber.

A squadron of royal archers ascends the battlements of the *Masjidi Darwaza* and sends a bouquet of burning arrows racing towards the stars.

Hope needs no chariot! It travels on the rays of Divine Grace!

*

Jharokha -e-darshan

Shahi Qila, Lahore

6th January, 1592; sunrise.

There are more than three thousand people standing quietly in the great quadrangle below the royal balcony. They have been streaming towards the great walls of the fort since sunrise to catch a glimpse of the emperor, who shall shortly appear on the balcony to reassure his subjects that the king and the kingdom thrive. The murmurs of a royal birth are audible in the crowd, and, anticipating an imperial bounty this morning, the crowd continues to swell.

The imperial guards, on foot and on horses, have formed double rows in front, and are looking towards the line of imperial elephants. As he does every morning, the huge Ceylonese tusker, Aitbaar, will raise his trunk and trumpet the emperor's arrival. Royal archers are concealed behind the granulated archers' slits in the fort walls, arrows strung on their bows, facing the crowd – they are trained to take out the eyes of a moving deer at five hundred paces.

A cry suddenly erupts from the patiently waiting crowd as Aitbaar trumpets. Jalal Ud Din Mohammed Akbar, emperor of *Sultanat Mughaliya, Padshah Ghazi Zillu'llah, Imam i adil,* steps out on the balcony in his imperial grandeur with the royal musicians marking a roll on their drums. As Akbar stands gazing at the assembly, a deafening roar of '*Padshah Ghazi Zindabad, Hukumat Salamat*' rises to the skies.

The assembled nobles, foot soldiers, and citizens throw themselves on the ground and perform the *zaminbos* obeisance to the emperor. The mounted *sowars* have lowered their lances to the ground and sit astride their steeds with bowed heads. The *ahadis* in their heavy chain mail are lined up just below the fort walls facing the crowd. Their royal pennants are lowered only for the emperor.

Several *qorchis* bearing golden trays overflowing with gold *mohurs* now stand just behind the emperor. As Akbar extends his right hand for a fistful of gold *mohurs*, the crowd surges forward. Soldiers of the imperial guard, restrained by the lowered sword of their commander, let the surging mass proceed. However, the mounted troopers are quick to canter a hundred paces forward and form another cordon. The emperor, his slightly bulging eyes shining with unconcealed happiness, is throwing great arcs of gold *mohurs* into the assemblage below. For the climbing, bending, jostling sea of humanity, the sky is filled with a golden shower!

Raja Man Singh of Amber, the military commander of Lahore Fort, canters to the centre of the milling crowd and, kissing his sword in tribute to his sovereign, commands, '*Takht Mubarak! Sultanat Mubarak! Zahur e Padshah Mubarak!*' or'Hail the throne! Hail the empire! Hail the birth of an emperor!' The surging crowd roars its approval.

*

Daulatkhana Diwan e khas

Shahi Qila, Lahore

6th January 1592, around noon

Several courtiers, including Raja Man Singh of Amber, the court poet and historian Abu'l Fazl, *Khan e Azam* Mirza Aziz Koka, poet laureate Abu'l Faizi, and Abdul Rahim Khanekhana, are sitting to the left of Emperor Akbar, and the revered mystic Mullah Mahmud from Indjan, with his two disciples, sits on the emperor's right. The emperor, in deference to the presence of Hazrat Mullah Mahmud, has preferred to sit on an elevated platform of silken dhurries on the floor, rather than on his silver throne in the *Diwan e khas.*

The noted mystic sits with his eyes closed and hands clasped in his lap. The emperor patiently waits.

For almost half an hour the mystic has not spoken, nor are there any evident changes in his expression. The eyes remain closed and breath, shallow. Gently, the Shiite saint opens his eyes and, looking directly at Akbar, speaks softly. 'Emperor, the birth of this prince augurs well for the kingdom. His birth is most fortunate and to be celebrated, as he is born exactly one thousand years from the birth of our Most Revered Prophet (Peace be upon Him) and in the *same month*, too! There can be no journey more fortunate than this, no life more blessed. The young prince is the Millennial Child of Munificence. But, Emperor, beware! Great munificence comes cradled in the arms of great virulence. If he follows the path of righteousness and the religious law, his life will be full of sweetness and splendour. Deviate, and he shall find the mighty oceans too small for his tears. Guide him, *Padshah*, for he is destined to bring eternal glory to your dynasty. The Moghuls will live for eternity through the acts of this Fortune's Child!'

The emperor, having listened with rapt attention, inclines his head in acceptance of the Divine's prophesy.

The emperor and his nobles scramble to get up as the spiritual cleric leaves the room in a swish of white robes and elegant fragrance.

Emperor Akbar, elated and troubled at the same time by the mystic's words, turns his back to the standing nobles and mumbles, '*Takhliya*.' The nobles depart silently, having witnessed the prophetic herald of a glorious future.

*

Prince Salim's royal harem

Shahi Qila, Lahore Fort

7th January, 1592

Early afternoon

In the subsidiary rooms of the royal harem, a child is born to the Kashmiri concubine, Zehrunnisa Bano.

The event goes unnoticed and unheralded, as the reign is bathed in the majesty of the young prince's birth.

Such is the spectacle of Providence...

*

Spirit of Fatima Banu Begum:

'Having narrated the events through my own voice to a sleeping Shahjahan, the Unfortunate Padshah Ghazi, imprisoned by his inglorious son, Aurangzeb, I must now retire to my corner in the step wells built by my great grandfather, Emperor Zahir Ud Din Mohammed Babur.

My spirit seems fettered in Shah Burj, for with all its magnificence, this decorated Burj remains but a shell for the most magnificent of the Grand Mughals now reduced to a decaying, sorrowing mass of flesh and bones.

At least my spirit is free!

The Sun is about to rise. I must leave.

But, the true story of Khurram continues...'

*

AWAAZE QAIDE PADSHAH

(The Voice of an Imprisoned Emperor)

Shah Burj

Agra Fort,

24th September, 1660

Twilight

My words shall not be numbered in a chapter.

I am 'We'... Much larger than a single number, as all Timurid Emperors are.

We are the realm, We are the populace, and We are the Majesty of the World!

Shadows, dancing on the golden ceilings and silver filigree of the walls, smirk not, for even in Our days of *lèse majesté,* We carry enough power to squash the burning wick which gives you life! Test me not with your flickering dance.

The licentious greed of a rebellious and deceiving son, the white snake nurtured and raised in Our fulsome love and protection, has bitten me.

Oh, how the *faqir's* words have come true! My beloved Arjumand had cautioned me, as she had cautioned our darling daughter, Jahanara. The head of the white snake should have been crushed by me long ago. But it was not to be.

It was ordained by the Will of Mighty Allah that We should suffer the poisoned fangs of this serpent, which has bitten and killed its very own brothers and emptied the nest. Arjumand, my shining beacon in heaven, how fortunate are you that you do not have to witness the sins of this devil born to us. But maybe, if Allah had willed for you to spend a few more years of your glorious life with us, the poisoned fangs of this serpent would have been coated with your love. Our sons, Dara, Shuja, and Murad would not have died.

My heart is broken, but not my will.

We have been bitten, but We are not dead.

The future holds much for me, as my *'Phuphi' Jannate Bahar* Fatima Bano Begum whispers to me every night, restless spirit that she is!

We shall write the words as Our story unfolds... I welcome every darkened hour as my beloved *'Phuphi'* flits around and whispers the joy of my childhood years. When my memory fails, or dims with the darkness of unmitigated pain, then she guides my quill to record the missing part.

We miss Shah Baba too. But I know that he will not come to visit me in this marbled prison of mine. He cannot bear to witness this wretched existence of a once proud emperor... His heart was too soft, and too full of love for me.

Hey, dark hours rush not by; and if you must go, then come back soon.

For We have so much to write!

But the naked truth is: 'We' have been reduced to 'I'!

I remain the emperor of my dreams, and of my future.

As my voice grows weak with the lesions of deceit and the excruciating hammer blows of a cruel Fate, White Serpent I condemn thee to hell!

As Allah is my witness, I record the events in my own hand.

Mirza A'la Azad Abul Muzaffar Shahabuddin Baig Mohammed Khan Khurram Shahjahan

Previously: *Shahenshah Al-Sultan Al-Azam Wal Khaqan Al-Muqarram Malik-Ul-Sultanat A'la Hazrat Abul Muzaffar Shahabuddin Mohammed Shah Jahan i Sahib-i-Quran-i-Sani Padshah Ghazi Zill'Ullah Firdaus Ashiyani Shahenshah-E-Sultanat Ul Hindiya Wal Mughaliya.*

*

(CHAPTER 3)

HUKUM-E-MULK BIDARI

(The Warrant of Exile)

The Imperial Palace

Shahi Qila, Lahore

11th January, 1592

Forenoon

There was fragrance in the air, as the floors had been washed with the cool waters of *Jumna* mixed with the subtle aroma of rose attar and the brisk smell of musk. The whole imperial palace was decorated with garlands of marigold and *kewara* running straight across the projections and lattices of the imperial walls. Long garlands of red roses, interspersed with strings of silver threads, hung in long strands of colourful symmetry across the palace.

The palace had been an ocean of gaiety and revelry over the last six days. The red burnt-brick walls of the Lahore Fort seemed to have been warmed by the winter sun, and served as a safe cocoon for the newborn prince. Formidable, today it seemed to welcome all into its loving embrace. The Moghul banner, in green with gold trims, fluttered in wild abandon from the ramparts, battlements, and abutments of the fort. Richly caparisoned elephants of the royal retinue, with *howdahs* of gold and silver, were stationed atop the battlements of the fort. Moghul cavalry and war elephants stood outside the walls in all their martial finery.

The six courtyards and the *charbagh* in the north-west quarter of the palace had been the scene of spontaneous singing and dancing by the ladies of the royal harem. The winter blossoms were in competition with the gorgeous colours of the harem, as they flitted from the cool gardens into the corridors and rooms of the imperial abode. The mighty Tatar women guards of the royal harem, formidable in their bulk and weaponry, were today magnificently attired in the deep crimson and purple uniform of the Royal Contingent.

The vast quadrangle immediately behind the main *Masjeedi* Gate had seen the assemblage of nobles with their standards and chosen soldiers performing the *tasliq-i-qar* for the emperor, every morning. Today, on the naming ceremony of the newborn prince, the *mansabdars* and the lesser nobles were ranged in order of seniority, with the senior most nobles being placed closest to the *Diwan i khas.* Their heralds and standard bearers stood just behind them and waited for the drum roll to announce the arrival of the emperor.

From the western side of the quadrangle emerged eleven elephants, of Akbar's *Khasa* cadre of a hundred and one elephants – these were handsome beasts from Ceylon and Africa, towering over the other five thousand elephants in the monarch's army. Fed on a daily diet of forty seers of rice mixed with five seers of *ghee* and five seers of sugar candy, and three hundred sugarcanes a day from September to March, these mammoth elephants needed two *mahouts* to control them during regular months, and five *mahouts* in the rutting season. Trained to fight and never retreat, these war machines could strike terror in the hearts of the most battle-hardened warriors.

Five troopers bearing the gold and green Moghul standard of a couchant lion against the rising sun marched swiftly from the *Diwan e aam* to a blare of trumpets. A few seconds later, the third Moghul emperor, Abu'l Fath Jalal Ud Din Mohammed Akbar strode into the forecourt, followed by Abu'l Fazl and the *Mir Bakshi*. The *khasa* elephants raised their gold sheathed trunks to trumpet and salute their master, whom they knew so well. After all, even at the age of fifty, in his thirty-sixth regnal year, the monarch often climbed onto the back of his elephants by jumping onto their trunks and catapulting himself onto their *howdahs.*

Emperor Akbar was resplendent in his *qaba* of aquamarine silk with a golden cummerbund, and a sash of shimmering orange flowing from his left shoulder to the ends of the cummerbund on the right. The rubies, emeralds, and other semi-precious stones embedded in the *qaba* and sash shone brightly in the sun, and the jade green royal turban with a huge, lustrous ruby adorning the gold aigrette was a personal favourite of the *Padshah*. A sheathed dagger with rubies and diamonds was tucked on the left of his cummerbund, as four *qorchis* carrying his quiver and bow, spear, sword, and mace followed ten paces behind.

As Akbar walked along the pathway of the quadrangle, twenty or more attendants emerged from behind the colonnades with *thalis* of gold filled with attar soaked rose petals. Their faces hidden by the colourful veils, they bowed and delicately spread the petals in his path. They were only entitled to shower petals on his august presence after symbolic initial felicitations from the royal ladies.

As he inclined his head, a smile played upon his lips. In the far distance, he could see his mother, the Grand Dowager, eagerly awaiting his arrival in the royal pavilion. Flanked by Prince Salim's Begum Rani Manmati, and her two granddaughters Shahzadi Shukrun Nisa Begum and Shahzadi Aram Bano Begum, the Queen Mother touched her lips and eyes in silent obeisance to the Almighty God.

Akbar walked along the pathway and the assembled *mansabdars* and other nobility bowed their heads and touched their hearts in supplication. Their personal standards and flags were also lowered, and would be kept lowered until His Majesty was visible. The upper and lower corridors of the royal apartments were now full of women from the *zenanakhana* who wished to have a glimpse of the emperor on this auspicious occasion. From the three thousand or so women inhabitants of the harem, many would spend their lives without ever having laid their eyes on the emperor.

As the *Padshah* climbed the twelve steps of the *Diwan i khas* and turned towards the silver doors of the harem, several hundred royal concubines and their assistants stepped forward and performed the *chahar taslim* – as prescribed by royal protocol. Joyful cries of '*Salamat, Padshah' and* '*Mubarak, Padshah*'filled the royal chambers.

The senior queens moved forward as Akbar reached the three gold inlaid marble steps of the Queen Dowager's apartments, and Prince Salim, wearing a ruby red *shast-khatt* and a golden turban encrusted with a string of rubies and diamonds, laid himself at the emperor's feet. Akbar, suffused with affection said softly, 'Rise, Sheikhu! My Child!'

Akbar stepped into the royal chamber of his mother, the Queen Dowager Hamida Bano Begum, and strode towards her. He stopped ten paces from her presence and raised his hand to perform the *kornish,* and the royal dowager swiftly rose and rushed to embrace her son, the emperor. Akbar's wives, Harkha

Sultan Bai, Ruqaiah Sultan Begum, and Salima Sultan Begum stood on the right with their eyes lowered and palms raised in *taslim.* Akbar acknowledged them with a soft '*Shukran*'and turned towards his two daughters.

'Bless you, my princesses,' he said, enveloping them in his embrace. Shahzadi Shukrun Nisa Begum, who was of marriageable age, shyly came close to him. On the other hand, his eight-year-old daughter, Shahzadi Aram Bano Begum, deftly caught his thumb and, pointing towards the golden cradle, asked, 'Your Majesty, why does my new doll cry so much?'

As the royal ladies tried to control their laughter, Akbar picked up his daughter in his arms and with a smile asked her, 'What do *you* think, my fairy? Why does your doll cry so much?'

'I don't know, A*bbu.* But Meher *dhai* was saying that my doll is tired of my talking!'

The emperor guffawed and, carrying the little princess in his arms, sat upon the marble throne.Though the emperor accorded the highest regard for his mother, the Queen Dowager, in the clearly defined royal protocol of the Timurids no one could claim the same honour as that of the emperor, in whose name the *khutba* had been read. In deference to such custom, the Queen Mother approached Akbar and placed a vessel full of diamonds and sapphires in the lap of the monarch, who gently inclined his head to acknowledge and accept the gift.

The Queen Mother took her place to the right, slightly below the marble throne, as the three wives of the monarch currently residing at Lahore Fort stepped forward and performed the *chahar taslim.* Three attendants brought forward golden trays filled with precious stones and gold ornaments. Led by Ruqaiah Begum, the other two queens also paid obeisance and touched the trays bearing the priceless gems onto the knees of the emperor, and withdrew.

It was time now for the new prince to be named; Princess Manmati, walking slowly and using the end of her crimson sari to cover her face, cradled the prince in her arms. As she neared the throne and prepared to kneel, Emperor Akbar rose with extraordinary alacrity and held her by her shoulders. 'Rise, Princess. You have made me and the kingdom proud. This child is just not any child, but is the future of our dynasty! May you live well, may you remain happy.'

Standing behind the screen of gold *jali*, Mulla Sayyed Mirza from Sirhind, having travelled continuously over the last five days to arrive on time, calmly instructed the chief eunuch, Saeed Alam, to stand near Princess Manmati. As the words of the Holy Quran filled the chamber, the chief eunuch helped the princess to place the infant prince in the arms of the emperor.

As the doting grandfather looked at the future of his kingdom cradled in his arms, an errant ray of the sun flung itself forth through the filigree work of the marble window and bathed the prince's face with a luminous, golden glow.

'*Subhan Allah!*' exclaimed the emperor.

'Magnificent! Truly magnificent!' could be heard from the lips of all assembled.

The emperor continued to gaze at the peaceful, glowing face of the infant prince, and his eyes grew moist and cheeks ruddy.

'He has brought me much joy. I shall call him Khurram, the Joyous One!' said the emperor softly, almost in a whisper.

'*Khushamdeed, khushamdeed*,' the cry went up from all those present.

Then, looking up, his royal countenance suffused with the softness of love and affection, the emperor stepped onto the main platform of the *Diwan i khas*. He stood motionless, with the prince cradled in his arms. The nobles and soldiers, with the sun glinting off their jewels and lances, waited expectantly.

'Khurram!' came the voice of the emperor.

'Khurram! Khurram! Khurram!' thundered the thousand voices, as the trumpets and drums joined the celebratory din.

Prince Khurram, with the beatific smile of a newborn's contentment, turned his head towards the emperor's chest, and slept.

He was, after all, to the manor born!

*

Royal Apartments

Shahi Qila, Lahore

Ten minutes later

Having returned to the royal apartments after acknowledging the tumultuous celebrations outside, Akbar turned to Ruqaiah Sultan Begum, his chief consort of twenty-eight years, and still barren.

As Akbar settled the young prince in Ruqaiah Begum's outstretched arms, he said, 'I am entrusting him to your care. Look after him, and raise him as your own son. Love him and teach him as his mother would. Separate him not from his mother, but bind him to you with your love. I know you are capable of all this and more, Begum, and therefore, I entrust you with our future.'

'I shall not fail you, Your Majesty.'

*

Shahi Qila

Lahore

26th February, 1592

Prince Khurram, the third son of Prince Salim, was to spend his infancy in the care and custody of the royal harem. His grandmother, Ruqaaih Sultan Begum, raised him not as a foster son, but as befitted a child born from her own womb. A wet nurse and twelve other female attendants were specially provided for the care of the infant prince. Even so, Rani Sahiba Ruqaiah Begum personally oversaw the bathing of the young prince, and it was a sign of her affection that the water in the basins of gold had first to be brought to the Rani Sahiba, who would dip in her finger to test the warmth of the water. The cradle of gold, with soft mattresses made from the feathers of the ruddy sheldeck and the feather down of geese and ostrich transported from the far-off lands of Persia and Africa, was set hardly ten paces away from the Begum's bed.

The harem eunuchs were the main transmitters of all news, and they seemed to have a supernatural affinity for catching snippets of information, from within and outside the harem. The *khwajasera* was very powerful, and at times they could be a law unto themselves. Although they were fastidiously loyal to the royal family, their hidden menace was a cause of perpetual concern for the harem inhabitants.

In such times did the senior eunuch of Prince Salim bring the news that Prince Khurram was in imminent danger of being poisoned.

'Majesty! May I have the privilege of a few words in private, please?'

Prince Salim, just back from the royal stables after an early morning hunt, looked at Qaid Akram, and said, 'Speak! What is it that troubles you?'

'Majesty, the winds are not favourable for the young prince.' Qaid Akram stood with his head bowed.

'Speak not to me in riddles, *khajasera*. I have neither the patience nor the time.' Prince Salim had stopped walking, and was looking hard at the poor eunuch.

Qaid Akram, well versed in the impetuous ways of the Moghuls, knew he was but a breath away from losing his head to a prince's sword.

'I am told, Your Majesty, that some women of the harem have an evil eye. And it is only the glory of the *Padshah*, the fortune of the young prince, and the fear of your mighty sword that keeps villainy away.'

'Who?'

The Chief Eunuch of Prince Salim stood trembling. He was cursing his luck at having touched upon this hideous secret; it would surely prove calamitous for all concerned, including him.

With his hands clasped in front, and eyes lowered, he said softly, 'Majesty, Zehrunnisa Begum from Kashmir is in the harem. She gave birth to a son just two days after the prince's birth. And, Your Majesty, there is a striking resemblance between them.'

Prince Salim remembered her well. She was from the hills of Kashmir – tall, fair, long limbed, and curvaceous. Dilawar Khan had presented her as he was on his way from Agra to Lahore. A slave girl, she used to perform in the evenings for the prince, and her singing and dancing so captivated the young prince's heart that he started spending almost every evening in her company. His sexual ardour, which had been dimmed by his love for opium and wine, found new vigour between the voluptuous thighs of the Kashmiri entertainer. This was resented by the three royal consorts, and the several hundred concubines of his personal harem. Messages emanating from the harem, and assiduously communicated by the chain of imperial eunuchs, had reached the emperor. The prince, in addition to his addiction for wine and opium, had cultivated a new iniquity – becoming the sex slave of a slave girl.

Without a word, Prince Salim turned towards the *zenanakhana* and in long strides had crossed the *char-bagh* and mounted the steps. A lover of flowers and shrubs like his great grandfather, Babur, today the colours and fragrance of the flowers were lost on him.

The delivery of another royal child in his harem was news to him. Since April of the previous year he had been campaigning in Sind with Khane Khanan Abdur Rahim, and had returned on the second of January to the royal court. Just three days later, on the fifth of January, the kingdom had celebrated the birth of Prince Khurram. The emperor was elated, first with the victory over Sind and the conquest of Umarkot, his birthplace, and then with the arrival of his royal grandson, the 'Joyous One'.

Prince Salim, revelling in his exalted status and the royal affection of the emperor, preferred the pursuit of new charms in the harem and wine cellars.

The Tatar women guards slammed their spears on the ground and bowed their heads as he passed by. The *khojas*, alerted by the Tatar guards, cried '*Baa dab, ba mulaizzah, hoshiar... Shahzade, tashreef farma*.' All along the harem, princesses and concubines straightened up, and their attending maids immediately started rubbing the priceless attars, brought from Esfahan, Kabul and Samarkand, onto the napes and wrists of the royal ladies. The Begums wondered what brought the prince to the harem this early in the morning.

Having crossed the main chambers of his three senior Begums, Salim strode inside the maze of smaller chambers provided for the concubines. Concubines and slavegirls stood motionless with bowed heads and palms raised in *tasleem*. The prince's stern face did not augur well, and the women were secretly happy that he had ignored their quarters today. Qaid Akram, afraid of the prince's wrath and fearing for his life, had developed a temporary limp, and was keeping a safe distance.

Prince Salim turned left from the corridor and entered a room shielded by silken curtains of purple and pink. He made a sign for the *khojasera* to wait outside. As he entered, he saw Zehrunnisa Bano bending by her bed and settling a deerskin patch over the little bundle that was her son. A small cry of pleasure escaped her lips and then, just as quickly, froze upon seeing Salim's angry visage.

Salim stepped closer to the sleeping infant and stared intently. Zehrunnisa Bano felt the frigid air of Lahore enter her soul. Please, Almighty... have mercy on my innocent son... the silent cry rose from the mother's heart. As if he felt the intense gaze of Salim, the infant moved his head and wrinkled his face.

Yes, there was an uncanny resemblance in the arch of the forehead, the unusually thick brow on a newborn's face, the sharp nose and the quaint turn of the lips. Even the curly brown fuzz on the head had the same swirls as the newborn prince. Much would change over the years, but then, who would take a chance with the fate of a kingdom?

As Salim drew his sword and closed his eyes in prayer, Zehrunnisa threw herself at the prince's feet, and implored, 'Majesty! Mercy, mercy! I beg of you, mercy, my love.'

'There shall be but one outcome, Zehrun... this child is unwanted, and against the rules of my harem. You know this very well.'

'My Prince, my love, my life... He is *your* son, born of our love, with *your* royal blood in his veins... my darling... please, lower your sword, sire.'

'You knew the rules very well, Zehrun... This should never have happened. You hid the truth from me. Know this – there is but one prince, and his name is Khurram.' The coldness in his voice numbed Zehrunnisa.

Zehrunnisa looked at her sleeping child and then at the dour face of the prince. As tears flowed down her cheeks, she thought back to the day in Pindi, two years back, when she was presented to the prince. Her life had taken on a golden hue as she became the prince's favourite and spent all her waking and sleeping hours in his robust arms. Love so tender and warm!

Salim could feel his resolve weakening, as he felt her hands gripping his thighs... even now she had the same magical effect on him. Steeling himself, he said, 'It will have to be done. There is no recourse. *Khoja* Akram, enter.'

As the eunuch waiting outside entered the room, a long wail erupted from her. 'My prince, take my life... spare my innocent son's life. He is innocent, Your Majesty. For the love of God, for the sake of our love,spare him, my lord.' The wails could be heard in the corridors and chambers of the *zenanakhana*. The harem women, in the dark venality of harem dynamics, were secretly enjoying the misfortune of the one who had lately enjoyed so much affection from the royal prince.

Salim looked down upon the bowed head of Zehrunnisa, and, feeling her trembling hands upon his thighs, he wavered. His eyes dimmed with gathering tears as he recalled their hours of love together. Delighting in each other's caresses, and glances brimming with love, endless hours had they spent together. His love for her had transcended to such a pass that he had been willing to rise against the emperor's severe displeasure at his alliance with this beautiful slave girl. In a moment of acrimonious rebuke, Akbar had taunted his son that his lust for a woman should not be mistaken for love.

The emperor's wrath was only tamed by his fear that Salim would be lost forever if he did not grant his royal permission to this contrastive bond. The Great Moghul could not lose an able son and heir to the guiles of a slave girl.

Prince Salim, with wisdom born of love, had persuaded his grandmother, the Dowager Queen, to prevail upon the emperor and grant his imperial assent to their marriage. The emperor, exasperated with the wayward behaviour of his three errant sons, gave his warrant but refrained from joining in the festivities. The royal court also remained cold and distant.

The prince, coming back to the present, sheathed his sword and raised Zehrunnisa by her arms. 'I love you, Zehrunnisa, and always will. The perfume of your love will remain with me always. To ensure your safety and our son's, we shall have to part. The emperor will decide as to...' He motioned for the eunuch to leave.

'My Prince, I have loved you with my life, even more... My love and my life are not worth your regal eyes but, even then, you have given refuge to this forsaken woman. I am the most fortunate amongst all to have been in your arms, and to bear your son. I am also the most cursed of all, to lose you when I need you the most.' The trembling in her body would not subside. The flood of her tears would not quell. Salim lightly touched her face, 'You have ruled my heart. And you shall forever be a fragrant memory for me. Raise my son with love and care. I name him Firdaus.' Freeing himself from her embrace, Salim bent and touched the cheek of his sleeping child, then quickly walked away. A moment longer, and his resolve would be smashed.

*

27th February, 1592

Outside the Shahi Qila, Lahore

The palanquin bearers carried Zehrunnisa slowly out of the massive gates of the imperial fort; she was accompanied by her infant son swaddled in blankets, two family bearers, a retinue of memories and a river of tears.

The harsh words of the emperor, as she knelt before him, still rang in her ears.

'You shall leave the fort immediately, and the city of Lahore forever. You will go as far away from here as possible, and never return. Your brother Mukarram shall be held hostage at Lahore, and any effort by you to return or to contact Prince Salim will warrant the death of your brother, as well as this child.'

'Now, hear more. You shall receive a pension of twenty-five thousand *dams* per annum, wherever you are. Your whereabouts will be recorded by the *Shahi Kotwal* and will be known only to me and the *Mir Bukshi.* The child will not be deprived of any necessities, or his life. Any deviation by you will see the devastation of your entire family. Now go forth, and live your life under the name of Nadira Begum *urf* Anarkali.'

*

THE THREE DOMED MOSQUE, KALANAUR. AKBAR'S 'KHUTBA' AS EMPEROR WAS FIRST READ HERE. 1556 A.D

(CHAPTER 4)

BAD'DUA

(The Prayers for Revenge)

The Three Domed Mosque,

Kalanaur, Suba Lahore

November, 1596

10:30 p.m.

The frigid winds of a cold November night swept through the little hamlet of Kalanaur.

A woman, veiled and wrapped in thick blankets, walked with hurried steps towards the silent mosque at the edge of the small habitation. She stumbled a little in the darkness but, gathering her blankets around herself, turned towards the mud tract that led to the mosque.

The old *fakir*,who sat in the thick grove of mango trees nearby, had today chosen to sit on the open veranda of the deserted mosque, leaning against a pillar. He watched the lady in the blankets climb the four steps and enter the stony concourse of the mosque.

The *fakir* knew that this woman had travelled far and had seen nobler times before she settled at Kalanaur almost four years back. Kalanaur had watched her arrival in the late spring of 1592 with interest; she'd had a tiny infant in her arms and a couple of male *khidmatgaars*. She had purchased a small piece of land with an ancient well, and her servants were able to grow barley and maize during the season.

The villagers also watched with interest as, twice or thrice a year, horsemen from the royal court at Lahore visited the woman and her household. They never stayed long, nor did they ever speak with any of the villagers, not even the village elder, Zaiman Daud, a distant relative of Mariam Makani, Hamida Banu Begum. Though the royal horsemen never revealed their purpose or identity to the locals, the imperial branding on their horses gave them away.

The woman stayed in a thatched house with several rooms and a courtyard at the front. A small hut had been made for her servants, the number of which had swelled over the years, along with goats and buffaloes. Now, there were three small huts in addition to her own dwelling. Her little boy, now all of four years, could be seen happily playing in the courtyard.

The *fakir* had smiled and made salutations to the young child once, when he had seen him riding on the back of a buffalo, escorted by one of the servants. The child had looked curiously at the old *fakir* curled up at the root of a massive tree, and had returned his salutations with a courteous, but haughty nod.

Such courtly behaviour from one so young! The old man smiled and gestured to the attendant to bring the little boy to him. The servant had heard much about the holy man in the village bazaar, and surmised that there was no harm in taking the child to him.

As the child sat in front of the ascetic, the *fakir* asked, 'What is your name, child?'

'Firdaus, *Jahanpanah*!'

The sage smiled, and said, 'I am not a *Jahanpanah*, child. I am just a seeker, and a poor old man. The *Jahanpanah* lives far away, in a big palace, and sits on a big throne.'

The child looked inquisitively at the huge, gnarled roots and, pointing them out to the *fakir* said, 'You also have a big throne, *Jahanpanah*, to sit upon!'

The *fakir's* eyes twinkled as he delved into his satchel and brought out a bunch of big, black grapes. Unlike any other child, Firdaus did not lunge for the grapes, but looked steadily at them. As the sage placed the bunch in Firdaus's hand the boy child bent low, and then with a formal '*Shukriya*', leapt up. After a few paces, he turned back and with outstretched arms offered the same grapes to the *Fakir*. Smitten, the *fakir* in his absolute munificence raised his weathered face to the heavens and blessed him. 'Firdaus, may the heavens endow you with kingship!'

The child happily ran to his keeper and was immediately hoisted upon the buffalo.

*

The woman gasped as she saw a silhouette sitting against the pillar, and froze. The shadow merely raised a hand in benediction and motioned her to go inside the hall for her prayers. She looked carefully at the swaddled bundle and realized that it was the same *fakir* she had seen several times sitting under the mango trees.

'Go, daughter. Finish your prayers in peace. You have nothing to fear here, except sin.' The old man spoke softly.

The woman bowed her head, and went inside.

For the next couple of weeks the *fakir* waited for her to come at night for her prayers, and the woman, on her way back, never forgot to wish him, '*Shab Bekhair. Allah hafiz.*'

One night, as November turned into icy December, the woman stopped near the ascetic as he sat propped against the old pillar. He looked at her from under the cloth he had wrapped around his face, and softly asked, 'Yes, daughter?'

'*Huzoor!* May I sit awhile at your feet?' the woman asked with lowered eyes.

'Sure, my child,' the mystic said as he gathered his legs close to him. The woman sat down hesitantly.

The veiled woman sat and just looked at her clasped fingers.

'Something troubles you, my child?'

The woman was silent, and then impulsively thrust a small parcel of cloth towards him. 'Sire, this is for you – you can use it to cover yourself, or to put under your head at night. This stone floor must be very cold and uncomfortable for you.'

The *fakir* nodded as he took the bundle from her hands and looked thoughtfully at her. Such a cultured voice belonged to richer climes, not to some thatched house in the forgotten fields of Kalanaur.

'Many thanks, daughter. May Allah reward you for your kindness.'

After a few moments of silence, and realizing her reluctance to speak freely, the old mystic probed again. 'Daughter, let us begin with your name. What *is* your name, child?'

'Nadira, sire.'

'Nadira... rare and priceless. What a fitting name for you.'

Nadira continued to stare at her hands. The *fakir* spoke at length. 'My daughter, I have watched you over these last many months, coming here to pray every night, elusive as a shadow, flitting from one patch of darkness to another. These are signs of a tormented soul. Of somebody, who has complaints against Allah. Or requests.'

'*Huzoor*... I come at night, because it is forbidden for us women to offer prayers inside the mosque and, initially, I was afraid that you might stop me, or report me to the learned *Aalim*. I preferred the night, for in the Holy Quran it says, "Come to me at night, after you have done your daily work. Spend the nights in prayer and worship, for your night is free."You know all this, and more, sire.'

'*Ameen*,'intoned the *fakir*.

Nadira looked towards the *fakir* as he slipped the cloth from his face. A dark, wizened face with a neatly trimmed beard could be seen. The eyes were black and shone with kindness.

'True, true. But there is something deeper and sinister, which claws at your inner heart, and sends you forth into dark, wintry nights to seek Allah's intercession on your behalf.'

Nadira flung back her veil and, with tears streaming from her dark grey eyes, cried, 'Yes, sire! I am a tortured soul. And I do weep, and I do cry and curse, and I lament for all that I have lost.' She put her face in her palms.

The mystic looked at the stars, and whispered, '*Ya Allah*, help this child,' and, turning towards the lady, he said, 'Unburden your soul, child. It is a heavy burden that you carry.'

Nadira wept softly, as she said, 'You must be wondering, sire, why I come here? I could have done it from the privacy of my home also, and not risked the wrath of the *Aalim* and the *Khadims*. I come here to seek revenge, for it was here that the *khutba* for Emperor Akbar was read, many, many years ago. And, hardly three hundred *dands* from here, was he crowned the emperor of Hindustan, sitting on the *Akbari Takht*! And, on that day, was my fate ravaged for ever!'

'You carry so much pain, daughter. Who are you?'

She turned her face towards the *fakir,* and, with tears glistening in her eyes, calmly said, 'I am Nadira, alias Anarkali! From the harem of Prince Salim.'

*

Winter turned to spring, and the resplendent *gul mohar* along with the silk cotton tree and the *gul-e-fanoos* trees were shedding their winter lethargy and donning new leaves. Roses, lilies, peonies, and irises were striving to compete with the shimmering red, blue, and gold of the people's spring attire.

Many nights had passed in solitude and prayers between the veiled woman and the *fakir.* The silent walls and pillars of the mosque, privy to thousands of confessions, appeals, prayers and conspiracies, strove to remain aloof from the pain, faith, and hopes brought inside its sanctified walls by the faithful. The old mendicant spoke little, but prayed to ease the suffering of this young woman, who risked her life every night to pray at the abode of Allah, the Almighty and Most Merciful. The woman too spoke little, but wept in silence at the cruel hand which Destiny had dealt her.

On one such night, Nadira sat in the shadows and watched the old mystic eat the wheat puffed balls fried in mustard, salt, and chillies that she now occasionally brought for him. Once, he had lightly admonished her to abstain from bringing food every day. His words still resounded in her ears. 'Nadira, my child... do not bring me food every day. Such luxuries as daily food and your company will distract me from my True Path. I prefer to remain hungry for His love and mercy. You are a child to me, and are always welcome... but saturate me not with worldly ties and the superficial needs of mind and body. If you must, then just give me some coarse bread to eat, once in a while.'

As the *fakir* brushed off the dry flakes from the floor and from his *chador*, he looked at the wooden staff lying next to her, and remarked with a twinkle in his eyes, 'The long stick that you carry, child, signifies a long journey. Don't tell me that you are preparing to go on a pilgrimage!'

'*Huzoor*, I am not fortunate enough to embark on a pilgrimage. I have neither the means, nor the will, to embark on such prodigious missions. I may leave on a quest.'

'Quest for what, child?'

'In search of justice. In search of my lost dreams. In search of a new life for my infant son. In search of the jesting courtiers who hound innocents to death.' Her voice was as chilled as the arctic wind.

The Mohammedan ascetic sat huddled, with nary a word. The silent walls and pillars, impervious to the mundane, now suddenly became alert. Nadira looked at the old man sitting, his face averted, and a rush of affection coursed through her.

'Father,' she said quietly.

A startled gaze, and eyes brimming with tears, searched her face.

'Father,' she said again, and shuffled closer to his feet. 'Your eyes seek answers which I do not know. You wanted to ask me all these months, but never have, the reason for my suffering. My unceremonious eviction from the *Shahi Qila* and my existence as a mere parasite on royal patronage is well known to you. I spoke not a word against His Majesty, and suffered every travail in silence. But now, these last six months have wrought havoc on my soul, and sanity.'

The *fakir* continued his silent vigil.

'As I told you earlier, my elder brother Mukarram was held hostage by the emperor to enforce my silence and loyalty to the Crown. Six months ago, in September, he took his own life by a guard's sword in the prison dungeons. The reason was not deprivation, but depravity. For three years he had endured the poisoned barbs of his sister being called a common prostitute, a slut and a whore. My name, Anarkali, given by the emperor at the time of sending me away, was variously interpreted as a luscious fruit, and its many sexual interpretations were daily thrust upon my brother. Slowly, his wife, and my mother, were also coloured in the same dye. That is when he decided to end his life of false ignominy.'

After a brief pause, she spoke again. 'He has a young wife and two small children.'

Silence prevailed. Only the walls and stones of the Three Domed Mosque clicked their sympathy in the creaks and sighs of a distressed soul.

Nadira continued softly, 'He was not weak, sire! He had endured three years of incarceration on my behalf – so that I could walk free. His only fault was that he was my brother! It would not have ended like this, had they not tried to sodomise him that night...'

'Enough said, enough,' rasped the old man. 'Who told you all this?'

'The palace slaves and eunuchs, sire! There are still many, within the palace, who secretly wish prosperity and health for me and my child.'

'Where will you go, my daughter?'

'To Lahore, father. My story must end from where it began.'

The *fakir* nodded, and then softly whispered, 'Name Firdaus as Firdaus Salim Sultan... Posterity shall remember him as the forgotten son of Prince Salim and his unfortunate love, Anarkali.'

'I will, sire. I shall leave in a few days, and may not be able to come again to meet you, father. Bless me, pray for us, and keep us in your thoughts, always.' Nadira could barely whisper the words through her trembling lips.

'Go with the blessings of Allah on your soul. And here, take this,' and so saying, delved into the recesses of his black blanket. He took out a silver amulet on a chain, and, raising it to the darkened skies, handed it to her.

'Place this around your neck. It shall protect you from evil and debauchery. You have called me father, and I look upon you as such, hence, know all – the skies, the stars, the night breeze, and yonder shrubs – that I protect this child with my own soul. To those who will bring you pain and suffering, You – the skies, stars, breeze, and shrubs – witnesses to my protection tonight, will remove such heathen within five *hijris* from such date. *Al-Madad, Ya Allah.*'

The *fakir* continued, 'And, for all the morsels that I have eaten of your house, I pray to Allah that as many centuries will remember your name, Anarkali. Neither Death nor Time will erase your tryst with Tyranny.'

The veiled woman quietly merged into the welcoming shadows, and was gone.

*

On Tuesday the tenth of March, 1597, Nadira Anarkali left Kalanaur with her young son, Firdaus Salim Sultan, and a few trusted retainers, for Lahore, a distance of twenty-eight *kos,* reaching her destination in just under ten days.

*

(CHAPTER 5)

DARIYA-E-NAKHRAE GUDAKHTAH

(The Rivers of Molten Gold)

Bhairon ka Sthan

Ichhra, one kos west of Walled City

Lahore

21st March, 1597

08:20 a.m.

Nadira stepped out of the octagonal room of the *caravanserai,* and drew her veil over her face. She had reached the village of Ichhra the previous evening, and had requested a night's stay at the *caravanserai.*

As her attendants placed the assorted bags, chests and vessels on the bullock carts, Nadira walked ahead with Firdaus by her side. She waited a while at the fork from where one road led to the *Masjeedi Darwaza* of the Walled City, and the other led towards the Chand Raat Temple, a few hundred yards further down.

As she waited for her small baggage train to arrive, Baqar Khan, her most trusted attendant, rode up and dismounted.

'Begum Sahiba, I have had a word with the *khidmatgaar* of the Hindu temple, and he awaits your arrival. I am told that the imperial squad does a check on the *serai* between eleven o'clock and noon. It would be most prudent if you could wait until the *Asir Namaaz*.'

'Thank you. Till then we can visit the bazaar. Please tell Mahmood to find lodgings inside the Walled City for the others.'

As the sun travelled on its western leg, and the time drew near for the *Asir Namaaz*, Nadira hurried back towards the Hindu temple known as *Bhairon ka Sthan* which stood a little away from the bustle of Ichhra Bazaar.

She had been informed that the temple was rarely visited, as it stood near the Hindu burning grounds. It had suited her purpose perfectly, for she had no wish to proclaim her return to Lahore and face the desiccating wrath of the emperor.

The temple priest came out to meet her, with a large black dog at his heels. Nadira, stopped at the sight of the vicious-looking dog. The priest spoke to her. 'Many *salaams* to you, lady. Please come in – do not be afraid of him... he just looks ferocious.'

Nadira still hesitated, her Mohammedan sensibilities unsettled over the close proximity of a dog, which was considered unclean in their religion.

The priest spoke again. 'Lady, you have sought refuge with us. Your servant, who now stands behind you, has elaborated upon your persecution by the court officials subsequent to your brother's death. This place is the Abode of Lord Bhairav, and He gives shelter to all those who are weak, deprived, and tormented. This dog, *TeevraDand*, is His vehicle, and Lord Bhairava, in all His Majesty, sits astride him.'

The priest gave a hard look at the attendant, Baqar Khan, as he laughed aloud at the prospect of a God sitting astride a black dog.

'What do you snigger at, Khan? You have yet not yet been blessed by maturity. Spiritual sense is seven oceans away from you.' The priest's ire was on the rise. 'You only want to see God in a golden cocoon... but it is not so, my dear friend. As your *Holy Quran* and our revered books teach us, God resides in every living being – He sees neither form, nor beauty – for all are His own. And, as for Lord Bhairav, He rides a dog for all others abhor it. It is in His nature to give shelter to the weak and persecuted, and to those who are shunned by the high and mighty. Wait! Hear it from your own people. Hey, Chooza Mastan, please come here and explain what a dog signifies.'

Nadira turned towards a group of ascetics sitting in a far corner of the temple courtyard, and watched a Moslem *fakir* attired in green with a black turban detach himself from the group and head towards them.

Nadira raised her palms in greeting, and the *fakir* nodded at her, transfixing the now suitably chastised attendant with smoke-filled eyes. 'A dog, my son, is the most loyal follower of his master, as we aspire to be of Allah and his Prophet, Mohammed, Peace Be Upon Him. He stays up nights, as the world sleeps, and prays for the wealth and wellbeing of his master. He prays that "*Ya Allah*, give work and good fortune to my master, for he gives me two morsels of food every day. I cannot speak his language to thank him, nor does he understand mine, hence, *Ya Allah*, in all Your glory, feed and protect my master." And, in our mystical world, he is known as *Fakire Begayer Himyan*, or a *fakir* without a beggars bag. And that, my son, is the dog for you in the world of mystics.'

Nadira turned towards the temple head, and quietly said, 'Thank you, sire, for permitting us to stay for a few days in this holy shrine, until we can seek proper accommodation within the city.'

'What is your name, lady?'

'Anarkali, sire, and this is my only son, Firdaus Salim Sultan.'

'Come with me, daughter. You can share the accommodation with my wife and daughters in the *zenana* quarters over there. And your two servants can stay in the small group of rooms behind the cowshed,' explained the priest as he led them towards his small cottage, which had a covered platform running around it.

'They will just stay the night, sire. Tomorrow, they shall proceed to the city to find work and accommodation.'

*

Akbari Mahal

Shahi Qila, Lahore

Preparations for Navroz Festival

26th March, 1597; late evening

Baqar Khan and another trusted retainer, Mazhar Khan, had started work as menial labourers with Bismillah Khan Turbegi, the *Mir Saman.* They had been recommended to the *Mir Saman* by Sheikh Qazi Obaidullah, a noted Shia cleric of the city, and owner of the huge mansion known as *Lal Haveli*. Since the *Navroz* festival would fall on the twenty-seventh of March, their appearance a week earlier had not generated many enquiries, and they were readily employed as manual helpers.

While the half dozen retainers of Nadira had taken quarters in and around the Shia *mohalla,* she continued to stay with the temple priest's family at Ichhra. The *Navroz* festival every year brought forth an army of merchants with their wares from many countries. Puppeteers, dancers, wrestlers, acrobats, and animal tamers from all over the eastern world descended on Lahore for the nine days of festivities. Many would be rewarded, and many old sinners pardoned, for this was the time of the year when imperial bounties were freely given.

Over the last three days, Baqar and Mazhar had worked with surprising effort and intelligence to gain the trust of the eunuch supervising the slaves and labour working inside the main quadrangle of the royal palace. Preparations had been going on for the past month, with master craftsmen and decorators converging on the royal court from the farthest corners of the realm and beyond. The fort complex was decorated in colours of green and gold, while the royal apartments and inner palaces boasted an ocean of colours casting their refulgence on the stout doors and stones of the fort.

The first day ceremony of the emperor's weighing in gold and precious gemstones would fall tomorrow, and several scores of attendants and craftsmen were busy stretching the silk and brocade tapestries and awnings near the Akbari Mahal and *Daulatkhana e Diwan e khas*, where the actual weighing would be done. Bales upon bales of silk, muslin, cotton, and brocade were spread over the quadrangle in giant heaps.

A line of slaves were carrying barrels of *ghee* and spices to the additional royal kitchens set up for the festivities, just behind the administrative section on the right. Baqar, having been given the extra responsibility of counting the *ghee* barrels, with their red-coloured neck collars, motioned Mazhar to put down a *ghee* barrel near the tent where he was standing. As Mazhar turned back to fetch another barrel, Baqar rolled the barrel on its side and sat upon it, wiping his brow.

Casually, he untied the coarse cloth wrapped around his waist, and emptied the gun powder mixture over the barrel. He dropped to his knees, as if to arrange the drapes of cloth spread on the ground, and carefully pulled out a few bundles of silk and cotton to cover the barrel from a casual observer. With a quick tug, he pulled away the red collar from the barrel's neck, and the five *seers* of ghee flowed freely into the heaped cascades of silken cloth.

He walked ahead nonchalantly, and again asked a slave to put down a barrel. Once the slave had disappeared behind the wooden partition, Baqar loudly called another slave to carry the barrel to the royal kitchens. Any chance observer would not have noticed the quick thrust of the iron spike into the barrel. A thin stream of *ghee* followed the slave as he carried the keg on his shoulders to the massive storage area.

'We do not have all night with us. We have to finish by nine o'clock, before the flower decorators arrive. So move your sorry limbs and get this work finished. And you, Baqar! Go to the *Diwan e khas O Aam* and tell Mian Masood that his team is required here urgently to hem the tapestries. Warn them that His Highness Prince Salim might come for a review any time soon.' The voice of the *Ustad* in charge of curtains and fabrics was fraught with anxiety.

Baqar Khan hurried across the quadrangle and turned towards the special pavilion being erected in front of the *Diwan e Aam*. He marvelled at the grandeur of the palaces, as the hundreds of yards of shimmering silks and brocades strung across the buildings, and hung from every arch and panel in alluring designs, caught the ochre rays of the setting sun, and danced a glittering farewell. Strings of gold and silver coloured leaves were strung in geometric patterns across the open areas and provided a radiant canopy.

He could now see the *chiraghchiyans* going about their business, lighting hundreds of lamps in the wall brackets and alcoves of the palaces. Torch-bearers, with their long-handled torches,were lighting the heavy wooden and iron torches fixed to the walls and ramparts of the fort. The Shahi Qila was slowly transforming itself into a sea of radiance and delight.

Baqar found the senior tailor, Mian Masood, buried under heaps of silk and sequined muslin. 'Janab Masood, the *Ustad* wants you urgently at the Akbari Mahal. You must hurry,' he added for good measure.

A sour-looking Mian Masood, eyes bleary with fatigue, emerged from under the mound of silk with which he was cohabiting, and, extending his neck, rudely squawked, 'Here, take this. Cut my neck and take it to your *Ustad.* And stuff it behind his buttocks. Come, take it.' The room erupted with laughter as his assistants either sunk under yards of silk, or perched upon ladders, chortled with glee.

Baqar could not help smiling, and said, 'Mian, you do it yourself. The heavenly smell there will galvanize you into action.'

There was more laughter as Masood, with a sigh, called to a young man – perhaps his son – 'Meraj! Just sew these together, and have it strung in diagonal stripes from here to the *Tosha Khana.* And, don't forget to lay the golden brocade at intervals of three. In the meantime, let me go and smell heaven.'

'Hey, *Ustad.* Where am I to hang these?' A young boy, hardly fifteen, pointed to a couple of huge silk paintings depicting a royal hunt.

Mian Masood pointed towards the pillars closest to the throne, and said, 'One on either side. The emperor enjoys these. Also, ensure that the rugs woven with strings of pure gold are laid from the steps to the throne. And, when the flower decorators come in, tell them to just edge the gold rugs with their petals, not cover them.'

As Mian Masood walked towards the quadrangle to enter the Akbari Mahal, Baqar, walking in the lee of the pillars, lightly pushed a huge silver *Shama i Kafuri* to the ground. As the three-yard-high candle stand with its eight wicks fell silently on the mounds of silk and muslin, flames erupted with an enormous *whoosh*. Baqar, catching the shadows amongst the pillars, raced in the other direction.

As the shouts and screams intensified, and workmen from all directions rushed towards the fire, he hurried back. Taking advantage of the utter chaos he snatched another flaming torch from its wall bracket and threw it onto the strings of silken cloth, bundled in layers upon layers of different sheens. Silently, he took to the far side of the shadows again.

The fire, fed by the silk, muslin, and brocade, leapt from one arch to another, like a fast, slithering snake. It travelled furiously across the fabric-draped roof, which fell in big tatters raging with fire onto the backs and bodies of the workmen trying to stem the flames with their turbans or *pattas.* This usually had a negative effect, with the turbans and *pattas* themselves catching fire.

The fire was travelling at a frenetic pace, and seemed to have engulfed the hall from all sides. Men, with their clothes and bodies on fire, rushed screaming and crying towards the open area separating the *Diwan e aam* from the *Toshakhana.*

The leaping flames could now be seen from outside the fort walls, too. There was a huge commotion from the streets as people surged towards the three main gates. Inside the fort, workmen, crew, soldiers, attendants, and slaves, all ran from different directions towards the fire.

Blazing people were stumbling and falling over the tent fabrics, ropes, poles, and mountains of dazzling cloth. As the flames travelled upwards on the cloth-decorated poles and devoured the canopies of silk and brocade, large swathes of burning canopies fell on the decorative materials stored underneath, as well as on the running, screaming horde. The burning swathes followed no regimen, and fell with confounding accuracy on humans and any other combustible material alike.

In a few frenzied minutes, the raging fire had reduced the proud grounds of the *Diwan e Khas O Aam* into a seething cauldron of untamed fire, as it raced towards the heavy silver and wooden doors of the *Toshakhana*. The royal *ahadis* guarding the *Toshakhana* stood resolute in front of the heavy doors, until fear and flames soon devoured them.

Mazhar, watching the rush of cooks and helpers from the kitchen area towards the *Masjeedi Darwaza*,slipped unobserved into the adjoining storage area and quickly opened a dozen barrels and kicked them around. As *ghee* poured out of the drums, he lit several long strings of cotton and threw them around the *ghee*-soaked floor. Fire, insidious as ever, licked its way around the floor and onto the welcoming barrels.

A royal archer, running across the broad battlement behind the royal palace, witnessed this act of deliberate arson and shot an arrow. Mazhar felt a searing pain in his left shoulder as the arrow pierced his workman's clothes. Stung, he fell onto a heap of burning rope as he tried to snatch the embedded arrow.

Immediately, he was on his feet again as fire engulfed his trousers and long shirt. In agony and consumed by fire, he careered across the fiery concourse.

In a short time, the forest of fire had travelled to the wood and coal cinder block, where huge mountains of coal and firewood had been stored for cooking purposes.

The emperor, along with Prince Salim, Prince Khusrau, and Prince Khurram, on horseback and surrounded by a phalanx of cavalry with matchlock men running alongside, were being escorted out of the *Masjeedi Darwaza* . The royal macebearers, traditionally responsible for leading the royal family, had been brutally pushed aside by the emperor's bodyguards as they formed a close phalanx around him and galloped through the huge gates. Princes Salim, Khusrau, and Khurram followed in his wake, surrounded by yet another detachment of *ahadis.*

The Dowager Empress, Maryam Makani, and the chief wives of the emperor and Prince Salim, were mounted on hastily assembled elephants and horses, with eunuchs, slaves, and attendants hoisting curtains around their *howdahs* and saddles. As they rapidly descended from the broad battlement of *Hathi Paer,* the mace bearers, running ahead, used their gold and silver maces with terrible effect on the assembled populace, irrespective of rank or gender. On Prince Salim's signal, a detachment of *ahadis* broke away and rushed to form a protective echelon around the royal ladies.

The hungry fire, devouring without respite, fed on the heavy wooden roof beams, the chests and furniture in the royal apartments, the wooden doors, frames, and ornamental screens in the seraglio and the royal apartments.

Hundreds of palace attendants, slaves, soldiers, and town people had formed a human chain from the *Diwan e Aam* concourse to the River Ravi, which flowed around the north wall of the fort, passing buckets of water and wet sand to quell the fire. Horsemen, with canisters of all sizes strapped to their horses, were galloping in and out of the mighty gates, delivering water to the front ranks of people engaged in fire fighting.

The heat was so intense and sustained that the gold and silver inlays from the ceilings, walls, frescoes, gilded furniture, and royal animal harnesses, from the inlaid doors, decorated walls and brackets, melted and flowed in thin, burning rivers of silver and gold onto the streets of Lahore.

*

At Ichhra, Nadira sat on the elevated stone platform encircling the shrine, and looked at the red cast of the night sky about her. In the distance, the Shahi Qila still sputtered and spat flame, as angry embers rose into the sky to find yet another perch to incinerate.

Baqar Khan, having arrived just a few minutes ago, covered in soot and ashes, with his clothes singed, lay prone on the ground. The enormity of his actions, and their possible ramifications, now haunted him. As he rested his head on his hands and looked at the fiery sky, he wondered if his end was near.

A sob escaped his lips as he recollected the vision of a badly burned Mazhar, with blazing clothes stuck on his back and head, running madly across the quadrangle, blinded by pain and fire. Baqar had watched helplessly, as Mazhar slowly folded into a warp, and collapsed.

*

Emperor Akbar, now mounted on his elephant, surveyed the destruction around him.

The molten rivers of silver and gold, still hot and liquid on the streets outside the fort, shone brightly in the moonlight.

(CHAPTER 6)

BIRBAL, EIN KHANAI TUST

(This Is Your Home, Birbal)

Akbari Darwaza / Maseeti Darwaza

Shahi Qila, Lahore

30th March, 1597

09:30 a.m.

Haze enveloped the Shahi Qila as the stone walls and floors still simmered from the gigantic fire, which had engulfed the major part of the fort just four days ago. Court drummers and musicians, unable to sit in the stifling heat of the *naubatkhana*, had lined the entrance, and were playing softly. The royal flag, guarded by a squadron of cavalry and foot soldiers, had emerged from the fort just a few minutes earlier.

The fort had been besieged with people in the street outside since the night of fire. They had come armed with small chisels, hammers, and knives to scrape the molten silver and gold from the street paving. The imperial guards had warned them off several times, but, like scavenging birds, they returned with renewed vigour. The more enterprising of them had brought spades and small rakes to scrape the street of its gold and silver streams.

The sounds of trumpets and kettledrums could now be heard from inside the fort, and the first of the trumpeters emerged, followed by the royal drummers. There was a flurry of activity as the soldiers gathered near the gate, unsheathed their swords, and raised them, as the twenty-one Moghul flag bearers marched out in procession. Behind the flag bearers marched a detail of camp attendants leading a lone camel carrying bundles of white cloth. Its sole purpose was to provide funeral shrouds for the animals and men that may die on the march, so that the monarch's eye would not behold carcasses strewn by the wayside, and thus make the campaign inauspicious.

The contingent of drummers, trumpeters, canopy bearers and the nine spare horses of the emperor were led out, followed by the twenty or so *bishtis,* who continually wet the ground on which the emperor was to pass.

Finally, the royal *ahadis* in their green and gold uniform, sitting proudly on their steeds, cantered out. These heavy cavalry units were the emperor's personal troops, and were an integral part of any imperial assault. Handpicked and brave, they formed the main body of the emperor's personal guard.

Two heavily caparisoned elephants, with the Moghul banner strung between them, emerged to shouts of '*Zindabad, Zindabad*', and lazily swayed their trunks, excited to be on the move again. Sitting on their *howdahs* were six sharpshooters with muskets and matchlocks, scanning the crowd and the surroundings for any visible threats.

Emperor Akbar, barely visible under a huge canopied *howdah* of gold encrusted with precious gems and gold tassels, rode into sight, seated on his favourite war elephant Hawai. Behind him sat two nobles, holding his personal sword, quiver, and bow. His full personal armoury, the *Shahi Qur*, was carried on four Bactrian camels, which themselves were escorted by nobles, imperial flags, and the *naqqaras.* The attending *mansabdars*, on their richly saddled horses, rode on all sides of the emperor with drawn swords. The Rajput chieftains in their colourful turbans secured the rear, as was their royal privilege, and carried glittering lances with *panchrangi* pennants streaming behind.

Roars of '*Padshah Salamat*'and '*Padshah Zindabad*' rent the air, as Hawai, used to such celebrations, majestically plodded onwards. Just behind the rear echelons of the escorting Rajputs came Prince Salim, riding atop his war elephant, *Qaimur*. A body of imperial *ahadis* rode in front, and to his rear.

The royal procession wound its way through the narrow streets of the Walled City, towards *Kashmeri Darwaza*. Emperor Akbar, with his heir apparent, Prince Salim, was en route to Kashmere to set up his court.

The Shahi Qila would remain bereft of its monarch for the next seven months.

*

Kashmeri Darwaza

Walled City, Lahore

30th March, 1597

11:40 a.m.

Nadira stayed inside the precinct of the old *haveli* belonging to Mian Shah Altaf, watching the people assemble near the Kashmeri Darwaza. A group of women, veiled and escorted by their eunuchs and palanquin bearers, stood near the broad veranda of the *haveli*. She moved forward and quietly stood at the rear.

The sounds of the emperor's procession came nearer, and the first of the standard bearers marched past. Royal attendants, with silver maces in their hands, could be seen running alongside, trying to push the spectators aside. A great shout of '*Shahenshah i Hind, Zindabad*' went up, and the veiled women moved closer to the road.

The eunuchs, shouting, 'Make way for the *Begums.* Stand aside,' jostled with the crowd, and cleared a small area for the women to step in. Nadira kept herself back, and watched as Emperor Akbar, with a benevolent smile on his face, swayed past. Oh, how many times had she seen the emperor in this classic pose, with his head inclined to the right and a slight smile or frown playing upon his face.

As Hawai came near the huge gate, he curled his trunk and gave a fearsome trumpet call. Alarmed, hundreds of pigeons, roosting in the roof crannies and crevices of the wooden beams, flew away in a flurry of flapping wings and floating feathers.

Coming closer now was Prince Salim on his richly arrayed elephant. The yak's tail banner flew merrily from the rear of his *howdah* as he sat staring straight ahead. There was a strained, tired look on his face, and Nadira knew that his indulgence in opium and wine had not abated. In fact, she thought, in these last five years his face seemed to have become more flushed and pallid.

Nadira could restrain herself no longer and threw up her veil. Disregarding the reproving stares of the gathered women, she wanted to shout 'Salim, my love! I love you so!' But no words came out. Tears, unbidden, were her only solace.

*

As *Qaimur* neared the arched portal of Kashmeri Darwaza, Prince Salim felt a tremendous urge to turn around, as if the roads left behind beckoned. Glancing to his left he saw a string of camels tethered together, carrying the first crop of watermelons. On his right were a group of traders sitting on their haunches, and the wooden toy shops behind them.

Just ahead, by the Kashmeri Darwaza, was a gnarled *neem* tree which leant to the right as if wishing to brush the royals goodbye.

His elephant was about to pass through the stone archway when Salim leaned and twisted around. At the far back he caught a flash of a tear-stained, beautiful, and achingly familiar face amongst a huddle of black-veiled women. He stood with a shout. '*Mahout*, stop! Stop, I said.'

The *mahout,* unnerved by the princely command, kicked the elephant behind his right ear, and called, 'Heda! Heda!'

Qaimur, heeding his *mahout*'s call, gave a low rumble and stopped. Salim stepped out of the seating canopy, and, holding the golden staff for support, gazed long and hard towards the group of women by the *haveli* wall. Partly obscured by the arch and columns of the gateway, Salim searched in vain for that one face which had kept him distracted and restless these past five years.

A cavalry officer rode up, as the escorting riders reined in their horses and milled around in apparent confusion at the prince's halt. Mounted archers and matchlock bearers were now surrounding the imperial elephant, and the *Sahiban i Ihtimam* had returned with their silver maces to keep the crowds at bay.

'Your Majesty! Please do not expose yourself. Is there a problem, Sire?'

'Rup Singh. Get the elephant turned around. And ride up to the yonder women there...' he said, pointing. 'Yes, yes, those in the black veils. Hold them. Hold them… Now, hurry.'

The assembled troops, following the line of Prince Salim's extended arm, made a dash for the motley group of women standing by the *haveli.* In fright, the women, eunuchs, and general towns people scattered, only to be surrounded by the riders of the prince's cavalry.

Rup Singh and his squadron of lancers raced ahead of the elephant as it started to turn around in the confined space of the accompanying troopers, musicians, and the gathered traders. The *mahout*, pulling the right ear of *Qaimur*,and with a sharp dig of his heel behind the head, goaded the elephant to turn back.

The royal trumpeters, on seeing the imperial elephant turn back, sounded the retreat. Salim, vexed at the prospect of losing Anarkali again, ignored the sounds of this sacrilege. As Salim neared the group of women and their attendants, he asked, 'Who answers to the name of Nadira *urf* Anarkali?'

Deep silence. 'I ask again… Who answers to the name of Nadira. Anarkali?' The prince's voice was stern and commanding.

The heads remained bowed. Salim gestured to his chief eunuch, Qaid Akram, and he stepped forward to lift the veils. There was pain and desperation in Salim's eyes as each upturned veil failed to quench his search for that one elusive persona. One of the women, unveiled and trembling from the fright and shame, whispered softly to Qaid Akram.

The eunuch turned to Prince Salim, and informed him, 'Your Majesty… this lady says that there was a tall woman here, who bared her face for a few seconds, but left immediately as Your Highness stopped. She is not known to these women, and seems to be a traveller from some other clime.'

Salim looked at the faces again, and with a glazed look sank back into his canopied throne.

Further ahead, Emperor Akbar frowned, having heard the royal buglers and trumpeters sound the retreat.

In the narrow bylanes of *Androoni Sheher*, a tall, veiled figure walked rapidly towards the welcoming folds of obscurity.

*

Dil Amiz Gardens

Across the River Ravi

30th March, 1597

Late night

'I cannot be mistaken, Sayyid... I cannot be!' Prince Salim paced the royal tent as Sayyid Abdullah of Barha stood near the huge silver candle stand.

Prince Salim glanced up and reiterated. 'Her face, glistening with tears, yet supremely beautiful – how can I ever forget? And I saw the same beauteous face, shining with love and longing in the midst of those black shrouded old women. Just as the crescent moon shines in the sweeping darkness of lonely nights, her face shone forth from the multitude of gross populace crowding the streets.' He paused and looked at Sayyid.

Sayyid Abdullah, sensing the disquiet in Salim's mind, preferred to stay silent.

'Sayyid, it has been five long years since I have seen her, or my little son, Firdaus. Why? Only because *Sahib i Hazrat, Jahanpanah* Jalal Ud Din Mohammed Akbar, exiled her forever! It was my biggest mistake, my biggest, to inform His Majesty about the child's birth.' There was bitterness in his voice.

'You did the right thing, Your Highness. If it had come to the emperor's knowledge through other sources, Anarkali and her child would have forfeited their lives. The emperor would not have allowed any shadow on the throne arising from a concubine's child...' Sayyid bit his tongue, as he realized the import of his words.

To his surprise, Salim did not fly into one of his monumental rages, but almost pleaded. 'So what, Sayyid? He was born of my blood... out of our love, and innocence. Thrones and empires do not create children... love does.'

'Yes, Your Highness. You are absolutely correct. But, you know the harem strictures and intrigues would have been fatal for them both. You are aware, Sire, that His Majesty will brook no violation on certain issues, this being one of them.'

Prince Salim spoke angrily. 'Then what about Prince Murad and Prince Daniyal? They are also born of concubines to my father, His Majesty. Why were Their Highnesses Bibi Kheira and Bibi Miriam not turned out from Fatehpur Sikri in *Hijri* 978 and 980 when Prince Murad and Prince Daniyal were born? And, Prince Murad, with his uncouth manners and intemperance, has been sent to the Deccan, as if he can win battles, where generals like *Khan e Khana* Abdur Rahim and Raja Ali Khan have been struggling for the last two years?

'And, Sayyid... do you know the latest? His Majesty is sick and tired of listening to the petty squabbles of Prince Murad and *Khan e Khana*, and has decided to replace them with Mirza Shahrukh of Badkahshan.'

Sayyid Abdullah started in surprise. 'Mirza Shahrukh? But he was thrown out of his own kingdom by the Uzbegs! How can His Majesty give him the command of Deccan forces?'

'Are you questioning the emperor's decision, Sayyid?' The words of Prince Salim dripped with menace.

'I beg your thousand pardons, Highness. It was not meant to be... How can I, a mere servant of Your Majesty, even imply anything as evil and sacrilegious as this? I have served, and will always serve, Your Majesty with my utmost devotion and sincerity. Please forgive me, Sire.'

He heaved a sigh of relief as he saw Prince Salim's face soften. These Timurids, thought Sayyid, are still nomadic in their heads, beliefs and loyalties. He was astonished at their sudden shifts in words and actions – one moment they could be plotting to murder their own father, and the next, they would be defending the same person with their lives. Step softly, Mian Abdullah, he cautioned himself.

Salim sat on the richly carpeted floor and looked with distaste at the *dastarkhwan* spread before him. The aroma of fragrant rice and mutton stew, with platters of clay-oven-grilled *kebabs*, failed to excite Prince Salim. Motioning the attendants away, he addressed Sayyid Abdullah.

'Sayyid, I think you should go back to Lahore. She is there, somewhere, and she must know that I love her yet, and have not forgotten about Firdaus. Her brother, what was his name, the one who was held hostage at Shahi Qila? Anyway, visit him... You should get some information about her whereabouts.'

Sayyid spoke in measured tones. 'Your Highness, may I suggest that I be allowed to accompany you for a few more days, to allay suspicion? The *Mir Bakshi* will definitely report my departure to the emperor in his early morning brief, and that may result in my immediate recall and interrogation.'

'Quite true, Sayyid. We shall discuss this a week from now.'

*

Bhairon ka Sthan

Ichhra

10th April, 1597

Evening hours; after dinner

As Nadira sat with the wife of the temple priest and her three young children in the quivering glow of a small earthen lamp, she took out a necklace of translucent pink pearls from her silk pouch and, holding it towards the poorly dressed lady, said, 'Ratna Devi, please accept this as a humble token of my love and affection for you all.'

'Oh, no, Nadira Begum. I cannot accept this!'

Ramadeen, the temple priest, who was sitting on the other side of a hastily drawn screen, gravely said, 'Dear Sister, we do not seek riches and favours from those who pass by us. Lord Bhairav provides for us – in fact, he provides for all of us. You came here as a guest of Bhairav, and as a dear daughter you shall depart.'

Nadira pressed the pearl necklace into Ratna's palm, and whispered, 'Keep it, sister, as a remembrance.'

Turning to the priest, she spoke softly. 'You have been most kind, Holy Priest. When I leave tomorrow morning, I shall leave a piece of my heart here. I shall depart with the blessings of Bhairav, and will return as a daughter coming home. May Allah provide you with a plentiful life. Bum Bhairav!'

'Bum Bhairav,' replied the priest as he picked up his rug and carried it outside to sleep.

*

The next morning Nadira, with Firdaus, departed with the golden rays of the emerging sun playing on the spires of the conical dome.

*

Laal Haveli

Near Morchi Gate

Walled City, Lahore

21st April, 1597

Afternoon

'Begum Sahiba, there is some disturbing news from the market,' panted Maqbool, the ancient retainer from the days of Nadira's childhood. He stood gasping for breath with his head bowed.

Nadira smiled at his abject dislike of all worries, either imagined or real, and waited for him to say more. He signalled his expectation of being heard by quizically raising one eyebrow.

'Maqbool, my old faithful, please tell us what you know.' Nadira's eyes twinkled as Firdaus, playing nearby, sidled up to her.

Maqbool almost gasped with relief as the words came tumbling out. 'Daughter, there is fire all around us. There are persons, rich and powerful, who are hunting for us.'

'Hunting, or searching for us?'

Expletives flew true and fast from Maqbool's betel-stained mouth as he sat down on his haunches and cast a worried look at Nadira. 'You are not comprehending the gravity of the matter, child, or you would not have been so silly about this issue. Do you know, a few nobles of the court visited the Shahi Qila dungeons a few days back, wanting to meet Mukarram, your brother, and when told that he had committed suicide almost two years ago have been searching high and low for you and Firdaus.' The long postulation left him almost wasted.

‘And what was the result of their search, Maqbool Mian?’

‘It is by Allah’sgrace that no one knows about you in this *mohalla*. Or you would not be sitting pretty like this.’ The rebuke in his words matched his shuffling gait as he walked away.

Firdaus too, got up and waddled away in an imitation of Maqbool.

*

Qurchak Shikargah

Near Nowshera

4th May, 1597

Early morning; before sunrise

Akbar shifted his arms as the attendant moved around to girdle the leather frock around his waist, from which his hunting sword would hang. The sky was still dark and the stars were marking their farewell with a rich brilliance. The sounds of an imperial camp coming to life were becoming evident, with the rattle of vessels and fires being lighted, the neighing and clatter of horses on the move, and the creak and groans of bullock carts returning laden with water and provisions.

The sound of several hundred feet assembling to form the *Qamargah*, and the loud calls of the attendant *shikaris* announced the impending royal hunt, as *qarawals* and camp followers made last minute checks.

The best huntsman of the realm, Haji Jamal Baluch, was accompanying the emperor this time and had reconnoitred over the last two days to find a suitable spot for the *Qamargah*. Satisfied, he had conveyed to the *Qarawal Baigi* a few suitable places to concentrate the hunt and had requisitioned almost a hundred male buffaloes, much to the puzzlement of the *Qarawal Baigi.*

Rai Durga Sisodia, who was the day commander of the camp and a valiant warrior with a *mansab* of four thousand troops, sought permission to enter. Akbar, having his riding cloak fastened at the neck, signalled to the eunuchs to let him through.

'Your Majesty, the *Qurawal Baigi* Mirza Ghazi Beg Turkhan also seeks permission to enter.'

At the emperor's signal, Rai Durga Sisodia and Mirza Ghazi Beg entered, performing the *kornish,* and Rai Durga announced, 'Your Imperial Highness! May it pleasure Your Majesty, that Yakub Shah Chak, son of Yusuf Shah Chak, the defeated Sultan of Kashmere, seeks permission to prostrate himself at your glorious feet.'

A look of displeasure crossed Akbar's face, but he asked, 'Where is he now?'

'He arrived after midnight, Your Majesty, with about a hundred armed riders, who were all arrested and quartered in the prison tents.'

'It is a good sign, Your Majesty. The prey itself walks in and submits himself, even before the hunt has begun. *Subhanallah*!' exclaimed the *Qurawal Baigi.* Mirza Ghazi Beg Turkhani was elated, as an auspicious beginning in his tenure as the Grand Master of the Hunt would invoke royal gifts and special privileges.

Akbar ordered that the arrested prince be brought in, and turned towards Mirza Ghazi Beg.

'What news of the hunt, Mirza?'

'The *qarawals* have all reported a good number of game, Your Majesty. There are tigers, leopards, mountain bears, and wild elephants. Smaller game – antelope and deer – are innumerable, but may not please Your Majesty. And your personal elephants, chosen from your imperial *khasa* stable, are already lined up for your inspection.'

Akbar nodded and turned towards the tent entrance as Yakub Shah Chak was pushed inside and thrown at the emperor's feet.

Yakub Khan extended his manacled hands and, in this prostate form, beseeched the emperor, 'Your Royal Highness, I seek forgiveness for my intransigence in the past, for all the troubles and losses caused to you by me and my clan. I seek your forgiveness, *Shahenshah i Hind*, most forgiving and magnificent of all rulers!'

Akbar's face remained stonily bereft of any emotion, as he recalled the pain and humiliation at the death of Raja Birbal by the Yusufzai's in the Swat valley almost ten years ago. His last meeting with Raja Birbal danced before his eyes:

Ibadatkhana

Fatehpur Sikri

21st October, 1585

Late evening

Wazir Beg Jamil, a mansabdaar of two thousand horses, finished reading from the petition sent by Zain Khan, commander of the Mughal army fighting in the Swat valley.

The emperor looked around at the seated nobles and tried to read their countenances. Half and half, he thought.

He addressed the Mir Arz, Wazir Beg. 'Tell me, Wazir Beg, you have just returned from the valley, and have fought the Yusufzai Pathans. What is your assessment?'

'Your Majesty, the Mughal troops fight with valour and have suffered many hardships. There is no unrest. The Pathans, fighting in their own territory with clear supply lines and knowledge of the terrain, have a definite advantage over us.' He waited for the emperor's reaction.

'Go on, Wazir Beg,' commanded Akbar.

'Majesty! Our numerical superiority is nullified by the narrow gorges that we have to pass through, and those are the preferred places for the Yusufzais to ambush us. It is difficult for our troops, mostly people from the plains, to cover more than five kos a day in hilly terrain. And, Your Majesty, they always attack from the slopes and sides of gorges as our troops are passing through. If I may reiterate, Your Majesty, they can be defeated and chased from these valleys if we can get additional cavalry.'

'What about cannons?'

'The cannons, Your Majesty, are not easy to deploy in the narrow gorges, plus it is very difficult to angle them up the sides of the hills. The ambushes are short and savage, with hardly any time to unhitch and manoeuvre the heavy cannons.'

'Quite true, Wazir Beg,' Akbar said thoughtfully.

Sheikh Abu'l Fazl, who had been listening with rapt attention and wished to alleviate the emperor's worries, spoke up. 'Your Majesty, I would be happy to lead the royal army and wipe off the Yusufzai curs, once and for all. With your permission, Sire.'

Before Akbar could answer, Raja Birbal, sitting across from the emperor and taking great interest in his bejewelled katar, smiled and said, 'Well said, Sheikh. If your sword is as mighty as your pen then, no doubt, the Yusufzais will be hard put to fight, and will readily vacate the Swat Valley. However, sir, your services are critical to the court and it will be the emperor's wish that you continue writing the most cherished and glorious chronicle of our age, the Ain i Akbari, to document these regal years which come once, maybe, in a thousand years.'

As the nobles applauded with soft cries of 'Subhanallah' and 'Ameen', Akbar let out a loud guffaw. 'Raja Birbal and Sheikh, both of you are blessed with wings of imagination, and also with a mighty tongue and a mighty pen, respectively! What we need now is the Fath Ul Mulk to preside.'

The collected nobles, all major grandees of the court, were immediately on their feet with drawn swords, clamouring for permission to proceed and wage war.

Akbar raised his hand, and said, 'If all of you are raring to go, then decide amongst yourselves. Choose two, and be aware that this campaign is being waged in far-off lands, in hostile terrain and against the treacherous Pathans.'

There was again a chorus of cries affirming their will to make war.

Birbal softly whispered in Akbar's ears, and Akbar spoke sharply. 'Now listen. Raja Birbal has suggested that this issue started between him and the Sheikh. So, let the dice decide. If it is an even number, Raja Birbal will go. If it is an odd number, then Sheikh Abu'l Fazl will depart. And, for the other general, I nominate Hakim Abul Fath to lead the army. If not my sword, at least its name will travel with the venerable Hakim.'

Hakim Abul Fath stepped forward and with a deep bow performed the kornish.

The dice was rolled, and the number four stared mockingly. The emperor was speechless.

In the echoing silence of the hall, there were two hearts which beat with trepidation – the emperor's, for he knew the travails that awaited Raja Birbal; and Raja Birbal's own, for an unpleasant knock in his rising heartbeats prophesied a long farewell.

With tears welling in his eyes, Akbar stepped forth and put his hand on Raja Birbal's shoulder. 'May the Grace of Allah travel with you, Birbal. Let Victory kiss your feet, and glory shine from your sword. My personal cannons and topchis will be under your command.' Unable to say more, Akbar turned away.

He had gone a few paces, when he turned around and, putting his right arm across his heart, hoarsely whispered, 'This is your home, Birbal. Come back soon.'

It was not to be.

The wringing of Yakub's manacled wrists on the stone floor jerked Akbar into the present.

'I have forgiven the treasonable acts of your clan several times, Yakub Chak. I forgave your father, Yusuf Shah Chak, and spared him death on the fervent pleas and a Rajput's oath of protection made by Raja Bhagwan Das Kachhawa to your father.

'When the imperial army under Raja Birbal, Hakim Abul Fath, and Zain Khan were battling the Yusufzais in the Swat valley, your band of marauders was actively fighting against us. You deliberately closed the Burliyas Pass with mountains of boulders and a strong garrison to stop the Mughal army from reaching Baramullah . These actions of yours resulted in the needless deaths of the Mughal soldiers, as well as Raja Birbal and Zain Khan themselves. It cost us millions of rupees.'

The emperor's face was flushed red with anger, and the protrusion of his eyes had become more pronounced as he almost shouted, 'And the most despicable act of yours, Yakub Chak, was the beheading of Raja Birbal and throwing his body in the deep ravines, never to be found.'

Boiling with rage, the emperor commanded, 'Tie him to an elephant. And have him fed to the tigers before we start the hunt.'

'Mercy, mercy, Your Highness, mercy! For the sake of my children, mercy!' grovelled Yakub Shah Chak as he was dragged away.

'Silence!' roared the emperor. 'What about Lala and Hiram Rai? They could not even perform the funeral rites for their father, in the absence of a body. Shut your mouth or I will have your lips sewn!' Akbar was trembling with rage.

For a fleeting moment, Akbar thought about Lala and Hiram Rai, the teenage sons of Raja Birbal, who had lost their father on the roll of a dice. Akbar, with all his regal paraphernalia, ruthlessness, imperial magnificence and sovereign command at his disposal, could never bring himself to face the two young sons of his closest companion.

*

The forest of Qurchak

Same day

Mid-morning

The *Qamargah*, with its semi-circle of drum beaters, buglers, conch blowers, and foot soldiers with spears and swords, as well as special riders bearing *gurj*, had started moving inwards to trap the encircled game. The *qarawals* estimated that at least a dozen tigers were in the circle, along with numerous leopards, deer, and antelopes.

Akbar watched from the edge of the circle, seated high on his huge war elephant, *Husn Bahadur*, as a tiger, alarmed by the advancing beaters, shot off across a patch of dried grass into the dense foliage beyond. A group of Kashmir musk deer snorted in fear and swung their heads in alarm. Their twitching noses could discern the presence of predators in close proximity, but they could not decide which way to run. They snorted and milled around in petrified confusion, until another roar from the thick clump of tall grass sent them careering away in a mass of brown fur and terrified eyes.

The *langurs* chattered excitedly amongst themselves at the sudden arrival of a couple of leopards on the high branches, and showed little fear at their presence. The leopards, acknowledging the right of these big, hefty monkeys on the forest trees, preferred to clutch the thicker branches of the poplar and willow trees while studiously ignoring the monkeys.

Suddenly, from the dense undergrowth on the left, a huge goat with long, corkscrewed horns charged a *sowar* seated on his horse. As the *gurj* bearer swung his mace at the goat's head, the curves of his *gurj* became entangled in the pirouetting horns and he was thrown from the saddle. The goat, stunned from the blow and fighting for its life, lowered its head and charged at the fallen man, goring him in his testicles and abdomen, and continuing to push his horns deeper with great shakes of its head.

As the man screamed and beat his hands on the ground, Akbar winced in sympathy. Just last year, he had been similarly gored in the left testicle by a *barasingha* as he had tried to wrestle it to the ground, and the memory was enough to send searing stabs of pain through his body.

Several riders had by now converged on the scene and had slain the goat. The injured man, almost disembowelled, was not expected to survive.

Akbar motioned for Haji Jamal Baluch to come forward.

'Haji Jamal, what huge beast was this? I have never seen the likes of them before,' queried Akbar.

'Your Majesty, this is the *Markhor* goat, generally found on the higher reaches of the snow mountains. You may not have given it much credence even if you had seen it earlier, because it is not royal game. It is generally found in the wilderness, and is not domesticated. Majesty, as the name denotes, it is commonly known as snake-eater, and is much sought after by villagers for its sponge-like cud, which is supposed to be an anti-snake venom.'

'For a goat, it has the massive power of a charging *Nilgai*! Haji Baluch, let us make this hunt even more interesting. Where is that perfidious son of a snake, Yakub?' questioned Akbar.

Mirza Ghazi Beg, who was riding close to the emperor's elephant, answered, 'Majesty, as ordered by you, he is roped to the sides of the mighty war elephant, Hawai.'

Akbar looked down from his special hunting *howdah,* and said, 'Good. Hawai knows his work. Tell the *mahout* to untie the prisoner and sling him onto Hawai's trunk, and to proceed diagonally across that clump of tall grass where the tiger is hiding. As he nears, the elephant must throw Yakub into the clump.'

'Yes, Your Majesty!' said the Mirza as he raced back to inform the trailing retinue of horses, elephants, buffaloes, and hunting cheetahs.

In a short while Hawai,with Yakub tied over his massive head, moved across the line of hunters and, espying Akbar seated on his stable mate Husn Bahadur, raised his trunk and gave a long trumpet. Akbar raised his arm in acknowledgement.

'Mahout, follow Hawai.'

Husn Bahadur moved forward with the mahout making small adjustments to avoid low hanging branches. As Hawai neared the thatch of long grass, one of the mahouts leaned forward to loosen the ropes and Hawai,with a swirl of his trunk, enveloped Yakub and lobbed him high into the air, to fall with a shriek into the cluster of jungle weeds, tall grasses, and tigers.

There was a mighty roar from an enraged tiger mingled with the agonized screams of a terror-stricken man. Within a few seconds, Yakub, badly mauled with his face and arms ripped bare, rushed out. The tiger, a full grown male over seven feet in length, sprang upon him from the thicket and pinned him to the ground. Akbar watched as, with one swipe of his paws, the tiger took out the intestines and pressed his face into Yakub's throat. The pitiful shrieks and thrashing of limbs ceased altogether.

Akbar watched in stoic silence as the tiger settled upon the inert body and started tearing out the flesh from the abdomen. It turned its blood-smeared face towards Akbar's mount for threat perception, and stared unblinkingly.

A quick word to the mahout, and Husn Bahadur turned around.

Mirza Ghazi Beg Turkhani, the grand master of this hunt, approached Akbar. 'Your Majesty, if we have your permission, then Haji Jamal Baluch has fashioned a new method of tiger hunting, which he would like to display.'

Akbar smiled with pleasure, for he knew that anything devised by Haji Baluch would be highly entertaining and novel in its execution. Leaning to the side, Akbar enthusiastically nodded his approval.

As Mirza was about to ride away, he reined his horse and haltingly asked, 'Your Highness ... the mode of hunting proposed by Haji Baluch is very dangerous and may prove fatal for him.'

Akbar replied with his usual equanimity, '*Qurawal Baigi*, if Haji Baluch is not afraid, then why should we stop him? And, remember, he is the best huntsman of the realm. Let him proceed.'

Mirza bowed low over the saddle and then galloped away to issue directions. The scramble of slaves drawing nets and beaters taking their positions in the hunting circle could be heard.

In about half an hour, the beat of drummers, buglers, and trumpeters commenced as they started to converge from three sides. On the fourth side, huge nets had been tightly drawn and roped across stout tree branches, and beyond them stood several lines of beaters and huntsmen.

Haji Jamal Baluch was brought into the emperor's presence, attired in a leather coat decorated with silver bells, and bearing only a lance and a long sword. The enormous bull that he was riding had pointed, sturdy horns which had been consecrated with red powder, and its neck adorned with garlands of marigold. Haji Baluch had a crude set of bridles and reins tied around the bull's head, and rode bareback.

Akbar, anticipating a stimulating performance, acknowledged the deep bow of the rider with a nod of his head, and threw down a gold coin.

Haji Baluch, riding his bull, moved forward surrounded by foot soldiers and drum beaters. The *Shahi Qur*, which had been following the emperor's mount from a distance, now moved closer.

There was a blur of striped yellow as a tiger sprinted across the thick trees and shrubs on the right, and merged into the rocky cleft ahead. The beaters and hunters, having sighted the tiger, increased the stridency of their beat and started drawing closer in a tighter circle. Interspersed amongst the beaters and foot soldiers were torch-bearers carrying long, wood-handled torches with large wicks of cloth dipped in *ghee,* which they now lit.

The tiger, unnerved by the constant clamour of drums, shouts, and trumpets blowing in close proximity, erupted from behind a group of large boulders, and, in his fright, knocked down a torch-bearer. The burning torch flew from his hands and fell on a drummer, setting fire to his cotton tunic. Amid the bedlam rode Haji Jamal Baluch astride his bull.

Akbar watched, fascinated, as Haji Baluch rode with much aplomb towards the snarling tiger, with his lance extended.

His bull, fed on a strong dose of opium and emboldened by the shouting, swaying mass of people advancing alongside, snorted and shook his great head in a furious paroxysm of bravado.

The tiger, snarling and roaring intermittently, retreated a few steps, and then with a lunging jump cleared the few rocks and a fallen tree, rushing towards the open side which was not encircled by beaters. The *harkaras* and foot soldiers started running inwards, constricting the three quarters circle into an area less than a hundred yards wide. At the end of this hundred-yard boundary were high strung nets of iron and hessian twine to bar the tiger's escape route.

The tiger, by now thoroughly bewildered and disoriented, made a rush at the net and, finding no way of escape, let out a mighty roar and raced around in a semi-circle. He turned and with a crouch faced the snorting bull as it ran in a half sprint and half dance towards the tiger. Pawing the ground and tossing his head, the bull would run belligerently and then suddenly skid to a stop sideways in an effort to psychologically intimidate the tiger with its massive proportions. Haji Baluch, holding on to the sides of the bull with his knees and free hand, swore under his breath and promised himself to take a stick to his young assistant, Chand Baba, for suggesting this peculiar hunt.

Akbar had moved ahead and was now mounted just behind the lines of *harkaras* and soldiers, who were maintaining a deafening clamour on their drums and trumpets. The tiger, entrapped between the high nets and the huge bull, preferred his chances against the bull and charged forthwith. The bull flicked his horns and the tiger, at the last moment, swivelled to escape the arc of the sharp horns.

Haji Baluch leant forward and tried to prod the tiger into attacking, but the tiger shrank back, snarling . Then, with a mighty roar and a leap, powered by his hunkered shoulders and legs, the tiger launched himself over the horns of the bull and straight into the body of Haji Baluch, who just had time to raise his lance across his face as the stinking, raw, and brutish projectile landed on him with an avalanche of flailing paws and snapping jaws. There was a tremendous crunch as the lance embedded itself in the tiger, and, unseated, Haji Baluch fell to the ground.

A powerful swipe of the tiger's paw had ripped open one side of Haji's face, and blood flowed freely. Dazed and concussed, Haji sat, unable to comprehend. He could see the tiger, with a part of the lance buried in its right front leg, roaring with pain and loping around on its three good legs. The bull, full of opium and fight, rushed at the injured tiger with his head lowered and horns carving mighty sweeps. The tiger, crazed with pain, swerved to its right and in one lightning moment attached itself to the bull's throat.

As the tiger tried to pull the bull down, the bull shook his head in enormous sweeps, and, even with almost four hundred pounds of vicious weight attached to its throat, refused to buckle down. The tiger was hobbling around in small steps, trying desperately to keep its hold on the bucking, swaying, snorting bull. Slowly, and perceptibly, the bull started faltering on his left leg.

Akbar had instinctively reached for his quiver, but refrained from unleashing a string of arrows, as he saw Haji Baluch rise and unsheathe his sword. Wiping the blood dripping from his face, Haji charged at the tiger with a loud cry, and swung with both his hands at the tiger's neck. In the clash of two huge grappling beasts, the sword missed its mark, and instead cleaved a deep furrow on the tiger's head.

Incensed by the attack, bleeding and stunned by the debilitating blow to its head, the tiger swung around to face the new threat. As Haji Jamal again smote with his sword, a pulverizing blow from the tiger's paw sent him spinning to the ground. Akbar again raised his bow.

The bull, in cataclysmic rage, rushed the tiger and with a mighty heave, tossed the almost four hundred pounds beast a good fifteen feet away. Continuing his deadly dance, he again charged and gored the tiger, pushing it several feet with his horns firmly planted in its belly. A few shakes of his great head had completely exenterated the intestines of the tiger.

In the dust and hushed silence, the tiger groaned no more.

As the minor hunters, beaters, and soldiers shouted in triumph, Akbar ordered his mount to move forward. When the royal elephant was but a few yards away from Haji Jamal Baluch, the emperor took off his string of lustrous pink pearls and threw it to the kneeling huntsman.

'Well done, Haji Jamal Baluch, well done. An entirely novel and exciting style of hunt have you shown today, and for this, I grant you five acres of land in the province of Chunar, in perpetuity.'

As Haji Baluch prostrated himself in grateful acceptance, Akbar spoke again. 'And, Haji, this injured bull is not to be killed. Have it attended to, and henceforth, it shall be known as *Syah Garz*.'

*

MORCHI DARWAZA. ALSO KNOWN AS 'MOTI DARWAZA'
CLOSE TO LAAL HAVELI AND LAAL KHOO.

(CHAPTER 7)

NAQAB-E-MULAKAT

(The Tunnels of Tryst)

Diwan e Khas, Subterranean Chambers

Prince Salim's Royal Apartments

Jahangir's Quadrangle, Shahi Qila, Lahore

23rd November, 1597; late afternoon

Prince Salim waited impatiently for the Jesuit priests to finish their lengthy imploration, as he watched Sayyid Abdullah Barha enter the *Diwan e khas* in great agitation. Father Xavier, intent on his entreaties, failed to discern the shift in the prince's mood, and was brutally cut short by Khubu Chishti standing just behind the small silver throne of the prince.

'Father, you have taken enough of His Royal Highness's time. He shall be retiring for his afternoon prayers and rest.'

Prince Salim, in a distracted voice, remarked, 'Priest Xavier, your request shall not go unheeded. I shall speak with the governor, Khwaja Shams Ud Din, and then decide on a time and date to visit your most revered church. Go in peace, Priest.'

Father Xavier bent low and saluted as he retreated from the royal presence. Most of the gathered minor courtiers frowned in disapproval. These *firangis* would never learn. A simple bow and three salutations also seemed an enormous chore to their leathered backs. Absolutely no grace or finesse.

The prince immediately beckoned to Sayyid Abdullah and, in a voice quivering with suppressed rage, which his close companions recognized so well, asked, 'Sayyid Abdullah Barha, where have you been idling away? We reached Lahore on the fifteenth of November, more than a week ago, and now you have found the time to show your presence? It has been four months since I relieved you from Bhimber to return to Lahore.'

Sayyid Abdullah performed the *kornish*, and answered softly, 'Your Highness, I have searched high and low, these past four months, for what your heart desired. And, by the Grace of Allah, I have news that will gladden your heart. A moment in private, Your Highness.'

Prince Salim, with a sudden gleam in his spiritless eyes, ordered tersely, '*Takhliya*.'

Sayyid Abdullah approached the prince as the others withdrew and, stopping about six yards away, drew a red scarf with gold and silver embroidery on it. The long-lost, but familiar smell of *Zabad* filled the space. Prince Salim rose quickly and almost snatched the scarf.

As he pressed the scarf to his face, his heart ached at the all too familiar smell of Zehrunnisa. Many times, as he had lain between her voluptuous thighs and buried his face on her taut breasts, he had inhaled her favourite fragrance.

The several cups of opium he had consumed since morning had heightened his sensibilities and tears were not far from coming. Clutching the scarf near his face, and with a faint tremor in his voice, he asked, 'Sayyid, where is she? Where?'

'Your Highness, she stays near the *Morchi Darwaza* of the old city in a *haveli*, with her attendants and possibly some relatives.'

'Does she have a little boy with her?'

'Not that I know of, Your Highness. She keeps a low profile and seldom goes out. All her purchases and other trivial matters are attended to by her servants.'

Salim, still clutching the scarf, turned towards his silver chair. 'How is she? Is she still the same? How did you find her?' The questions tumbled out.

Sayyid Abdullah took a deep breath and then, settling the turban on his head, chose his words carefully. 'Highness, I have seen her just twice or thrice, and only in veil. But her carriage and deportment is of a noble woman, and there is an aura of peace wherever she be...'

Prince Salim almost sobbed as he cut Sayyid's statement short. 'Yes, that is my Zehrunnisa! Serenity and love flowed from her and enveloped her. Her sweet laughter and playful nature are a reflection of her native Kashmere. Lovely, colourful, scented, and welcoming.'

Sayyid Abdullah smiled, happy in the prince's joy, and with much candour announced, 'Your Highness, veiled as she is in her appearance and conduct, it was not easy to find her. In fact, Sire, when I heard that you had started the return journey from Kashmere in late September, I had given up all hopes of finding her. Several days and nights I spent in solitary despair – despair at the thought of having failed you, and your trust defiled by my failure in locating the one that your heart weeps for. But, just a fortnight ago, I chanced upon a bangle seller's shop near the *Lahori Darwaza*, where a statuesque lady was trying on bangles, aided by a female servant. Out of idle curiosity and guided by the Hand of Allah, I paused to look. And there, as she tried out a pair of bangles on her left wrist, I saw your ruby ring with the words "HRH Prince Salim Akbar" engraved on the shank. As I stepped forward for a closer look, the lady quickly withdrew her hand. She looked at me with panic clouding her grey eyes and swiftly walked away. I made no attempt to stop her, since the ensuing commotion would have compromised my search and her identity. I also did not follow her, but sent my trusted *sowar* Habib Ullah to follow her home. This he did on foot, and, after many false detours and stops, he finally watched her walk into her home.'

'And how did he surmise that this again was not a decoy, but her home?'

'Your Highness, she petted the goat that was tethered inside the entrance, and the goat also nuzzled her hands. Her female attendant, who had accompanied her to the market, came out with some fresh laundry which she strung across a string *charpoy*. Regular household chores, Highness. And, Habib Ullah waited until well past midnight, but there was no further movement.' Sayyid sighed with evident satisfaction.

'And where does she stay, Sayyid?' Salim asked excitedly.

'She stays in a part of the big mansion near *Morchi Darwaza*, known as *Laal Haveli*, Your Highness.'

Sayyid Abdullah, his face shining with unmitigated glee, continued, 'And, Your Highness, Allah is with you. Shahi Qila is connected to *Mochi Darwaza* through a tunnel which is located just beyond the royal *hamam*, Sire.'

'Wonderful!' exclaimed Prince Salim as he clasped his most trusted companion by the shoulder.

With a deep bow, Sayyid announced, 'You will be further pleased, Majesty, to know that *Morchi Darwaza* is also connected to the *Lal Khoo* located in that particular *haveli*, by means of an old tunnel.'

'Allah be praised!' exclaimed the prince as he embraced Sayyid Abdullah, and he took off his enormous emerald ring and pressed it into the palm of his now favourite courtier.

*

Laal Haveli

Near Morchi Darwaza

Androoni Sheher, Lahore

24th November, 1597

5:30.m.

The early morning birds in search of the scurrying worms, the rustle of sheets hastily thrown, and the sizzle of kitchen fires being stoked declared the beginning of a new day. Nadira, having just put aside her holy book, gathered her prayer rug.

Her female attendant, Biwi Jaffer, entered the room with panic written all over her face. 'Begum Sahiba, there is a person outside who claims to be from the royal court, and wishes to see you. Urgently.'

'Did you not tell him, Biwi, that I cannot and will not meet strangers. That he should speak with Baqar or Maqbool?' The irritation in Nadira's voice came through clearly.

'I did, mistress, but he is not willing to listen. He was...'

Nadira screamed as the door was flung open and a man in rich robes entered. He had pulled the long ends of his turban across his face so that only his eyes and forehead were visible. Startled out of her wits, Nadira opened her mouth to scream again, but the man raised a finger for silence and his imperious eyes, accustomed to deference and obedience, willed Nadira to remain quiet.

From the folds of his cloak, he took out a piece of gold jewellery and extended it for Nadira to see.

'A moment in private please, Begum Sahiba.'

Surprised beyond words and with disbelief writ large on her face, Nadira signalled for her servant to leave.

Nadira's eyes were glued to the gold aigrette which he held, and his words 'I am Sayyid Abdullah of Barha, and I am here at the command of His Highness, Prince Salim,' barely registered with her.

She held out her hands for the aigrette she recognized so well. Her eyes flickered with memories, recalling that night when Salim, after an impassioned bout of drinking and sex, had lovingly plucked this *serpench* of gold and dangling rubies from his turban, and placed it on her forehead.

The messenger coughed politely, and said, 'His Highness shall meet you this afternoon. You know the tunnel from *Laal Khoo* to the *Morchi Darwaza*?'

'I do. But *Morchi Darwaza* is hardly a ten minute walk from here...'

Sayyid cut her short. 'Begum Sahiba, you should know better... you are not a novice. Take the tunnel route, and wait just under the arched exit for *Morchi Darwaza*. Bring no one but your trusted maid, Biwi Jaffer, and if need be, Baqar Khan. Please be there just after *Zuhr* prayers. *Allah hafiz*!'

He was gone as quickly as he had come. Nadira, overcome by the sudden developments, felt her head spinning. Realizing that she still held the *serpench*, she rushed out only to see her attendants huddled in anxious trepidation, and the messenger nowhere to be seen. With a quick reassuring smile for her servants, she turned back.

*

Hamam, Royal Apartments

Shahi Qila, Lahore

Same day; Zuhr

Prince Salim, preceded by several bodyguards, walked briskly through the vaulted corridors of the royal *hamam* and, entering a small dark hall, waited for them to open the tunnel slab. Sayyid Abdullah moved to the far corner of the room, and, reaching inside a lamp alcove, searched for the small lever. He tugged at the iron ring hidden beneath the lamp holder, and the stone slab across the miniature doorway folded downwards on its hinges.

As Prince Salim was about to enter, he turned around and asked Sayyid, 'Have you sent a contingent to guard the *Morchi Darwaza*?'

'Yes, Your Highness,' replied Sayyid Abdullah. 'A squad of mounted *ahadis* and *bandooqchis* have been stationed there. Also, spare horses from your personal stable have been sent without the imperial insignia.'

Prince Salim bent to pass through the small opening and Sayyid, holding the prince's scimitar, continued, 'The *hamam* too, Your Majesty, is secured by the Barhas and handpicked soldiers of Raja Ram Das Kachhawa. They have been instructed to let no one enter until we return.'

The prince, escorted by his personal bodyguards, some of whom were bearing lighted torches, moved carefully through the uneven stone paving on the floor. Rawal Sal Darbari, a minor Rajput noble, quickly took a lighted torch and moved ahead.

'Thank you, Rawal,' acknowledged Salim, as he increased his pace.

Salim looked around at the subterranean passage and remarked, 'Sayyid, this tunnel is quite clean and well maintained. Who looks after it? Certainly not the *Mir Saman*.'

'No, Highness. Maintenance of all war material, including escape tunnels, safe houses, and identified pleasure gardens are the responsibility of the *Mir Bakshi*. There has been no special cleaning done as your visit has been kept secret.'

Passing through several such slab openings, each of which was then left guarded by a pair of royal troopers, Prince Salim soon reached a dead end, where the tunnel turned left and steps had to be mounted to the suite of rooms and first floor *naubatkhana* inside the *Morchi Darwaza*. Just past the first twenty steps, the stairway turned sharply right for another flight of twenty-five steps to the ground floor of the structure.

To the right of the landing stood a recessed doorway, guarded by a minor Rajput noble whom Prince Salim recognized as Keso Das Maru, in his trademark turban of mustard yellow. As Keso Das paid obeisance, the prince's bodyguards quickly took their places over the stairway and the huge central foyer of the *Morchi Darwaza*. Rawal Sal Darbari moved down to secure the tunnel passage, while Sayyid Abdullah Barha took his position at the entrance of the recessed doorway, motioning for Keso Das Maru to move upwards to the central foyer.

As Salim stepped forward to open the door, he was restrained by a quiet, 'Your Highness, please wait.' Sayyid, sword in hand, motioned for two troopers to join him, and then with a sharp crash opened the door. Having surveyed the room, he withdrew, and held the door open for the prince.

Prince Salim, as if in a stupor, strode silently into the vaulted room, his eyes set on the figure in turquoise blue standing silently in the far corner. Salim ignored the maid, his eyes searching for those familiar, graceful lines that he knew so well.

Nadira had heard the commotion outside, and suffered the barging through the door of armed men. Her morning had passed as if in a fluff of misty clouds, the reality and suddenness of Prince Salim's reappearance in her life a magical streak. She dared not lift her gaze, for fear that disappointment lurked nigh.

Taking a deep breath, Nadira slowly lifted her eyes and they dwelt on the figure of Prince Salim. The prince appeared bewitched, as he took in the deep grey eyes, the beautiful oval face with the high cheekbones and sharp nose, truly Persian in its profile rather than Kashmiri, the full lips capable of providing so much pleasure, the cream and peaches complexion just as enchanting as ever; definitely, the years had been kind to her.

With small hesitant steps, Nadira moved towards Prince Salim, and as he smiled with an ecstatic sparkle in his eyes, Nadira flew into his waiting arms. Those five long years of separation telescoped into a few moments of unbridled happiness, as they held each other in rapturous glee.

'Oh, Zehrun... I have missed you so. Missed you so much,' was all that Prince Salim could manage, as he clung to the softness of Nadira and kissed her all over her upturned face.

Nadira, with tears streaming from her eyes, and her lips quivering at the touch of her beloved Salim once again, fiercely clutched at his back, and sobbed, 'My lord, I have missed you every single moment of these five years, as only Allah knows. I begged, and I prayed to Allah, and in moments of despair I cursed too, for just one more glimpse of you. I wanted to be held by you once again, and to smell your scent once...'

'Zehrun, my love, you are nibbling at my beard.' There was merriment in his voice.

Laughing and crying at the same time, she playfully held a good patch of his beard between her teeth and moved her hands across his chest.

Having removed her veil and the high Persian turban that she wore today, Salim looked deep into her eyes as he moved his fingers around her chiselled lips and traced the soft contours of her face. Drawing her closer, he let his fingers slip into the cascade of her perfumed hair, nuzzling her slender neck with his lips. As she arched her back, she took hold of his golden *chogha* and tugged hard. Smiling, Prince Salim left her neck and sought her lips. Swooning with pleasure, Nadira moved her hands inside his *chogha* and explored the expanse of his chest and midriff.

Salim, sucking on her lips, suddenly let go and asked, 'Zehrun, how is Firdaus? Where is he?'

Unbuttoning his inner garment, she replied, 'Firdaus is fine, Sire! He is strong and healthy, and has your deep brown eyes. I did not bring him today, as I feared that this could be a trap.' But the joy on her face was genuine.

With a sigh of satisfaction, Salim roughly pulled her against his chest and, reaching behind, cupped her buttocks. Nadira remembered the sensitivity of Prince Salim's left nipple, and playfully scratched it. Salim jumped as if he had been seared with a red hot iron, and, in retribution, hungrily chewed on the bodice covering her breasts as he thrust his hand between her legs.

He looked around the sparsely furnished room and, noticing a low wooden cot, pushed her towards it. His fingers had been busy untying the strings at the back of her long tunic. Her silken trousers, in matching shades of turquoise with silver threads, were not far in coming off. As Salim beheld Nadira in her naked loveliness, he could not help but exclaim, 'Such magnificence of beauty comes once in a millennium, Zehrunnisa! *Subhanallah*!'

As she spread her thighs for Salim to enter her, she whispered softly into his ear, 'My lord, beauty, as you know, lies in the eyes of the beholder. It is your inner grace and innate innocence that sees beauty in someone as unadorned as me. Aahh, my love, gently, please...' Her whole body arched as Salim entered her with a passionate thrust.

The wood and iron beams, frames, rafters, and the elaborately drawn cornices of the stone roof witnessed the hungry and breathless lovemaking of this star-crossed couple. Even centuries later, in their derelict and forgotten state, they would whisper amongst themselves at the tragic but exuberant love of Prince Salim and Anarkali, which they witnessed over several such afternoons. When stressed beyond endurance, the old walls and roofs would shed tears and creak and groan in their stony grief.

*

(CHAPTER 8)

SAYA-E-SHAHZADAH

(The Prince and his Shadow)

The Jesuit Church

Lahore

Christmas Eve, 1597

The symphony of harps and mandolins, and the soaring pitches of the church choir came struggling through the clamour and bedlam of the royal procession. Prince Salim, mounted on his war elephant, Sipah Salar, gestured for the *mahout* to kneel the elephant down. Immediately, the torch-bearers, *sowars* and *Sahiban i Ihtemam* surrounded the elephant, and broad steps of silver were placed for the prince to step down. Prince Salim, glittering with jewels on his scarlet *Shahajida*, nodded to the crowd paying obeisance on their knees, and waited for the Jesuit priests.

Father Xavier, Father Goes, and Father Pinheiro, in their fluted robes and vestments, moved forward and performed the obeisance. A robed monk, carrying the sceptre, preceded the procession as it slowly moved from the porch of the church into the nave inside. Two young boys, holding long candles in silver stands, moved them across in circular motions with Latin chants to ward off evil.

A few junior clergy and Jesuit followers, standing within the nave, frowned as the Moslem and Rajput nobles accompanying the prince streamed in.

A young priest in his clerical smock remarked rudely, 'Now we have Saracens and pagans visiting our House of Worship? Just look at them. Swords, lances, and pikes in a church!'

'Softly, my fellow priest,' cautioned an older Jesuit. 'You really would not like to be skinned alive now, would you?'

The naïve priest ignored the warning, and continued to stare belligerently at the troops now crowding the nave and the transept. The older priest continued. 'Not only will you be skinned alive, inch by inch, with mustard and chillies being rubbed into you to keep you conscious and screaming with pain, but you will be sewn into a carcass of a donkey, mule, or cow, and then paraded through the streets on a cart. I have seen Emperor Echebar ordering one of his minor nobles accused of misappropriation being sewn inside the skin of an ass with my own eyes. Now, step back and stop staring, or I will clobber you well and good.'

The new priest, cringing at the prospect, stepped deep into the rows and started chanting '*Spiritus Ducentia Protégé Me*' with fervent clicks of his fingers. Some of the soldiers looked askance at the strange sounds coming from the black-smocked priest, which caused further consternation to him. In a few moments, clicking and chanting, he was gone.

Prince Salim was standing at the wooden filigree screen which divided the nave from the chancel, and waited patiently as Father Francis Xavier, old and bent, sprinkled holy water and recited the *Adoro Te Devote*, 'Godhead here in hiding, whom I do adore; masked by these bare shadows, shape and nothing more...'His robust baritone, now hoarse with age and the weakness of a recent illness, fell and rose in a pleasing cadence.

With great pomp, Prince Salim was ushered inside the chancel, and he was shocked and amazed at the empyreal sight of Jesus Christ on the Cross, sparkling with the reflected light of several hundred candles. He stood as if in a trance, with eyes closed and arms crossed, for several minutes. The choir, at a signal from Father Pinheiro, swung into the lilting melody of *Ave Maria* and Prince Salim started to sway rhythmically. As the song entered its second section, Prince Salim raised his arms and moved in the manner of dervishes. Khubu Chishti, one of the two nobles allowed inside the sanctuary with the prince, whispered urgently in his ears, 'Majesty! Let us go, or these *firangis* will scatter false reports of your turning into a heretical Jesuit! Please hurry, Your Highness.'

'I am not so fickle as the revered emperor to fall in and out of spiritual love with every new religious book and *Brahmin* that crosses my path. However, it is time for our amusement. Let us bid goodbye to the good priests.' Salim turned to thank the senior priest.

Father Xavier held a small golden sceptre in his hands and, presenting it to the prince, remarked, 'Your Highness, we have been privileged today with your presence, as also the continuous support from your father, the Great Emperor Echebar. This, Highness, is a small gift from us to thank you for all your support and encouragement, these past many months.'

The prince accepted the golden sceptre, and the silver inlaid words, encrusted with rubies, sprang forth: '*Ad Maiorem Dei Gloriam*'.

At the prince's raised eyebrows, Father Xavier clarified. 'It means, Your Highness, "For the greater Glory of God".'

*

In the great fort of Lahore, the cutting winter chill of the north-western mountain ranges of Karakoram and Hindukush was welcomed with glowing hearths and fire pits. Men, huddled in sheepskin cloaks and arm covers of treated leather, went about their business of stoking coal, tending foundries, driving sheep, and manning the battlements. Women, their colourful attire thwarted by the bluster of winter, found refuge around *sigris* of iron with silver inlays and the warmth of harem gossip.

The sun, as if hung on opium, rarely made an appearance, and in deference to the seasonal eminence of its frosty visitor, decided to lie in torpidity.

Prince Khurram, enjoying the companionship of his father, Prince Salim, and his revered Shah Baba – Emperor Akbar – devised ingenious ways to escape from the cloying embrace of the imperial harem.

Prince Salim, in the lee of his father's shadow, and separated from his love by imperial ire, nevertheless sought warmth and love in the grey eyes and smiling lips of Nadira *urf* Anarkali.

Abul Fateh Jalal Ud Din Mohammed Akbar, Padshah Ghazi, with his heart set on the Deccan kingdoms, deliberated on turning his energies and the Mughal might on the subjugation of these tiny kingdoms, which were swollen with treasures of gold and diamonds from their quarries, mining pits, and river beds. In fact, several travellers and courtiers had portrayed the brown, barren mountains of Deccan as virtual vessels of rubies, emeralds, gold, and diamonds, to be vanquished and plundered in great measure.

What they did not tell the monarch was an old saying prevalent in Khandesh, that anyone who stayed in the Deccani states for more than three days was destined to warp and die there. In hushed whispers, over hissing fire pits in the dead of night, it was also murmured that the waters of Deccani states carried *bewafai* in them.

The black soil of this land proudly proclaimed the accuracy of this fact. *Peregrinus Cave!*

*

Maidan Diwan e Aam

Shahi Qila, Lahore

29th December, 1597

11:45 a.m.

There was a silence which hung in the vast arena of the *Maidan Diwan e Aam*.

Emperor Akbar, after hearing the petition of Rao Mulkh for amnesty from harvest taxes in the *Suba* of Lahore, had subsided into one of his silent spells, with his eyes staring over the heads of the assembled nobles and courtiers. Seated on his silver throne, in the royal pavilion, his eyes passed over the colourful turbans of the *mansabdars*, and came to rest on a violet turban, fastened in the peculiar Persian fashion of a dome.

There was an unease in the ranks of the minor nobles standing close to the violet turbaned youth, as they felt the eyes of the emperor on them. Many fidgeted, as several looked down and waited with trepidation. The emperor, lost in his thoughts, let his eyes wander towards the sea of simple white turbans on the opposite end of the huge garden. As a special *durbar* this day, representatives of the adjoining villages had been permitted entry to petition for remission of harvest tax for the year on account of the widespread pestilence, and its resultant losses and destruction.

From the cloistered corridors, which enveloped the garden on three sides, Akbar watched the hurrying figure of Mirza Anwar Turani approach the royal pavilion. He quietly watched as the *ahadis* on protection duty stopped the Mirza, and after a few words escorted him to the steps of the pavilion. Sheikh Abu'l Fazl, officiating at the Diwan today, received the scroll and read it. With a slight smile, Sheikh climbed the nine steps of the royal pavilion, and, paying obeisance to the emperor, apprised him, 'Your Majesty! The Old Khan is dead.'

Akbar's reverie was broken, and he exultantly asked, 'What is the source of your information, Sheikh?'

Sheikh Abu'l Fazl gestured towards the bearer of the scroll, and replied, 'Majesty! Mirza Anwar Turani, distantly related to the Old Khan, has been especially sent from Kabul by our governor, Daulat Khan Lodi, with this news. It also informs that upon the death of Abdullah Khan Uzbeg, his son, Abdul Momin Khan, has been declared the ruler and rules from the ancestral seat at Aghrapur.'

The Sheikh, unrolling a more elaborate, but smaller scroll, continued. 'Your Royal Highness, the new Sultan Of Turan sends his greetings, and promises an envoy to the Court of the Great Moghul after the forty days of ritual mourning. His Highness the Sultan also reiterates that he will honour the treaty signed between Your Majesty and his revered father, and while stating his oath of not interfering in the Mughal dominions of Kabul and Kandahar, requests the same assurance from you with respect to Badakshan and Balkh. He further states, Your Majesty, that they will continue to honour the Hindukush as our mutual borders. His Highness commends all good fortune and majesty to your reign.' Sheikh Abu'l Fazl Allami furled the scrolls.

Akbar listened in smug silence. The ponderous weight of safeguarding his north-western borders and the *sarkar* of Kabul and Kandahar from the greed and avarice of the Uzbegs had now almost vanished with the death of Abdullah Khan Uzbeg. Shouldering the responsibilities of an infant empire, beset with rebellions and aspiring chieftains from the young age of thirteen, Akbar had valiantly fought the odds and emerged victorious, but nature had taken its toll for his labour, and left him with a permanent limp in his left leg, and a head that always hung to the right. His bowed legs were a legacy of his Mongol origins and penchant for riding bareback for long hours.

The emperor instructed the Sheikh, who motioned for Mirza Anwar Turani to step forward. Performing the *Kornish*, Turani stood with hands clasped. A silk bag with tassels in royal green and gold was brought to the emperor, who briefly touched it before it was presented to Mirza Anwar Turani.

Akbar, in his loud, booming voice announced, 'Mirza Anwar Uzbeg of Turan, you have brought glad tidings. Abdullah Khan Turani rose in arms against our might many years ago, and we had to compel him to withdraw beyond the Hindukush, as our revered ancestors had done. When he failed to comprehend our Divine Faith and raised questions on our beliefs, we sent Miran Sadr and Hakim Khushhal to his court, to refute the charges of apostasy, with the words:

'"Of God people have said that he had a son; of the Prophet some have said that he was a sorcerer. Neither God nor the Prophet has escaped the slander of men – Then how should I?"

'Abdullah Khan of Turan, with all his greed for power, riches and empire, was still a good king. He carried that most vital of regal traits – he was a man of his word. He never reneged on his treaty with us, and we respect him for that. Mirza Anwar, you are rewarded with fifty gold *mohurs* for your troubles, and for the *Suba* of Lahore, we declare a complete remission in harvest taxes for the next one year.'

Jubilant shouts of '*Padshah Salamat; Hukumat Salamat*!'filled the vast concourse and bounced off the stone walls.

In the royal harem, the Begums and concubines touched their eyes in reverence, as they murmured prayers for the emperor's health and longevity.

As the emperor descended the steps of the royal pavilion and moved inside the pillared cloisters, a noble in a violet turban walked briskly away towards the *dak* stables near the main gate.

Settling the heavy violet turban on her head, Anarkali fingered the straight backed, long and pointed dagger which hung so invitingly at her waist. Next time, maybe, she could get a little closer to the emperor.

In her native Kashmere, on any given day, she could pierce an apple with a thrown dagger from forty paces. Lahore was less windy; a definite hit at fifty paces could be managed.

Her Persian *Qubbedar* turban had ensured her immunity from the frisking and scrutiny of the royal *ahadis.* The violet resembled the imperial purple which the minor nobles who had migrated from the Safavid court wore with so much pride, and was well respected in the Mughal court.

She quickened her steps. The last thing she wanted was a conversation with a well-meaning, friendly courtier.

*

Mirza Kamran's Baradari

West bank of Ravi, Lahore

28th March, 1597

10:15 a.m.

The royal barge carrying Prince Khurram sailed upriver escorted by two smaller boats filled with troops in Prince Salim's service. Just the day before, a royal messenger had arrived with the emperor's wishes that young Prince Khurram should join Prince Salim for a few days and participate in the hunting expeditions, as well as having horseriding lessons under the attentive eyes of his father. In compliance of this royal wish, Prince Salim had immediately dispatched a small squad of his personal troops to escort Khurram to the river pavilion.

The barge docked at the pier, and the six-year-old Prince Khurram, chased by his foster nurse, Jameela Anga, ran towards the beautiful pavilion set amidst lush green gardens. He could make out the figure of his father, Prince Salim, emerging from between the colonnades, flanked by his nobles and bearers. Jameela Anga, upon seeing the prince, stopped her chase and stood at a distance, watching.

Prince Khurram, clothed in soft muslin of light yellow with silver embroidery, and with a pert little red turban on his head, raced down the vast spread of green grass, with his little arms and legs flailing. Prince Salim, wearing a broad smile, hastened down the shallow steps of the pavilion and scooped Khurram into his arms.

Prince Khurram, clinging happily with both hands, buried his face in Prince Salim's neck and inhaled the wondrous smell of his father's favourite fragrance, *Argajah*. Khurram loved its smell, and often, in the confines of the harem, would pester Queen Ruqaiah to instruct his attendants to apply the same perfume on him. Queen Ruqaiah, in her turn, would kiss and appease him with the words, 'Khurram, my joyous Prince! Why should you use a manmade fragrance, when you carry Allah's sweet scent on you? Don't you know, my little one, that you are blessed with regal sovereignty and eternal fame?' And Prince Khurram, with his large expressive eyes, would smile happily at her, and puffing out his little chest, would walk around Begum Ruqaiah's apartment with his hands clasped behind his back, in perfect imitation of his revered Shah Baba. This always drew loud applause for him and Begum Ruqaiah, with her harem attendants, would laughingly bow and perform the *kornish* to him.

Prince Salim kissed him and gently put him on the ground. Immediately, Khurram clutched the open folds of his robe in alarm and tugged as he saw another boy, very like him, peering from behind the glittering robes of Prince Salim. The other child, dressed in green and white, also observed Khurram with puzzled eyes.

Each child looked baffled as he searched the other's face. While Prince Khurram was fair with a chubby face, large expressive eyes, and the hauteur of imperial lineage, the second child was of Prince Khurram's height and build, with the same chubbiness around the face and large, expressive eyes. But he was much fairer, and had the impish restlessness of a six-year-old.

To Jameela Anga, standing a hundred paces away, the two boys looked almost like twins. While one was clothed in the finery of nobility, the other carried his ordinary, but well-cared-for clothes with easy grace. To her practised eye, Prince Khurram with his longer hair, curling at the nape, looked the sturdier of the two.

Prince Salim knelt down, and, bringing both of them close, he smiled at Khurram, and said, 'Khurram, my son, this is your new friend, Firdaus. And, Firdaus, this is my son, Prince Khurram.'

Wide eyed, Firdaus enquired, 'Sire, is he a real Prince?'

Salim ruffled his hair, and answered, 'Yes, Firdaus, sweet child. Khurram is a real prince, and will be just like your elder brother.'

'But, Your Majesty,' Firdaus said with a puzzled frown. 'I have no elder brother. Nor a sister.'

'Well, Firdaus, you now have one,' said a cultured voice, as Nadira Begum emerged from the main octagonal hall of the *Baradari* and performed the *taslim* for Prince Salim, and a delicate *salaam* for the young prince. 'Welcome, Prince Khurram.'

Khurram, steeped in royal etiquette, made a small bow, and gracefully replied, 'Thank you, my lady. We wish much of Allah's grace and bounties on you.'

Nadira stepped forward and, taking both of Khurram's hands in her own, blessed him. 'I, too, wish for you many years of glorious rule, and the unwavering protection of your father, His Majesty, Prince Salim.'

Khurram had never seen a woman as beautiful as this. Though surrounded by the prettiest women, including queens, concubines, and slaves in the royal harem, Prince Khurram had yet to see a lady with such beauty, charm, and grace. With a child's innocence, he blurted out, 'My lady, you are so beautiful and nice. You must come and stay with us at Shahi Qila. I will show you my pet parrot, which can speak Persian.'

Begum Nadira burst out laughing, and, taking Khurram's face within both her hands, kissed him on his forehead. 'Thank you, my royal prince. I shall definitely visit you.'

She turned towards Prince Salim, who was watching with a half smile, and said, 'Your Majesty! He is just like you. Precious, and charming.'

Prince Khurram moved closer to the silently watching Firdaus, and, taking his hand, said 'You must also come with us, Firdaus, for there is so much to do there, including eating.'

Firdaus's eyes lit up, and a smile crept upon his lips at the prospect of a new playmate. Ever since he could remember, the dour Daud Khan, Jaffer Biwi, and Maqbool Mian with his waddling gait were the only companions he'd had. Only Maqbool Mian with his funny walk and funnier oaths offered some respite from tedium.

Nadira, listening to the childish banter and the innocuous reference to eating, gestured to a waiting maid to lay provisions for food in the garden outside, and, taking both children by the hand, announced, 'The prince must be hungry after his long journey over water. Come, let us go in the garden and try some watermelons and pineapples. And, if you are really hungry, then we can have some stuffed Afghani bread with mutton stew and egg curry garnished with cashew nuts.'

'And, mother, can we have some kebabs, too?' enquired Firdaus. 'The ones that Maqbool Mian makes with the eggs stuffed inside? Prince Khurram will also love them.'

'Sweetheart, how do you know for sure that Prince Khurram will like them, too?' she asked, as she led the two boys to the garden.

'Because, mother, I like them.' The simplicity was overwhelming.

Prince Khurram did not forget to bow to Prince Salim, as he happily clung to the other hand of Nadira, and skipped along to the shade of the fruit trees where rugs and victuals were quickly being arranged for the famished princes.

Prince Salim had a contemplative look on his face, as he watched his sons walking together in apparent companionship. Only Allah knew what the future held for them.

The *syces* holding the Prince's horse came forward. It was time now for the hunt to begin.

*

Mirza Kamran's Baradari

Next day

Morning hours

Prince Khurram and Firdaus looked at each other surreptitiously, and then with equal aplomb stared ahead. The painter, Nur Ud Din Teherani had been highly recommended by the celebrated poet and faithful follower of Prince Salm, Khwaja Mohammed Shirazi, famously known by his poetic name 'Urfi'. He had recently come from Persia, and his portraits of the reigning Safavids was the last word in royal portraiture.

At Nadira's suggestion the previous night, Salim had sent for Nur Ud Din, as he required a painter who could be absolutely trusted, and was relatively ignorant of the Mughal harem. For the last hour, Prince Salim had been seated with both the princes standing on either side of him for this royal portrait. Salim could feel the restlessness of his young sons, as they wished for this ordeal to end and their hunting lessons to begin. Since early morning, they had excitedly been watching the preparations with horses, elephants, palanquins, and weapons being readied for the hunt.

Nur Ud Din Teherani sat on the grass with the cloth canvas spread on a long, low table before him. The cloth had earlier been treated with a painting compound to give it an even, glazed base, and the under drawing in red and black was complete. The thin first coat of water colour had been applied to the under drawing, and the painter now contemplated his subjects with the eyes of a surgeon. Each crease, line, cleft, and fold had to be perfectly aligned for the human form to develop. Each colour, accentuated or diffused, had to melt just right into the gold, silver, and multi-coloured threads of intricate embroidery on the royal suits.

His palette was a veritable storehouse of minerals, dyestuffs, extracts, and hybrid pigments. The reds on the prince's tunics came from mercuric sulphide and red lead, while the royal blue *qaba* of Prince Salim was a mix of indigo and natural lazarite. The *patta* at the waist, of bright yellow, was a magnesium salt of euzanthic acid, extracted from cows' urine. As he dabbled his brush in the gold dust, the intricate and sophisticated detailing of stars, sequins, and Persian floral patterns emerged in their golden splendour.

Three of Teherani's apprentices sat behind him and mixed the binders with the pigments to ensure their even spread. While the pigments were nearly odourless, the sickly, sweet smell of gum arabic and gum tragacanth swept the colours, and would remain steadfastly over many centuries, even as the coloured subjects would demise, decay, and move into oblivion with the passage of time.

Nur Ud Din could feel the restrained desire of the two young boys to break into a run, chase lions, climb *Jamun* trees, and do all those things which normal, ebullient six-year-olds did. As he put in the colours, with quick flicks of his wrist, the similarity between the two young princes was amazing. Wearing identical, gold-embroidered red tunics with yellow *pattas* at the waist, and carrying bejewelled daggers in golden sheaths, they looked every inch the Timurids descended from the haughty warrior clans of the feared Taimurlane and Genghis Khan.

Adding the finishing touches, he took a final look at the royals, to transpose those same expressions onto the finished painting in the final hours before submission. Closing his eyes, he recapitulated – Prince Salim in his *qaba* of royal blue with a white turban and gold aigrette, smiling slightly, his eyes quizzing the future; the sturdier of the two younger princes in his red tunic and orange turban, with the hint of imperial disdain in his brown eyes; the other prince, in a similar red tunic and green turban, the fairest of them all, with eyes shielding some unknown pain – they would all come alive on the square piece of cloth before the sun was down.

Gathering his brushes, he stood up and performed the *kornish*, and remained that way as Prince Salim rose and, with a nod of acknowledgement, proceeded towards the river pavilion. Prince Khurram and Firdaus Salim Sultan merrily jostled along in their father's shadow.

*

Mirza Kamran's Baradari

The Royal Suite

Same night

Nadira settled herself more comfortably in the crook of Salim's arms, as she traced small, dainty patterns on his muscular chest. The smell of their perfumed bodies mixed well with the perspiration from their frantic lovemaking, when Nadira had thrown her thighs around the groin of Prince Salim. Brushing her hair from her face, she quietly remarked, 'It was really very brave of Khurram to save Firdaus from the bucking and rearing of that skittish horse. For a moment, I thought that Firdaus would fall and be terribly hurt by the rearing and kicking of that beast.'

'Yes, it *was* good of Khurram to ride out and control Pari.' Salim turned on his side and pulled Nadira closer.

'I do not mean to interfere, Your Highness, but I would be glad if that vicious horse could be removed from the royal stable. One day it will surely bring grief to someone.'

Prince Salim smiled in the darkness, as he recollected the day's events. 'Pari is a mare, and a battle-hardened veteran. You see, Nadira, these Arabian war horses are very sensitive to any change in attitude or riding misconduct. She must have felt some change in her handling by Firdaus, which made her shy and neigh.'

Nadira was up in a flash. The terror in her eyes was real. 'Shy and neigh? Why, she almost knocked out the teeth of that *syce* who rushed in first. She was kicking and biting, and shouldering everyone who came near. Had it not been for Khurram, Pari would have snorted the *djinns* out of your fierce warriors.'

Salim laughed delightedly, and moved his hands to explore the soft contours of her rounded buttocks and shapely thighs. Pushing Salim onto his back, Nadira straddled his thighs and with tremulous fingers guided his rigid shaft inside her.

The night was still young.

*

In another suite of the royal apartment, Firdaus and Khurram played chess by candlelight.

'Firdaus?'

'Yes, Prince?'

'What did you mean when you said "I shall repay you"?'

'Well, Prince, I meant exactly what I said.' Firdaus leaned forward, his eyes earnest. 'When you rode in from behind and hung onto Pari's bridle, I thought you would fall and get crushed under her hooves. But, you held on until Pari quietened down. I am telling you, brother, I was so scared that I wanted to just jump from that crazy horse and run away.'

Prince Khurram looked deep into his eyes. 'Firdaus, we Timurids take our words very seriously. You are my brother, and you owe me nothing.'

Firdaus, eyes shining with tears, said seriously, 'I meant what I said. You saved my life, and I shall repay you. I shall give my life for you.'

Khurram smiled happily, and, wiping a runaway tear from

Firdaus's cheek, turned his attention to unsettling Firdaus's rook on the chess board.

Jameela Anga, pretending to sleep in a corner, smiled at the childish banter of the young Timurids, and curled herself up on the hard floor.

Around the *Baradari,* and on all roads approaching the royal gardens, the fierce Afghan warriors Lala Beg Kabuli and Khwaja Dost Mohammed kept a strict vigil. The river front was secured by Sakat Singh Kachhawa and his three hundred *sowars.*

*

(CHAPTER 9)

TAATTUL-E-SHAHI

(The Royal Interlude)

Raja Man Singh's Palace

Akbarnagar, Capital of Subah Bengal

18th May, 1598

Evening hours

The rider, coated in dust and the assorted debris of a long journey, rode low over the neck of his tired horse, as he galloped at full pelt towards the main gates of the city palace. His leather messenger's pouch, secured by a wax seal, was around his waist and rested in the front of the saddle. Two swords, worn on either side, edged upwards as the messenger leaned further into the neck of the horse. The Mughal insignia on the saddle covering proclaimed that the rider was from the

Mughal Court of Lahore.

As he thundered past the sentries, a cry went up. Jumping down from the saddle, he faced the encircling soldiers and cried, 'I carry an urgent letter for Mirza Raja Man Singh of Amber. I demand admittance on behalf of *Bhai Sa* Sakat Singh Kachhawa.'

The sentry commander, sheathing his sword, pointed to a broad sweep of road outside the gates and remarked, 'His Highness is visiting the site of Hadafe Mosque which is under construction. Today is Monday, hence labour payments are being made and, if you hurry, you might find him there. Otherwise, come back here.'

'Many thanks, brother,' said the messenger, as he sprang on to his horse and clattered out again.

*

Construction Site

Hadefa Mosque

Same evening

In the flickering light of the earthen lamps, Mirza Raja Man Singh read the handwritten note a second time, and found that the re-reading had not diluted the venomous portends of the words.

Rubbing his tired eyes, he read again:

In the service of His Highness, Mirza Raja Man Singh of Amber, Governor of Subah Bengal, Bihar and Odisha: 20th April,1598

Most Honourable Mirza,

Khamaghani!

I send this missive to you with the hope that the divine blessings of Maa Bhawani and Lord Krishna shall grace your valorous form and bless you with all success and fame.

I take this opportunity to remind you that ever since you deputed me to the court of Prince Salim, I have served him faithfully and to the best of my insignificant ability. In each syllable and action of mine I have upheld the honour of the Kachhawas, and the prestige of our Jharshahi flag nurtured with the blood of our ancestors.

My allegiance to you is unquestionable, and all these past years I have closely followed His Royal Highness Prince Salim in all his crusades, only because of the responsibility that you placed on my shoulders many years ago.

The safety and wellbeing of your adored sister, Princess Man Bai, has been a constant source of worry for me and for the three hundred Kachhawas who ride with me. Prince Salim's avarice for women and the throne is well known, and carries much pain for His Majesty Shahenshah Akbar, as well as for all those Rajput nobles who wish honour and loyalty to be their companions.

Sire, be advised: in these past two months, Prince Salim has been clandestinely meeting with a Kashmiri dancer, who goes by the name of Nadira urf Anarkali. Earlier, the trysts were being held at Lahore in secret passages, but are now on frequent trips to the royal gardens and Shikargahs beyond Lahore.

It is mentioned with regret that Rawal Sal Darbari and Keso Das Maru of Mewat have been actively involved in facilitating these unethical liaisons. Raja Ram Singh Kachhawa has also been providing protection to these meetings. Things have come to such a pass that these afternoon trysts are now referred to as jinsi muamalaat.

In the second half of March, His Highness Prince Salim camped at Mirza Kamran's Baradari on the west bank of Ravi for more than a fortnight. Some of the minor nobles, including

Lala Beg Kabuli, Khwaja Dost Mohammed Teherani, and Zamana Beg were entrusted with the perimeter security, and I was tasked with securing the riverfront.

With utter dismay I report, Sire, that the dancer, Nadira urf Anarkali was a constant companion to His Highness, along with her son, who is almost the same age as young Prince Khurram. In fact, if camp sources are to be believed, then there is an astonishing resemblance between Prince Khurram and this young child.

There was one good fallout of this whole episode – the attendants and personal eunuchs of Prince Salim were heard marvelling at his abstinence from wine and opium during this period, and are gladdened by the fact that Prince Salim is much happier and more tolerant now, towards one and all.

This matter begets significance as the emperor is unaware of this development, and may not be so pleasantly disposed to this royal interlude, considering Prince Salim's aberrations in the past. To my uncivilized eyes, Sire, it seems that immense precautions are being taken to keep this liaison hidden from the emperor's eyes. That this matter precedes our knowledge of the past can also not be ruled out.

I could not be a silent witness to the betrayal of his nineteen wives by earlier marriages, and the perceived threat to our Rajput sister from Jodhpur, Princess Manmati Rathore and her young son, Prince Khusrau, on account of this dancing girl's sorcery, hence this missive to you.

Hukum, there is no better judge in my eyes to decipher the long term implications of this besotted quagmire than you, since you have the emperor's ears, and can help dispel the dark clouds hovering on our clan, and our tenuous hold on the Mughals through marriage.

I leave it in your capable hands, Bhai Sa, to do as you please. I could trust no one with this information, hence I have sent my younger brother, Roop Singh with this missive.

Please forgive me if I have exceeded my brief.

In your service, I remain, a loyal Kachhawa.

Jai Bhawani!

Sakat Singh Kachhawa

1600 Zat / 300 Sowars.

Raja Man Singh folded the parchment and said, 'This letter is dated the twentieth of April. Why did it take you almost a month to reach here?'

Roop Singh, faint with fatigue, licked his lips before answering. 'Your Highness. When I set out from Lahore, I was told that I would find you at Rohtasgarh in Bihar, and therefore I reached Rohtasgarh first. There I was told that you had left for Akbarnagar, and I followed you here, Highness.'

Raja Man Singh nodded as he called for his horse, and instructed Roop Singh, 'Stay here for a few days. What has been done cannot be undone, so rest for a while, and then return to Lahore. You shall carry a reply from me.'

He turned towards several attendants. 'Bhau Singh, arrange for Roop Singh's stay in the royal guest house. Make sure he is comfortable.'

He mounted his steed and rode away, surrounded by a small detail of his Rajput warriors.

*

Ruqaiah Begum's Apartment

Shahi Qila, Lahore

16th June, 1598

Afternoon hours

Prince Khurram snuggled close to his grandmother on the gem-encrusted seat of the silver pillared swing. This year, early monsoons had set in and there was great rejoicing on the streets. The first of the showers lashed the fiery stones of the buildings and the parched fields in a carpet of large sized drops. Errant raindrops, searching for companionship, drifted in mischievous spurts onto the people lining the corridors, porticos, and *jharokhas* of the palaces, mansions and thatched huts, with equal joy.

Sipping the chilled *Khus* sherbet from his silver tumbler,he plucked a pinch of raw, green mango powder and sprinkled it liberally on top. Finding the taste perfect, he grinned happily at Ruqaiah Begum and proffered his tumbler.

'Try this, *Ammi Huzoor*, it is better than the flax seeds you have every night to loosen your tummy.'

Ruqaiah Begum smiled at her grandson's sauciness, and in mock severity called out to her attendants, 'Get me a bowl of dried resins. It seems young Prince Khurram's head has become unglued, and needs to be fixed again!'

They both dissolved in fits of laughter, with Khurram spilling his iced sherbet on her fine bodice of Chinese silk.

As they rocked together in companionable silence, Khurram took out a long, red feather and tickled under her heavy chins. The fragrance of *Zubad* filled the vaulted terrace and sparred for dominance with the earthy smell of fresh monsoons.

Begum Ruqaiah Sultana looked fondly at her grinning grandchild, and remarked, 'Your feather carries a wonderful smell, Khurram. Don't tell me that you have bathed your African Parrot in *Itr,* and then plucked his feather.'

'No, *Ammi Huzoor,* this scented feather is a gift from my friend, Firdaus.' Having said this, Khurram immediately looked up in alarm. The strict admonitions of his father, Prince Salim, to avoid any reference to Firdaus, came rushing back to him.

It was not the name, but the alarm on Khurram's face which led Begum Ruqaiah to probe further.

'And who is this new friend of yours, Khurram? I have never met him.'

'Oh, *Ammi Huzoor*, he is just a small boy like me, who was there for the hunt. He is gone now.'

'Gone where, Khurram?'

Prince Khurram jumped down from the swing, and, with a cheery, 'I do not know, *Ammi Huzoor*! The fat, fatter, fattest *khojasera* Ghulam Hamid might be able to tell you!' rushed down the steep stairs to play in the courtyard below.

Begum Ruqaiah Sultana counted the drizzling raindrops, as her eyes sought answers to questions unknown.

*

Royal Apartments

Same night

Jameela Anga was drenched in perspiration as she came out of Ruqaiah Begum's apartment.

The questioning had been close and direct. There was no room for lies or prevarications. The supremacy of the harem in all matters pertaining to the wellbeing of the emperor was well established, and obfuscations or deceit were severely punished.

The glowering visage of Begum Ruqaiah Sultana again spun before her eyes, as she mopped her brow, and cursed the nineteen wives of Prince Salim who were unable to satisfy his lust and keep him away from the wretched dancer's charms.

*

Shikargaah

Virkgarh (14 kos NW of Lahore)

28th October, 1598

9:40 p.m.

'I knew the coming of Raja Man Singh in terrible urgency to the royal court would have some malefic purpose. The old Sheikh, flattering his way to the emperor's side and bent upon tarnishing my image, must have joined the Raja in creating monumental lies. The emperor's usual affection has been replaced by a subtle wariness.'

The words spoken in subdued anger further increased the misery of a tearful Nadira, as she sought the hands of Prince Salim.

'Your Highness, I can feel the onset of a terrible calamity! My lord, I think Destiny will again tear us apart, and bring me to ruin.' Nadira was unable to stop her tears, beset by past memories of separation and the impending prospect of a calamitous future.

'Why do you weep, Zehrun? There is no power in this world that can keep us apart. You worry for Firdaus? You should not, considering that I have fathered him, and have never...'

Salim's words were cut short by a sobbing Nadira. 'Sire, how can I forget that morning when you raised your sword to kill a month-old innocent baby? It was still your child. How can

I forget the harsh words of His Majesty, Emperor Akbar, as he turned out a young woman with an infant son, a prince, to live in the fringes of civilization?'

Nonplussed, Salim pulled her closer. 'Hush, my darling. Those were wretched times, and I, in the exuberance of youth, could not fathom the depths of my love for you. The unwritten Timurid rules of harem eclipsed my sanity and my love during that period. What else can I say?' The remorse and helplessness in his voice engulfed all those years of irredeemable anguish.

Salim, with his pathological hatred for his father building up once again inside him, roughly seized Nadira by her arm and threw her face down on the large bed. Climbing behind her, he parted her buttocks and thrust his engorged penis inside her, even as she whimpered in excited pain. Hunching down on her like a *sowar*, he continued to pound against her soft buttocks, as his fingers mauled her breasts squeezed against the bed.

Coming inside her in violent shudders, he stretched himself on top of her body and let her perfumed softness envelop him. Gently, he rolled onto his side, pulling Nadira against his chest. As she arched her back, buttock and thighs against him, he reached out in the darkness searching for his turban. With one hand, he removed the heavy gold aigrette adorned with a rose made of small rubies and diamonds, and, closing Nadira's palm over it avowed fiercely, 'Zehrun, from my turban have I put my *serpench* in your hands as my honour rests with it. Keep it with you, until I redeem it. I have plans to seek a separate territory as my kingdom, with the emperor's pleasure. If denied, then I will resort to arms and cleave a kingdom of my own.'

Nadira, all sensualities doused, sat up in alarm and clutched his hand. 'Allah have mercy! I wish no such thing from you, Highness. How can you even think of rebelling against your own father? The emperor! Have you considered the might of his army and the resources at his disposal? Perish that thought. I will not have you rising up against your father, no matter what the future holds for me or for Firdaus. I will not, I will not!'

Prince Salim, clenching his jaws, was already drawing the sketch of his kingdom in his heart.

*

Diwaan e Khas

Shahi Qila, Lahore

30th October, 1598

9:20 a.m.

Emperor Akbar stared at Sheikh Abu'l Fazl and his voice, pregnant with vicious spikes, cut through the equanimity of the learned Sheikh.

'Old friend, we leave Lahore in four days. Maybe for the last time, who knows, but *Allah*! I have reigned from here for more than fourteen years, and every stone, every shadow is known to me.'

Looking wistfully at the silent, towering walls of the Shahi Qila, he added, 'The death of Abdullah Khan Turani has relieved me of my worries from the north-west, hence, my presence at Lahore is not necessary. Prince Salim has also become indolent with the cushioned life at the royal court. As a matter of fact, we have all become lazy and complacent and need to be in the rigours of marches and battles, to sharpen ourselves.'

He continued, 'This is the right time to tame the Rana of Mewar, as also to annex the kingdoms of Berar, Bijapur, and Golconda. The royal harem and the court rides with me, but you must stay behind to administer a few things before proceeding to Deccan. Prince Murad should be immediately sent back to the royal court at Agra or he shall ruin himself with the filthy opium and wine. He will either accompany you back to Agra if the situation permits, or will travel alone if you have to stay back to sort out matters between the different commanders.'

Fixing Abu'l Fazl with his torrid gaze, Akbar coughed. 'There is this delicate matter of Anarkali and her son, Firdaus. In a month's time from now, have them slain.' The stare remained. 'You may thereafter proceed to Deccan.'

'Yes, Your Majesty.'

*

Mohalla Teer Garran

Near Morchi Gate

2nd November, 1598

Past noon

'What do you mean, you can't find her?' There was bafflement and panic in Prince Salim's voice.

Zamana Beg, reining in his shying horse, said, 'Your Highness, since early morning we have been combing *Mohalla Shia* where *Laal Haveli* is located, as well as the surrounding areas of *Mohalla Teer Garran* and *Kaman Garran*. There is absolutely no trace of her.'

'What does the landlord say?' rasped Prince Salim.

'He says that she left early morning, the previous day. Firdaus and her few attendants were also with her. What disturbs us, Highness, is the statement of a milkman, with his cow sheds at the southern end of this street, who says that he saw a group of Mughal *sowars* in black and mustard uniforms surround her.'

'Black and mustard. These are the colours of Keso Das Maru's men. Quick, bring them to me at Meher Bagh.'

*

Meher Bagh

A few hours later, Keso Das Maru of Mewat with his band of *sowars* presented themselves before Prince Salim. The morning detail of troopers only remembered coming across a small party of travellers comprising a statuesque veiled woman with a child and her half dozen attendants. After routine questioning they were allowed to go.

*

Diwan e Khas

Shahi Qila, Lahore

5th November, 1598

9:00 a.m.

There was total bedlam outside the *Diwan e Khas* and the royal apartments. The mighty Moghul court would move for Agra tomorrow and thousands of soldiers, slaves, labourers, and attendants were toiling away in shepherding the mountains of weaponry, tentage, kitchen paraphernalia, furniture, royal wardrobe, granary, and thousands of livestock for meat and victuals supply en route.

The *Mir Manzil*, with two advance teams, had left a couple of days earlier, to identify and prepare the stages for halt of the imperial train. The statistics were mindboggling. Almost a hundred thousand men and women, in thousands of carts, with elephants, camels, horses, pack mules, and on foot, would be travelling covering eight to ten *kos* daily. The emperor's personal luggage was being loaded on seven hundred camels and two thousand bullock carts, with the royal ladies and the harem inmates employing another five hundred camels and a similar number of bullock carts for their personal belongings. This train, from head to tail, would be about twenty miles long and a hundred thousand strong, and to the circling birds above it would look like a monstrous centipede with the motley colours of green, gold, red, orange, mustard, and white signifying the different religious and ethnic groups comprising this imperial juggernaut.

Into this maelstrom of hyperactivity entered the Jesuit priests, Father Francis Xavier and Father Pinheiro, with a few clerical attendants.

There were looks of consternation and disapproval on the faces of the attending courtiers at the appearance of these priests.

Having taken their positions at the back of the court, they waited patiently. The *Vizier* Sheikh Abu'l Fazl Allami was quick to question their presence.

'Jesuit priest, Xavier, how dare you come to the throne of the Mughaliya Sultanat, in the august presence of His Majesty *Shahenshah e Hind* Emperor Akbar, without prior intimation or permission?'

Father Xavier, old and tired in his sixtieth year, but with his face radiating youthful vigour, performed the *kornish* and addressed the emperor. 'Your Majesty, I seek a thousand pardons from you regarding my unannounced presence today. I was informed last night that you may advance your departure and leave on Friday the sixth of November itself. In my haste to meet you, I could not follow the protocol, for which I seek your pardon.'

The booming voice of Akbar rang out. 'You are a good man, Priest. Come forward and explain.'

The Jesuit priest stepped forward into the central aisle, and, performing the court obeisance, submitted, 'Your Majesty, I seek your permission to travel with you to your new court at Agra.'

The emperor looked hard at the frail priest, and remembering his sickness on the return journey from Kashmere the previous year, tried to dissuade him. 'Oh Priest! This is a long and hard trek over several hundred *kos*, to be covered over several months, and unfit for a fragile priest. Remember, you fell sick on our return from Kashmere last year and I had to especially nurse you back to health?'

'As *I* nursed you back to health when you fell sick on the same journey, Your Majesty!' Having said this, the priest lowered his eyes, but not before Akbar caught a glimpse of twinkling amusement in them.

He gave a loud guffaw, patting the cushion on which he sat. 'True, *fakir*, true! You did nurse me to health first. Now, prepare to accompany us. *Mir Saman*, arrange four Bactrian camels for the priest, and place him just behind the royal troopers guarding the harem. Is there anything else that you need, Priest?' There was merriment in his voice.

'You are most kind and benevolent, Your Majesty. There is just one thing which tugs at my heart as we go. We wasted fourteen years in your royal court, with the wisdom of true faith and salvation being expounded to you, in the form of Our Father, the Son, and the Holy Ghost, but having misled us since the beginning, you gave no relevance to the teachings. I am answerable to the Holy Cardinal, and I am now being asked as to what I have achieved in these past fourteen years at your royal court. Has it all been in jest, Majesty?'

The emperor's eyes had turned bloodshot and so protuberant that it seemed as if they might explode out of their sockets. The face, normally gentle and affable, had taken on a terrible visage. With brows knitted, and clenched jaws, Akbar roared, 'We are not answerable to you, or your Holy Cardinal, or to anyone else on this Earth! We, the emperor of Hindustan, Defender of the Faith and God's Own Shadow on Earth, will not listen to your bunch of concocted stories and miracles.'

Gripping the arms of his throne, Emperor Akbar was almost standing in rage.

Father Xavier looked stricken at this violent manifestation of the jovial emperor. He had never, never expected such a venomous assault from the normally placid ruler. The whole court quailed at this frightful sight, and the black-turbaned *ulemas*,with their hands across their chests, quietly started reciting the holy *kalmas*.

Taking a deep breath, Akbar sat down. But, the words came in angry bursts. 'Who asked you to waste your time here? Your Cardinal? Then take your woes to him. Did we not grant you permission to build your church, and spread the word of your religion, without fear of reprisal? In fact, we granted you the right and privilege to exercise your religious beliefs under our protection. And, even when you converted that Moslem girl, what was her name, to your creed...'

'Grace, Your Majesty,' reminded Sheikh Abu'l Fazl from the foot of the throne.

'Yes, Grace. That was her name. Did we stop you? I could have ordered for your bones, and the bones of your followers to be separated with hacksaws and then be fed to the starving hyenas in the royal zoo, or your head to be stomped to a bloody pulp by an elephant, but we refrained. We let you enjoy the pleasure of my benefaction. And now you have the impunity to say that you wasted your years with us?' The angry flush was again coming back on Akbar's face.

Many of the Jesuit followers accompanying Father Xavier had become incontinent with fear, as the old priest, trembling in fear and reciting psalms of protection, sought permission to leave the court with a thousand apologies.

At Akbar's nod, the priest slowly retraced his steps, never turning his back to the emperor, and performing *taslims* in rapid succession.

Several dark splotches were left on the highly polished marble floor, marking the previous positions of the incontinent priests. Palace attendants quickly scrubbed the floor clean with perfumed water to mask the odour. Acute incontinency in the *durbar* hall was a frequent occurrence.

The younger followers had pulled their clerical cowls over their heads, but still could not resist shivering in morbid fright as they passed the forty hangmen with leather nooses standing just beyond the last pillar of the *Diwan e Aam.*

Before retiring for the night, Father Francis Xavier noted in his ecclesiastical diary, 'The emperor is jovial in laughing, and monstrous in anger.'

As his head hit the soft pillow, he marvelled at the gigantic canvas of the Mughal psyche, who never referred to themselves as 'I', it was always the royal 'We'.

Tomorrow, they would depart.

*

(CHAPTER 10)

MAUT, NIZDE MAN MAYA!

(Death, come not near!)

Village of Gulyana

Three kos south of village of Gujar Khan

2nd February, 1599

11:25 p.m.

The thunder of many scores of hooves shook the small village of Gulyana, as fifty riders rode into the sleepy hamlet, where the residents, tired after a hard day's labour harvesting their wheat and millet crops, had settled in for the night. The leader turned sharply to the man in peasant's clothing riding behind him and asked, 'Which way now?'

The man, with the ends of his turban drawn across his face, pointed south, where the silhouette of a small *haveli* could be seen in the distance. Riding swiftly across the narrow country lane, they surrounded the double storeyed mansion. A lone watchman sleeping outside lunged for his spear, but one of the riders tackled him on the ground and pressed a dagger to his neck. The man, wide eyed with fear, folded his hands in submission as he felt the dagger lightly pierce his skin.

'Where is she?' hissed the trooper.

Closing his eyes in shock, pain and fear, the man croaked, 'She is on the upper floor.'

'And her attendants?' The dagger pressed harder.

'Spread on the ground and upper floor.' The terrified man could feel the warm trickle of blood seeping through his under vest.

'And the landowner and his family?'

'Munshi Khemchand with his family left yesterday for Gujar Khan. Family marriage.' The watchman winced in pain as the trooper pressed his knee into his chest.

The next moment his head lolled sideways as the dagger was thrust deeper, and the head savagely spun to one side. A low moan and a warm gush of blood gurgled from his slit throat, as the *sowars*, silent as shadows, streamed into the open courtyard and into the rooms.

The thud of leather boots and iron clubs mingled with the shouts and screams of men and women, as they were roughly pushed and thrown into the courtyard. A few children started crying. A larger section of the guard had rushed upstairs and found Nadira, sitting terrified and wide awake, shielding Firdaus behind her back in one of the smaller ante rooms. The female attendant, Jaffer Anga, sat hunched in a corner, petrified.

Willing herself to speak, Nadira addressed the lead soldiers. 'Who are you? What do you want?'

'We come from the royal court at Lahore. Are you Begum Nadira, *urf* Anarkali?' asked a soldier who had a scar running down his left cheek.

'I am Begum Zehrunnisa from the harem of Prince Salim Sultan. And how dare you come in here!' exclaimed Nadira.

The soldier gave a short, wicked laugh. 'Royal harem, indeed! You are just a dancer with luscious thighs, who opens them for anybody who has two rupees to spare.' He approached closer. 'I have two rupees on me. Will you give me a quickie, Anarkali?' He leaned down and, roughly grabbing her breast, squeezed hard.

Nadira knotted her fist and drove it straight between the legs of the soldier with all the strength she could muster. She felt her hand jar as it squashed his testicles against his groin. The soldier, hooting with pain, let go of her breast and hobbled into a corner clutching his genitals. The other sepoys laughed in cruel merriment.

Two of them moved forward and caught hold of her arms, dragging her to stand upright. Firdaus clutched at the skirt of her *kameez* and started crying.

'Take your dirty hands off me!' screamed Nadira, as she pushed and shoved against the soldiers restraining her. The soldiers only tightened their hold and dragged her from the room.

'Firdaus! Firdaus! Please do not take me away from my son, please...' her wails shattered the stillness of the cold February night, as she was pushed down the steep stairs.

Firdaus, crying bitterly, tried to run after her and, stumbling in the trailing bedsheets, fell on the hard, stony floor. Jaffer Anga, catapulted out of her petrified state by the plaintive wails of the child, rushed to pick him up in her arms. She scurried down the stairs to find a hysterically crying Begum Nadira on her knees, imploring the guard commander to let her be with her son. The other members of her household staff, including Baqar Khan and Maqbool Mian, were sitting in various stages of dishevelment and injury. A few minutes before, when Maqbool Mian had remonstrated in his earthy language, an iron-clad fist had silenced him with a glancing blow, and he was now sitting quietly nursing a badly bruised face.

As soon as Firdaus saw Nadira, he scrambled out of Anga's arms and ran to her. Nadira, still on her knees, clasped him to her bosom and rocked back and forth.

Motioning to the huddled servants, the guard commander said, 'Tie them up and gag them. And, you,' he said, motioning to the terrified huddle, 'if you create any trouble, or raise an alarm, we shall come back and kill you all. Understood?

'Take the woman and the child outside. Get some blankets and warm clothing from inside.' He gestured to Jaffer Anga. 'And, you – go and help them.'

Baqar Khan and Maqbool tried to get up and say something to Nadira, but they were clubbed down viciously. Nadira, holding Firdaus close to her chest, was being pushed outside, when she turned and called, 'Bum Bhairav!' Another shove. Baqar was looking askance at her, even as he held one hand above his head to ward off another blow. Crying bitterly, she called out again, 'Bum Bhairav!' This time there was a glimmer of understanding in his eyes, as he called out, 'Yes, Begum Huzoor. Bum Bhairav!'

Nadira screamed as she saw the inert body of Gopi, the night watchman, with his throat slit, and congealed blood on the stony floor around his head. Pulling Firdaus close to her and covering his eyes with her hand, she shuffled quickly towards the saddled horse being held for her.

As she tried to lift Firdaus into the saddle, he was rudely taken from her and a sepoy said brusquely, 'The child rides with me. You get up on the horse.'

With defiance writ large on her face, she faced the soldier. 'No. My son shall ride with me.'

The soldier held her roughly by the neck. 'Shut up, woman. Just get up and ride.' Plucking a few sheets and a warm blanket brought by Jaffer Anga, he threw them at her. 'Here, the night is cold. Cover yourself properly.'

Firdaus clung tightly to her hand, and would not let go. Nadira, judging the ruthlessness in the eyes of the soldiers around her, and their uncouth ways, feared for Firdaus's safety. She quietly kissed his forehead, and, wiping his tears, spoke softly. 'Firdaus, my son, listen to me. These are bad men, and they will harm us if we do not do as they say. We are travelling together, and tomorrow I shall find a way out of this mess. Now, my brave son, go with this person. I shall be riding just behind you.' She fastened a heavy woollen cloak around Firdaus, as Jaffer Anga wept bitterly and caressed Firdaus's head. Wracked with sobs and unable to bid farewell to her mistress and her beloved Firdaus, she simply knelt and planted a kiss on both his cheeks and placed a small fur cap over his head.

In a few minutes, they rode out into the darkness, never to return.

*

Hamid Gul Afghani, the guard commander entrusted with the arrest of Nadira Begum, covered the eighty *kos* to Lahore in seven days. During this period, the posse of horse riders eschewed the regular caravan routes and rode through fields and villages, stopping just long enough to rest their steeds and prepare some food. Nights were spent in either open fields or within the precincts of village mosques. Nadira was not touched again, as Hamid Gul Afghani, fearing the *Vizier's* brutal retribution in the event of any complaint, gave strict orders for her protection.

The soldier with the scar grimaced in pain at every contact with the saddle. His tender testicles lost no malice in making their pain felt.

They reached the outskirts of Lahore on the evening of the tenth of February 1599, and encamped in the deserted compound of a Moslem school.

*

Saadat Shah ki Haveli

Androoni Sheher (Walled City)

Lahore

12th February, 1599

Morning

Sheikh Abu'l Fazl stepped out of the dark dungeons into the wintry sunlight and fresh bracing air of a cold February morning. The last hour had been distinctly uncomfortable for him. The sight of a young woman and her child in fetters had clearly assailed his sensibilities and tenets of honour. He had immediately ordered for the fetters and manacles to be removed from the woman's hands and legs.

His questioning of this beautiful lady had yielded no results. To his discerning and cultured mind, the Mughal nobility could have been better employed than in chasing and punishing defenceless women and children. Having spent the better part of an hour in procrastinating, he reluctantly turned towards the dark dungeons once again.

Nadira sat on a stone slab, with the unchained fetters lying strewn on the stony floor. Thick and oil-coated manacles on long iron chains hung suspended from the walls. Rats, the size of mongooses, boldly peeked from behind the slabs and coils of rope scattered around the filthy dungeon. Neither sword nor spears, nor the breath of death, frightened these denizens of the dark as they went about their business of scavenging with impunity.

She looked up as the Sheikh sat down, fear and anxiety clouding her beautiful grey eyes.

Unable to meet her gaze, Abu'l Fazl gripped his chair and spoke in a monotone. 'Begum Nadira, the emperor spared your life and that of your son seven years ago, and ordered that you leave Lahore never to return again. You have disobeyed his royal decree wilfully, and stand convicted of gross infraction of royal command, and, to a certain degree, of sedition.'

'Where have I erred, sire? My only crime is that I came back to Lahore, in search of my lost love. In deference to the emperor's wish, I stayed away from the imperial seat. For many months, I stayed in the old *haveli* near *Morchi Darwaza* with no hidden need to press myself into the Mughal designs of deceit, chicanery, and ruination. I made no effort to meet my beloved, Prince Salim, although I had carried the seed of his love within me for nine months, just as Princess Manmati and Shah Begum did for Prince Khurram and Prince Khusrau. I did not pursue the prince but suffered in silence, living a life of ignominy. Why? Only, sire, in abiding respect of the emperor's command. Had it not been for that fortuitous glance that day in March, Prince Salim would not even have dreamt that I still existed. It was Providence, sire, which spoke for me. And Allah's will is supreme, in case you have forgotten, learned Sheikh. Neither kings nor emperors, nor generals, nor mullahs, can prevail upon the writ of Allah!' She paused to collect her breath.

The Sheikh regarded her with hooded eyes. There was no satisfactory rebuttal to her statements, but he took refuge in the easiest indictment. 'The merits of love are not under debate, Begum, nor are you qualified to elaborate on the will and powers of Allah, for he is beyond the scope and comprehension of human intellect, and certainly beyond the qualifications of a *nautch* girl. The fact remains that you have deliberately disobeyed the emperor's direct command, and should therefore be punished by death.'

Nadira clutched Firdaus close to her, and looked at the Vizier with trepidation in her eyes. Her young and beautiful frame trembled with dread.

Abu'l Fazl could not bring himself to pronounce her death warrant. He spent a few moments looking at the heavy gold aigrette of Prince Salim, which she wore so proudly as a brooch on her bosom. At this moment, all his senses rebelled at the very thought of putting a young woman and her innocent child through the traumatic wheels of Mughal justice. Tyranny is closer to the truth, surmised the disgusted Sheikh.

Abu'l Fazl sighed, and standing up, formally proclaimed. 'Begum Nadira, the emperor's order will prevail. I bear you no ill will, and I am bound by oath to execute His Majesty's directives. But, take heart, there is always justice and hope in Allah's eternal court. *Khuda hafiz*.' He turned around and stumbled up the steep, flagstone steps.

A weeping woman, softly sobbing, and a young child with a bewildered, frightened face were all that remained in the fear-infested cells of injustice.

*

The *Vizier* stopped at the iron gates near the entrance to the secret dungeons, where Hamid Gul Afghani stood with his guard detail.

The dark, thin face of Sheikh Abu'l Fazl was drawn with lines of grief, as he quietly commanded, 'The woman shall not be chained, but keep the dungeon securely guarded. Permit her to wash under *Khoja* Pir Ali's security. Feed them well. The child shall be sent to *Shahi Qila* on the morning of the eighteenth of February for beheading, and take her to the isolated, decrepit area south of Shahi Qila, and have her walled alive. Do this on the night of the eighteenth.'

The Afghan soldier touched his breastplate in acknowledgement, as Abu'l Fazl walked with rapid steps to his waiting horse.

The two tears he shed for Nadira and Firdaus on that stony ground would seal their future, and change the course of Mughal history for ever.

*

Subterranean chambers

Saadat Shah Ki Haveli

Thursday, 18th February, 1599

Early morning; sunrise

Two of the burly Afghani guards were trying to restrain Nadira as she kept lunging for Firdaus, who was being forcibly taken, biting and screaming, from the dungeons. Nadira, hissing like a serpent with rage and spitting bubbles of froth from her mouth, was heaving and clawing at the soldiers holding her. Firdaus, his listless legs trailing behind him, was being dragged over the stairs, and was screaming, '*Ammi*, *Ammi*, please... I want my *Ammi*, please!'

Twisting to her left with all her strength, she viciously bit the wrist of the guard and yanked her right hand away in one sweeping motion. Using the pivotal force of her twisting body she slammed into the soldier, sending him staggering over the low stone slab, to lie spreadeagled on the floor. In a flash, she was running towards the stairs, foaming at the mouth and shouting in a guttural voice, 'Leave my son alone, you sons of mongrels and filthy pigs. Leave my son, you bloody wretches born of a jackal's womb! Leave him, I said.' She caught hold of the scabbard of the guard nearest her and tried to pull him down. Another guard, moving swiftly from the side, savagely hit her on the shoulder with the hilt of his sword. Unmindful of the pain, with only the crying, tear-stained face of her beloved Firdaus dancing before her eyes, she clambered again over the steps.

'Firdaus, my son... wait... don't drag him so, you bloody sons of whores, he is only a child.' She caught the hand of a soldier who tried to push her away and pulled with all her might. The soldier, caught off guard, fell tumbling down the stairs. Another soldier caught her leg from below and started dragging her down. Spinning around, she kicked out with her other leg, catching him square on the nose. There was a soft crack and a spurt of blood.

'The bloody whore needs to be taught a lesson. Hold her. I will fuck her brains out.' As one soldier gripped her neck from above, the trooper with the bloodied nose came hurtling up the steps and kicked Nadira in the shins with his iron boots. She crumbled on the steps, faint with pain and shock, as she saw Firdaus being lifted up and carried away, with a hand clamped over his mouth, tear-stained eyes wide with fear. The soldier now held her by her hair, and, twisting his fist around it, grappled Nadira to the floor. With his forearms across her throat, he dragged her backwards, the rough edges of the stone steps leaving marks on her back.

Paralysed with grief and stricken with horror, her eyes remained riveted to the stairs. Her mouth could only made strange gurgling sounds as her clothes were torn off her body, and the man with the bloodied nose dropped his close-fitting pyjamas and roughly spread her thighs.

For the next two hours, she was as a frothing, mumbling carcass, as man after man emptied his dirty seed inside her.

The only thing she remembered was the tormented face of Firdaus and his cascading tears.

*

At around nine o'clock that morning, *Khoja* Pir Ali came to get her dressed. His eyes, used to the cruelties and debaucheries of royal courts, flinched at the sight of Nadira. In place of the once beautiful dancing girl with her enchanting eyes and smile, lay the battered body of a common prostitute, with bruises all over her body and her pubic hair matted with the semen of a dozen men. Her eyes, still suspended on the image of Firdaus, did not register the *khoja*'s presence.

At Pir Ali's instructions, a bucket of cold water was thrown over her. Muttering and sputtering, a dishevelled Nadira sat up, groaning at the weight of misery upon her. A couple of hours later, Nadira was escorted out of the dungeons, dressed once again in clean clothes, and covered by a black-veiled gown.

The veil could not hide the contentment in her eyes, as she left for her rendezvous with death. The grief and pain of separation were left behind in the *haveli*'s dungeons for the rats to feed upon. Death was a welcome visitor.

*

Ahata e Khilwat Khana

Northern end, Shahi Qila

18th February, 1599

10:30 a.m.

Sheikh Abu'l Fazl placed his hand on Abdur Rehman's sleeve, and spoke in measured tones to alleviate the sea of troubled questions lurking in his son's eyes. For the past several minutes he had been trying to explain his actions to his disbelieving son, who had never known his father to even contemplate such actions as he was being asked to undertake now.

No amount of persuasion or justifications had worked initially, as Abdur Rehman refused to believe the course of action being advised by his father. The profusion of treacherous actions, illicit liaisons and ruthless revenge in the Mughal court was well known to Abdur Rehman, but the developing scenario completely appalled him in its ruthless devilry.

Sheikh Abu'l Fazl, sensing his son's reluctance, summed up his current actions in a single sentence. 'My son, you know I have never questioned the most fortunate emperor's wish at any point in my life. Though this act of mine is disgraceful, I will live with it. I also commend you to perceive this as another one of your father's follies and forgive me, if ever the truth be found out. In my heart, and in my prayers, I shall seek forgiveness every day for this disgrace which shall be attributed to me.' He sighed and said in a choked voice, 'I despise myself for this, but what must be done, must be done.'

Abdur Rehman looked at him for a long moment, and then stepped forward to embrace him. Bowing low, he retreated. In the anteroom of this House of Seclusion, he grabbed the almost senseless child and roughly pulled him into the secret passage which led to the *Laal Burj* on the northern end of the western periphery. It was but a short walk from the secret exit of this octagonal tower to the River Ravi, which flowed near the base.

Ashamed of his betrayal, Abu'l Fazl dismissed the *Waqia Navees* waiting in the antechamber, and picked up a quill to write the missive himself.

The quill flew over the parchment from right to left in the celebrated calligraphy of Sheikh Abu'l Fazl:

To the Most Fortunate, Bejewelled, Illumined Ray of God, Protector of the Realm, and God's Own Shadow On Earth, Shahenshah e Hindustan, Padshah Ghazi Abu'l Fath Jalal Ud Din Mohammed Akbar:

This is to inform Your Majesty that the small work entrusted to me has been completed this morning.

The other responsibility of brickwork entrusted to me shall commence tonight.

With my utmost felicitations at Your Exalted Feet,

I remain,

Your true servant,

Abu'l Fazl Allami

Vizier, Sultanat Mughaliya

It was the first time in Sheikh Abu'l Fazl's distinguished life that he had abhorred the execution of his emperor's command.

*

A few minutes past noon, Sheikh Abdur Rehman walked out of the complex of rooms at the octagonal base of *Laal Burj* with a large sack carried between two attendants. The sack, dripping blood, left a documentary trail from the room to the pier, where a river boat was moored for a quick escape.

The flagstoned floor of the small room where Abdur Rehman had brought Firdaus was splattered with blood, and swords dribbling with gore were thrown against the wall. Small fragments of bones came across as froth in the red pools of blood, with small chunks of flesh sticking to the walls and floor.

Reaching midstream, the attendants carefully lowered the bloody sack into the swirling waters of Ravi, as Abdur Rehman touched both his cheeks in the Moslem gesture of repentance.

The sack sank with the weight of deceit.

*

Abandoned Garden of Qayamat Khan

Four kos outside the southern periphery

of Andruni Sheher, Lahore

18th February, 1599

Past dusk

The small detachment of Afghan troops under Hamid Gul Afghani, entrusted with the escort of the condemned Nadira, had been camping here for the last few hours. An advance guard under Afghan Mubarak Sarwani had been posted to this deserted and lonely *Bagicha* of Qayamat Khan Ghaznin for the last three days, engaged in the protection of the perimeter and approach roads. A hundred or more labourers under the court architect Mohammed Kasim Khan had been sent here for preliminary preparations, and had raised a wall about seven feet high built of stones and rubble, almost two hundred feet long. A space of about twenty feet across had been left incomplete, which would be filled in once Nadira was embedded alive.

The soldiers had taken over the few apparent neglected mud and stone buildings within the premises, and had turned them into temporary barracks. There was an unusually heavy guard at a two room set, which had served as Afghan Mubarak Sarwani's abode until a few hours earlier. Now, Begum Nadira was held captive in these quarters.

The principal guards were stationed around the small cottage, even as Hamid Gul sat on a wooden bench toying with his prayer beads, out of habit. The senior commander, Afghan Mubarak, was walking around the part-constructed wall, giving last minute instructions.

A few minutes later, two riders preceded the arrival of Vizier Sheikh Abu'l Fazl. As the escorting cavalry rode in with the Vizier and the *Sadr i Sudur* Mohammed Bakhtaruddin, the clink of shovels and chisels became more pronounced, and the underlying lethargy of the camp vanished.

Afghan Mubarak Sarwani and Hamid Gul approached the nobles as they dismounted from their horses, and performed the simple *taslim*. Signalling torch-bearers to lead the way, the small party made its way to the section of the wall that had been left untouched. The labourers silently withdrew to the shadows and sat on their haunches.

Abu'l Fazl picked his way through the rubble, testing the stones and grit with his toes. At one point, he bent down to run his fingers through the thick slurry of lime and mortar, and, apparently satisfied with its viscosity, nodded abstractedly and moved on. He picked up an iron bar and slammed it against a part of the stone wall, only for a few flakes of lime and mortar to descend aimlessly. Clapping his hands free of dust, he turned to ask, 'Where is the architect Mohammed Kasim Khan?'

Pointing towards a group of labourers working in the far shadows, Hamid Gul replied, 'He is standing in the shadows, there, sire... the stones are being chiselled to a uniform size. Should I call him?'

'Yes, please do.'

A trooper ran to find Mohammed Kasim Khan.

Sheikh Abu'l Fazl, with tired eyes, asked of Gul Hamid, 'Where is she? Has she been prepared?'

'Sire. She is kept in custody at yonder barracks. And, as advised, we have been giving her a cup of *poshtu* every two hours to drink. She is barely conscious now, and speaks incoherently.' Hamid Gul looked down, and then continued. 'She just keeps calling out, "*Al-madad*!" She answers no questions.'

Abu'l Fazl glanced at Bakhtaruddin Khan and nodded. Looking upwards into the dark night, the Sheikh saw black clouds flitting across the dazzling moon. How very apt, he thought. The moon entombed by her own natural ally, the clouds. He ordered Mubarak Sarwani, 'Lead the prisoner out, but give her a chance to say her last prayers. And, you, architect Kasim Khan,' he gestured to the architect hovering nearby, 'ensure that the wall is raised immediately. I do not want to make a spectacle out of it.'

He addressed Mubarak again. 'The *Sadr i Sudur* and I have to identify her. Let's get this over with quickly.'

As Hamid Gul and Mubarak Sarwani marched towards the makeshift barrack, Kasim Khan hurried to get his masons and apprentices ready.

The flaming torches sputtered a little as heavy raindrops fell. The Sheikh noted the sparse clouds and concluded that the raindrops were just casual visitors.

In a few minutes, a woman in black robes was dragged out by a couple of troopers. Abu'l Fazl and Bakhtaruddin Khan hurried towards the prisoner.

The woman was dragged to within a few paces of the Vizier, where she remained suspended on the arms of the soldiers, with her knees buckled and legs splayed behind her. Her head rolled to one side and soft, unintelligible sounds came from her throat.

'Lift her veil,' Sheikh ordered tersely.

Hamid Gul stepped forward and threw the veil back over her head. The fair, oval face of a blindfolded woman, with spittle running down her tilted face and her hair in disarray, was illumined by the flaming torch brought dangerously close to the *Sadr i Sudur*'s pointed beard. Squinting against the heat and brightness of the flame, Bakhtaruddin's eyes were riveted to the heavy gold *serpench* which was fastened to the front of her black tunic.

Abu'l Fazl spoke loudly. 'What is your name, woman?' There was no answer.

The same question, repeated by Hamid Gul, elicited no response except for a few feeble murmurs of '*Al-madad*! *Al-madad*!'

Abu'l Fazl remarked to the commanders, 'I see a lot of bruises and marks on her face. What happened?'

'Your Honour, there was a scuffle with the guards this morning, as her son was being taken away. She was like a tigress defending her cub and it became difficult to contain her. A little force was used.' Hamid Gul did not elaborate further on the sexual denigration of Prince Salim's *nautch* girl; if he had there would have been hell to pay.

Sheikh pointed to the large gold aigrette fastened on her tunic, and ordered, 'Afghan Mubarak, take off this *serpench* of Prince Salim's. It shall be submitted to the emperor as proof. *Sadr*, are you in agreement?'

Bakhtaruddin Khan nodded his acquiescence, as the aigrette was handed over to the Vizier.The wily old Sheikh immediately pressed it into the sweating palms of the fat *Sadr i Sudur* with the words, 'Bakhatruddin Khan, you shall leave as soon as possible for the royal court at Agra, and shall personally hand it over to the emperor on my behalf, as evidence of the enwalling of Nadira *urf* Anarkali. Is that clear?'

'It shall indeed be an honour for me, *Hazrat* Vizier. I shall leave tomorrow.'

'Good. Then it is settled.' Turning towards the sentry commanders, Sheikh instructed them curtly, 'Proceed. And tell the masons to expedite. I don't think I can stand this for very long.'

Half dragged and half pushed, the woman was placed in the middle of the opening, and two stout bamboo poles were hurriedly secured around her to keep her upright. Her hands were made to clasp the bamboo poles at waist level, and then her wrists tied to the poles with strong hessian rope. Masons, apprentices, and labourers quickly started placing the stones and rubble mixed with lime and mortar paste from both sides, at a feverish pace. Within fifteen minutes, the immediate wall around Nadira Begum had been raised to her waist level.

As Abu'l Fazl watched in resigned dismay, the wall rose up to her neck, and then in another ten minutes had completely enveloped her. As the last of her head disappeared, Abu'l Fazl walked a few paces away and vomited. *Sadr i Sudur* Bakhtaruddin Khan looked on with interest. He must relate to His Majesty, the emperor, this weak-hearted display by the skinny Vizier.

There was no point in waiting now, the Sheikh thought. The air pockets within the walls would keep her alive for an hour or more in her semi-conscious state. Beyond that time, the special slurry of lime, mortar, and rubble would have strengthened to such an extent around the stones that any attempt to dislodge them would be impossible, especially for an oxygen-starved body.

Signalling for the horses to be brought, he directed the major part of his escorting cavalry to stay behind until sunrise. With a last look at the silent wall, he mounted his horse and raced away, ignoring the salutations of the workmen and the soldiers.

The *Sadr i Sudur*,with a little help from the assembled troopers, hoisted himself on his horse and chased the receding shadows of the Vizier and his bodyguards.

*

There was no merriment in the deserted gardens of Qayamat Khan that night. The masons and workers had long rested their equipment, and slept on the hard ground. Tears, silent as the trees, coursed down many a cheek that night. The soldiers, keeping vigil, were also silent, and ate little of the food cooked for them over campfires.

The cottage of Afghan Mubarak Sarwani was the only place where extra food was served that night.

*

(CHAPTER 11)

ZUBAAN-E-KHAMOSHI ILAHI

(The Silent Voice of God)

Intezar Gah

Shahi Qila, Lahore

9th April, 1599

7:50 p.m.

Sheikh Abu'l Fazl Ibn Mubarak was busy handing over parchments sealed with red strips carrying the small, round wax seals of the imperial office. The attendants and *Mushrif* stood behind the provisional *Subedar* Khwaja Shams Ud Din, as imperial orders were stacked in order of importance and geographical *subas*.

The *Mir Saman*, the officer in charge of the royal furniture, had already submitted the list of imperial furniture and was now present to witness the final discharge of duties of the Sheikh, prior to his departure for Deccan the next day. As a matter of interest, Abu'l Fazl was informed that the reams of paper used for the *Mir Saman*'s report, if stretched over open ground, would run for almost a *kos*.

Sheikh sighed heavily as he passed the last parchment over to *Subedar* Khwaja Shams Ud Din, and stretched his back. Now the time had come for the formal change of authority in the province of Lahore. The Vizier beckoned one of his liveried attendants to step forward, who respectfully extended a golden tray.

The Vizier took the tray, which held a ring of solid gold with ten large iron keys, and turned towards the governor.

'I, Sheikh Abu'l Fazl Allami Ibn Mubarak do hereby formally hand over the charge of *Shahi Qila* and the *Suba* of Lahore to you, Khwaja Shams Ud Din, in the name of our emperor, Abu'l Fath Jalal Ud Din Mohammed Akbar, Defender of the Faith, Protector of the Poor and Upholder of Divine Justice, to honour and protect with your life, this north-western province of the Mughal Sultanate. In good faith, I give you this.'

'In good faith, I do receive, to defend and to honour, the *Suba* of Lahore and the *Shahi Qila*. In the name of His Imperial Majesty, Jalal Ud Din Mohammed Akbar, God's Own Shadow On Earth, and *Sahib i Islam*. So help me God.' The words spoken by Shams Ud Din carried high notes of reverence and allegiance, as he accepted the proffered keys of *Shahi Qila*.

The assembled nobles and court attendants murmured, '*Ameen, Ameen*!'as the Sheikh and *Subedar* embraced.

Sheikh Abu'l Fazl tightened the *patta* around his waist, as he addressed Shams Ud Din, 'I shall leave early tomorrow morning for Berar. Please send a courier immediately to His Majesty at

Agra, informing him of my departure and the subjugation of the Afghani Pathans near Pir Panjal. The satchel of diamonds and precious stones received as *nazranas* after His Majesty's departure is also to be sent. If need be, provide a light escort.'

'Yes, sire.' Shams Ud Din collected the sheaf of royal parchments intended for safe custody with the *Subedar*. They contained the *Farman-i-Sabtis* and other imperial orders of a confidential nature. 'I do hope the Vizier's preparations are complete for a long and tiresome journey?'

'Don't you worry, Shams Ud Din Khan. Preparations have been going on for the last two months, and if I do not travel soon, then the packed baggage shall come undone!'

'Go in peace, Sheikh Ibn Mubarak! May the road shorten to reach your destination.'

*

That same night a group of Jesuit priests came to the palace of Sheikh Abu'l Fazl Ibn Mubarak on urgent business.

They were directed to the mansion of the new Governor Khwaja Shams Ud Din Khan, where their histrionic protestations over the disappearance of a recently converted girl, Grace, were met with a stoic silence and absolutely no assurances.

*

The next morning, just after sunrise, a large column of horses, elephants and bullock carts, escorted by light cavalry, rode out of the *Masjidi* Gate and took the less travelled road to Ujjain, skirting the provinces of Rajputana and Khandesh, before cutting across central Deccan to reach the headquarters of Prince Mirza Murad at Balapur in the province of Berar.

The Sheikh and his son, Abdul Rehman, travelled on caparisoned elephants, whilst the principal wives of the Vizier rode on the other draft elephants that followed. The household slaves, attendants, and escorting soldiers rode on horses or on the baggage carts.

Passing to the west of Dilli, a large part of the harem and household entourage peeled off towards Agra, and the remaining procession comprising the Vizier, his son, and the escorting soldiers increased their pace. Entering the mildly forested borders of Khandesh on the twenty-sixth of April, the Sheikh wisely changed to swift horses.

*

Bhairon Ka Sthan

Ichhra, near Lahore

1st May, 1599.

9 p.m.

The temple priest Ramadeen scuttled towards the small earthen lamp burning feebly in a corner. Had he imagined it, or was the muffled call for real?

Yes, there it was again. Shaking his sleeping wife by the shoulder, he motioned for her to quietly follow him. Nearing the rickety wooden door, he removed the iron bar wedged against it and stepped out, pulling the door closed. Peering ahead of the flickering lamp, he could just make out some huddled shapes.

'Who are you all?' he asked cautiously.

'Greetings, Holy Priest! I am Baqar Khan of Begum Nadira's household.' The priest immediately recognized the voice.

He hurried down the cobbled platform, and cried, 'Hey *Bhagwan*! What brings you here in the dead of night, Baqar Khan? I hope all is well?'

'Yes, Sire. All is well.' There was sorrow and pain in the man's voice.

Ramadeen extended his lamp, and the second man lowered the cloth draped around his face. The scarred face of Ibrahim Khan was unveiled, and Ramadeen excitedly beckoned them towards the rear of the shrine. Anxious and afraid at this unexpected visit, Ramadeen said hoarsely, 'Well, Baqar Khan, where is Begum Nadira? I hope she and little Firdaus are keeping well?'

Baqar Khan and Ibrahim looked at each other in dismay. 'We were hoping to get some news about her from you, sire.' The voice of Ibrahim came through softly as they both looked at Ramadeen intently.

Ramadeen gripped Baqar Khan's arms tightly. 'What's happened, Baqar Khan? This is a matter of great concern for me... Let me sit down.' Placing the dying earthen lamp on the ground beside him, Ramadeen sank onto his haunches and leant against an old barrel.

Baqar snuffed out the dying flame with his fingers and settled his considerable frame alongside Ramadeen's. In low tones, Baqar Khan narrated the sequence of events from the time they moved to *Laal Haveli* to the midnight capture of Nadira from the *Haveli* of Thakur Khemchand. Ramadeen listened with rapt attention, and his eyes clouded upon hearing of the brutal treatment meted out to Nadira Begum and Firdaus.

Ibrahim continued as Baqar Khan stopped and looked at the ground in stony silence. 'Holy sire, as Begum Nadira was led away, she turned many times and said, "Bum Bhairav".' The priest looked at him in astonishment.

'We, too, were surprised by her utterances, but then we assumed that she was trying to convey a message to us. To meet us here. Or, something to that effect. The Afghani guards who were surrounding her could not comprehend her salutations of "Bum Bhairav" and hence paid no heed to our exchange. We hoped that maybe she could be found here, or at least some message from her. But it is not so. The wretched Afghans must have killed her. Or, worse!'

Ramadeen quietly wiped away a tear with his sleeve, and enquired of them, 'Brothers, the night is long, and you must be tired. You can rest the night here. Have you eaten? Let me see what I can provide for you.'

Baqar Khan put a hand out to restrain him. 'Please do not worry, sire. We carried flattened bread of gram and fresh jaggery with us.'

'So what, a glass of warm milk will not hurt you.'

Ratna Devi, the priest's wife, stood silently by the door. Without a word, she poured two large tumblers of warm milk from the large earthen pot, which was simmering over dying embers. As she handed the glasses to her husband, the pain of Nadira's torturous fate haunted her.

Baqar and Ibrahim Khan had spread their blankets on the open platform outside the shrine, and, finishing their milk, went across to the well where pitchers of water were kept for washing clothes and utensils. Returning, they folded their hands in the fashion of the Hindus, and said, 'Sire, thank you for your hospitality, as always. We shall leave before daybreak tomorrow, so please do bless us, holy priest. You will have to bear with us for a little while, holy priest, as the departing words of Begum Nadira haunt us night and day. We shall come here every month on the eighteenth for news of the Begum. And, sire, please do pray to your God for her safety, and that of little Firdaus, wherever they may be.'

'Go with the blessings of Lord Bhairava, Baqar Khan and Ibrahim Khan. May your quest be fruitful.'

*

The night stretched long and hard for Ratna as she sat by her wooden chest and looked at the pearl necklace given to her by Nadira. The kind words of the beautiful lady with the grey eyes kept coming back in nauseating waves and she could well imagine the horrible tortures which the Afghans must have wrought upon her and the little angel, Firdaus. Lost in her thoughts, she picked up the necklace of pink pearls and caressed it with her fingers, as if her touch could erase Destiny's pain.

Two hours before sunrise, as Baqar and Ibrahim rose to leave, they saw the priest sitting in front of the black idol of Lord Bhairava. In the fulgurating light of the silver lamp and the stillness of this moment, the eyes of Shree Bhairava were pregnant with speculative predictions.

*

The Royal Shikargah

Dihari, Near Jalnapur, Berar

2nd May, 1599

8:50 a.m.

Sheikh Abu'l Fazl and his troops thundered into the precincts of the royal shikargah. A few hours earlier, four escorts from the prince's bodyguard had approached the Sheikh's camp near Jalnapur, and had apprised him of the swiftly deteriorating health of Prince Murad. Wasting no time, the Vizier had left the camp immediately, but as he reined his horse in the forecourt of the hunting lodge, he realized that he was too late.

Several attendants and soldiers were squatting or standing near the covered porch of the circular lodge in various stages of despair. They scrambled to their feet and stood silently, with bowed heads, as the Vizier jumped off his horse and half ran towards the porch. Seeing the Mughal standard furled in a corner, he stopped mid-stride and enquired, 'Why does the royal standard lie unattended and unguarded?'

A dark-skinned attendant stepped forward and in a broken voice, said, 'The Prince dwells no more, *Huzoor*.'

'Fool! Unfurl the royal standard. The prince is dead, but the emperor lives. The Sultanate lives!' The barked command galvanized the soldiers and attendants. Immediately, the royal standards and insignias were unfurled as the heralds and *qorchis* took their assigned places around the royal abode.

Abu'l Fazl entered the prince's chamber to be assailed with the mixed scents of herbs, ointments, disease, and incense. On the large silver-canopied bed lay the still figure of Prince Murad. The *hakim* tending to the young prince stood up as Sheikh approached. Two *ulemas* softly chanted incantations from the Holy Quran, as several fly whisk bearers softly moved their feather whisks near the prince's face.

Sheikh Abu'l Fazl leant down to check for a pulse, but found no sign of one. He grieved at the sight of the prince's emaciated face and frame, a young princely life ended in the dregs of wine and self-ruination. He stood looking for a few minutes, as prayers for the departed flew from his lips.

Bowing his head, and raising his palms to the heavens, he touched his cheeks and eyes in absolution. His voice was soft, as he asked, 'When did the prince pass away?'

'Just as the sun had crossed its first latitude of ascension, sire, about two hours ago.' The *hakim* continued, 'For the past two months, sire, we had been doing everything possible to reverse the damaging effects of the wine, but there was no improvement. Last week, as we received the imperial order banning the service of wine and opiates to the young prince, May Peace Be Upon Him, he went into withdrawal symptoms of tremors and disorientation. Finally, two days ago, he slipped into a deep coma, from which he never came out. We did our best, sire.'

Sheikh nodded and indicated for the face to be covered.

'The heat must not affect the body, *Hakim*. Please start your embalming process immediately for the body to be sent to the royal court at Agra.' The *hakim* nodded at the Vizier'swords, and, paying obeisance to the inert form of the dead prince, shuffled out of the room.

Sheikh Abu'l Fazl, lost in the transgressions of Life and Death, slowly dipped a quill in the silver ink pot in order to officially inform the emperor.

*

Jharokha e Darshan

Agra Fort

14th May, 1599

5:45 a.m.

Emperor Akbar nodded his approval as the cavalry of *Mansabdaar* Shah Beg Khan Turrani cantered past the seated monarch. Holding a *mansab* of five thousand *Zat* and three thousand *sowars*, Shah Beg Khan and his troops, in their distinctive turquoise blue turbans, had smartly executed close order drills. Shah Beg's Persian steed, Albela, had performed a lively equestrian dance, much to the delight of the emperor.

The emperor leaned forward as he saw the distinctive *naqqara* war drums of his favourite cheetah, Samand Manik, approaching from the east. The war drum beaters, with their waists covered in tiger skin wraps, played a martial cadence as they preceded the open palanquin of the ennobled cheetah. Samand Manik was being carried on an open palanquin between two horsemen, as his liveried servants, holding maces and bells, ran at his side. Wearing a gold collar encrusted with precious jewels he sat licking his lips. With some innate, rare instinct he looked up at the emperor and emitted a low growl as he went past. Akbar quickly threw a fistful of gold coins for his attendants to recover.

Just behind him came the newly decorated cheetah, Chitt Ranjan, with his set of war drum beaters. Seated on a decorated cart pulled by four liveried attendants, Chitt Ranjan stretched himself on the *Qashqai* carpet, and lazily tugged at his golden chain. In a recent hunt, Chitt Ranjan, in pursuit of a deer, had jumped a ravine of twenty-five yards and brought down his prey. The same day, Akbar ordered for drums to be beaten in front of him and for him to be granted several privileges.

Behind him rode Sayyid Ahmed of Barha who was the noble in charge of the *Khasa* cheetahs. A large contingent of *khasa* cheetahs in their brocaded saddlecloth followed him, and as he reached in front of the emperor's seat, he dismounted and performed the *kornish*. The cheetah keepers, too, genuflected on their knees, and then marched away.

The emperor could not hide his delight, and stood up. His lusty bellow of '*Subhan Allah*' was echoed by the hundreds of people assembled there. The cheetahs, upset by the noise, growled and strained at their leashes, as the *Doriyas* tugged hard on their chains to bring them under control.

Wearing bright red and gold-embroidered saddlecloths in muslin, the *Tuzis*, famed hunting hounds from Persia, high stepped their way past the emperor, as their keepers continuously bowed and performed the *taslim*. Riding in a decorated cart pulled by his keepers came Mahuwa, the emperor's favourite bloodhound gifted by the Portuguese. The large, red-coloured, European hunting dog with his drooping ears and lips rode majestically, sitting on a Persian rug. His habitual melancholic expression was in stark contrast to the shimmering red coat he wore, and the sparkle of his ruby-encrusted gold collar.

Five years before, when he was barely two years old, Mahuwa had accompanied the emperor on a deer hunt in the forests of Toda. Bred purely for hunting deer, wild boar, and small carnivorous animals, its mettle had been tested that day as they chanced upon a full grown tiger hiding in the tall bamboo grass. Cornered, the tiger had sprung at the head of emperor's war elephant, Nahir Khan, and with brute force pulled its head almost to the ground. Jumping down from the struggling, bellowing elephant, Akbar attacked the tiger with his sword. Mahuwa, who was running at the emperor's side, flung himself at the tiger in a bundle of raw, vicious power. The tiger, incensed by the dual attack, turned on the emperor with a ferocious roar. Mahuwa, with the intellect of a hunting dog, pounced on the weakest part of his prey, clamping on the tiger's tail. As Akbar deflected the clawing, snapping attack by the savage beast, Mahuwa hunched down and, with all the might of his broad jaws, severed the tail from the tiger's body.

Roaring in agony, the tiger spun around and rolled on the ground. A flailing paw smote an excited Mahuwa across its head, almost shearing off his right ear. A few grandees had joined the emperor, and the roaring, rolling tiger was pierced and disembowelled by several swords.

In recognition of his valour, the emperor had ordained that he be given the privileges of a minor noble, and entrusted to the care of six liveried servants. In his private conversations with Mahuwa, Akbar always called him *Jaanbaz Bahadur*,and over the next several days, the court and private gatherings were rife with embellished accounts of "the Tale of the Tail".

Smiling affectionately, Akbar saw the rest of his favourite dogs, Fenni, Kallua, and Bachawa move past him with royal disdain.

Akbar waited, with much anticipation, the arrival of the dancing soldiers of south-eastern Bihar. These soldiers of the Birhor tribe were basically hunters-gatherers, and were expert bowmen. Averse to riding horses, they were intrepid foot soldiers and trackers. Initially, they had been assessed to be trained as cavalry archers, but when the news reached the *Mir Bakshi* that the Bihors were animatedly discussing the quantum of meat available from the well-fed war horses, the idea was quickly dropped. Dressed in their tribal finery of colourful loin cloths, bare chested, and wearing several strings of colourful beads, they swirled, swooped, and hopped in small circles whenever they passed in review for the emperor.

Their short stature and aboriginal looks were a curiosity amongst the hardy Turqis, Afghanis, and Persians of the Mughal army, and hence they were nurtured as a special contingent within the *mansab* of Raja Man Singh, *Subedar* of Bihar and Bengal. Their expertise with poisoned arrows was much feared even by the boisterous Turqs, Pathans, and Afghans.

Akbar felt the nervous presence of a person behind him. Turning, he saw the commander of his personal *Qur* waiting apprehensively for his attention.

'Yes, Sangram Singh. What is it?'

'Your Majesty! Sardar Abdur Rehman, son of the worthy Vizier, seeks your audience, Majesty. He says that he has urgent news for you.'

The emperor's heart sank.

Rising swiftly from his silver throne in the *jharokha*, he walked into the adjoining chamber. Covered in dust and fatigue, Abdur Rehman stood trembling with a blue kerchief tied around his wrist.

Akbar staggered, and then, in a voice shaky with emotion, asked, 'It is Prince Murad?'

Abdur Rehman remained silent and still, not daring to look up.

Akbar clenched his eyes shut as tears spilled over. Choking, his hoarse whisper was barely audible. 'Oh, Murad! My son! What is this that you have done?'

Knotting his fist, he held it against the frescoed walls as he groped his way blindly into the sanctuary of his rooms.

Pain, faithful as ever, accompanied the emperor into his sanctum.

*

Rang Mahal

Illahabas Fort

23rd May, 1599

11:40 p.m.

There was much merriment and laughter as the wine flowed freely and silver cups of opium mixed with wine were served in plenty. The assembled guests of Prince Salim, mainly his chief courtiers, were jubilant. The news of Prince Murad's death was a welcome respite from the scorching heat of a torrid summer.

In the three storeyed Rang Mahal, the halls, balconies and stairwells were ablaze with lamps in glass bowls of red and blue. Every solemn cornice and carved niche had been lit by small earthen lamps which bravely held their own against the much bigger candles and silver stands with wicks as thick as thumbs.

The inebriated voice of Zamana Beg came ringing through the double colonnaded walkways. 'The night is young, Your Majesty, and your glorious chapter about to begin. There is none in this realm to challenge you... The throne is but a march away.'

'None, none,' echoed the fawning courtiers.

Prince Salim, ensconced in the comforting lap of opiate-induced ecstasy and the dreams of a mighty empire, called for more wine.

'Come hither, you beautiful wench, let me see your wares.' Prince Salim slurred as he grabbed a passing slave girl and groped under her bodice. Finding her breasts warm and firm, he tore open her bodice and buried his face between her breasts. The girl was livid with shame and disgust, but could only silently suffer the depravations of a filthy mind.

As the night progressed, the levels of debauchery also increased. The line between decorum and lewdness had been crossed much earlier, as the nobles, emboldened by the perversities of this decadent Sultan, had carried off the royal slaves and *nautch* girls for their own enjoyment. Eventually, only Prince Salim was left slumbering in the huge hall with semi-naked attendants and the debris of a lascivious court.

*

The emperor's bedchamber

Akbari Mahal

2nd June, 1599

Past midnight

It was a clear night sky with stars shining brightly and a cool breeze blowing in from the swollen Ganges. The monsoons had been rich and there was much rejoicing in the kingdom, as the farmers could now look forward to a spell of comparative comfort.

Over the past two days, Akbar had been unable to summon Debi Brahmin for his nocturnal visit due to the incessant rains. Today, as he waited for Debi Brahmin to be hauled up, his thoughts went back to his stay at Shahi Qila, Lahore, where Sufi Taj Uddin would be similarly hauled up on ropes for night-long discussions. Much had he learned from the simple teachings of the Sufi saint.

In a few minutes, Debi Brahmin was slowly hauled up on a wad of blankets secured by thick ropes. As he came parallel to the emperor's window, a signal from the sentry stopped his ascent. Suspended in mid-air just outside the emperor's window, he performed his obeisance and waited for the emperor to speak.

Akbar greeted the saint with folded palms in the traditional Hindu manner. 'Welcome, saint Debi Brahmin, welcome. We are fortuitous indeed to be blessed by your presence, sire.'

The Brahmin looked squarely into the emperor's eyes, and with great equanimity replied, 'I wish I could bless your dynasty to continue and prosper for thousands of years, but I cannot, Great King.' Abruptly, he became silent.

Masking his concern, Akbar guardedly asked, 'What deters you from blessing us, holy priest? You are well aware that the bounties provided by Allah to a select few are to be shared amongst fellow brethren.'

The saint laughed. 'Easier said than done, O King! When have you shared your bounty with your subjects? Your treasure rooms are overflowing with gold, diamonds, *mohurs*,and precious gems, while several of your fellow brethren go to sleep on an empty stomach. No, do not aspire to say anything, Great King, for you are also human and prone to all such failings. Enough of this... Now, tell me what disturbs you.'

Akbar dejectedly answered, 'You know my cause of distress, sire.'

Brahmin looked at the emperor with grim eyes. 'I do, Great King.' He seemed lost for a few moments, then addressed Akbar again. 'You must be prepared to be stung by the barbs of truth, King, if you wish to know the reason.'

Akbar nodded.

'Then, listen.' The saint drew his white shawl closer to himself. 'The death of Prince Murad is not an act of omission. The rulings of Fate have been converging for many years now, and the untimely death of Prince Murad is a direct result. In your days of glorious ascendancy, you plundered, raped, and slew hundreds of innocents, for no fault of theirs. And the latest, brickwalling an innocent girl and having her son butchered and thrown in the river! God knows how much truth there is in it.' The sage paused.

Akbar kept quiet. His cascading tears were Brahmin's answer.

The saint's eyes and voice softened. 'I know, Great King, the waves of repentance clouding your mind. You see, you are just a player in the celestial universe, and you have done, or will do, exactly as ordained in your destiny. And the leaves of your destiny are not chapters from yesterday, but the writ of several lives over thousands of years. What happened yesterday, or will happen today, had been ordained right at the time of your birth. Now, hear this, Great King. In your previous life, you were a Hindu ascetic named Mukund Brahmachari.'

'What!' exclaimed the astonished emperor.

'Yes, Great King. I am telling you this to put your mind at ease. As I said, in your previous birth you were a Hindu ascetic named Mukund Brahmachari. One day, while having milk, you mistakenly ingested a cow hair. Mortified at your perceived sin, you committed suicide.'

Akbar's mouth was hanging open. Debi Brahmin continued. 'Committing suicide is a heavier sin than mistakenly ingesting a cow hair, and hence, you were ordained to be born a *malechh*. But, because of your past good deeds, you were born royal, with the power to do good for many. What do you know of the Illahabas Fort? You think you built it? Wrong. You were guided by Providence to build it as a refuge for the weak and the struggling, at the most sacred place – Sangam! The holy confluence of the Ganga, Jumna, and Saraswati.' Brahmin stopped as he saw utter amazement in the emperor's eyes.

The saint continued. 'The construction of this fort was your act of penance, and it shall remain a shelter for many centuries after you are gone. There were twenty favoured disciples with you, Great King, who shed their mortal bodies as you committed suicide, and followed you in your afterlife. They have taken rebirth around you, and remain your well-wishers in this life, too. They surround you and protect you, and have either predeceased you or shall die soon after you leave this mortal world. Your souls will remain interconnected in this world and the celestial journey beyond. My salutations to you, Sage Mukunda.' He bowed deeply with folded hands.

Debi Brahmin paused to reflect, and then quietly said, 'And Prince Murad's death? It was the silent voice of God.'

*

(CHAPTER 12)

SIKKA DAR CHAH

(Coins in the Well)

The Royal Palace

Agra Fort

6th July, 1599

10:00 a.m.

The time was drawing near for the imperial army to move from Agra. Preparations, as if for war, had been going on for the past six months. In the seven years since Prince Khurram's birth, the royal household had seen the birth of two other princes, Jalandher and Shahriyar, from royal concubines. As the eunuchs were fond of saying, however, 'Only the fusion of royal blood can create royals – the others are just roughage.' This pronouncement from the *khojas* was like poisoned veal to the harem concubines, as well as to the queens not descended from royalty. Had the eunuchs not enjoyed the emperor's confidence, the harem would have wiped them out many centuries before.

Prince Khurram, now all of seven years old, had just recuperated from a severe attack of smallpox. As he accompanied the emperor, along with Prince Khusrau, on his journey to the Deccan to annexe the kingdoms of Ahmednagar and Berar, he had been afflicted by the disease, which steadily became worse. The army camped for almost three weeks while skilled physicians accompanying the army and the emperor's own physician, Hakim Humam, treated Khurram. As he recovered, and the customary bath was given, there was much rejoicing in the Moghul camp, and the emperor himself chose to give gifts and monies to the nobles, troops, and the needy. The emperor had small flowers made of gold and silver, which were showered on the assembled troops and *mansabdars*. That such master goldsmiths and such a cache of gold and silver travelled with the Moghul army was a testimony of its opulence and depth of preparedness.

Though Prince Khurram accompanied the emperor onwards to the Deccan, he was restrained, on account of his recent illness, from taking part in the few military skirmishes which happened near Malwa. The prince, unable to stay away from the battle, would wear his armour and prepare for battle every day, but the royal instructions to the *ahadis* guarding the enclosure forbade such adventures. Prince Khusrau was riding with the army, on an elephant surrounded by the rear echelons of the Rajput cavalry and infantry of the Uzbegs and the Afghans. As the citadels of Ahmednagar and Berar held, a fierce battle ensued with the Regent Chand Bibi, who fought with such valour and ingenuity that the Moghuls preferred to accept her capitulation on simple terms.

In such a colossus of war and politics, Prince Khurram was left alone in the royal camp with his personal bodyguards, the wounded, the service staff, and the shallow pock marks on his face.

The prince sat upon a small rock in the shade of a tamarind tree and watched the continuous activities of a city assembling to move. Though Shah Baba had set July as the month of departure, the royal court and the harem had been preparing for imminent departure since the previous September. Khurram, in the early years spent with his Shah Baba, had seen the court and the imperial army move several times. The addition of the harem to the royal entourage would be a new experience. After all, it meant the movement of almost seven thousand people, including the concubines, *khojasaras*, cooks, attendants, and slave girls. With the imperial army and the royal court, it was almost a hundred thousand strong megapolis on the move.

As Khurram looked at the worn bricks and battlements of the fort, it reminded him of Shahi Qila at Lahore, and he thought of the times he had run out of the chamber where he was made to sit and learn the history of his ancestors, the principles of statecraft, and Islamic theology. His young mind had wandered over the hills and plains of far-off lands as Mulla Qasim Beg Tabrezi gave him lessons in the history and geography of lands across the mountains.

Though Khurram was fluent in Persian, his knowledge of Turqi, their ancestral language, was a cause of despair for his father, Prince Salim, and was practised a bare minimum with his foster mother, Ruqaiah Sultan Begum.

The prince heard the stories of his ancestors, the great Taimurlane and Genghis Khan, with unusual interest and never tired of hearing their battle exploits and war strategies. As Mulla Qasim Beg related the tales of valour and bloodshed on the mountains and plains of Transoxania, Prince Khurram could feel himself astride the *peony* horses of his ancestors, rushing across the plains with his lance extended and his revered yak's tail fluttering behind his saddle. The sweat of the horse's flanks and its streaming breath could be felt by him, as he raced across the battlefield in the wake of his ancestors.

His sessions with his early tutors, Mulla Qasim Beg and Fathullah Gilani, filled his young mind with wonder, as they narrated visions of ships with two hundred oars, of the speed and strike of lightning, of chariots pulled by scores of horses, and of the distance of the sun and the moon from Earth.

One day, as the learned Mulla Qasim Beg, a disciple of the much venerated Mirza Jan Tabrezi, tried to explain to the young prince about the spherical shape of the Earth, it led to a mammoth debate in the harem, consuming the combined intellect of the harem inmates and the several resident scholars of the court.

'Hazrat, if the Earth is round like the egg of a duck and, as you say, people stay and sail all around the egg, then why don't they fall off from the lower side of the egg? Are they bound by ropes or do they have glue on their *kafshs*?'

'Your Highness, it is the way of the universe.'

'Then it is not possible. Can you walk on the ceiling, Hazrat, upside down?'

The learned Mulla Tabrezi kept his eyes lowered and looked sideways at Hakim Ali Gilani, the physician scholar, for assistance. Gilani, for all his knowledge of Egyptian and Turkish pharmacopoeia, was unable to help.

After a long pause, Mulla Tabrezi slowly replied, 'No, Your Highness.'

'Good. Then you must spend your time in finding the answer to this riddle. Shah Baba will be delighted if you can resolve this problem, or suggest ways to keep people safe from falling off,' shot back the prince as he quickly rose from the rug and with a small bow ran out of the room.

The next day, Ruqaiah Sultan Begum had to personally instruct the five-year-old Prince Khurram to attend to the narratives of the learned scholars . The education of a Moghul prince could not wait for the secrets of the universe to unravel.

Ground near Diwan e Aam

Agra Fort

15th July, 1599

Ever since the *Maktab* ceremony of Prince Khurram on the ninth of May 1596, which fell four years, four months, and four days from his birth date, the emperor had closely watched the academic progress of his favourite grandson, and the kingdom's best scholars, physicians, and theologians had been provided for his academic pursuits. When Khurram turned six, Akbar appointed a senior military commander, Mir Murad Juwaini, for archery lessons, and Raja Sullivahan for swordsmanship, spears, and wrestling.

The skies were heavy with dark rain clouds as Prince Khurram waited for the *Shahenshah i Hind* to emerge from his afternoon prayers. Early that morning, the emperor had expressed his desire to witness the military prowess of his young grandson, and the first watch after noon was fixed for the demonstration. The palace guards formed a cordon near the inner entrance gate, and the assembled nobles stood expectantly waiting for the emperor to arrive.

As the prince fingered the arrows in his quiver, he looked at his archer's ring absently. Made of white jade and inlaid with tiny streaks of ruby, the thimble-like ring rode smoothly on the young prince's fingers. Though Raja Sallivahan stood just behind him, today, Khurram missed his archery master Mir Murad very much. He could still remember so clearly his softly spoken words, 'Hold steady, pull back, aim, pull right back, aim, hold your breath, steady, shoot!' If all went well, Khurram thought, he must inform him of his success at Lahore Fort.

His reverie was broken by the sudden quietness that descended on the gathering. From the tiny doors of the unassuming Akbari mosque, the emperor emerged and strode towards the large quadrangle where the prince and the nobles stood. As was his habit, he flicked a silver coin into the large main well as he passed by. Even today, the prince could remember his explanation word for word: 'Khurram, I do this as a matter of courtesy to the well... it provides succour to all the inhabitants inside the fort, and is our lifeline. Remember, in times of war and siege, this well shall provide the means to survive. And escape.'

'Escape? Escape to where, Shah Baba?'

'Listen to me carefully, my dear Khurram. There is a tunnel inside this well, high and wide, which will in times of war, Allah forbid, take you to Sikri and Mathura. There is a fake exit on the other side of the Jumna, to confuse enemies if they ever discover, and follow. There are parcels of gold hidden behind specific, marked bricks, which are known only to me, the *Mir Bakshi*, and the *Mir Manzil*. So will you know, when your time comes.'

Khurram felt a hand on his shoulder as he bowed before the emperor. He lifted his eyes to see the smiling face of his adored grandfather. The emperor nodded to the other assembled courtiers as the first of the raindrops fell.

'Proceed.'

Khurram nodded and picked up his bow and an arrow with a large head. Raja Sallivahan, after bowing to the emperor, selected a bow, the head of which was wrapped in cloth. An archer moved up with a flaming torch and, as the Raja pulled the string back, he stepped forward and ignited the cloth-wrapped arrow head. As the burning arrow shot upwards, Prince Khurram, in a split second, drew his specially tipped arrow, sighted and released the string in a smooth, coordinated motion.

The arrow streaked upwards and clashed with the burning arrow. The combustible mix of gunpowder on the nose of Prince Khurram's arrow ignited, and both burning arrows fell downwards.

'Do it again,' commanded Akbar, and immediately the same procedure was repeated. This time, again, Khurram's arrow found its mark and fell burning to the ground.

'Well done, my child! You will make a warrior yet!' the pride in the emperor's voice was evident. Beaming with joy at the praise from his beloved grandfather, Khurram bowed low.

Akbar strode towards the low table on which several weapons were laid. Swords, scimitars, daggers, shields, short spears, and shields with the royal emblem had been displayed. Akbar tested the blade of a long sword and gestured for the prince to choose one. Khurram, in his enthusiasm to please Shah Baba, picked up a wicked-looking scimitar and ran it through the air.

The emperor stepped back and raised his sword. The young prince, forever in awe of his beloved grandfather, also stepped back and tried to imitate the emperor's stance. As Akbar had a weak left leg, which he favoured, he slid his right leg forward and the prince, too, immediately switched from his natural left foot forward stance to that of the emperor.

'Khurram. I am sure Raja Sallivahan has taught you the principles of effective sword play. Now, raise your sword and show me,' said Akbar, as he tensed for an attack from Khurram.

As the import of the emperor's words hit Khurram, he threw down his scimitar and flung himself at the emperor's feet.

'Shah Baba, I have never raised my eyes against Your Majesty, how can I raise a sword?' the tremulous voice of a seven-year-old spoke up.

As ecstatic shouts of '*Padshah Ghazi Zindabad*' and '*Sultanat Salamat*' from the courtiers and *ahadis* rent the air, a misty eyed emperor bent down to raise the future of his dynasty.

*

(CHAPTER 13)

TUKHM-E-BAGHAWAT

(The Seeds of Rebellion)

Two kos from Agra Fort

10th July, 1600

11:40 a.m.

Prince Salim had been informed of the heightened activity along the ramparts, abutments, and battlements of the Agra Fort the previous evening. A temporary vigil tower had been erected, soaring eighty feet into the sky. This tower was made of hardened bamboo poles and wooden planks, secured by strong hessian ropes and leather chains. A small detail of sharpshooting archers and musket men had been stationed on the covered platform while the ground was secured by a large troop of Afghani and Uzbeg cavalry. Their mission was to keep an eye on the preparations going on inside the seventy-foot-high walls of Agra Fort, and to decimate visible targets.

The Mughals had learned this war craft of building temporary watch towers from their bitter enemy of the past, Sher Shah Suri. He had captured the almost impregnable fort of Kalinjar by challenging its lofty perch from a hastily erected temporary tower which was staffed with excellent archers and musket men. The continuous barrage of musket shots effectively subdued the resistance from Raja Kirat Singh's mixed troops of Bundelas and Rajputs. The impregnable fort of Kalinjar fell, but the valiant Sher Shah also lost his life in a freak accident at the vigil tower.

About half an hour back, Prince Salim, escorted by his own cavalry and with Sayyid Abdullah in attendance, had ridden out to about a *kos* from the Agra Fort, and had reviewed his personal cavalry practising close formation drill. Satisfied with the battle readiness of his troops, he had wheeled his charger towards his camp and galloped in full battle array over cultivated fields and fruit gardens, leaving destruction in his wake.

As they rode into the camp and towards the royal tent, a trumpeter blew three short blasts to signal the prince's arrival. A *syce* and several slaves ran forward to help him dismount.

The prince sat in his tent sipping a tepid glass of sherbet, and ruminating over the tragic developments of the last fifteen months. The recurring, maddening pain of separation from his beloved Anarkali, and her subsequent murder and that of Firdaus at the emperor's behest tore into Prince Salim's body and soul like an ever-present knife.

The emperor's abrasive neglect and contemptuous treatment of Prince Salim's love spurred Salim into withdrawing from the Mewar campaign and raising the flag of rebellion.

Plundering, sacking, destroying, and in open rebellion, the prince had marched towards Agra.

Salim stared into his silver glass and for the hundredth time vowed revenge on the emperor and his close associate, Sheikh Abu'l Fazl. His eyes turned bloodshot as he crushed the silver tumbler into a misshapen mass.

There was a hesitant knock on the wooden panel of the tent as Sayyid Abdullah and Khubu Chishti sought permission to enter.

'My prince... Majesty, may I take the liberty of addressing a few words to you, even though it may sound grievous to you? Please allow me, Sire, as I suffer the burden of unsaid words.'

'Speak, Khubu. You are my foster brother and childhood companion. Speak.'

Having assuaged the sycophantic cravings of Prince Salim, Khubu continued. 'My prince, we have been camped here for almost eight days now, and the men are getting restless. They can smell the kitchen fires of Agra and the tinkling of ankle bells on courtesan's feet. It is unwise to delay any further, Majesty.'

Sayyid Abdullah also voiced his concern. 'Your Highness, there are reports that cannons have been turned towards the vigil tower, and several heavy cannons have been moved up on the battlements and are directed towards us.'

'Khubu, I am well aware of the desires of my men. I also want to taste the delicacies of the royal kitchen and the soft touch of my queens. But we are not being welcomed as honoured guests, or as a royal son returning home, in my case. Our withdrawal from Mewar without performing our responsibility of conquering it has not gone well with His Imperial Majesty. My father has probably been briefed by that scavenging rogue, Raja Man Singh, with all sorts of deceitful stories and brazen lies as to our motives. That is why the gates of the fort have remained shut to us.'

Abdullah Barha, in overwhelming zeal, spoke up. 'We can take the fort easily, Your Majesty. There is only a skeleton force of about twelve thousand irregular troops, of which only five thousand are properly trained. There are many within the fort walls, Majesty, who shall welcome your return and rule of the empire.'

'Are you completely insane, Abdullah Barha? Or are you still swimming in opium sodden drinks? Have you considered the fortifications? Are you not aware of the heavy cannons and the immense armoury inside? Have you forgotten that all the *ustads* of archery, musketry, and gunnery, having retired from active service, are residents within those great walls? That the royal guards and *ahadis* entrusted with the treasury and the royal harem will give no quarter and fight us with everything at their disposal?' Salim's voice cut scathingly across the tent. 'Even at this moment, royal troops could be marching on us from Bundelkhand and Malwa,' he continued, 'while you stand here dreaming your bedevilled dreams.'

Regaining his breath, Prince Salim again directed his ire at the unfortunate Sayyid. 'Have you considered the consequences of such an act? Assaulting the emperor's own fort in his absence? He will pulverize you and then feed you to his pet cheetahs.'

Sayyid Abdullah and Khubu Chishti hung their heads and waited to be dismissed from the young prince's presence. Their discomfiture was alleviated by the sudden opening of the tent flap and the entry of a royal attendant.

'Your Majesty. Please pardon this intrusion, but the observers have sent word that a small mounted detachment flying the royal flag are coming this way.'

'Prepare to mount. A hundred *sowars* only.'

The terse order from Salim sent both the nobles scurrying. Salim watched their retreating backs with narrowed eyes. At times he wondered if his greedy and foolish accomplices would one day lead him to his destruction.

Prince Salim rode out, flanked by his ranking nobles Khubu Chishti, Zamana Beg, and Sayyid Abdullah Barha, along with five score chosen cavalry. The standard bearer with the Mughal flag rode ahead as the other nobles were spread a horse's length behind the prince in adherence to royal protocol.

The prince stopped just a few paces behind the last *kos minar* on the Ajmere-Agra route and waited for the detachment to arrive. In the distance he could see a small party of people on horses and camels, numbering not more than forty-five, travelling at a leisurely pace. Salim knew this was a deliberate tactic to show the peaceful intentions of the advancing party.

As they came nearer, Salim could make out the figure of Mir Qulich Khan, Emperor Akbar's faithful fort commander, at the head. The fort commander wore no armour, and similarly those accompanying him were also not in chain mail. Their swords were sheathed.

Mir Qulich Khan, now almost fifty-five years old, dismounted from his horse and walked slowly towards Prince Salim. At twenty paces he stopped and performed the *chaar taslim* and waited.

'Welcome, Qulich Khan! Noble servant of the empire, welcome.' Prince Salim was quick to put the fort commander at ease.

'Welcome to Agra, Your Highness. As a humble servant of His Majesty, *Padshah I Hind*, I welcome you to the borders, Sire,' the deep voice of Qulich Khan recited. It was said that his voice was so rich and sonorous that it could be heard across the fort ramparts if he ever issued a challenge during night hours.

Smiling at the old devil's play on words, Salim smilingly asked, 'Why only to the borders, Mir Qulich? Will you not allow me to meet my revered grandmother, the Dowager Empress, and my mother, the most honourable Mariam Uz Zamani, Mir Qulich?'

'Your Highness, I am commanded by His Imperial Majesty, Emperor Jalal Ud Din Mohammed Akbar, Protector of the Realm, to permit no one to enter except with his personal permission issued under his *Muhr Uzek*.I am bound to his command, just as you are, Your Highness.' The old faithful, Mir Qulich Khan, had singularly conveyed the imperial message in clear terms.

Salim's eyes narrowed at the implied denigration in the well-camouflaged words. He had not missed the immediate reminder in 'Your Highness' addressed to him, against the 'Imperial Majesty' used for his father. Zamana Beg rode up on the prince's left and whispered in his ear. 'Your Majesty... let us take this dithering old fool as a captive, now.'

Salim dismissed him with a scorching look and rode forward. He forced himself to say with a smile, 'I completely understand, Qulich Khan. The emperor's words are sacred to both of us. You must do your duty.'

'Yes, Your Highness. And I bring you many priceless gifts from the royal treasury and from the most noble ladies of the harem. The emperor will be pleased to know that you passed this way.'

At a gesture from Qulich Khan, the camels knelt down and the straps holding the massive iron trunks and boxes strapped to their backs were quickly undone. More than twenty trunks and boxes of various shapes and sizes were slowly carried forward and laid at Salim's feet.

Qulich Khan spoke again. 'These are just a few humble gifts, Your Highness, from the garrison of all those items which please your royal senses... jewels, gems, ornaments, and precious commodities. You will be happy to know, Sire, that your most revered grandmother, Dowager Empress Mariam Makani is even now, as we speak, preparing to come and meet you.'

Salim stiffened, and stared hard at the fort commander. 'Tarry not, Qulich Khan! Send a messenger now to my beloved grandmother, that she need not trouble herself at this juncture. I am leaving immediately for Illahabas Fort, and shall pray to Allah to meet her soon in better times.' After a brief pause, Salim continued, 'And Qulich Khan, please do send my deepest regards and faithful servitude to His Imperial Majesty at Malwa. Now, go forth, immediately.'

'As you command, Your Highness. May your onward journey be with the Hand of Allah upon you.' And bidding so, Mir Qulich Khan performed the salutations once again, and rode back to the fort at a gallop, his retinue following in his wake.

*

Mir Qulich smiled. He recalled the consternation on the young prince's face as he heard that his beloved grandmother, Mariam Makani, was preparing to come to him. In his present state of treachery and rebellion against the emperor, Salim was in no condition to answer her regal admonitions, and sought the easier way out.

*

As the gifts from the fort were laid before Prince Salim, he swallowed the bitter bile which rose in his throat. Only one chest contained precious stones and ornaments of gold, while the other twenty chests were full of mangoes, pomegranates, dry fruits, cascades of silk and brocades, and in high insult – a chest laden with muslin wrapped opiates.

That same night, Prince Salim with a few *ahadis*, Zamana Beg, and attendants hastily boarded a river barge for Illahabas and ordered his army to follow in quick order over land.

*

(CHAPTER 14)

MINAR-E-KASA-I- SIR

(The Tower of Skulls)

Khwabgah

Fatehpur Sikri

13th August 1601

Forty minutes past midnight

The thick curtains of silk and muslin parted slightly, as a young but wearied voice asked, 'Shah Baba, can I come in?' The emperor turned and smiled as he saw young Prince Khurram silhouetted against the light of the dimmed earthen lamps. Behind him loomed the huge figure of Ehteram Beg, commander of the night sentries, and an old faithful whose grandfather had marched with Babur from the distant hills of Ferghana almost eight decades ago.

'The prince carries a dagger, Your Majesty. He is unwilling to hand it over,' said Ehteram Beg, his soft voice belying his monstrous form. In his turban, he stood almost seven feet tall and four feet broad at the shoulders. It was said that he had once pulled down a camel to the ground with sheer strength. It was a sign of the emperor's favour towards his adored grandson, Prince Khurram, that he had not been disarmed by force. Even Prince Salim, the heir to the throne, was not permitted to carry weapons in the emperor's presence.

Akbar sat and motioned for Khurram to come closer. The visibly distraught prince walked slowly to his side and stood tightly clutching his *yalekh*. Akbar took his arm. 'What is it, Khurram? You seem upset.'

The specially designed ventilation shaft directed cool air over the bed and the fragrance of *chameli* wafted through. Every two hours, a fresh bunch of *chameli* wrapped in muslin cloth was lowered into the shaft to diffuse the aroma. The guard commander silently withdrew.

The prince looked at Akbar and softly murmured, 'I am scared, Shah Baba. I heard the screams of men and the wailing of women a few minutes ago. I checked over the parapet and along the corridors, Shah Baba, but I could not find anything. And then I heard it again. I came here to protect you.'

Akbar smiled and pulled him closer. 'Protect me! Indeed, you will. I know, Khurram, that you will pray and tend for me until my last breath. And now you must know about a royal secret. It is passed on from one emperor to his successor, orally, but never, never recorded in the court chronicles. Come with me.' And Akbar led Khurram by the hand to the pillared balcony running around his first floor bedchamber, *khwabgah*.

'But why, Shah Baba?'

'Because the secret is too big to fit inside books.'

As they stood and looked towards Anoop Talab on their right, Khurram asked, 'Tell me, Shah Baba, what is the secret that cannot be contained in the thousands of books that you have down below, in the royal library?' The question seemed to amuse the emperor.

'The *kutub khana* downstairs, Khurram, is a vast ocean of knowledge from across the seas and the distant mountains. Learned scholars, as bright as the sun, have laboured for years and years to distill their knowledge into these books. And that is why my bedchamber is above the library, so that I may sleep on a bed of knowledge, which I never had a chance to learn when I was young.'

Khurram frowned at this information, and in all sincerity asked, 'But, Shah Baba, was Mulla Beg Tabrezi and Hazrat Fathullah Gilani not there to teach you?' A brief pause, and the prince muttered again, 'Or maybe they were too young then.'

Akbar stood looking at the shimmering waters of the Anoop Talab, and reminisced about Raja Tansen, who for many years had made this fort of stones and miracles sway to the lilt of his celestial voice. Since his death several years ago, the sounds of laughter, happiness and music had also fled from this great fort. He stared at the silent walls as if willing them to speak.

Sighing wistfully, he put his hand on Khurram's shoulders and said, 'I never had a chance to learn. When I was barely two years old, I was abandoned by my father, Firdaus Ashiyani Shahenshah Humayum and my mother, Mariam Makani, in the desolate and barren battlefields of Samarkand. It was my father's brother, Hazrat Askari, and Begum Sultanum, who took me into their home and looked after me as their own son for the next two years. Their love was so rich and engulfing that never did a tear from my eyes fall to the ground. Their palms were always there to cup my sorrows.'

Khurram listened in silence and reverence. For him, Shah Baba was the epitome of all that was grand and imperial in this world.

Akbar looked into the distance at the Tehra Gate which opened towards the small hillocks and meadows of Khanwa village. His thoughts went back to the day in February 1585 when he had ordered these gates sealed forever. There had been numerous complaints to the *Mir Bakshi* by night sentries of frantic rattling of the iron chains on the wooden gates. When the troops on night duty challenged these spectral visitors for identification, they were always met by silence. Extra troops were posted along the crenellations and arrow loops for night-long vigils, but nobody was ever seen. This continued for several years with no predictable timing or frequency, and in the wake of the unease of the night sentries, he had finally ordered the gate to be permanently sealed.

Akbar rested his hand on the stone railing, and his face clouded with the sorrow of a grieving king. A sigh escaped the emperor's lips as he thought back over the last eleven months' travails with his rebellious son. Since the previous August, Prince Salim had risen up against him from the fort of Illahabas, and was trying to form a parallel kingdom within the principality of Illahabas and Chunar. Akbar, saddled with the debilitating Deccan wars, and softened by his love for the appointed successor, chose to ignore it. In April of this year, Salim had decided to further broadcast his independence and had started bestowing titles on his close followers. He proclaimed himself as Sultan Salim Shah Ghazi – Warrior of the Faith; the title of *Abu al Muzaffar* or 'Father of Victory' would not be long in coming. When Salim started minting coins in his own name and the Royal Seal was changed to carry the title 'Victor of the World and the Faith' it was the last straw for the beleaguered emperor. Leaving Abdul Rahim Khanekhana as the Deccan commander and Sheikh Abu al Fazl in charge of the garrison, Akbar hurried towards his capital, Agra, covering the distance of five hundred *kos* in just a hundred days. Now camped at Fatehpur Sikri, just twelve *kos* from his capital, the emperor thought with distaste of the harsh measures which Salim's rebellion demanded.

His reverie was broken by searing, sharp cries of anguished men and the clash of steel upon steel. Sounds, like distant thunder, of men in battle raged across the walls from Tehra Gate side. Khurram was in the tight embrace of the emperor, as both looked in terrified wonder towards the village of Khanwa, beyond the sealed gates. The horrific screams of wounded and maimed men cut across the dark night, as the clash of swords and the terrified trumpets of wounded elephants and fallen horses merged with the cries of '*Al Fateh*' and '*Jai Bhawani*'.

Not a single light could be seen from the village of Khanwa, which seemed to have shrunk into a veil of blackness, and nothing seemed to stir beyond the great walls of the fort. Within the fort, most of the exterior ramparts and battlements were now awash with lighted torches and the harsh shouts of *qorchis* and *bakshis* readying troops for imminent battle. There was a flurry of activity in the grounds between the royal apartments and *naubat khana*, as imperial guards and *ahadis* rushed around securing their weapons and horses for battle. In the royal apartments too, lamps were being lit and the Tatars and the Uzbegs were forming a secure battery of small cannons aimed towards the grounds sweeping up from the *Diwan I aam* and the Royal Mint.

Akbar pulled Khurram close, as he felt a shadow on his left. He turned to see the hulking presence of his night commander, accompanied by more than two score of *ahadis* in full armour, crowding into his bedchamber and onto the covered pavilion where he stood.

'It is not safe here, Your Majesty. Please come with us.' The tone in Ehteram's request was deferential, but firm.

'Fetch my sword. Secure Prince Khusrau and light up the *Diya Firdausi*.' Akbar's demeanour had changed. From a wronged father mourning the intransigencies of his rebel son, he had transformed into the undisputed emperor of Hindustan.

There was a flurry of shouted commands, and a hundred or more guards, waiting outside the chambers, rushed to obey the instructions. Prince Khusrau, the eldest son of Prince Salim, had also accompanied Akbar back to Sikri, and was encamped in one of the royal apartments. Soon, an escort of armed *ahadis* had secured the prince, as several guards rushed to cover the entrances to the seraglio.

The *Diya Firdausi*, a massive seventy-foot-high oil lamp, constructed with interlocked sections of wood and steel, was hastily being hoisted upright by the sentries. This huge lamp was a constant fixture of the Moghul army when the emperor was in command, and moved along with him. In all war camps, it was lit every evening close to the emperor's crimson royal tent, and proclaimed to all those who had the audacity to gaze upon the imperial army that the Grand Moghul, was encamped.

As the *Diya Firdausi* sputtered into flames, the din of battle subsided just as suddenly as it had begun. For a few moments there was complete unnerving silence, and then the fort rang with the soaring cries of '*Allah u Akbar*'as thousands of soldiers from the ramparts, battlements, stables, and the garrison accommodation raised their swords and beat their shields.

Prince Khurram clutched the *yalekh* of the emperor and looked into the taut face of his Shah Baba for assurance. Akbar nodded at him and turned to his night commander. 'Now hear this. Secure all gates, the treasury, and the royal offices. Mount extra guards along the fort and at the royal harem. Gates will not be opened tomorrow morning until the fort inhabitants have presented themselves before me. Tell the *Darogha* that all leaves and exits are cancelled for the next sixty days. *Takhliya*.'

As Ehteram Beg bowed and left to carry out his orders, the *ahadis* also withdrew to beyond the curtains of the bedchamber.

Akbar ruffled Khurram's hair affectionately, and said, 'This is our secret, Khurram, passed down orally from one king to his successor. The sounds of battle that you heard today celebrate the valiant crusade that my grandfather, emperor Zahiruddin Babar, fought against the famed Rajput king, Rana Sanga, and the other powerful kings of Rajputana, who had rallied under Rana Sanga's banner to throw us out of Hindustan. Emperor Babur, with his few thousand valiant and dedicated followers, defeated an army five times as strong. Know this, my prince, whenever there is a Moghul emperor residing in this fort, the great warrior spirit of Emperor Babur shall rise in the dead of night, and remind us of the valour and sacrifices of our ancestors to claim this land as our own. Forget not, Khurram, that our ancestors paid with their blood and the sacrifice of leaving their motherland and all that was dear to them, to carve out this empire for us.

'In centuries to come, the spirits of our crusading ancestors and Emperor Zahruddin Babur shall rise from time to time, and awaken the world to our majesty and power. The night will shrivel, and the moon disappear, when the swords of the victorious will tear the skies with their roaring disdain!

'Remember one more thing, Khurram – these events will never be chronicled in the court records. It is forbidden.'

'How did this happen, Shah Baba?'

Emperor Akbar again looked towards Tehra Gate, and said softly, 'It all began with the Battle of Khanwa, in 1527.'

*

Flashback

The Plains of Khanwa,

17th March, 1527

9:10 a.m.

Babur, astride his horse Shamsher, shielded his eyes from the blazing March sun, and concentrated on the miniscule movements in the ranks of the Rajput army arrayed before him. Babur considered his disadvantage as the sun, in its travel from east to south, was blazing directly into their eyes. He looked upwards and silently cursed the vultures and the other carrion birds wheeling above with their raucous calls, invoking the humans to shed blood and feed their hungry souls.

Staring ahead, Babur ordered his Mir Bakshi *to spread the word. In a few minutes, iron shields and javelins were being manoeuvred to catch the rays of the sun and deflect them onto the eyes of the enemy war elephants standing dead ahead in the Rajput lines. Shielded by the five hundred war elephants ranged as the first echelon of the Rajput assault, it was difficult to ascertain the activities of the infantry and cavalry jostling for space behind them.*

The two armies had stood at battle length for the past three days, but on each day had withdrawn by late afternoon. Today, Babur could feel the restlessness of his men, as well as the skittishness of his horses who could smell battle and death.

A brief order, and the sixth, seventh, and eighth lines of cavalry raised their bows and unleashed an umbrella of fire-tipped arrows. As the arrows fell just short of the massed elephants they trumpeted and moved in alarm at the small fires erupting before them. The harsh cries of Rajput commanders exhorting their troops to advance merged with the clamour of war drums and the excited snorting of horses and men.

As Babur watched, the lightly armoured war elephants began to move forward. His eyes searched for the elephant carrying Rana Sanga, but he could discern none carrying the royal howdah or the dull yellow flag of Mewar with its rising sun. His experienced eyes swung from the centre of the Rajputs to their right, but could detect no singular group of royals.

Without needing further instructions, the topchis *under Mirza Quli Khan, and the matchlock men under Mirza Mustafa Rumi had rushed forward and had taken their positions just behind the chained carts and the forward echelons of the cavalry. The first volley from the Moghul cannons were just range finders, while also attempting to slow the advance and discourage the possibility a full charge on the Moghul positions.*

The tufangchis, *having set up their wooden tripods between the iron chain fastened carts, were now firing at will into the approaching elephants. Babur, having fathomed the lumbering gait of the Indian war elephants from the previous year's battle of Panipat, had put three ranks of matchlock men with their tripods mounted on small wooden wheels which could be pulled and stationed in any direction. As the first rank of* tufangchis *discharged their arms, they quickly withdrew with their matchlocks, leaving their tripods in position for the second rank to squat behind them and fire. The* tufangchis *had practised and perfected the art of cleaning their barrels and priming their flash pans in under forty seconds.*

Then, again, the three rows of mounted Tir-Andaz *unleashed another flight of arrows, angled vertically to have a sharp trajectory and descend straight into the milling mass of Rajput infantry closely following the elephants. The Rajput cavalry were concentrated on the left and right wings of the advancing foot soldiers.*

Suddenly, from the extreme right of the Mughul army, a squadron of almost one thousand cavalry under Mir Quli Sistani detached themselves and charged towards the left flank of the Rajputs. After covering more than half the distance, they suddenly swerved left and cut across the front of the Rajputs at full gallop and receded into the distance, leaving a trail of dust behind them.

The Rajputs raised celebratory shouts, assuming that the Mughals had been scared into desertion. What they failed to notice were the iron claws and spiked iron balls left by them in the path of the advancing elephants.

Babur smiled grimly and extended his sword with a small jerk. The topchis, *after firing their initial salvo, had been patiently waiting for the front echelons to come within the range of their heavier cannon balls. These cannon balls, some of them weighing as much as thirty-five seers, carried much destructive power, but their range was limited to about eight hundred yards. As the bigger cannons thundered, there was immediate turmoil in the Rajput ranks. Some of the elephants were struck directly, and though they wore iron armour on their trunks and across their sides, they erupted into a bloody mass of flesh, bones, and stinking innards.*

Goaded by their mahouts, the elephants, fed on opium mixed with jaggery and rice, lumbered into a run. The second salvo was even more devastating as the heavy cannon balls smashed into the heads and howdahs of the war elephants, blasting the elephants as well as their riders into smithereens. The surviving elephants, convulsed with fright and pain, were now stepping onto the iron claws and spiked balls strewn behind by Mir Quli Sistani's horsemen. As they stepped onto these iron traps, which easily perforated their soft under-paws, the elephants screamed in pain. As they staggered, they tumbled to their knees, and with the weight of their howdahs on their back, slowly keeled over onto their sides and lay trumpeting in agony.

Some of the elephants, scared by the flash and sound of the Mughal cannons discharging in front of them, fled in apparent turmoil and blindly pummelled their way through the ranks of their own infantry, killing and maiming by the score. Their great trunks, now swishing in wide arcs, were engulfing soldiers and throwing them ten or fifteen feet up in the air, only for them to be eventually trampled upon by the advancing foot soldiers or cavalry.

The Rajput chiefs, sensing that the Mughal right flank had been weakened by the desertion of twelve hundred sowars *a few minutes earlier, commanded the Rajput cavalry on the left flank to advance into the Mughal right wing. Raising cries of* 'Jai Bhawani' *the Rajput horsemen rode towards the Mughal flank.*

A basic flaw in the Rajput war calculations became apparent. While the Rajput horsemen preferred to fight with swords, which were good at close quarters, and with barchis, *which were good at close and medium distances, the Mughal cavalry were expert bowmen, and could shoot their arrows over relatively longer distances. Hence, as the Rajputs charged, the Mughal cavalry from the right flank – the* Barangars *– as well as from the centre – the* Qol *– let loose a fusillade of poison-tipped arrows.*

Though several Rajput horsemen fell to the arrows, a major part of the Rajput cavalry clashed with the Mughals. Such was the ferocity of their assault that for a few minutes it seemed as if the Mughal lines would be broken. But Babur, sensing the panic in his right wing, ordered the Tarahs *to join and assist the besieged right wing. Meanwhile, Mir Quli Sistani and his twelve hundred horsemen had ridden back behind the Moghul vanguard, and were even now waiting for fresh orders. A quick word from Babur sent a rider rushing to the other reserve contingents, sending half of them into battle against the rampaging Rajputs on the right wing.*

Babur watched in stupefied awe as Rajput soldiers, dismayed at the havoc being wrought by the Mughal cannoneers, flung themselves into the mouths of heavy cannons in an effort to silence them. The Mughal gunners, battle-hardened Turks, Afghans, and Uzbegs, could not but admire such formidable and audacious courage. Small pieces of human flesh and bone were spattered in the close vicinity of the disabled cannons as they lay mangled and smoking on the battlefield.

From the centre of the Rajput formations, a heavy posse of cavalry galloped towards the Mughal right flank, where the fighting now was at its most lethal. Babur immediately signalled his qarawals *to cut across the racing Rajput cavalry and blunt their attack. As the* qarawals, *being expert archers, approached the charging Rajputs, they swivelled in their saddles and shot arrows at a blistering pace. Even on a hard gallop, they could shoot an arrow every five seconds.*

In the meantime, the Mughal Tarahs, *who had joined the battle on the right wing, had squeezed the Rajputs between themselves and the Moghul flank. Rajputs, brave as ever, made no move to withdraw from the battle, but continued to fight until they were either slain or lay maimed on the blood-soaked earth.*

As Babur followed the qarawals, *he saw the yellow pennant of Rana Sanga being carried by two riders in the midst of the Rajput horde. In an instant, he was into a full gallop with his sword raised, hunched over the neck of his stallion. The* Mir Bakshi, *with three thousand mounted warriors of Babur's own clan from Ferghana, gave chase. Babur, and his three thousand* sowars, *cut deep into the middle of the Rajput mass. The* Qol *and the* Jaranghars *of the Mughal army then advanced headlong into the centre of the Rajputs, cleaving a path that was to rule Hindustan for the next three hundred years.*

The clash of steel and the shrieks of wounded, dying men permeated the plains of Khanwa.

The circling vultures above, now assured of a royal feast, had ceased their raucous cries and were now patiently waiting for the living to retire.

The battle waged for ten hours and, as darkness was setting in, Rana Sanga, with close to eighty wounds on his body and almost unconscious, was forcibly taken away from the battlefield by Rao Maldev.

The battle was over.

As Babur surveyed the battlefield with its gory entrapments, he vowed never to let his successors forget the valour of his warriors on this day. If need be, his spirit would visit to keep the memories alive.

In the tradition of his Mongol ancestors, he ordered for a Tower of Skulls to be made.

The carrion birds now had a befitting throne.

*

(CHAPTER 15)

ASHK NAMI MANAD

(The Tears Will Not Stop)

Agra Fort

Akbari Mahal

14th September, 1601

Past midnight

As the clink of swords being drawn from their scabbards reached the Mughal emperor, his hands, even in his somnolent state, reached for the jewelled dagger by his side. He lay alert, his eyes adjusting to the dim shadows of the moonless night.

Jalal Ud Din Mohammed Akbar felt wetness on his cheeks, and looked towards the ceiling, trying to find the source of the leakage. The intricately designed Persian motifs, replete with the bright colours of green, red, and gold, twinkled innocently in the reflected glow of the silver *diya* burning behind the silver filigree mesh.

The emperor sat up and realized that the wetness on his cheeks and pillow were his own tears. As his grip on the dagger softened a low moan escaped his lips. Immediately, there was a rustle of silk behind him and again the clang of drawn steel.

'Your Majesty! Are you all right, Sire?' the cautious voice of Sentry Commander Ehteram Beg cut sternly into the night.

'Yes.'

Ehteram Beg made no move to retire from his position. The past twenty minutes or so had been full of nervous anxiety for him, as soft sounds of deep anguish had emanated from the royal chambers. He had, with the temperance born out of clanship and extreme devotion, been brave enough to part the thick silk and brocade curtains with the tip of his sword, and peer through the thin white muslin at the restless figure of his emperor.

Akbar, in the twilight years of his life, was being destroyed from the most unexpected quarter – the intransigence and rebellion of his own son and heir apparent, Prince Salim. He, Emperor Jalal Ud Din Mohammed Akbar, the Most Fortunate of Kings, God's Own Shadow on Earth, Defender of the Faith, Apostle of Justice and Mountain of Precious Divinity, had been reduced to a snivelling, weak monarch, prone to long periods of desolate solitude and melancholia.

A terse order and Ehteram Beg withdrew from the curtains.

For Akbar, sleep had vanished to be replaced by an incessant throb in his heart of searing memories and buried pain. As he collected the brocaded gown from the foot of the large silver gilded bed, his eyes fell on a piece of navy blue fabric with tiny scribbles on it, secured firmly to his bed post.

Akbar's eyes blurred with harboured tears as he recalled the day, almost twenty-seven years before, when Prince Salim, all of four years old, had scribbled on a navy blue silk face towel and presented it to him, in the fashion of a revered mystic, with the words, 'Majesty! Let these words of mine be like the shield of Allah for you. May all your troubles be gone forever!' The assembled Begums had laughed and blessed the young prince, while the harem eunuchs and slave girls had smiled fondly at the solemn words, spoken with such sincerity and grace.

Akbar had laughed and answered with much seriousness: 'I am indebted, Sheikhu, for your blessings and good words. May all that you have said come true. I shall also pray that my Sheikhu Baba grows up to be an emperor, not only of a vast kingdom and immense riches, but also a king of good deeds!'

Begum Salima Sultan could not resist but add, 'And a hundred beautiful Begums!'

The fleeting smile on Akbar's face at these long-lost memories slowly turned into a frown as he faced the grim realities of the past twelve months. How could Sheikhu, his first born and heir to the throne, rebel against him, the emperor – his own father?

Although disturbing news had been coming from the royal camp at Ajmere, where the prince had encamped for the last four months and had been indulging in frightening bouts of drunkenness and debauchery since August of the previous year, Akbar had chosen to ignore it as the trappings of youth. But now his mind went back to a hot, humid day in April at Burhanpur Fort.

*

Flashback

Diwan e khas

Burhanpur Fort, Deccan

10th April, 1601

Just after sunset

'Your Majesty, you cannot forever ignore the growing indiscretions of Prince Salim.' Sheikh Abu'l Fazl spoke softly as he saw the troubled look in Emperor Akbar's eyes after having heard the contents of the urgent document sent by Raja Man Singh from Ajmere.

'I know, Sheikh, I know. I am truly at a loss to understand his wayward mind. I wonder who can bring Sheikhu to his senses again.'

'My lord... Majesty. For a servant of opium and wine, there is no master, except the impending fatality of ruin.' The bitter statement of Sheikh Abu'l Fazl was cut short by the sharp command of Akbar.

'Enough, Sheikh! Do not forget that Prince Salim is my son, and is entitled to all the rights and respect which his noble birth commands. I am well aware of his past weaknesses, which, to an extent, lies with every child born in kingly wealth.'

Akbar looked at the crestfallen face of his closest courtier, nay, his closest friend, and felt sorry for having rebuked him so sharply. He knew that Sheikh Abu'l Fazl meant well, and, in fact, Prince Salim deserved a harsher chastisement not only for his wanton ways, but also for nurturing treasonable thoughts against His Majesty.

Akbar walked out on to the covered burj *and looked towards the swollen Tapti flowing furiously by. In the diminished light of a wilting moon he watched the debris of a ruined dominion pass, as pieces of logs, unpegged squares of thatched roofs, carcasses of dogs, lambs, and bloated cows rushing by in writhing agony. Curse of the Deccan, mused Akbar. Floods, famine, or plague were the annual destiny of this accursed state.*

Akbar missed his capital, Agra, with its teeming populace of learned scholars, singers, dancers, men of wisdom and men of spiritual high craft, warriors, rajahs, and nobles. Deccan, on the other hand, had only death and pestilence to offer, along with the stubborn cowardice of the five Shah dynasties ruling the Malwa kingdoms of Ahmednagar, Berar, Bijapur, Golconda, and Bidar. These sultanates preferred to stay within their forts and suffer the siege, rather than come out fighting. It was also their strategy to commence heavy shelling from their battlement-mounted cannons after sunset at the Mughal camp, with small groups of specially trained troops laying mines and spikes along the periphery of the forts to ambush the Mughals if they ever tried to rush the fort. Hundreds of crippled elephants, horses, and maimed imperial soldiers were testimony to the gruesome efficacy of these war tactics.

For Akbar and his invading army of Turks, Afghans, and Rajputs, such wars were a slur on their pride and battle prowess. Many times, the Mughal cavalry had openly galloped across the face of the forts, well within arrow flights, but the defending garrison had hardly ever struck at them. Khanekhana Abd'ur Rahim frequently compared the Deccanese with the Karonda berry – there was nothing tasty in this berry, yet people tried to pluck them from their prickly stems.

Akbar shuddered as he watched the furiously raging Tapti sweep the debris away. It was as if his dreams of a glorious empire were being tossed and shaken in the whirlpool of Time.

*

Agra Fort,

Akbari Mahal,

14th March, 1602

1:15 a.m.

The tears would not stop.

Akbar rose from the chess board with a heavy sigh. 'Well done, Khurram. You have cornered me again. The emperor yields.'

Prince Khurram wore a sombre expression. He knew that the emperor was heartbroken at the rebellious pursuits of Khurram's father, Prince Salim. Each day, there were fresh reports coming in from the provinces of Illahabas and Chunar of excesses, and intrigues of an independent court being commanded by the intransigent prince.

He watched as Shah Baba walked out onto the covered terrace.

Rain drops in the balmy spring night played a soft contralto in the background, as rain water, collected in the crevices and corners of the palace roof and overhanging carved archways, splashed in the fish-scaled basins created in the flagstoned courtyards.

As Emperor Akbar stood with his head inclined slightly to the right, and gazed at the splashing water in the scaled basins, now made silver in the passing moonlight, tears flowed unbidden from his eyes. The past eighteen months had been suffused with miserable news of Prince Salim's continuing rebellion and his treasonable act of setting up an independent kingdom governed from the great fort at Illahabas, which Akbar himself had built almost eighteen years earlier.

The emperor raised his eyes and looked towards the moon scurrying amidst the rain-laden clouds – how time had flown and circumstances transformed! It seemed only a fortnight ago when Salim, as a proud fourteen-year-old prince, had followed in his father's wake seated upon a gold caparisoned elephant into the newly constructed fort.

*

Flashback

Illahabas Fort

11th November, 1583

Friday, 2:00 p.m.

As they crossed the main gate, small brass cannons fired a welcome salvo in the emperor's honour. Two grey pigeons sitting atop the Ashoka Pillar fluttered their wings in disapproval, and, cocking their heads, flew away. As the emperor's elephant lurched its way towards the west gate and the royal apartments, Akbar swivelled in his seat to watch Prince Salim and Prince Daniyal following on their royal elephants.

Akbar was amused to see that prince Salim's elephant Kalighat had stopped in front of the Ashoka Pillar, and Salim was gazing intently at the stone edict. The prince's mahout, now aware of the emperor's silent gaze, immediately prodded his elephant to move forward.

*

Same Day

Illahabas Fort

Just before Magreeb Namaz (4:30 p.m.)

Emperor Akbar, followed by Princes Salim and Daniyal and the escorting noblemen, including Raja Birbal, walked slowly towards the Royal Mosque near the Main Gate. As they were passing by the stone edict, Prince Salim hastened to the emperor's side and called softly, 'Father, Your Majesty! What is this tall pillar for?'

Emperor Akbar took him by the arms, and, turning towards the massive sandstone pillar, said, 'This pillar was made many hundreds of years ago by another great king. His name was Ashoka.'

Emperor Akbar, with his tremendous curiosity and interest in all historical, astrophysical, and religious matters, was a huge mine of information collected over years of interaction with masters of these sciences. Though an illiterate himself, his knowledge on a vast array of subjects astounded even the critical teachers and mullahs of faraway lands.

Salim squinted into the setting sun, and remarked, 'What funny inscriptions are there on this pillar! It seems as if an army of ants has meandered over its face while it was still wet!'

Akbar's loud laughter rang out. 'Sheikhu, these scrawls, which seem meaningless to you, are the ancient king's instructions to the populace of his time, written in the venerable script of Brahmi.'

'Sire. Did this king come from beyond the mountains in the north, as we did?'

'No, Sheikhu. This king also ruled from the river Indus in the west to the mighty snow-covered mountains of the east. His dominion spread over many rivers, mountains, and great cities, and extended much further to the south than we have ever been.'

Prince Daniyal, then all of eleven years old and attired in a dazzling orange and green chogah with a brilliant red patka around his waist, chipped in. 'Your Majesty! Does that mean he was more powerful than us? Did he have more cannons and horses?'

'No, my child. Cannons and gunpowder were unknown to them, and he had a weak cavalry. But, he had more than five thousand war elephants and expert archers. It is said that his archers were so swift, and of such numbers, that they could blacken the sky and hide the sun with their flights of arrows. He was a great king and a brave warrior, but he also became weak and emotional in his final years. He took the shelter of Dharma, or religion, and put away his sword. It did not bode well for his successors, and over time his kingdom was lost.'

'But, father, even you are religious. Does that mean we could lose the forts and palaces someday?' The worried countenance of Prince Daniyal brought a smile to the faces of the emperor and his accompanying nobles.

Akbar had had a soft spot for his youngest son, Daniyal, since from the age of twelve months he had been put under the care of Raja Bharmar of Amer and his queen, as a signature gesture of faith and kinship with the Royal House of Amer. The corners of Emperor Akbar's lips twitched in merriment as he replied to this innocent question, so pregnant with tales of the future.

'No, my young Prince! I follow religion, but I have not forgotten my sword! And, always remember, that your sword is your most loyal companion. You are Timurid princes, descended from the Great Taimur and the most powerful Genghis Khan... it is your destiny to subjugate, conquer, and rule! Religion, or Dharma, is your wise counsellor, which shows the righteous path to rule. But rule must be enforced with the might of the sword.'

Princes Salim and Daniyal listened with close attention to these words. Though the emperor's voice had been low, the intensity of his gaze and the pitch of his tone had conveyed the heavy import of these words. Unwittingly, Prince Salim's hand curved against the golden hilt of his sheathed sword.

Sheikh Abu'l Fazl stepped forward, and, with a bow to the emperor, spoke. 'Young princes, many kings will come, and many will go, but the glorious reign of your father, His Majesty Emperor

Jalal Ud Din Akbar, will shine like the radiant sun for thousands of years to come. This stone edict is only fifteen dands high and made from the sandstone quarried from the suba of Chunar. But the deeds of Your Most Noble Father, Shahenshah I Hind, defy the very heights of the blue sky! Many such minars will be required to encapsulate even one year of his lofty reign.'

Raja Birbal and Raja Todarmal, standing behind the emperor, squirmed with undisguised disdain at the abject sycophancy of Sheikh Abu'l Fazl. His verbal ramblings and loquacity had become a covert joke of the royal court. Many of the courtiers wondered as to how Emperor Akbar, normally so astute in state matters, could not see through the false contours of the Sheikh's words.

Sheikh Abu'l Fazl saw the sneering contempt in the Rajas' eyes, and, like a coiled serpent, spat, 'And see here, Your Majesty! Our very own Raja Birbal has inscribed his name on this pillar – he aspires to be in royal company.' He pointed towards the bottom left of the stone edict.

Raja Birbal, bewildered, stepped forward and peered closely at the spot, where all eyes were fixed. It was true. In between the Brahmi script were two lines in Persian. He turned to the emperor and said, 'Your Majesty! I have absolutely no idea as to how my name came to be inscribed here.'

'Certainly you can read Persian, Raja Birbal?' the mocking tone of Sheikh Abu'l Fazl was not lost on the royal retinue.

Keeping his eyes firmly fixed on a spot near the emperor's knee, Birbal replied, 'Majesty! It shows my visit of eight years ago, when you invested me with the responsibility of ensuring proper work during the initial construction of this fort. I had applied for a month's leave for a personal visit to Tribeni, and you most graciously honoured me by delegating this most honourable task. The inscriptions were done without my knowledge or sanction, Your Majesty!'

Prince Salim leaned forward and read aloud the Persian script engraved on the pillar. '982 AH – arrival of Raja Birbal from the Royal Court of Emperor of Islam, Emir of the Faithful, Shadow of God on Earth, Abul Fath Jalal Ud Din Mohammed Akbar Padshah Ghazi, on a personal visit to Tribeni, with the Padshah Ghazi's sanction.'

As Akbar smiled and walked forward, evidently satisfied with Birbal's answer and the context of the words inscribed, Prince Salim cast a contemptuous glance at Sheikh Abu'l Fazl; the old serpent was back to his tricks again, thought the young prince. As his eyes narrowed with derisive malevolence, he promised himself that one day his name would be inscribed on this pillar of the ancient warrior king.

It was time now for the khutba to be read in the emperor's name, for the first time in this fort in the Friday evening prayers.

*

Akbari Mahal, Agra Fort

14th March, 1602

1:45 a.m.

Emperor Akbar turned away from the veil of rainfall obscuring the flitting moon and stepped back into his bedchamber. The lone candle inside the silver filigree lamp cast patterns on the frescoed walls. Akbar, in his melancholic state, knocked the silver lamp to the floor and gazed balefully at the dying flame as it dared him once more with its last, twisted dance.

He walked over to the silver trunk and prised open the lid. Inside, flung across his personal swords and daggers, was the last *nishaan* sent by Prince Salim from his camp at Etawah just a fortnight ago. Akbar unrolled the sleeve and stared at the golden letters written on the red muslin in Prince Salim's neat script. Though he could not read, the deceitful words of his son stabbed his heart with a searing pain. He could recall each word for its deceptive sheen:

Serviced at the Feet of My Most Revered Father and Guardian, Refuge of the Universe, Protector of the Faith and Emperor of Hindustan, Jalal Ud Din Mohammed Akbar:

I have spent my entire life of thirty-three summers and winters under your benevolent protection and nurturing hand, as the most fortunate of princes and auspicious shadow as your first born son, born unto you as a divine blessing from Hazrat Sayyed Salim Chishti, may his soul rest in peace, to serve, to honour, and to revere the most Glorious King of Kings.

Akbar winced at the villainy of his son's words and the reference to the great Sufi mystic Hazrat Sayyed Salim Chishti. How could a child born of the blessings of a revered mystic carry such malevolence within?

In your name, and under your flag have I ruled from Illahabas, and have tried to uphold and increase the glory of your reign, as a most obedient servant of the Realm, and a trusted son of the Great King.

I have not been favoured by your grace and blessings for almost two years now, and I wished to appease my heart and resurrect my flagging spirits by setting my eyes upon Your Majesty. And, with this wish only had I set forth from Illahabas.

I have received your commandment today, to proceed back to the garrison at Illahabas with my retinue, and as always, I shall uphold your words to the last drop of my blood.

I have always been, and shall always remain, a mere shadow of your Divine Presence, and hold no wish than to be graced again with your Most Fortunate Gaze.

I am sending my most trusted lieutenant, Mir Sadr Jahn, with this epistle, and to convey my words in person before Your Majesty, that I remain , with unswerving allegiance, your faithful son and trusted servant,

Sheikhu.

Akbar folded the parchment and gazed morosely at it. He well remembered the advance of Salim's army of over thirty thousand troops, dragging their heavy and medium cannons with them – even a fool would have deduced that this was not the homecoming of a favoured son, but the military campaign of a marauding force.

The disgraceful events flashed before his eyes:

Spies had been bringing news of impending preparations within Illahabas Fort of a potential war campaign, much before Salim had set out for Agra. The significance of increased recruitment of troops, including archers and cavalry, along with a huge quantum of work for swordsmiths and iron forgers, the incessant display and purchase of battle tested horses and war elephants, along with induction of some Portuguese artillery men, was not lost on the host of imperial spies masquerading as tradesmen, troopers, and palace attendants within the forts of Chunar and Illahabas.

Though Akbar had been concerned about the impending arrival of Prince Salim's army, and a possible civil war, he had kept his emotions under check, and had shown no great measure of anxiety, even as messengers scurried on a daily basis with reports of forced marches and battle plans.

Akbar waited.

As soon as Prince Salim camped at Etawah, about forty kos *before Agra, to regroup his forces prior to the final assault, Akbar struck.*

Overnight, forty thousand royal troops of the emperor's own garrison, with an additional twelve thousand ahadis of the emperor's personal bodyguard were assembled in battle array. Messengers on swift horses were sent to neighbouring mansabs to report with their sanctioned troops immediately. Well aware of the need to signal his readiness for battle and the superiority of the imperial forces, the emperor ordered for the heavy field cannons to be test fired outside the city walls. War elephants in huge contingents were daily paraded outside the city limits and were trained to trumpet in unison, bringing fear into the hearts of all those witness to this spectacle. Rumours flew thick and strong, abetted in no small measure by the emperor's studied silence, that the emperor was determined to decimate the rebel army and publicly execute the erring prince and his cohorts.

Having ridden through the night, a large contingent of imperial troops, led by Mirza Qulich Khan, appeared on the fringes of Salim's encampment at early dawn.

Roused from his opium-induced slumber, Prince Salim was hardly in a fit state to give a coherent reply, but the stern demeanour of Mirza Qulich Khan in full battle armour, carrying the harsh words of Emperor Akbar to immediately halt his advance and return forthwith to his garrison at Illahabas, was not lost on Prince Salim.

Fully awake, the prince assured the military envoy of his peaceful intentions and adherence to the emperor's command.

The very next morning, Prince Salim had sent Mir Sadr Jahn with his nishaan to the emperor, pledging eternal allegiance.

Over the next forty hours, Prince Salim, along with his army, generals, and sycophants, retraced his journey back to Illahabas Fort.

*

Left alone, he caught one of his favourite pigeons, and, with a flick of his wrist, broke its neck. A grim smile appeared on the emperor's face.

*

It was time now for Sheikh Abu'l Fazl to be recalled from the Deccan campaign and to be present in the royal court at Agra, thought Akbar, as he clapped his hands to summon a royal attendant.

The next morning, a *waqia-navees* prepared the imperial order for Sheikh Abu'l Fazl's presence at the royal court. By midday, the royal *firmaan* had already travelled ten *kos* towards the Deccan.

The ravines of Bundelkhand were thirsting for blood.

*

(CHAPTER 16)

BAD'DUA-E-PARSI

(The Persian Curse)

Sironj

Haveli of Gopal Das Nakta

5th August, 1602

7:20 p.m.

'Sire, I see no reason why you should leave your personal troops behind, and plan to proceed with the raw troops of *Faujdar* Nakta. They are neither well trained nor battle tested,' said Jabbar Khas Khail.

'Because they have to be trained some day, by someone, so I might as well speed up the process.' Sheikh Abu'l Fazl spoke with a smile.

'Sire, there is frivolity and obstinacy in your words. Forgive me, but your actions are beyond our comprehension. It is not advisable to proceed through the forested terrains of Malwa without a proper escort. The words of Jabbar Khais have merit.' The chief officer, Asad Beg, of the Sheikh's military escort spoke up.

The Sheikh smiled at his escort commander, and, stroking his white beard, said, 'Your words also have merit, Asad Beg, and I am truly humbled by the concern shown by all of you, but I must proceed with all haste to Agra. The emperor awaits my presence, and each day and night hangs heavy on me. I will travel with a lighter escort, and hence, will travel faster.'

Asad Beg, having accompanied Sheikh Abu'l Fazl Ibn Mubarak in all his recent campaigns against Ahmednagar, Asirgarh, and the fortress of Maali, was well acquainted with the fearless, and at times, reckless attitude of the Sheikh. That those forts, considered invincible, had fallen to the Mughal army in the Deccan was due in no small measure to the ingenuity and bravery of this frail and slender Sheikh.

A small smile played on his lips, as he recalled the dark, moonless night, when Sheikh Abu'l Fazl, with a small detachment of Afghans, had scaled the walls of Maali fort, using a circuitous and camouflaged route from the infamous Saapin Hill. True to its name, Saapin Hill had serpentine gullies and small, rocky ravines, which were infested with snakes and huge jungle lizards. The smile became broader as he recalled the string of abuses in Persian and Turqi let forth by the Sheikh, when his searching fingers had dislodged a resting snake from its cosy crevice in the fort walls. Wrenching the snake, he had flung it away, only to have it fall on some unsuspecting soldiers climbing behind. The oaths and curses which followed in Afghani and Pashtun were no less colourful.

The gentle voice of Sheikh questioned, 'What makes you smirk, dear Asad? Don't tell me that visions of your Kashmiri slave girls have travelled so far with you?'

Asad Beg, with his head bowed but his smile in place, replied, 'No, sire! I was only thinking about your clambering up on the walls of Maali fort, and your encounter with the unsuspecting snake.'

The Sheikh roared with laughter. ' I really do not know, Asad... who was more frightened. The snake or me!'

'The snake, obviously, sire. He had never been abused in such chaste Persian before.'

The room rang with laughter, and the *Faujdar* of Sironj, Gopal Das Nakta, added, 'Sire, do you know that Sironj is infested with scorpions and snakes? It is said that half the reptilian population of Hindustan resides within a *kos* of this city. In fact, several houses and huts have been abandoned to the scourge of these snakes and scorpions – the residents preferred to shift to some other nearby settlements rather than be guests of these venomous reptiles.'

Jabbar Khas Khail observed, 'Oh, no wonder our horses and elephants were so restless today upon entering Sironj... They are normally tired after a hard day's march.'

Sheikh Abu'l Fazl straightened his leg on the *diwan* and said, ' Well, it is settled then. I shall proceed tomorrow with a light escort, and my personal bodyguard will return with you, Asad Beg, to Burhanpur.'

Asad Beg was on his feet. 'What foolishness is this of yours, my learned Sheikh? I am not abandoning you in the middle of your journey, no matter what you say.' The indignation in his voice was evident.

All eyes were on the Sheikh as he murmured thoughtfully. 'You have no choicc, Asad Beg. I command you to return to Burhanpur and report to Khane Khanan Abdur Rahim with my military escort. Write a note to him, which I will personally sign and put my seal to, that I am proceeding with an escort of the troopers freshly recruited by *Faujdar* Gopal das Nakta of

Sironj, and that the returning military detachment should be better put to use in quelling the Bidar Shahis.'

All the commanders close to Sheikh Abu'l Fazl stared in dismay at each other. Though they realized that the Sheikh's mind was made up, and he would not relent, they agonized over the unknown dangers lurking in the mountainous tracts of Malwa and the ravines of Bundelkhand.

As would become evident a week later, Destiny had again prevailed.

*

Forest Tract

Sarai Berar

11th August, 1602

1:15 p.m.

Sheikh Abu'l Fazl, surrounded by his new escort, had passed the settlement of Karera about an hour ago, and was now looking for a suitable place to rest for a while and offer his afternoon *namaz.*

As he squinted against the high afternoon sun, he saw a clearing just ahead to the left, and lifted his hand to signal a stop. The small retinue of about two hundred mounted escorts and fifty attendants on five elephants, slowed down.

As he dismounted, a *syce* ran up to hold his horse's bridle and his personal servants rushed to prepare a small meal and to place his worship mat. Abu'l Fazl was aware that each such stop would put him behind by almost two hours, and he must reach a safe village or settlement before sunset.

As the Sheikh performed the last of the prayers, and took the Prophet's name while rubbing his eyes with the palm of his hands, he felt the presence of someone close by. He opened his eyes to see a semi-naked mendicant in ochre robes sitting at some distance from him, with a wooden staff and a brass vessel on the ground next to him.

The Sheikh nodded politely and rose to his feet.

The bearded mendicant continued to stare at him with a look harbouring on pity, and then gently beckoned him. Sheikh Abu'l Fazl, having himself been raised on the threshold of a mosque, was always courteous to learned scholars and holy men.

As he neared the sage, the holy man spoke softly. 'Brother, travel with caution, as there could be trouble on the way for you.'

Sheikh Abu'l Fazl stopped short, and with equanimity, asked, 'Sir, are you an Oracle? Or have you been blessed with divine powers to foresee the future? Or, are you a *behroopiya* sent to lead travellers astray?'

The half-clad monk peered at him and again softly proclaimed, 'Tomorrow itself you will know. Turn back, for Death beckons.'

Abu'l Fazl looked at him quizzically, and with a half bow, withdrew.

As the ochre-robed mendicant watched him mount and ride away, he drew spears with his fingers on the earth. In that small parcel of land, the black soil of Malwa carried blood-coloured spears.

*

Forest tract, near Antari

Eight *kos* from Gwalior

Friday, 12th August 1602

Early morning; 5:20 a.m.

The Bundela warriors, numbering about five hundred, were preparing their mounts and checking their weapons. Bir Singh Bundela, their renegade chieftain, was busy counting the feathers of the black crow sacrificed last night. He smiled as the feathers numbered thirteen, an odd number, which indicated success in the venture.

The tradition of sacrificing crows, cockerel, and cats to propitiate the gods before any major campaign or journey had travelled with the Bundelas from the deserts of Rajasthan more than two centuries ago, when they had plundered and subjugated this hilly, inhospitable terrain. Wild, wily, and cunning, with a vicious streak born out of rough living, the Bundelas had no qualms in robbing, plundering, murdering, and raping all who, unsuspecting, crossed their path.

The advance of Sheikh Abu'l Fazl Ibn Mubarak from Sironj onwards had been monitored by the Bundelas on a daily basis. Village *Pradhans*, goatherds, roadside merchants, and *sarai* owners were all informants of the Bundelas, and the passage of any large force, rich merchant's caravan, or royal retinue, was regularly reported to the Bundela chiefs. The Bundelas would assess the information, and if the target was lucrative enough, they had no compunction in waylaying the travellers.

Bir Singh had been much surprised when told that the Vizier was travelling with a very light escort, and all the troopers seemed to be young and inexperienced. He had been expecting a much heavier escort of at least five hundred armoured *sowars*.

Before mounting, there was one more ritual to be followed.

Bir Singh Bundela stood with his back to the sacrificial fire, and flung the crow's carcass over his left shoulder. The immediate cries of '*Jai Maa Bhawani*' assured him that the carcass had indeed landed in the fire pit. Without looking back, he jumped onto his horse and galloped away.

If all went well, then Prince Salim would have the head of his father's Vizier,and he would get to sit on the Orchha throne.

*

Sarai Vir

Near Antari, eight *kos* from Gwalior

Friday, 12th August 1602

9:34 a.m.

Mirza Mohsin, one of the few soldiers from the initial escort still accompanying the Sheikh, was galloping back to him. He had been sent ahead to scout and was clearly alarmed as he sped across the sparse bushes of the rocky landscape.

Reining in his horse, he yelled, '*Huzoor*, turn back immediately. There is a large group of men, dressed for battle, riding this way!'

Afghan Gadai Khan rode up. 'How many *sowars*, Mirza?'

'More than five hundred, and all are wearing armour, carrying heavy arms.'

Sheikh Abu'l Fazl spoke aloud. 'This is Bundela country, and Raja Ram Chand of Orchha is not in revolt against His Majesty. Why would he attack us?'

The worried voice of Gadai Khan cut through. 'But he is not really enamoured of us, either. None of the Rajput clans are, as a matter of fact. It could also be his recreant younger brother, Bir Singh Bundela. He is a brigand and a lout.'

'You are right, Gadai Khan. They were carrying no flags or royal signages. Must be that traitor, Bir Singh. And, sire, waste not your time here... Let us flee, while we still can.' Mirza Mohsin seemed desperate to escape.

The Sheikh turned his horse towards the scout, and said, 'Mirza, it does not become you, as a veteran soldier of His Majesty's army, to speak of fleeing. Go, if you must, but I shall never run like a scurrying mongoose.'

Gadai Khan Afghan, an adherent of many years, brought his steed close to the Sheikh's charger, and said, 'There is still time, sire. We are not adequate in numbers, or weapons, or...'

'Khan Afghan! Since when have you started weeping like a woman? Are not our swords of superior steel, and our flags of the majesty of the emperor of Hindustan, Jalal Ud Din Mohammed Akbar? Tell me, will you ride on to Agra and show your cowardly face to the emperor? Will you? Do you want me to cower like a desert jackal and slink away? You and I, and all the others with us today, were born for greater things than to run and hide like cowards!' As Sheikh said these words, he swung his sword in an arc around his head, and roared, '*Allah u Akbar*!'

All the accompanying attendants and troops, infused with new vigour, unsheathed their swords, and cried, '*Allah u Akbar... Fateh*! *Fateh*!'

The Sheikh spurred his horse into a canter, and his personal escort spread themselves in a diamond formation around him. As they covered about half a *kos* over the stony ground, they espied the Bundelas in battle array, ranged on the edge of the forest. Against the sun, their silver chain mail armour shone with the green foliage of the forest behind them.

Gadai Khan swerved his horse in front of the Sheikh's, forcing him to rein his steed. Again, there was panic in his voice. 'Sire, they are too many! Please take a small detachment and turn west... Raja Rai Singh with two thousand troops and Rai Rayan with another one thousand troops are camped hardly four miles from here. You will be safe there. I shall fight these infidels and try to keep them engaged for as long as I can... Just take a small retinue, sire, and go!'

There was a resoluteness on the Sheikh's face as he replied. 'Have I come thus far, only to seek refuge from these scavenging hyenas? The emperor has raised me from the doorstep of a mosque, and brought me into the exalted radiance of his court... for what? To race like a stricken cheetah from the bows and arrows of cowards? I shall fight.'

'What work do you have here? Your presence is required by His Majesty... This is a soldier's work... Be gone, be gone...' cried Afghan Gadai Khan in desperation, the grace of courtly language forgotten.

'Speak no more. I shall fight and win. Or, die like a brave soldier!' The words were barely out of his mouth when he broke his horse into a full gallop.

Gadai Khan, Jabbar Khas Khail, Mirza Mohsin, Zaffar Baig, and other close attendants ranged themselves around him as they charged after him along with the remaining cavalry. The five *hulqa* elephants carrying supplies and attendants lumbered behind.

'Steady, steady... hold your charge... let them get closer,' shouted Bir Singh as he watched the Mughal troops charging at them.

'*Tau*, they are fools to be rushing at us... Look, they are hardly two hundred, and not even equipped for battle. They wear no armour, and carry no lances!' a surprised Bundela chieftain exclaimed as the Mughal troops drew nearer.

'Or very brave,' muttered Bir Singh Bundela as he watched the approaching Mughals from under the brim of his helmet. He raised his sword, and cried, 'Hold, hold... steady... hold... Now, Chaaarge!'

The opposing soldiers met with a clash of horse flesh and bracing steel. Roars of '*Jai Bhawani*' and '*Allahu Akbar*' rent the air as the Sheikh and his close followers, wedged in a diamond formation, rode deep into the Bundela ranks.

The Bundelas, armed with spears and long swords, were able to fell or dislodge a large number of the charging Mughal cavalry, as the raw recruits from Sironj and their untested horses either rode directly into the extended spears of the forward echelons of the waiting Bundelas, or, in abject fear, swerved away, only to be shot from behind by the archers.

As the escort, few in number and virgin in matters of battle, was thwarted or brought down by the vanguard of the Bundelas, Sheikh Abu'l Fazl and his dozen close followers were separated from the main body. The Bundelas, led by Bir Singh, swung around to hem in the Sheikh and his few remaining followers. Their retreat cut off, the Sheikh had no option but to race towards the cover of the forest looming ahead. They crashed through teak, sal, and khair and hung low over the necks of their horses as they forged a way through the low hanging branches of the trees.

Bundelas, with superiority in numbers and well versed with the local topography, slowly encircled the escaping Mughals and finally closed in on them at a sparse clearing full of overgrown weeds and thorny shrubs. As the Sheikh wheeled his horse around to face the pursuers, a spear thrown by a charging warrior pierced his left side, just under the shoulder blade. Reeling from the pain, Sheikh swung his scimitar in a wild arc and slashed the arm of a Bundela warrior who was riding close to him. Gadai Khan placed his horse on the left of the Sheikh and tried to pull the spear out from where it had lodged itself. The excruciating pain, the hardships of the last four years of the Deccan campaign, the travails of travel over the last fortnight, and the wrenching of the embedded spear were more than the frail body of Sheikh Abu'l Fazl could take. He toppled from his horse to the ground, and Jabbar Khas Khail, riding in the lee of Sheikh's steed, immediately dismounted and carried the wounded Sheikh into the shade of the neighbouring trees. As the Sheikh spouted blood from his mouth, he turned his weary eyes towards Jabbar Khas and, through bloodied spittle, whispered, 'Khail... tell the emperor that I fell to treachery... fought... my family needs m...' And his life ebbed out with the dribbling flecks of blood.

*

'Speak. Which one of these is Sheikh Abu'l Fazl?' asked Bir Singh Bundela, as he held a cowering *mahout* who had been seized while trying to goad his elephant away from the battle field. The *hulqa* elephants from the emperor's stable were merely transport animals – the war elephants constituted the *khasa* contingent and were deployed in the imperial fort at Agra as well as on the campaigns of Deccan and the siege of Mewar.

The *mahout*,with a scimitar drawn across his neck and a thin red line of blood coursing down his tunic, was almost on his knees with fright. As Bir Singh pressed his scimitar deeper, the *mahout* pointed towards one of the bodies lying amongst several.

Jabbar Khas Khail peered from behind the thick forest foliage as Bir Singh prodded the Sheikh's body with the tip of his scimitar. He kicked the head of the slain Sheikh, and his green and gold turban rolled away. Jabbar Khas could not bear to see this wretched pillager dishonour the Sheikh in death and, drawing his dagger from his *patta*, he threw it at Bir Singh.

As Bir Singh fell to his knees with the dagger embedded in his right cheek, Jabbar Khas erupted from the foliage in a blur of his swirling long sword and short, personal lance. He caught the first Bundela with the thrust of his sword, and extended his lance into the unguarded thighs of another warrior leaning over to help Bir Singh to his feet. He rushed at another adversary and smote him with the blade of his sword. As the Bundela tried to parry with his shield, Jabbar's blow glanced off the shield across his jaw, ripping it into a few bloodied fragments of flesh and bone.

Bir Singh, with blood flowing freely from the gaping wound on his cheek, plunged his lance through the unprotected back of Jabbar Khas and, with a ferocious cry, threw him to the ground. Raising his scimitar with both hands, he plunged it deep into Jabbar Khas Khail's back.

Turning towards the slain body of Sheikh Abu'l Fazl Ibn Mubarak, he stepped forward and, with a deep stroke, beheaded him. The emaciated head of the dark and slim Sheikh, eyes still open in the terrible pantomime of death, rolled away. A few Bundela warriors, emboldened by the sight of the defenceless body, kicked the decapitated head around.

As Bir Singh jumped onto his horse, he ordered, 'Send the head to Prince Salim at Illahabas. Tell him, also, that as I have stood by him and fulfilled the promise made to him, so must he remember the promise made to me.'

*

Diwaan e Aam

Agra Fort

13th August, 1602

10:40 a.m.

'Ba'adab, Ba Mulahiza, Hoshiyaar... Shahenshah e Hind, Sultanat e Auliya, Abu'l Fatah, Jalal Ud Din Mohammed Akbar, tashreef la rahe hain... Hoshiyaar!'

The trumpet calls of Aitbaar, the emperor's favourite elephant, could be heard as six heralds bearing the Mughal flag entered the Hall of Public Audience. Emperor Akbar, followed by his ten bodyguards bearing his personal weapons, strode into the royal sanctum in the Hall of Forty Pillars. As Emperor Akbar ascended the throne, his courtiers and visiting noblemen bowed low, performing the *kornish*.

The emperor sat and surveyed the assembled courtiers. There seemed to be a chilling silence in the assemblage, as if everyone was waiting for a cloud to burst. Akbar settled his legs, and once again scanned the lowered heads. As was befitting, the Great Mughal never favoured anyone with his direct gaze... his eyes always looked ten inches above, since a direct gaze from the Great Mughal had only two meanings – either immense munificence or grievous harm.

Hakim Humam, the monarch's personal physician, standing in the first row, raised his eyes and then just as quickly lowered his head as he saw the emperor's glance settling on him. Perplexed, Akbar swung his gaze to the far corner on the left as a man dressed in white quietly stepped out and with bowed head slowly walked forward.

In the Timurid fashion, this harbinger of calamitous news wore a blue kerchief on his left arm. As he walked towards the throne, his steps faltered and then, with great effort, once again moved forward.

Recognizing the *Vakil* of Sheikh Abu'l Fazl, Akbar stood up in consternation and without waiting for the customary salutations, asked, 'Daud Khan! All is well?'

'*Jahanpanah*, Sheikh Abu'l Fazl is no more.' The hoarse whisper was hardly audible.

'What?'

The desperate cry of the emperor shook the court. Akbar, in his disbelief and anguish, turned ashen. He caught the silver pillar of the throne for support as he felt the ground tremble, and, steadying himself, he leaned forward menacingly.

Daud Khan quailed at the sight of the wrath writ on the emperor's face.

'Your Majesty. The Sheikh was slain at the treacherous hands of Bir Singh Bundela. He was waiting to ambush us with five hundred cavalry at Antari, near Gwalior.'

Akbar's face had darkened, and his low growl was full of menace. 'Were the Mughal troops unable to protect my Vizier?'

There was complete silence in the court.

'Have we come to such a pass that the royal troops can no longer stand the treacherous arrows and lances poisoned with the shame of deceit? That their swords blessed with the spirit and blood of the Great Taimur and Genghis Khan cannot shield us from the villainy and rot of despicable curs infesting our forests and living off our munificence? Are we Timurids, or are we not?' Akbar's roar was like thunder passing by.

There was a great shout of 'Timurids! Death to the Bundelas!' from the assembled nobles, *ahadis*, visiting court officials from different *subas*, and the citizenry of Agra.

Emperor Akbar shook with colossal rage, and his face turned a dark shade of red, as he looked at the sea of flashing swords and the repeated roars of his generals and soldiers demanding Bundela blood.

'Your Majesty! Sire! The Sheikh's last words to Jabbar Khas Khail were: "Tell His Majesty, the emperor, that I fought and died like a soldier." These were his lasts words.' The *vakil* Daud Khan sobbed as he finished.

Akbar visibly tottered, and a cry of deep sorrow and desolation escaped his lips as he heard the parting words of his faithful companion, advisor, and most trusted courtier.

With tears streaming down his face, Akbar turned and stumbled towards his royal quarters. His personal retinue, taken by surprise, hurriedly arranged themselves around him. The courtiers, similarly surprised at his sudden withdrawal, bowed low to the retreating back of the grieving emperor.

Shuffling along the stone corridors of the fort, Akbar kept mumbling, 'Sheikhu, what have you done?'

*

Royal Apartments

Agra Fort

15th August, 1602

5:40 p.m.

Hakim Humam and the other physicians stood just outside the antechambers of the emperor's royal apartment, with the Uzbeg and Tartar harem guards in close attendance. Begum Sultana and Bibi Daulat Shad Begum were in the antechamber but were afraid to enter. The emperor had neither eaten nor slept for the last forty-eight hours.

Footsteps could be heard in the stone corridor as a eunuch approached carrying the silver hookah and jewel-encrusted stool of Raquiah Begum, the first of Akbar's queens. The senior eunuch of Ruqaiah Begum, Ishrat Ali, came forward and stood to one side of the stone alcove, where a small lamp had been kept burning continuously over the last two days by Mariam Uz Zamani, the Rajput queen of Emperor Akbar, as an offering for the emperor's health. Ruqaiah Begum, with a hand on young Prince Khurram's shoulder, and her portly frame enveloped in the auspicious green of the Moslems, entered the bedchamber of the grieving emperor.

Prince Khurram froze as he saw his Shah Baba, bereft of his royal robes, accoutrements, and stately honour, writhing on the floor with soft moans of suppressed grief permeating the melancholic aura of the room. Wide eyed and aghast he stood, unable to register the enormity of the searing, burning anguish tormenting the very soul of the unvanquished, glorious emperor of Hindustan.

Sultana Ruqaiah Begum could feel the stiffening of Prince Khurram's shouders as he continued to gaze at his beloved Shah Baba suffused with an agony that none could contain or extinguish. Khurram, in shocked silence, cast his eyes across the room and its evident disarray. The royal turban of turquoise and gold with its large emerald was flung in a far corner, as were the royal robes. His scimitar, the *Mulk ul Fateh*, was unsheathed, and lay dangerously close to the emperor.

Impervious to the presence of the queen and the young prince, Akbar, his face buried in the rich Persian rug, whimpered softly. 'Sheikhu, how could you do this to me? I have loved you, Sheikhu, with all my heart... If you wanted the throne, you should have killed me... Why did you kill Abu'l Fazl? Why? Why?'

Numbed beyond words, Prince Khurram leaned heavily on the queen, his foster mother. Unable to take his eyes off his cherished grandfather, he took a few faltering steps towards the emperor prostrated by the mephitic treason and perfidy of his son and heir apparent. Sultana Ruqaiah Begum watched the shaken prince bend down and reverently place the royal turban on a corner of the silver-canopied bed. The prince gathered the robes of silken burgundy and the royal *patta* lying on the floor and, folding them across his arms, came and stood by Ruqaiah Begum. She quietly took the robes and placed them on the silver table.

Prince Khurram again knelt by the emperor's side and reached out to sheath the emperor's scimitar, but hesitated. Acquainted with the respect, honour, and responsibilities the emperor's sword commanded, he silently withdrew his outstretched hand. Lightly touching Akbar on his shoulder, he bowed his head in obeisance and stood up.

As he walked past the queen there were scars of hatred on his heart; how could his father cause so much pain to *his* father? Were not the bonds of blood and kinship greater than the avarice of gems, *subas*, and the ruby-encrusted silver throne?

As Prince Khurram walked past the waiting *hakims*, *vaids*,and Raja Man Singh of Amer, with reflections of violence and hatred in his eyes, Hakim Humam stared gravely at his retreating back. He turned around, and met the apprehensive gaze of Raja Man Singh.

The seeds of the dynastic rebellion, fratricide, and rapacious greed had been sown.

'What must be, must be,' murmured Hakim Humam as he lowered his head to pray.

*

Diwan e Aam

Illahabas Fort

20th August, 1602

1:40 p.m.

The call of a court herald could be heard outside. Prince Salim, reading a petition, raised his eyes as he looked towards the entrance.

Three men clad in armour and bearing a box covered in red satin turned onto the central aisle leading up to the throne. Just behind them, carrying the Bundela flag, marched six soldiers.

Kotwal Amir Beg Turqi, standing at the far end of the pavilion, pounced upon the flag bearer and threw him to the ground. The other soldiers quickly surrounded the Bundelas.

'How dare you raise the Bundela flag in the king's presence?' roared Amir Beg Turqi.

Hulasi Singh Bundela, a nephew of the renegade chieftain Bir Singh, had been entrusted with the task of carrying Sheikh Abul Fazl's decapitated head to Prince Salim. Facing the enraged *Kotwal* he spoke loudly enough for the courtiers to hear. 'I am in the presence of Prince Salim, who is the Governor of Illahabas, Bihar, and Orissa provinces. The emperor resides at Agra.'

'Silence, Bundela! Or you shall join your ancestors.'

Hulasi Singh Bundela, untamed and proud, spoke even more loudly than before. 'Save your breath, Turqi! You scare us not with your fiery breath. We are Bundelas, and our swords speak for us. Here, take this, and present it to Prince Salim. Our chief, Bir Singh Bundela, has sent it with his compliments.' The satin-covered box was thrust into the hands of Amir Beg Turqi.

Nonplussed, the *Kotwal* walked towards Prince Salim.

'Open it,' commanded Prince Salim.

As another courtier stepped forward to open the box in the *Kotwal*'s outstretched hands, the putrid smell of death and decay assailed the court. The courtier, averting his eyes, speared the head of Abu'l Fazl and raised it from the box. As Salim looked upon the maggot infested head of the slain Sheikh, he laughed and exclaimed: 'Throw the head of the learned Sheikh in the latrines.'

*

Haveli of Sheikh Abu'l Fazl

Jumna riverfront, East of Agra Fort

22nd August, 1602

2:00 p.m.

The three wives of Sheikh Abu'l Fazl heard the *ulema* recite the *Faateha e Janaza* according to Shi'ite rites, and as the resonant voice of the *ulema* carried the words, '*Allaahum-maghfir lahu warhamhu, wa'aafihi, wa'fu'anhu, wa 'akrim nuzulahu, wa wassi' mudkhalahu*,' the finality of the Sheikh's farewell descended upon the gathered relatives, nobles, and attendants.

Standing close to his father's bier was Abdur Rehman. His hands were protectively thrown around the shoulders of a handsome, fair boy of about ten or eleven years, who stared at the dark red blotches on the white funeral shroud.

While the Hindu and Kashmiri Begums wept softly behind their veils, and the Sheikh's only son, Abdur Rehman, recited the *Faateha e Janaza* with the Shi'ite cleric, the youngest wife, who was of Persian origin and a dabbler in the wicked science of mystic potions and curses, recited her own litany of malefic words in Persian.

As the cleric finished his prayers, and the congregation swung their necks in supplication, the Persian wife threw up her veil and, in a voice hoarse with venom, cursed: 'Salim, as you have cut asunder the body of my husband and provider, with the trunk interred at Antari and the head buried at Illahabas, so do I damn you and your descendants to eternal strife, to cut the hand, limbs, and tongues of all those whom they hold dear, to wallow in the impending sorrow and destruction of their own selves, to be ravaged by the maggots of Fate and the sacrilege of your actions... I damn you for ever!'

A widow's curse could never be allayed.

The Persian curse would endure.

*

(CHAPTER 17)

DARBAR E SHAITAAN

(The Satanic Court)

Diwan e khas

Illahabas Fort

10th March, 1604

Early evening

Prince Salim struggled to sit up and extended his hand for support. A royal attendant standing behind moved to help and, in doing so, knocked over the silver bowl of arrack kept close to the prince's bolster. As the sweet, decaying smell of the Arabian fermented spirit hit his nostrils, Prince Salim opened his eyes in drunken pleasure and exclaimed, 'What delight is there in this beautiful toddy, that it soothes the souls of emperors and slaves alike.'

Prince Salim sank into the arrack suffused mattress again, and a thin stream of brownish spittle from his mouth stained the golden sequined sheet.

His courtier and close confidant, Sayyid Abdullah of Barha, propped up the delirious prince and softly whispered in his ear, 'Majesty... please rise. You know that Sulaiman Sirhindi is here from the emperor's court. Let him not carry tales to the imperial court.'

'Tales! What tales, Sayyid?'

'Your Majesty. You know that the emperor favours Prince Khusrau. He has already decided to appoint Khusrau as the next sovereign, no matter how unworthy he may be. Raja Man Singh of Amber also regards it as a matter of right for his nephew, and poisons the emperor against you with talks of licentious behaviour at your noble court. A few bowls of arrack are exaggerated into mighty oceans of perfidious liquor being consumed at this court. Please, Your Majesty, rise, and dismiss the assembly.'

'Sayyid Abdullah, do you forget that I rule with the pleasure of Allah, the All Merciful and Most Gracious? What fear have I of the *Padshah Ghazi*? Have I not minted coins under my own sovereignty, and granted you lands and titles under my Royal Seal?'

'Yes, you have, Your Majesty. And we continue to flourish under your immense bounty. But I caution you, Sire, that the great king at Agra is looking for reasons to impose sanctions against your authority.'

Prince Salim, intoxicated, staggered to his feet and fumbling for his dagger shouted, 'I rule with the authority of my Timurid ancestors and the Will of Allah. From today, Illahabas shall henceforth be known as Allahabad – the Abode of Allah.'

The assembled nobles, visiting dignitaries, and royal attendants proclaimed, 'Allahabad, Allahabad, may your reign be eternal, King Salim.'

*

The next morning, royal heralds with drums around their necks and escorted by soldiers stood at village squares, traveller's *serais*, and important highway junctions; in the roads, lanes, and passages of the city, proclaiming the royal *firmaan*:

'Now, hear this: In the name of Prince Salim, King of Illahabas, Jaunpur, Bihar, and Orissa, Scion of His Majesty, the emperor, Jalal Ud Din Mohammed Akbar Padshah Ghazi, the name of *Suba* Illahabas stands changed to *Suba* Allahabad, *Suba* Allahabad. Now, hear this, hear this!'

Carried on the winds of insurrection and royal infamy, the proclamation swiftly made its way to the Imperial Court at Agra.

*

The Hall of Forty Pillars

Allahabad Fort

17th April, 1604

Early evening

Prince Salim was being helped out of his riding robes and leather weapons girdle by his favourite slave girls, Qaseema and Chandni. As Chandni came close to unbuckle the *patta*, Salim let his hands roam idly over her buttocks.

The two slaves slid closer to Prince Salim and lightly caressed his thighs – it was rarely now that Prince Salim found pleasure in the sensual curves of his harem. It was mostly opium that sent him to bed rather than passion. Qaseema pushed herself against him and lightly slid her fingers inside his robe. Prince Salim, still standing, quickly curled his hands around her waist and pulled her closer as Qaseema sensuously buried her face in his chest. Chandni, not to be ignored, ventured lower, and Salim felt the first stirrings of desire after many days.

Salim continued to caress and explore the waist and buttocks of Qaseema with one hand, while with the other he fondled the ripe breasts of Chandni, swollen with desire.

Qaseema and Chandni exchanged smiles; they would be surely rewarded today.

The sun was setting over the horizon, and the red glow mingled with the softly rippling waves of the Jumna. The lamp illuminators, carrying long candles with silver handles, discreetly went around lighting the wicks in lamps of silver, brass, and polished copper. A small signal from Qaseema sent them scurrying away from the hall.

Chandni, the more adventurous of the two, took Prince Salim's rigid member in her hands and, wrapping her fingers around it, gently nudged the prince onto the bolstered silver diwan on its marble slab. Salim roughly put his hand on the hem of her silk bodice and ripped it away. Her milky white breasts spilled out. Qaseema, who was still entangled in the folds of Salim's inner vest, found his nipple with her lips, and Salim gurgled with delight.

'Drop your skirts,' he ordered.

Divested of all garments, Chandni and Qaseema renewed their ministrations of the prince's body, with frequent gasps of delight and appreciation, as they continued to explore, and be explored, by roving fingers, gaze, and lips.

A soft cough from the arched doorway interrupted the tangling of limbs, and Prince Salim sat up, gathering his robe around him.

'Yes,' he enquired, buttoning his robe as the two attendants withdrew behind the brocaded curtains, darkened by evening shadows.

'Your Majesty... There is an imperial courier from the *Khane Khanan* Abdur Rahim.'

Salim watched with unease as the courier from *Suba* Burhanpur approached. His heart skipped a beat as he saw a blue handkerchief tied on the courier's wrist, signifying death.

The messenger stood with bowed head, and Salim waited.

When he could wait no longer, Salim exclaimed, 'Speak, messenger! Why hast thou tied the blue kerchief on your wrist? What accursed news do you bring?'

The messenger slowly recited, 'Your Majesty, on behalf of *Khane Khanan* Sheikh Abdur Rahim, it is with profound grief that I inform you of the untimely and sad demise of your younger brother, Prince Daniyal, on the eighth of April, at a hunting lodge near Burhanpur. We grieve for your loss, Prince.'

Salim leaned back nonplussed for a few moments. Though he was aware of Daniyal's precarious condition, brought about by excessive drinking and consequent liver trouble, he had never thought the end would come so quickly. Salim exulted; the road to the imperial throne at Agra was now clear.

Straining to keep the joy from reflecting on his countenance, Salim replied in a faltering voice, 'What dismal news is this! Daniyal, oh, my youngest and most beloved brother... What ruination has come.'

And then, turning to the silent messenger, he said, 'Rest. And then leave for Burhanpur, to be with the *Khane Khanan*. In moments of woe and misery, willed by Allah, we need to be together, as one. My heart cannot find the joy to reward you for your toil and hardships in bringing forth this message, but go in peace.'

As the messenger performed the obeisance and withdrew from the chamber, Prince Salim turned towards Chandni and, grabbing her roughly by the waist, turned her around and penetrated her from behind. As she gasped in pain, she realized that the prince had never seemed as engorged or as rigid as today.

Salim leaned over her, and, crushing her breasts in his hands, chortled with glee.

*

In the Shahi Qila at Agra, there was darkness and pain.

*

Diwan e Khas

Agra Fort

18th April, 1604

11:40 a.m.

'Your Majesty! The empire demands your unflagging strength and towering spirit, Sire. We are all devastated by Prince Daniyal's demise. It was the Will of Allah, and who should know this better than your own self, *Zille' Illahi*! Your continued abstinence from any victuals is a matter of great concern to all of us, and Hakim Gillani, in his disquiet about your health, has also not eaten for more than two days now. We entreat you, Majesty, to please accept a few morsels of food, in acceptance of the realm's desire.'

The haunted eyes of Akbar looked at Hakim Ali Gillani standing quietly in a corner, and he asked, 'Do you have a balm for my soul, Hakim? Can all your medicines and potions give me back a mere two minutes with my son Daniyal, again?' Akbar paused, and then wearily answered his own question. 'No, you cannot, Hakim Gillani. You cannot.'

Akbar turned his melancholic gaze on to Raja Man Singh and in a barely audible whisper said, 'Tell me once again, Mirza Raja Man Singh. What happened?'

'Your Majesty, in accordance with your *Shahi Farmaan* issued to Abdur Rahim Khane Khana, prohibiting the supply of wine and opiates to the young prince, he was moved to a royal hunting lodge in the vicinity of Burhanpur Fort. A strong guard was posted to enforce the embargo on wines, and the few attendants and soldiers who were smuggling in wine and opiates in their turbans were severely punished.

'Khane Khanan, as a worried father-in-law, tried to counsel the prince many times, but it always ended in acrimonious arguments and accusations of gross neglect. The prince devised a novel way of importing wine into his chambers. He bribed a musketeer of the royal guards, Murshid Quli Khan, into smuggling wine in the barrel of prince's favourite hunting musket, which he affectionately referred to as *Yak au Janaza* – or 'just like a bier'. In fact, Sire, he was so enamoured of this flint gun that he had the following couplet engraved on its barrel: "From the joy of the chase with thee, life is fresh and new; To everyone whom thy dart strikes, 'tis the same as his bier."How prophetic were the words, Your Majesty.

'This wretch, Murshid Quli Khan,' continued Raja Man Singh, 'expecting monetary rewards, did as he was told. He put double-distilled wine in the barrel of the musket and carried it for Prince Daniyal, little realizing that the rust and gunpowder remnants within the barrel would make for a lethal combination with the wine. Regrettably, Sire, Prince Daniyal was dead as soon as he consumed this poisonous mixture.

'The erring soldier, Murshid Quli Khan was executed the same day,' he added softly.

The emperor sat with his eyes closed.

'*Takhliya*.'

The Royal Shikargaah

Forests of Shankargarh

30 kos from Allahabad

11th May, 1604

Hoshiyaar stood absolutely still as Prince Salim took careful aim at the tigress resting in the clump of *sarpat.* Evidently indolent after satiating her hunger from a fresh kill, the tigress was lazily smacking her lips and gazed at the small hunting party with disinterested eyes. Turning her head, she yawned, the low grumble exciting the gathered monkeys into a fresh round of shrill chatter.

Her head snapped as there was a loud roar from the musket fired by the prince. She tried to scramble to her feet by digging her front paws into the hard earth and pushing with her hind legs. There was a gaping wound on her neck, and blood spurted out from her open mouth as she let out a rumbling roar. There was the thunder of another discharge as the musket fired again, and this time she rolled over on her side as the musket shot hit her just below the ears.

'Brilliant shot, Your Highness! Just brilliant!' exclaimed Syed Abdullah as he rode forward with his lance extended.

The mahout urged Hoshiyaar, the enormous Burmese elephant, towards the kill as several *qarawals* and troopers surrounded the slain beast.

'*Masha Allah*!She is almost eight feet in length!' Shezer Khan, an experienced *qarawal* exclaimed.

Suddenly there were shouts of 'Hoshiyaar, Hoshiyaar,'as the small body of troops guarding the rear frantically wheeled their horses around. The prince's war elephant trumpeted and lumbered around to face the impending threat as the royal troopers and assembled *qarawals* spread themselves in a protective formation around the prince.

Zain Alam Khan, a veteran of many battles, shouted, 'Archers to the trees! Archers, take to the trees!'

Immediately, several of the minor *shikaris* and mounted archers climbed into the high branches of the *peepul*, banyan, and *sheeshum* trees for a vantage position. One of the archers called down, 'I see a dozen riders and I see the Mughal flag.'

Soon, a small posse of royal troopers flying the Mughal flag of green with a golden couchant lion crashed through the thick foliage. Riding in front was the Vizier Sharief Khan of Prince Salim's court. He had a blue kerchief tied on his wrist.

Jumping down from his horse, he performed the *kornish* and spoke softly. 'Forgive me, Your Highness, I bring terrible news. *Shah Begum* committed suicide yesterday evening by consuming an excess of opium.'

There was not a flicker of emotion on Salim's face.

*

Triveni (Confluence of Ganges, Jumna

and the mythical Saraswati)

Near Allahabad Fort

15th August, 1604

Late evening; 10:15 p.m.

Shardi Beg, Keeper of the Royal Barge, sat near the stern and watched the twinkling lights of Allahabad in the distance. The huge fort with its many torches, earthen lamps, and suspended cauldrons of bronze carrying large burning wicks seemed to tower on the right. To the left, and in the distance, shimmered a necklace of twinkling nights from the flickering glows of earthen lamps from the houses on the riverbank.

Shardi Beg should have been happy, but he was not. He had served with Emperor Akbar since the campaign against the Bengal rebels, almost twenty years before. Then, he had swiftly carried the emperor's trusted general, Todar Mal, and his attendant troops to Munghyr via the Ganges waterways up to the port of Teliyaghat, considered the Gateway to Bengal.

He remembered that evening when the *Jagirdar* of Patna, Masoom Khan Kabuli, who had joined the Bengal rebels, was brought to the riverbank in iron fetters. He could still envision Raja Todar Mal reading the emperor's *firmaan* received through royal couriers a few weeks previously, condemning Masoom Khan Kabuli as *aasi*. The regal but cultured voice of Raja Todar Mal, even in battle, flashed through the boatsman's eyes:

'Masoom Khan Kabuli, you have abetted the enemies of state and reneged on your oath of loyalty to the emperor, Padshah Ghazi Jalal Ud Din Mohammed Akbar. You have spurned the faith His Majesty anointed you with. The emperor bestowed on you the Jagir of Patna, but you have preferred to collude with those who are enemies of the Sovereign Majesty. For this, you are declared an aasi, *a common criminal, and this is how you shall be recorded in history. For your treacherous liaison and seditious correspondence with Mirza Mohammed Hakim of Kabul, your perfidious limbs shall be separated, one by one, from your treacherous body.'*

At a signal from Raja Todar Mal, Masoom Khan was struck with a shield and he fell on his knees. Two soldiers extended his fettered arms. Aasi Masoom Khan screamed his apologies to the heavens and the gathered troopers, but the emperor was too far away in Agra to heed, and the circling eagles even less interested.

Two swords came crashing down and both his arms were severed just below his shoulders. A limbless aasi, *spilling blood from the gaping wounds where his shoulders used to be, fell on the sands.*

Raja Todar Mal spoke coldly as he ignored the specks of fresh blood spewed on his face and moustache. 'Take him away to the water. He must die by drowning.'

Incoherent with pain, and quickly losing blood, aasi *Khan Kabuli was swiftly dragged into the river and left to drown with flailing legs and missing arms. The gurgle of treason ended in a few bloodstained bubbles of river water.*

Shardi Beg shook his head and spat a stream of tobacco into the softly lapping waters of the Jumna. When carrying the royals, he always preferred to anchor in the Jumna, as it was deeper. He could not afford the risk of hitting a sandbar in the shallow Ganges, with royals on board.

The reason for his discomfiture was the scurrilous ways of this court... so removed in functioning, decorum, and grace from His Majesty's court at Agra. To him, this court was a den of thieves and malefics, sycophants and losers.

Ah, what would he not sacrifice just to hold the main sail of the emperor's barge again! He always considered his services to the emperor as a divine chapter, for it was in the same year that Emperor Akbar initiated the *Illahi* calendar. His appointment to the province of Allahabad had also been by imperial command, from His Majesty himself, as a favour to his Sheikhu Baba.

Well, so much for Sheikhu Baba... this serpent in a prince's guise, mused the Keeper of the Royal Barge as he shot another stream into the silently protesting waters.

The strains of soft music and the cadence of ankle bells wafted from the royal quarters, where Prince Salim and a few other nobles were enjoying the gyrations of the royal dancers. The garrulous laughter and opium laden conversation of the nobles was supplemented by occasional giggles and sensual sighs from the courtesans.

'Yo, Girdhar. Lower the main sail to quarter. There is a slight breeze now, the boat shall heave.'

‘Yes, master,’ replied Girdhar, as he and his son, Shyamu, rushed to lower the main sail to stabilize the barge.

Suddenly, there was some commotion at the royal jetty. Shardi Beg turned to see a rush of people with lighted torches, and shouts muffled by distance. He straightened up and saw a boat pull out from the jetty.

There were shouted commands from the several boats ranged around the imperial barge carrying the prince’s bodyguards. A couple of these boats closely surrounded the vessel while three or four, Shardi could not make out how many in the darkness, rowed noisily towards the oncoming boat.

The royal boatmen and soldiers watched as the new boat was first surrounded, and then escorted, towards the royal barge. As it drew near, the escort commander shouted a few commands and the guard boats drew away. A few of the handpicked sentinels of Prince Salim drew their swords and moved towards the bow.

‘Secure amidships,’ cried the Keeper of the Barge, and immediately two of the surrounding boats closed in from port and starboard. The soldiers clambered aboard and encircled the royal quarters with a cluster of them taking positions near the entrance.

The visiting boat approached, and Shardi Beg saw that the escort commander, along with a few of his men, had already boarded it.

‘Keeper of the Barge, request permission to board,’ cried the commander.

‘What business do you have on the royal barge?’ queried Shardi Beg, as he squinted to see in the darkness beyond the torches.

A court noble, whom Shardi recognized as Zamana Beg, shouldered his way forward and spoke. 'There is urgent news for the emperor, Keeper. Lower the steps.'

'Disarm yourself, and just two of you come up the nets. Not the steps,' ordered Shardi Beg, and a climbing net was lowered.

Zamana Beg and another person, who was dressed as a long distance courier with saddle bags and a water *bishti*, were pulled aboard.

The clatter of so many people on deck had alerted the assembly downstairs and the music stopped. Prince Salim on unsteady legs, held by Sharief Khan and Khubu Chishti, and preceded by half a dozen minor nobles, appeared on deck.

The assembled soldiers, boatmen, and nobles bowed low.

'What is it, Zamana Beg?' slurred Salim.

'Your Majesty, this is Hari Chand, a courier from the Agra court, and he brings disturbing news.'

Prince Salim tried to shrug off the supporting arms of his friends, but gave up. He turned his bloodshot eyes towards the messenger, and commanded, 'Speak.'

'Your Highness... His Imperial Majesty, Rajadhiraj Shahenshah Akbar, started on a military campaign against Your Highness on the tenth of August, five days back.' The man did not look up as he spoke.

'Who comes with him?' Salim's tone had become alert.

'He rides at the head of seventy thousand imperial troops, with over two hundred cannons. There are several proven generals with him. But, Your Highness, he sails with the royal barge and a small escort of the Mughal navy. The army moves over land.'

'Why have you come? Who has sent you?' came the query from Sharief Khan, ostensibly the Vizier of Prince Salim's court.

'Sire, my father, Ram Adhir, was a *syce* in the royal stables, and Prince Salim mounted his first horse guided by my father's hand. We have stayed loyal to you, Your Highness, and I rode night and day to warn you.'

Salim furrowed his brows and asked, 'What else do you know?'

Hari Chand lowered his eyes and spoke softly. 'Your Highness, as His Majesty was setting out for the royal pier astride his elephant, he turned to the thousands upon thousands of his *sowars* lined in the quadrangle and beyond and shouted, flourishing his sword, that this expedition was a crusade against flummery and false titles, against treason and pseudo courts, against disobedi—'

Prince Salim straightened up with a jerk, and cried, 'Psuedo courts? Pseudo courts? You have the temerity to stand before me and utter these words? The mountains quail before me, and mighty kings travel over many hundred *kos* to seek the shelter of my hand, and you, an infidel wretch, have called...' Prince Salim, in his umbrage, could not bring himself to utter those hated words.

He turned to Zamana Beg, and said, 'Behead him. He shall pay with his life for sins.'

Hari Chand, in a babble of words, sobs, and incomprehension, threw himself at the prince's feet, wailing for forgiveness. Salim withdrew his gold brocaded shoe and stepped back. His fear, anger, and ego, a deadly combination in the best of situations, wrote another sentence in the satanic court.

Zamana Beg, snatching a long sword from one of the soldiers, dragged Hari Chand over the gunwale, and with a two-handed blow severed his head from his trunk.

'Make for the fort,' commanded Salim.

'Unfurl the main sail. Man the mast,' croaked Shardi Beg.

Numbed by the events they had witnessed, Girdhar and his son jumped to obey. As they pulled at the rigging and untied the knot, the main sail billowed and caught the stiff breeze from starboard.

For a moment, the barge tilted to port, and Prince Salim, who was tottering in his intoxicated state, fell face down on the deck.

Cries of '*Tauba, Tauba,*'and '*Lahoul vila qubat*' followed the attempts by Zamana Beg and a quaking Sharief Khan to help Prince Salim to his feet.

As Salim stood up and wiped some blood from his lips, he turned towards the keeper, and asked ominously, 'Who was responsible?'

Shardi Beg could not help but look towards the main mast, where Girdhar and his son were now cowering. Salim followed his gaze.

'Behead them,' he said roughly as he struggled to find his way downstairs.

As the soldiers dragged Girdhar and Shyamu towards the stern, waves of derision and loathing swept over Shardi Beg. He quietly drew his dagger across his jugular and toppled backwards into the shamed river.

The satanic chapter was now complete.

*

In a corner of the lower deck, behind the silk and brocade curtains, prime minister of the Sultanate and headsman of the kingdom, Sharief Khan, examined his soiled silk trousers. False titles! He wrung his hands, and sobbed in silence.

False titles. Pseudo courts. And Padshah on the move.

He vowed to arrange a swift horse for Kabul. Via Gujarat.

*

IRAJ FORT. BATTLE BETWEEN THE BUNDELAS AND IMPERIAL TROOPS. OCTOBER, 1602 A.D.

(CHAPTER 18)

KHUSHBU-E-SEV

(The Scent of Apples)

The Inner Apartments

Akbari Mahal, Agra Fort

18th August, 1604

11:20 p.m.

A thin sheen of sweat shone on Prince Khurram's face and tightly muscled chest, as he thrust deeper into the warm recesses of the Kashmiri slave girl lying spreadeagled under him. Tonight he had chosen this girl, with the full, round breasts and milky white thighs, over the several Persian, Moslem, and Rajput slave girls available in the harem.

The *khoja sara*, having divined the restless mood of the prince, had brought this Kashmiri girl, and whispered, 'Your Highness, this girl is special – a virgin, she comes from the mountains of Kashmir and carries the scent of the apples with her. Look at her breasts, Your Highness, firm and succulent, just like the ripened fruit.'

'What is your name, girl?'

'Aaliya, Your Highness,' was the reply of the half girl, almost woman, as Prince Khurram reached out to fondle her breasts.

Continuing to stare at her, Khurram squeezed her breasts. A soft whimper escaped her lips as her nipples swelled against his palms.

'Send her to me. And, *Khoja* Hamid, find me a lush pomegranate, too.'

'Yes, Your Highness,' the eunuch Hamid had replied to the retreating back of the young prince. What is it with the Mughals, he had thought – this weird fascination for pomegranates over three generations? First, the mighty Emperor Akbar's attraction for the courtesan, Nadira Begum, and calling her '*Anarkali* – the pomegranate bud', and then his scion, Prince Salim, having dared the emperor's wrath over his illicit liaisons with Anarkali, almost to the point of open rebellion. Now, the third generation of Mughals was seemingly attracted to this wintry fruit which allured with its juicy, red, pearl-like pulp, but actually hid a bitter seed inside.

The slave girl, Aaliya, selected at the age of eleven years by the roving eunuchs of Prince Salim, and thereafter trained in the consummate art of sexual pleasures in the harems of Lahore and Agra, arched her back and ground her pelvis against the thudding groin of the young prince. Prince Khurram continued to push deep inside her, and she lightly raked his back with the tip of her fingers and raised her face to nibble at his chest. She was now starting to find pleasure in the continuous rhythm of his coitus, and the soft whispers of endearment and sighs emanating from her lips were not contrived.

Khurram flexed his elbows and leant down to kiss her inflamed nipples. She arched her back and pushed her breasts into his searching mouth. Khurram straightened up and roughly grabbed her breasts, continuing to tease her swollen nipples.

As his pounding became heavier, faster and deeper, Aaliya whimpered in pleasurable pain, and opened her eyes to see the prince breathing heavily with a demonic, mesmeric glint in his eyes. She clutched his hips and surrendered herself to the tumultuous sensations arising from deep within her.

'I shall tear you apart, limb by rotting limb, Bir Singh Bundela. I shall tear you apart,' cried the young prince as he hammered against the writhing buttocks of Aaliya, and finally came inside her in great shuddering jolts.

*

In the royal apartments at Allahabad fort, his father, Prince Salim, while sinking in and out of opium-induced slumber, was murmuring, 'I shall go to Illahabas, and not Mewar.'

The huge banners of silk strung across the roof swayed mildly in approval.

*

As Khurram rolled on his side and pulled the girl to lie with her head on his shoulders, his eyes, in the weak candlelight of the room, smouldered with unconsummated fury. He had not forgotten, nor ever would, the debilitating sorrow of his most revered Shah Baba at the news of Sheikh Abu'l Fazl's murder. His father Prince Salim's complicity was a source of concealed contempt for the young prince, and the flames of hatred had not diminished in these past twenty months. His eyes flickered as he remembered.

Flashback

Diwan e aam

Agra Fort

18th August, 1602

12:15 p.m; just before Zuhr Namaaz.

Prince Khurram, standing below and to the right of the imperial throne, watched as emperor Jalal Ud Din Akbar stared at the crowd of courtiers, generals, and ahadis *ranged before him. Akbar, attired in mourning robes of white, wore a plain green turban, with a single string of diamonds lacing the curves of the gold aigrette.*

Akbar had not attended court since the news of Abu'l Fazl's cowardly murder had reached him on the thirteenth, and this was his first appearance. His eyes were red and swollen, and, normally prominent, they seemed cocooned in a rim of kohl around the lids. Though not an alcoholic, his cheeks today carried the tell-tale puffiness of a habitual drunkard. His head, in his state of melancholy, dropped even further to the right. Across his knees, in its bejewelled scabbard, lay his royal scimitar, Fath Ul Mulk.

'We, as the emperor of Hindustan, and Defender of the Weak and Poor, as the Slayer of Injustice and Tyranny, do demand from those assembled here their unquestioning loyalty and ceaseless endeavour to punish, to slay, to fetter, and to chain Bir Singh Bundela and his clan. Who steps up?' The gruff voice of Akbar shook the court.

The mighty growl from Akbar had sent shivers down the spines of the gathered Umrahs, *as Akbar, by directly addressing the court, had violated the court decorum of the* Chagatais. *It was unheard of for the emperor to ignore the subtle protocols of the Mughal court and speak thus, unheralded, and indicated the urgency and gravity of the matter.*

Several nobles stepped forward. Akbar's eyes rested on Asad Beg, the escort commander of Sheikh Abu'l Fazl, who had rushed to Agra upon hearing the news from Sironj with a handful of trusted soldiers. The main body of his troops would arrive in a couple of days.

'Asad Beg, you have failed me, and you have failed the Sheikh, who was entrusted to your protection. You have been remiss in your duties.'

'Jahanpanah, my lord, I was unwilling to let the Vizier e Mulk travel alone with the untrained troops of Newta, but...'

'There are no buts, Asad Beg... You were the military escort, and qualified to judge the situation. The harboured boat cannot tell the wind which way to blow. You have erred.' Had the courtiers stood close enough, they would have seen the tears waiting to spill out from Akbar's eyes.

As Asad Beg stood with bated breath, dreading the impending words of amercement, Akbar, in his celebrated role as a judicious and forgiving sovereign, envisioned the derisive mirth with which the Sheikh must have spurned the escort commander's request. His heart softened, but not his eyes.

Akbar turned his gaze towards the nobles who had stepped forward, and addressed Raja Rai Rayan. 'Raja Rai Rayan, you were closest to him with sufficient troops, but Destiny had other plans for our Sheikh. Had the winds of fortune favoured us, the Sheikh would have joined your troops and Bir Singh would have been strung up on the Fort gates.' Akbar's voice had grown hoarse. 'But Allah willed otherwise.'

Rai Rayan moved forward, and spoke. 'Your Majesty! It is my duty to avenge the Sheikh's death, and alleviate your grief. Permit me, Majesty, to proceed.'

Akbar gazed at him for what seemed an eternity in the absolutely silent court. Prince Khurram, seething with fury but encumbered by court protocol, stood motionless with his hand on the hilt of his personal dagger.

Rai Rayan spoke again. 'Your Majesty! For nearly forty summers have I fought under your shadow, and braved as many winters in the lee of Your Majesty. In your youth, I scaled the walls of Chittor with your advance guard. I have served in Bengal and Bihar as your Subedar. From the elephant stables, Sire, you have raised me to your exalted court. I shall die, but I will never let Your Majesty down.'

Akbar rose slowly, and said, 'Raja Rai Rayan, this matter of Bir Singh and his treacherous tribe is now given to you. You will move forth immediately, with sufficient troops, to search and annihilate these scavengers, to destroy, plunder and annex their wretched lands, and to remove their malefic shadows, descendants, and women from the lands of my realm.' The full might of the Mughal empire could be heard in every word.

Rai Rayan performed the chaar taslim, and then turned swiftly to mount his horse tethered near the Dak Chowki at the inner gate.

Cries of 'Allahu Akbar' accompanied the galloping hooves.

*

The Fort of Iraj

On the Betwa River

4th October, 1602

7:30 a.m.

Bir Singh Bundela sat astride his horse facing his clansmen and the assembled troops. His son, Jhujjar Singh, stood on the ramparts near the three main cannons placed on the fort walls, facing the imperial army gathered on the plains below.

'My brothers, and fellow Bundelas. Oppressed is our lot, and barren lands our home. Our mothers, sisters, wives, and innocent children are made to hide in forts such as this, or worse, in the jungles and deserted villages. We know no luxury, but, *we know* freedom*! The Mughals, with their mighty armies and fancy weapons, led by lecherous old men who covet their own sisters and aunts, have never been able to subdue us. But they follow us like scavenging jackals and hyenas.*

'We have gifted the head of that warmonger Abu'l Fazl to Prince Salim, and, it is known all over the Mughaliya lands and beyond, that this single act reduced the great Emperor Akbar to a blabbering fool on his royal floors. We fear not the Mughals – they fear us.

'Pain is not new to us, and fear is not known to us. We are five thousand – they are seventeen thousand. Now, hear this, Oh Bundela warriors – we fight for our freedom, we fight for our honour, we fight for our lands, and we fight for our Sun. Each one of us, blessed by Maa Bhawani, carries the speed of the Wind and the strength of the Heavens with us... WE FIGHT WITH HONOUR, WE FIGHT FOR HONOUR!'

The rousing words of Bir Singh Bundela were answered by the boom of cannons, as the first volley was fired from the fort.

The mighty gates of Iraj Fort were pushed open, and the creaks and groans of the burdened iron hinges were lost in the roar of the Bundela cavalry as they clattered forth carrying their diagonally striped pennants of yellow and black.

*

The Bundela warriors swung to the left of the fort, and rode about half a kos *along the Betwa river. The Mughals in battle array watched this new manoeuvre of the Bundelas with trepidation. Over the last three months they had been led on a fruitless chase through Baroni and Datiya, crossing jungles and ravines, and frequently ambushed by the fleeing Bundelas.*

Rai Rayan, sitting atop his elephant in the vanguard of the royal army, gestured with his sword to encircle the Bundelas between them and the Betwa river. Zamindar Sujan Singh Panwar of Berchha, who was holding the left flank, rode up to Rai Rayan's elephant and shouted, 'Sire, this must be a trick of Bir Singh. There could be additional troops waiting to ambush us from behind.'

Rai Rayan shouted down. 'From where, Sujan Singh?'

Sujan Singh gestured towards the small forested hills beyond Iraj fort, and said, 'From beyond those hills, sire. The village of Dhuni lies there, and it is a familiar setting for Bir Singh... one of his sisters is married there.'

'Sujan Singh, the village of Dhuni is a good day's march from here. Hold your station on the left.'

As Sujan Singh rode off to his designated flank, Rai Rayan shielded his eyes from the sun and followed the progress of his troops. The Mughal artillery was still in its place and was returning the cannon fire from the fort. The elephants and oxen assigned to these artillery pieces were now being brought forward to push and pull them closer to the fort.

As they came within matchlock distance, the armies fired at each other. The archers, following the Mughal cavalry, rushed to the front and shot arrows into the Bundela echelons. The Bundelas, with the war tactics of offering a smaller target, turned smartly towards the arrows and raised their shields in a protective umbrella. A few Bundela horses and riders fell.

The Bundelas turned once again and galloped along the banks of the Betwa in a thin stream of three or four riders abreast. To the Mughal generals it seemed as if a long and thin tail of warriors was streaming against the azure waters of the Betwa. They gave orders to pursue.

As the Mughal cavalry and heavily caparisoned elephants came near the riverside, they were met by a fractured mass of muddy ditches and camouflaged trenches, which held poisoned iron spikes. The struggling elephants and horses were easily getting entangled in these poison pits, which tore apart the hooves and under-pads of the war animals. The horses and elephants, crazed with pain and fear, milled around in frightened chaos. An enraged royal elephant picked up a Mughal rider in his trunk and threw him into a spiked ditch, where he was immediately trampled upon by the heaving mass of an army in disarray. Not satisfied, the tusker swung his head again and dislodged two riders from their horses. Trumpeting, it angrily trampled them underneath its huge paws.

The gates of Iraj again drew open, and fresh squadrons of cavalry poured forth. They bore into the left flank of the Mughals held by Zamindar Sujan Singh Panwar and Jamal Khan, son of Khan Zaman. As they hacked and cleaved their path into the Mughal cavalry, the difference between the Bundela troops and the imperial troopers became evident.

The Bundelas, being fierce, independent warriors, needed no instructions to assail the enemy. Their one objective was to kill or maim as many as they could. They were fighting for their lives.

The Mughal soldiers, on the other hand, were trained to fight in rigid echelons, and looked up to their chieftains for directions. Their one objective was to survive the day. They were fighting for money and plundered loot.

Sujan Singh Panwar reeled at the fierce Bundela onslaught and galloped away with his fifteen hundred riders, leaving the Mughal left flank undefended. Jamal Khan, assessing vulnerability, roused his followers and made a brave charge into the ghoulish mass of the shrieking Bundelas. The clang of swords and the screams of dying men and animals remained the all-pervading sound.

As Jamal Khan leaned down to spike a Bundela warrior he had just unseated from his horse, a sharp, stabbing pain made him wheel around. Rewati Raman, a minor Bundela chief, had thrust his lance into the unprotected abdomen of Khan. As Jamal tried to pull out the embedded lance from his stomach, a two-handed blow from Rewati Raman's scimitar neatly severed his right forearm from below his elbow. Jamal Khan toppled into the dust with the embedded lance guiding him with infinite accuracy into the realms of macabre death.

The initial body of Bundelas who had ridden out from the fort and along the banks of the Betwa now wheeled around and engaged the right flank and rear of the Mughal troops. Bir Singh and his men did not cut deep into the Moghul lines, but skimmed across the outer ranks of the imperial soldiers, cutting them down with impunity. By the time the middle and inner ranks arranged themselves to charge, the Bundelas disengaged and rushed off. The few royal soldiers who were foolish enough to pursue were quickly encircled by groups of Bundelas and mercilessly hacked to pieces.

A short trumpet call, and the Bundelas streaked towards the opening gates of Iraj Fort.

The Mughals, in unusual disarray, limped towards their staging ground, half a kos *from the blood-washed basins of the Betwa.*

*

Iraj Fort

Same night

11:35 p.m.

The cannons boomed once again from the battlements of the silent fort, camouflaging for a few minutes the recurrent whimpers and groans of the wounded and the crippled.

Towards the rear of the fort, a band of soldiers with pick axes and hammers, were toiling at a fortified wall, which had been partially breached by blowing up a few drums of gunpowder a few minutes earlier.

*

Mughal Camp

One *kos* from Iraj Fort

Same time

Zamindar Partap Rao, on night vigil with his troops, looked at the flame-spouting cannons of the Iraj Fort, and spat in disgust. Bloody idiots, he mused, expending their ammunition on an enemy that was out of their range.

As his troops had not participated in the battle and were rested, he decided to send a large posse of archers and cavalry ahead to reconnoitre, and to ensure that the Bundelas were not preparing for a night assault.

The cannons of Iraj continued to spew fire and iron nails into the cold October night, without aim or purpose.

*

Iraj Fort

12:48 a.m.

Stooping low through the small breach created in the fort wall, Bir Singh Bundela walked through the debris, leading his horse by the bridle. His son, Jhujjar Singh with a few chosen body guards, had gone ahead. The calm waters of the Betwa, and the forested hills beyond, silently beckoned the beleaguered warriors.

Shrouded in blankets against the October chill, the Bundelas slipped quietly into the moonless night.

The cannons, handled by a skeleton crew of the walking wounded, continued to vomit in derisive mirth.

*

Royal Apartments

Akbari Mahal, Agra Fort

27th April, 1604

1:20 a.m.

As Khurram cradled the young Kashmiri girl, Aaliya, in his arms, a faint smell of apples permeated the air. He turned his face into her tresses, but they smelled of jasmine and lavender. He nuzzled her long neck, but could smell only jasmine. He pulled her closer and softly ran his hands around the curve of her buttocks, and onto her thighs. The smell of apples seemed to pursue his roving hands.

Aaliya, in light slumber, moved closer to Khurram and draped her shapely thighs over his legs. She moved her head a few inches and settled comfortably in the crook of his shoulders as he sought her breasts with his hand. Yes, thought Khurram, the smell of apples is unmistakable and is definitely coming from my hands!

He moved his hands over her breasts and leaned to kiss her turgid nipples. As his lips teased and caressed her swollen nipples, the smell of apples from his hands cupping her breasts once more assailed his nostrils.

He put his finger under her chin, and softly kissed her closed eyelids. As she nuzzled closer, Khurram cupped her face in his hands and gently bit her on her lips. She smiled in slumberous pleasure and tried to open her eyes. Instinctively, her hand reached down to hold his rigid member.

'Hey, girl. Wake up.'

She smiled, and, caressing his swollen penis, gently traced her fingers over his groin, where the first wisps of pubic hair were making their appearance.

'I am awake, Your Majesty... and, so are you.' His penis throbbed in her warm hands.

'Tell me, Aaliya... why is it that the scent of apples is on my hands ever since I made love to you? You can smell it too, I am sure. Your body smells of the harem jasmine and lavender oils, but this scent of apples follows me.'

Aaliya sat up and, putting her hands on Khurram's chest, softly said, 'Your Majesty, when I was seven or eight years old, I gave water to drink to a tired *fakir* who was sitting under a tamarind tree. I also gave him my half-eaten apple as he looked weary and hungry to me. The *fakir* blessed me and said, "Child, the first man who loves you will forever carry the scent of your apple until his dying day. He will never forget you, and shall remember you on his dying breath."'

Khurram smiled and pulled her astride his inflamed member. As she sank onto the tumescent penis and put her hands on his muscular chest, she exclaimed happily, 'My young prince – I know now that you love me.'

'Yes, I do, Aaliya,' whispered Khurram as he reached out to knead her breasts.

*

(CHAPTER 19)

KILLATE ABE RUD E JUMNA

(Shallow Flows the Jumna)

The Royal Encampment

Banks of River Jumna

Two *kos* from Kalpi

19th August, 1604

Just before midnight

In the hot, humid, August night, Akbar was finding it difficult to sleep. He tossed around on his bed and, finding no respite from either the suffocating heat or the mental trauma of fathering a rebellious and recalcitrant son and heir apparent, Akbar partially opened his worry laden eyes.

The fan bearer, dozing in his servitude, felt the eyes of the emperor upon him. Not daring to open his eyes, lest his soporific state be deduced, he changed his position on the floor and started pulling the fan with renewed vigour.

Akbar rose and stepped outside the royal tent. Since he was travelling by boat, the regular paraphernalia of a Mughal army on the march was missing, as was his enormous war tent. The temporary tent put up here was neither as commodious nor luxurious as his crimson war tent. Surrounding him on all sides were the tents and shelters of the nobles and the five thousand cavalry sailing with the emperor.

Just three days before, on a moonless night, the imperial barge had drifted from its moorings and had struck a sandbar on the starboard prow. The other barges of the royal navy, as well as the boats and barges of the *Amirs* and the escorting troops, quickly closed in and the emperor was transferred to a hurriedly pitched tent on the river shore.

A fusillade of shots was fired by the musket men of the emperor's personal bodyguard to alert the imperial army, which was quartered hardly half a *kos* away. It was a Mughal martial strategy that the imperial army on land always followed the royal barge in visual sight. The gunshots fired from the shoreline immediately brought forward the advance troops of Rajputs and Uzbegs who were on sentry duty, and, finding the emperor ensconced on the muddy, sandy shores, quickly set up a defensive perimeter.

The night breeze felt laden with rain to Akbar, and he welcomed the signs. The monsoons were much delayed, and the cultivators and general populace were growing restless – the empire could do without a bad monsoon, thought Akbar.

He might yet have to relax the tax on land if monsoons did not appear soon. As he paced about on the muddy shores, his prized elephant Bal Sundar trumpeted. Akbar smiled as he remembered his favourite war elephants, Bal Sundar and

Saman, being forcibly loaded onto their respective barges with two female elephants to keep them company.

Of these two huge war elephants, Bal Sundar was quite a character. Though ferocious in war, and capable of tolerating terrible pain, so essential in the emperor's war elephant, he provided moments of comic relief. His favourite pastime was to shower his *mahout* with mud and miscellaneous debris, especially when the *mahout* was freshly bathed, or was having a meal. The *mahout*, Govindraja, was an equally devious character, and, after every such shower, would carefully wrap Bal Sundar's bale of sugarcane in a brightly sequined cloth of red silk and lay it before him. The *khasa* elephants, especially those of the emperor's own retinue, were trained to pay obeisance to the emperor. Bal Sundar, mistaking the bright silk to be the emperor's accoutrement, would go down on his front legs and repeatedly trumpet in salute. After a few choice abuses, Govindraja would reverentially untie the bundle and, touching the cloth to his forehead, would fold and put it away for another day, another ruse.

Akbar walked towards his two war elephants, both chained to huge stalks of wood, murmuring his customary elephant speak. Bal Sundar and Saman both squealed in delight and started shaking their great heads.

The *ahadis*, following Akbar at a distance, watched the emperor gently stroking the extended trunks of the mammoth beasts with soft whispers of endearment. One of the *ahadis* commented to another, 'Look at them... it seems as if the beasts are smiling.'

The others peered into the darkness, and Kambaksh Durrani, who had served the emperor for many years, remarked, 'That is so. Men, beasts and birds... all are ruled by His Majesty.'

'All, excepting his own son.'

In a split second, the speaker, Ali Mardan, distantly related to the disaffected courtier Al-Badauni, was on the ground with a couple of swords at his neck. An Afghan by birth, he had recently been admitted to the personal bodyguard of the emperor at the express request of Al-Baduani.

As Akbar watched from a distance, he saw an *ahadi* being dragged away. He looked at Kambaksh Durrani, and, satisfied with the unperturbed posture, walked further on.

He wished he had worn the heavier shoes – these soft shoes were not meant for squishing around on the muddy shores. As he stepped onto drier ground, he saw a small fire being lit in the distance. Akbar looked keenly, and saw a man, possibly a *fakir* carrying a staff, going around the fire. He quickened his pace.

Akbar stopped when he was about sixty feet away – the half-naked *sadhu*,a Hindu saint, was sitting cross-legged before the fire, and throwing twigs into it. Akbar shuffled his feet, and the sage looked up.

The *sadhu*,who had piercing black eyes and long, matted hair, beckoned him closer. 'Come, my child,' he said.

Akbar walked up and greeted him with folded hands. The *sadhu* unwrapped another rug from his small parcel of belongings and spread it on the rough ground. He indicated for the emperor to sit.

Both of them sat in silence as the sage continued to throw small sticks and twigs into the fire. After a few minutes, he looked at Akbar, as if expecting some questions.

'Revered saint... why do you keep throwing twigs into the fire without purpose? I see you utter no *aiyats* or prayers. What is it that you seek?'

'I seek to quench the hunger of Fire. You see, Fire has a great hunger, so great in fact, that it devours its own feet! Do you understand, my child?'

'No, sire. I just see you idly throwing twigs, for no purpose.'

'There is a purpose, child. I can see Fire demanding huge amounts of firewood for the funeral pyres, and wood for the coffins, for yonder army that follows you. I am trying to satiate Fire's hunger by feeding him wooden sticks, twigs, and prayers for the dead, so that these sons, brothers, and husbands who follow you, clad in arms, maybe spared the fate of death. And Fire, satiated.'

Akbar was stunned. The depth of the saint's words and their implied ramifications left him speechless. The *sadhu* continued to throw twigs and sticks.

After a few minutes, Akbar asked him, 'Most revered sage... This means that the voyage does not augur well for me?'

'This voyage is but a small ripple in the larger voyage of life, *Shahenshah*!'

'Please call me child, sire. I had forgotten how it felt to be a child.'

The saint smiled faintly as Akbar continued. 'You do not have to say anything, revered sage. I know the portends when I see one. I know that hitting a sandbar is an inauspicious beginning, and maybe I should wait a few more days before embarking.'

The sage turned to face Akbar, and quietly remarked, 'Who knows the beginning? Who knows the end? Who can define what is good and what is bad? The beaching of your barge on that sandbar, which seems a bad omen to you, must be perceived as a boon to your poor soldiers who would be thanking God, in His Eternal Majesty, of the few more days that they have been blessed with.'

The *sadhu* returned to his task of throwing twigs into the fire.

Akbar fingered his rings and spoke to the burning fire. 'I chose to travel by river, as it is monsoon and the Jumna runs deep. It is not in spate because the river Chambal, which enters the Jumna near Etawah, is still dry due to inconsequential rains. Otherwise, there would have been no sandbar collision.'

'Child, listen carefully. Jumna, the River Goddess, is a Divine Mother for all of us. Though she is the sister of Yamraj, the God of Death, she abhors fighting and bloodshed amongst her children. She abhors the idea of a father setting out to fatally punish his son with arms and gunpowder, no matter how untrue, disobedient, and evil that son may be. She knows that you will crush his worthless head under the mighty feet of your war elephants, and in doing so, undo all that you have striven for in these last forty-five years. She also knows that your mother needs you at Agra, hence... *Shallow flows the Jumna*!'

Tears were rolling freely down Akbar's cheeks as he remembered his last meeting with his mother, the Revered Mariam Makani, confined to her bed, and gasping for breath due to her respiratory disorder.

'Go, my son, go. Your mother calls.'

The mystic raised his hands to bless Akbar, who had wordlessly bowed in obeisance.

As Akbar got up to leave, he quietly turned towards the dark waters of Jumna, and, bowing his head in reverence, brought his right palm to his chest.

And, shallow flowed the Jumna!

*

Same night

Royal Tent on Jumna bank.

Ever since his return from the mystic's presence, the emperor had not been able to sleep. The future of his kingdom, which he had so assiduously acquired through valour, stealth, and guile, seemed to be possessed of a dark shadow. Akbar was no novice to the world of spiritualism, and was blessed with a psychic cloak of his own. He well understood the words of adepts and master, as well as their theologies of Faith and Fate.

He turned towards the flame burning in its silver vessel and willed his eyes to sleep. It seemed as if only moments later he was awakened by the call of the sentry commander from just outside the tent.

Akbar snapped, 'What is it?'

'Your Majesty, the *Mir Bakshi* requests your audience. There is an important report from Illahabas.'

'Let him enter, *Qorchi*.'

The *Mir Bakshi* prostrated himself, and spoke. 'Blessed am I, Your Majesty, at beholding your divine self with the welcoming rays of dawn.'

Akbar nodded, and asked, 'What is the report about, Khane Khanan?'

'Your Majesty, this report has been sent by Abdul Qasim, who is the personal fly whisk bearer of Prince Salim, and a faithful spy in Your Majesty's army. The news is disturbing, as it seems to imply that a sacrilege committed by Prince Salim has offended the Hindu majority of Illahabas and its satellite areas. May I read the report, Sire?'

Akbar, festooned with worries and doubts, merely nodded his head.

'For the eyes of Mughaliya Shahenshah and Padshah Ghazi, Jalal Ud Din Mohammed Akbar, Sovereign of the Realm! Padshah Salamat!

It is with utmost regret, and a sense of personal disgrace, that I submit this report to your ethereal eyes.

On the ninth of August, His Highness Prince Salim, while attending the Hall of Public Audience, was apprised by the usurpant Wazir, Sharief Khan and Khubu Khan Chishti, about a Hindu Temple of Lord Hanuman, the monkey faced God of the Hindus, which lies just outside the south-west corner of Allahabad fort...'

Akbar interrupted curtly, 'Tell the writer that it is Illahabas Fort for us. Continue.'

'...just outside the south-west corner of Illahabas Fort. As soon as His Highness was informed about the "sleeping" position of the deity for hundreds of years, the young prince ordered the statue to be transported inside the fort, and to be consigned to the dungeons. There was much disaffection within the court, as well as outside, between Hindus and Moslems alike.

The next morning, a group of slaves was sent to raise and bring the statue inside the fort. Dusk fell and nothing was achieved. In the evening, Prince Salim was apprised by Sharief Khan in the Diwan e Khas of the failure, and Prince Salim, vexed and agitated in his highly inebriated state, rode out to the temple with all the court nobles and a fresh group of slaves and oxen.

This temple, as Your Majesty may be aware, predates the presence of our Most Revered Padshah Jannat Makani, Zahir Ud Din Mohammed Babur and His Most Regal Descendants, by many hundreds of years. This temple, with the sleeping statue of Lord Hanuman, was discovered in the year 1119 AD, almost four hundred years ago, by a much venerated Hindu saint, Maharaj Balagiri. Legend says that as soon as Maharaj Balagiri, who was also known as 'Baghambari Baba' (for he wore tiger skin) drove his trident into the sandy shores near the fort, he felt the presence of a Divine Being. As he dug with his hands, the peacefully supine statue of Lord Hanuman appeared from underneath. All efforts then, and since, to raise the recumbent statue have failed. This idol is much revered and a temporary shelter has been raised.

The fresh efforts to dig and raise the idol, with the help of scores of slaves, court wrestlers, and baggage oxen, only led to the statue embedding itself deeper into the ground. Frustrated and incoherent with rage, Prince Salim committed the sacrilege of flinging vituperative abuses at the deity.

The silent, angry stares of the slaves, merchants, Rajput nobles, and troops were a precursor of troubles to come.

The next morning, as the news spread, there was widespread consternation and anger at the Prince's blasphemous behaviour.

As I write my report to Your Highness, the prospect of a Hindu rebellion, led by the Rajputs, is a very real situation. There are dark rumours of an armed uprising on the second of October, on which date Dussehra falls this year. This date has been carefully chosen as it symbolizes the victory of Good over Evil.

I shall keep Your Imperial Majesty informed of all developments, and pray for a long and victorious reign of our Most Revered Al-Sultan Al-Azam, Imam I Adil, Padshah Ghazi Zil'Ullah, Abu'l Fath Jalal Ud Din Mohammed Akbar, Sultanat Salamat!

Your most obedient servant,

Investigative Chronicler

And a speck of dust on your Golden Realm,

Abdul Qasim Khursani'

Emperor Akbar kept quiet, and thought for a few minutes, as the *Mir Bakshi* remained standing, waiting for further orders.

Grimly, Akbar said, 'Let the Gods speak. Let Salim cook in his own stew.'

The *Mir Bakshi* paid obeisance and withdrew, bewildered. It was the first time ever in recalled memory that Akbar had referred to Prince Salim as anything but Sheikhu.

The Gods were indeed speaking.

Royal Camp

Banks of the Jumna, near Kalpi

20th August 1604

10:30 a.m.

Akbar was still in a quandary as to his immediate course of action. He had visited the Hindu *sadhu*'s site early in the morning and had seen no tell-tale signs of the fire pit from the night before... no ashes, no smouldering embers, no heat signatures on the ground. But, yes, carefully tucked beneath a stone slab was a large piece of raw silk in royal blue. It was so incongruous in these muddy, desolate surroundings that Akbar picked it up. Immediately he was assailed by the sweet fragrance of the lavender attar which his revered mother Mariam Makani always wore.

Tears welled in his eyes at this sweet reminder – a parting gift from the learned sage. Akbar's mind was now made up as he gave rushed orders to break camp and return to the fortress at Agra.

Mother is calling...

*

(CHAPTER 20)

BAYAAN-I-ASAD BEG

(Report of Asad Beg)

Kutubkhana **(Library)**

Agra Fort

24th August, 1604

10:40 a.m.

Prince Khurram entered the *Kutubkhana* and walked slowly through the rows upon rows of beautifully bound volumes of Persian, Arabic, and Turqic manuscripts and scrolls with small, triangular flags of silk dividing the different sections. These marker flags were in different colours to denote their importance – purple for those in which the emperor had personally shown interest, green for books on Islamic traditions and religions, golden for books relating to different lands, their philosophies and geography; the most important colour code was red, which denoted the section preserving the *Shahi Firmaans, Mansurs, Nishans, and Parvanahs* of the Imperial Court. Some of the official reports, considered critical at the emperor's orders, were also bound in red muslin and preserved with the royal manuscripts.

'Your Highness, welcome. We are graced by your noble presence today, Sire!' the chief librarian bowed low and performed the *chaar taslim*.

'Thank you, *Mir Kutub*! It is nice to see the emperor's most cherished books so well looked after. You do know that the emperor is hastening back to Agra on account of Her Majesty, Mariam Uz Zamani's indifferent health?'

'Yes, Your Highness. We are aware of His Majesty's arrival by tonight, or tomorrow afternoon. We are told that he is but two stages away from his royal abode. And, Your Highness, may Allah, in His Grace and Mercy, provide many more years to Her Majesty, the Dowager Empress.'

Prince Khurram looked around at the library attendants standing with heads bowed, and inquired of the chief librarian, '*Mir Kutub*, I wish to see the official report submitted by Commander Asad Beg on the Bundelas.'

'Yes, Your Highness.' The chief librarian gestured to an attendant.

The attendant appeared in a few moments, and, bowing low to the prince, handed over a red muslin wrapped scroll to the *Kutub Mir*.

The librarian carefully unwrapped the scroll and led Prince Khurram to a low divan with gilded bolsters. As the prince adjusted his sword and sat down, two attendants quickly moved behind a screen and started pulling the silk banner suspended overhead for air circulation.

Khurram unfurled the scroll and started reading:

'The Royal Fort

Gwalior

6th July, 1604

In the service of His Imperial Majesty, the Mughaliya King and Padshah Ghazi, Jalal Ud Din Mohammed Akbar, Sovereign of the Eternal Reign...

Under orders from your Imperial Majesty, I proceeded from your Eternal Court at Agra to the forests and rivers of Bundelkhand. In my search for truth, which Your Majesty so richly desires, I visited all the known and unknown places in thy kingdom, from where treacherous serpents had raised their ugly heads against Your Majesty and your empire.

It is with utmost respect, and the highest fear, that I submit to thee the spiels of lies, treachery and folly which our generals have committed over the last two years. And, it is only with my knowledge of your goodness and lofty spires of forgiveness that I venture to point an accusing finger at the royal camp, far removed from Your Imperial Presence, where the flame of perfidy was first lit, and then nurtured, to claim the life of one so innocent and gifted as our Vizier Ul Mulk, Sheikh Abu'l Fazl Ibn Mubar ak, may he rest in peace.

It is true that Rai Rayan did enter the ravines of Bhind and Moraina with the imperial army put at his disposal. The wings of Raj Singh of Kachhawa and Ram Sah Bundela provided the flank guards against the fleeting, but severe attacks from the Bundelas.

In several encounters, the cowardly criminal Bir Singh was defeated and barely managed to escape with his hide and horse from the wrath of your imperial troops. They tried their best to thwart the imperial army by poisoning their own wells, which not only endangered our soldiers, but several villages in that region were wiped out on account of this heinous act of the fleeing Bundelas.

Seeking shelter in the fort of Iraj, they were besieged and then singularly defeated in a day-long battle fought along the banks of the Betwa. As the imperial army prepared to storm the fort early next morning, Bir Singh and his wretched followers, sheltered by the hand of treachery, breached the fort walls and escaped.

The fort was captured next morning, and the surviving enemy soldiers annihilated, but a grave mistake was committed by the general – Rai Rayan. Instead of pursuing the Bundelas, who would have initially trekked slowly to escape detection, and hence could not have covered much distance in the four intervening hours, the Moghuls failed to set their swift horses in pursuit. All three generals were remiss in their duties, and careless in their obedience of your orders to destroy Bir Singh Deo, as they preferred to sit and rejoice in the comfort of their victory than to purge with blood this curse of the Bundelas.

After wasting over a week at Iraj, and making Indarjit the fort commander, with a holding garrison of two thousand troops, the generals Rai Rayan Patr Das, Raj Singh Kachawa, and Ram Sah Bundela retired with their cavalry to the fort of Gwalior.

In the investigations directed by Your Majesty, it has been established by inquiries with several pradhans, daroghas, *and* dak chowkis *in the region, that Bir Singh initially took refuge in the village of Dhuni, about eight* kos *from Iraj. He was sheltered by the local warlords, and by the extended family of Chaturbhuj Shreshtha, into which his sister is married. After staying for a week, and with the departure of the Mughal army to Gwalior, Bir Singh fearlessly rode back to Datiya.*

With utmost regret and shame, I venture to report that there he was received with much kindness and warmth by Prince Salim, who was encamped at Datiya on his way to Agra.

As such matters are in shrouds of deceit and veiled from the eyes of the virtuous, may I hasten to add that Her Royal Highness Begum Salima Sultan, who was travelling with the prince, was completely ignorant of the above tryst. Please forgive me, Majesty, if I have crossed the threshold of my service to Your Grace.

It has also been established that sowars *from Prince Salim's entourage frequently carried* nishans *to Rai Rayan and the Kachhawa noble, urging them to desist from any extraordinary or severely damaging action against the Bundelas.*

As I will never have the courage, or the will, to disguise anything from Your Imperial Gaze, I humbly submit that Rai Rayan Patr Das, on being apprised of the custom of my investigative duties, did try to lead me astray with trays of gold mohurs and jewels.

I write this not as I rue my destiny, and my honour, in protecting the Vizier Ul Mulk, but as a loyal soldier in Your Majesty's service.

I submit myself to the mercy and benefaction of Your Majesty!

In words and deeds, your eternal servant,

Asad Beg'

*

(CHAPTER 21)

SUTUN-E-MUNKASAR

(The Shattered Pillar)

The Royal Pier

Jumna river front, Agra Fort

9th September, 1604

8:43 a.m.

The emperor was expected to arrive by dawn, but the blue expanse of the Jumna to the right of the Agra Fort remained deserted, save for small barges and boats, which had sailed last night under orders from *Mir Bahri* to receive the emperor from the river bracket nearly ten miles downstream.

The *Mir Bahri*, Mustaid Khan Turrani,was himself sailing in a galley with handpicked *ahadis* to welcome and escort the emperor back to his royal court. As he stood by the lower mast pole on the deck, Mustaid Khan pondered his future.

The beaching of the royal barge on a sandbar had caused hours of serious anxiety to him, as it reflected on the boatmanship and training of his boatmen. Allah knew, thought Mustaid, that the very best of crew had been sent, and the barge had been minutely inspected for leaks, corrosion, or structural flaws. For almost a week, he had spent long hours weeping and fretting over his doomed fate. However, the news of Akbar's intention to return on account of Her Majesty, Mariam Makani's worsening condition, and the devastating rain squalls, had been received with a great sense of relief. Nevertheless, doubts about the emperor's reaction to the sailing fiasco nagged him time and again.

Reports of the emperor's return were received almost daily. The emperor had initially sailed back towards Agra; special couriers sent by the Agra Fort Commander Qulich Khan intercepted the royal armada just before Etawah and conveyed the news that Her Majesty, the Queen Dowager, was not expected to survive for long.

Akbar immediately switched to travelling over land in a bid to hasten his return. Unfortunately, the same night, heavy thunder showers and squalls set in, almost ruining the provisions and gunpowder of the imperial army, which were stored in hastily erected tents. The thunderstorm and squalls continued unabated for three days, leaving the imperial camp in ruins.

Jumna, joined by a raging Chambal, a major tributary from the hilly tracts of Bundelkhand, was in spate. There were reports of spontaneous whirlpools and swift currents from the coastal populace. The imperial army had no option but to halt.

After five days of ruinous rain, Akbar could wait no longer. Since the ground was muddy and treacherous with rain-filled craters, elephants were ruled out. Horses, too, with their fragile legs more suited for sprinting and cross-country travel over visible ground, could not quickly cover inundated fields and rain-filled ditches. The emperor again switched to his barge.

The thoughts of the *Mir Bahri* were broken by the loud cry of the *Panjari* posted in the crow's nest on the main mast.

'Hail, the emperor! I can see the royal flag,' cried the lookout, cupping his hands.

The blare of trumpets, rattle of kettledrums and cries of '*Manzil Mubarak*! *Padshah Salamat*!'announced the arrival of the emperor, as the green and gold Mughal flag of the couchant lion against the rising sun was hoisted on the yardarm of the royal flotilla.

*

Mariam Makani's Royal Chamber

Royal Harem, Agra Fort

10th September, 1604

4 a.m.

Emperor Akbar called anxiously, 'Hakim Gilani... come quickly! She is opening her eyes.'

Hakim Gilani, standing by the door, rushed to her side and took her wrists in his hands. The emperor, sitting at her bedside since yesterday morning, stood up and leaned closer. The Empress Dowager, as if sensing Akbar's presence on her left, turned her face towards him. She opened her eyes and gave a wan smile.

Akbar looked at the still, smiling face of his mother, now in her seventy-eighth year, and felt the knot of overpowering grief tightening his throat. Her face remained unlined, a lying testimony to all the hardships which she had endured as a nomadic empress ever since her marriage to the tragic *Arsh*

Ashiyani, Emperor Humayun. Her stoic demeanour had been like a permanent umbrella for the young Akbar, and had shielded him from the arrows of fire, treachery and deceit.

Hakim Gilani, eyes red with unshed tears, quietly put her hand back on the bed, and started reciting the *kalma*.Wails and lamentations arose from the queens, concubines, and female attendants assembled there, as the finality of her death struck home. Great heaving sobs wracked the emperor's body as he continued to hold his mother's lifeless hands. Hakim Ali quietly closed her vacuous eyes.

The deafening silence from the *naubatkhana* at dawn announced the tragedy to an anxious city. While news of the Empress Dowager's critical illness had been known to the citizens for almost a week now, spiced up by daily reports from the palace eunuchs and city merchants to the court, the city had continued to believe that the good fortune of their God-King would not allow any unfortunate event to arise.

An anxious, silent crowd was gathering on the royal grounds facing the *jharokha* for their daily sighting of the emperor. The crowd grew restless as the royal balcony remained deserted. Finally, a group of horsemen in white robes emerged from the main gate.

The *Makhdum-Ul-Mulk*, wearing a blue kerchief on his wrist, slowly rode to the midst of the silent thousands, and, surrounded by his eleven *ulemas* sporting black turbans, cleared his throat and spoke. 'This morning, at *Sehr*, Her Imperial Majesty, the Queen Mother, Maryam Makani' left us to join Allah, at her rightful place in the Celestial Empire. Our emperor, Al-Sultan Al-Azam, Wal Khaqan Al-Mukarram, Sahib-i-Zaman, Jalal Ud Din Mohammed Akbar, Padshah Ghazi, remains in sovereign rule, and thanks you from the depths of his heart for your sharing of his colossal grief. At the same time, be advised that all forms of entertainment are banned for the next seven days. The *Salat-Al- Janaza* shall be read just before *Zuhr namaaz*, in the royal forecourt. May Allah bestow His immense mercy on the departed soul and our *Padshah Ghazi*.'

As the words of the funeral prayer faded, the emperor, shorn of hair, beard, moustaches, and eyebrows, bent down to lift the wooden coffin of his mother, laden with strings of gold, silver, and flowers.

His grandson, Prince Khurram, bore the coffin from the other end, as all the *Umeras* surged to put their shoulders to the royal casket.

One thousand four hundred of the *Umeras* had shorn their heads in honour of the *Arsh Ashiyani Mariam Makani*, and as a show of solidarity with their grieving emperor.

(CHAPTER 22)

TU BUZDIL EI!

(Thou Art a Coward!)

Diwan e Aam

Agra Fort

9th November 1604,

10:40 a.m.

The *Diwan e Aam* was crowded with nobles, plaintiffs, soldiers, and court attendants. As far as the eye could see, the concourse was full of colourful turbans and glittering lances. Scabbards in gold, red, black, and emerald green swayed ominously with their lethal residents and the forecourt was resplendent with the Mughal insignias of the couchant lion, and pennants in green and gold.

There was a sudden flurry of intense activity outside, as the *naqqaras* announced the arrival of a court grandee. Soon, the royal standards of Prince Salim could be seen, paraded in front of the war elephant carrying the prince. As they approached the forecourt, the prince dismounted and climbed the seven steps to the Hall of Public Audience.

Salim walked with measured steps to within fifteen paces of the imperial throne, and stood with bowed head. His fifteen-year-old son, Prince Parvez Mirza, stood slightly behind him, and gazed curiously at the attendees and paraphernalia of the magnificent court. Well versed in Timurid protocol, he did not raise his eyes to gaze at his grandfather, the emperor.

The voice of the *Mir Tozak* rang out. 'In the grace of His Majesty, *Shahenshah e Hind*, Jalal Ud Din Mohammed Akbar, prostrates his beloved son, the Governor of Illahabas, Bihar, Bengal, and Odisha, Prince Mirza Salim Sultan.'

Emperor Akbar watched with a faint smile as the renegade prince of several years prostrated himself in full court. He let the prince remain in the *zaminbos* posture for a few moments too many – the surrender must be absolute and unconditional. There was complete silence in the court as a hundred pairs of eyes darted between the recumbent form of the errant prince, and the compelling majesty of the emperor.

As Akbar descended from his throne and walked with outstretched arms towards the prince, there was a palpable sigh of relief from the royal ladies of the harem, who had assembled behind the stone filigreed upper chambers in large numbers to witness the historic return of the recalcitrant son.

'Rise, Sheikhu, rise.' There was happiness and relief in the emperor's voice.

The Prince rose to be embraced by a smiling Akbar. 'I have erred, Your Majesty. Please forgive me.'

The emperor held his shoulders and looked him over with affection. 'Welcome home, Sheikhu. The sun may disappear every evening, but it reappears the next morning.'

The highly descriptive pun was not lost on Prince Salim, as, teary eyed, he whispered, 'You are most kind and forgiving, Majesty.'

The voice of the *Mir Tozak* rang out again. 'Prince Mirza Parvez, son of Prince Mirza Salim Sultan, submits to the affectionate protection of His Majesty, *Shahenshah e Hind*, Protector of the Realm, Abul Fath Jalal Ud Din Mohammed Akbar, *Padshah Ghazi*!'

Prince Parvez, in his youthful energy and the intimidation of the moment, almost threw himself at the emperor's feet. Akbar, his face radiating happiness, quickly brought him up in a warm embrace.

Holding him at arm's length, he cupped his chin, and said, 'Well, Parvez, I can see that you have been tutored well by Sheikh Abu'l Fazl. I saw you last as a sweet child of twelve, now you are a fine young man!'

'At your service, Majesty,' the prince replied with formal courtesy.

Akbar walked back to his throne, with Prince Salim and Parvez following. Cries of '*Mubarak, Mubarak*,' rose from the assembled nobles and the royal ladies sitting in the upper floor behind stone filigreed screens. The prince and his son took their customary privileged position to the right, and nearest the throne.

The *Mir Tozak* stepped forward, and, unrolling a golden tasselled scroll, announced, 'The governor of *Suba* Illahabas, Bihar, Bengal, and Odisha, Prince Mirza Salim Sultan, does present at the glorious feet of our monarch, the lavish gifts of his affection and allegiance. The mightiest of the war elephants – four hundred of them!'

'*Masha Allah*!' exclaimed Akbar, delighted, as the first and the most monstrous of the war elephants raised his trunk in salute.

'His name is Qaimur,Majesty, and he is as fierce and bold in battle as his form suggests,' Prince Salim proudly informed him.

There was genuine delight on the emperor's face as the other 399 elephants passed in squadrons of twelve.

As the other gifts of gold *mohurs*, a rare, priceless diamond, and trays of precious stones were laid at the emperor's feet and then whisked away, many of the nobles who had painted Prince Salim as a renegade and a traitor to the favours of his father, softened their revulsion at this open display of subjugation and familial affection from the prince.

It was almost close to the time for *Zuhr* prayers when Akbar rose for his afternoon meal. While dismissing the court, his regal voice boomed. 'This is a most fortunate day for us. The return of Prince Salim to the Timurid court augurs well for his safety and long life.' He cast an oblique glance at the startled face of Salim – the implied threat was not lost on him.

He continued. 'To mark this day of rejoicing, we order that the imperial kitchens be made open for a period of three days to the people of Agra. Let there be feasting and music.'

The emperor turned for the aisle leading to his personal chambers in the seraglio. Prince Salim and Prince Parvez followed him inside.

The *Mir Bakshi*, *Mir Saman*, and the *Mir Bakawal* hastened to initiate preparations for a city feast.

*

The midday meal had taken the better part of an hour, as the royal ladies fussed over Prince Parvez and Prince Salim.

The sudden transformation of a child into a handsome young prince of marriageable age ensured a lively discussion during lunch.

Akbar, recognizing the importance of this occasion, did not dine alone but preferred to eat in the company of Prince Salim and the senior Begums.

Begum Salima Sultan playfully caught Prince Parvez's cheeks and announced, 'I have found the perfect wife for our handsome prince.'

This announcement was met with much merriment and a host of questions from the curious Begums. Salima Begum happily replied, 'Who could be better suited for our handsome prince than Iffat Jahan Banu, pretty daughter of our beloved Prince Murad, may he rest in peace.'

Prince Parvez flushed a deep red as Akbar stopped eating and looked speculatively at Begum Salima. Thoughtfully, Akbar opined, 'It is indeed a good match, Begum. However, the pain of the prince's loss is very recent and we need more time. But send out the word to Habiba Banu Begum Sahiba that this match has our approval.'

The hall resounded with shrill cries of '*Mubarak, Mubarak*!' as the royal Begums raised their open palms in thanksgiving. Begum Ruqaiah, following tradition, immediately took off a large jade ring and gave it to a passing attendant to mark this happy event.

The emperor finished his meal and beckoned for Prince Salim to follow him.

The moment they turned a corner, Akbar held Prince Salim by the collar of his *qaba*, and dragged him into an adjoining room.

Holding him against the wall in a vice-like grip, Akbar slapped him hard on his left cheek. Frothing with rage, he shouted, 'How dare you disobey me, Sheikhu? How dare you?'

Pinned to the wall by Akbar's immense strength, Salim could only look with dread at the frightful sight of an enraged Akbar with red, protruding eyes and flushed cheeks. The vein in his temples stood out.

'You, like a mongrel in heat, have forgotten your roots? You have spent these last four years raising the banner of revolt against me? Me! Your father!' The room resounded with another hard blow. 'Raised under the hand of my all loving protection, bred on the love that I had for you and living off the riches of your father and his ancestors, you dare to defy me?'

Akbar released Salim and felled him to the floor with a flurry of hard punches to the face and head, sending the prince's violet turban rolling into a corner. Akbar again hauled him up and shook him like a leaf. 'You make a mockery of my mother's death and come here to pay your obeisance? To gift me what already belongs to me? You marched against me with seventy thousand men, and the mere apprehension of facing me sent you scurrying back to Illahabas Fort? You coward! You dream of annexing my kingdom while I am still alive? Huh? Stop dreaming, and surprise yourself. You are nothing but a slur on the Timurids. Just a black shadow which happens to ruin my evening years.'

Trembling with rage, Akbar again slapped him hard, and shouted, 'I should have had you hanged for your treasonable acts, Salim, but the river of Timurid blood stops me. Thou art a coward, Salim, and a disgrace to your ancestors.'

There was no court historian present at that moment to record that for once in his life, Akbar did not refer to Salim as 'Sheikhu', but by his given name. The myth would have been broken.

His powerful shoulders hunched, Akbar stalked out of the room. Locking the door behind him, he warned, 'You will be confined to this room until you learn to live without wine and opium. It will help you realize your true worth and the misery of your past actions.'

He summoned two of the female Tatar guards accompanying him inside the seraglio.

'You will stand guard at this door, and not let anyone in without my express permission. No ladies of the royal harem or otherwise, no visitors, no opium, and no wine. Prince Salim will not be allowed outside this room until I say so.'

Turning towards the other Tatar and Uzbeg female guards of his personal security detail, he instructed, 'Secure the corridors, and inform the *khojasera* of my instructions.'

*

By dusk Prince Salim, opium deprived, was banging on the door and walls, demanding release.

*

At the same time, in one of the anterooms of his royal apartment, Akbar looked at the three people standing before him.

'Raja Sallavihan,' spoke the emperor, 'you are a physician with impeccable credentials. I entrust Sheikhu to your care for the next ten days to rid him of this affliction, which has already consumed two sons of mine. Sheikhu is now my only surviving son, and possible heir to the throne.' For a few moments, Akbar's voice failed him.

Raja Sallavihan and the two attendants stood with bowed heads.

'I have full faith in you, Raja, and your healing touch.' Gesturing towards Arjun, the barber, and Rup Khwass, the servant, Akbar continued. 'Both of you shall provide all comfort and services to the prince, except the provision of wine and opiates. You shall be suitably rewarded. Or punished.'

His voice breaking, the emperor simply said, 'Just give me back my son!'

*

On the fourth evening, Akbar himself entered the room with a silver cup of wine, devastated by reports of the prince's worsening health and attempts at suicide. His turban and rings of diamond and precious stones, deemed as possible aids to suicide, had been confiscated by royal order.

The constant diffusion of aromatic incenses in the room failed to camouflage the smell of vomiting and diarrhoea. Foremost, was the smell of a decayed human.

That night, Akbar wept as he had never wept before. The only intelligible words were, 'I have poisoned our future with my own hands, today.'

*

(CHAPTER 23)

SHUGUN-E-FIL

(The Behemoth's Prophesy)

Riverside grounds

Agra Fort

20th September, 1605

6:30 a.m.

The emperor stood smiling at the elaborately carved, overhanging balcony for his daily *jharokha e darshan.* The milling crowd was restless in its energy, waiting expectantly for the much vaunted fight between the elephants of Prince Salim and his ambitious, disaffected son, Prince Khusrau.

The trumpets blared as the emperor took his seat with his favourite grandson, Prince Khurram. Soon, there was the rattle of kettle drums, announcing the arrival of Prince Salim, mounted on his favourite war horse, Dilsangar, and surrounded by a phalanx of armed followers, all wearing white turbans. His massive Burmese war elephant, Giranbar, wore no armour and came at a steady run from the Lahori Gate side. Fed on a huge dose of opium, it stood snorting and thumping the ground with his large forefoot. The two mahouts permitted for this fight were trying their best to keep him restrained.

Soon, from the Khirji Gateside, rode Prince Khusrau on his white stallion, Sulaiman, with a knot of close followers riding behind him. His huge war elephant, Apurva, was similarly driven by two mahouts, and hardly wore any armour. Though enormous in size, it looked weaker and more civilized than the beastly Giranbar. The Rajput following of Prince Khusrau was evident from the colourful turbans of his attendants, as they formed a crescent on the opposite side of Prince Salim.

The emperor, with an almost mystical affinity for these mammoth creatures, preferred this sport above all others. In fact, even princes were not permitted to hold elephant fights without express imperial permission. Such permissions were rarely sought. He ran his experienced eyes over the two combatants, and was glad that he had appointed his mighty war elephant, Ranthamban, as the *Tapancha*, or referee, for this fight. It was onc of his own innovations, and it might come in useful today.

Zamana Beg, positioned to the right of Prince Salim, leaned forward and smirked. 'Your Majesty, our Giranbar looks hungry enough to eat the other elephant.'

'And, why not, Zamana Beg? The mahouts have fed him with enough opium to fight not one, but six elephants at the same time.' There was satisfaction in Salim's voice.

Giranbar had seen the other elephant trumpeting and shaking his great head, and raised his massive forelegs in a challenge, almost unseating his mahouts. The senior mahout unleashed a volley of choicest abuse, and for good measure, tapped him hard with his iron rod behind the ears.

'For today, Giranbar is a Rajput elephant... just as drunk on opium, and floating on false courage as the demented Rajputs in their cavalry charges.'

Zamana Beg winced at Prince Salim's reference to the 'demented Rajputs', conveniently ignoring Zamana Beg's own Rajput past and family. The years after conversion had still not robbed Zamana Beg of his deep respect for his lineage. Only the exigencies of life and service at the Mughal court had forced him to convert.

*

In the throng of Prince Khusrau's supporters rode Sheikh Abdur Rehman, with a fair boy of about thirteen trailing behind him on foot. In the aftermath of Sheikh Abu'l Fazl's heinous murder, he had been recalled to the royal court at Agra, from Deccan.

With his innate abhorrence of Prince Salim as his father's murderer, he had gravitated to the opposite camp of Prince Khusrau where he enjoyed the company of the diplomatic Raja Man Singh of Amber, and the scintillating exchanges of an exasperated emperor with his irascible foster brother, Mirza Aziz Koka.

He straightened up on his mount, as he saw that the fight was about to begin.

*

Prince Salim, clad in white with a matching turban speckled with gold brocade, and sporting a red *patka* around his waist, rode up to the emperor and, dismounting, performed the *kornish*. Akbar accepted his salutations with a smile as he waited for Khusrau.

In deference to royal protocol, Khusrau made obeisance after his father, and waited for the emperor's acknowledgement.

Akbar was now beset with anxiety, as he watched his son and grandson in an armed face off. Would the elephants today become symbols of the future?

He dreaded the outcome.

*

At a nod from the emperor, the royal trumpeters blew a note, and the elephants took their positions in the middle of the parade ground. The Jumna flowed to the rear, and in front were the fort walls. Sitting high above in the overhanging covered terrace was the emperor with Prince Khurram. Both sides to the left and right of the contestants were packed with people from the opposing camps of the two princes.

Giranbar and Apurva stood face to face, separated by a low mud wall, specially constructed for this purpose the previous evening. The emperor's war elephant, Ranthamban, in his role as the *Tapancha*, was stationed in one corner, and also seemed ready for a fight.

To rousing shouts of '*Kill, Kill*,'the elephants charged at each other, easily breaking the mud wall between them. Their heads met with a ferocious thud as their trunks grappled in an effort to twist and snare. Apurva, being the smaller of the two, bent his foreknees and then immediately rose, driving his pointed, iron-sheathed tusks into the sensitive underlip of Giranbar. Anguished, Giranbar reacted by extending his trunk to wrap the first mahout and flung him into the air as the second mahout, precariously perched on a heaving Apurva, drove his iron goad into Giranbar's trunk and deliberately slashed downwards, ripping it.

The exultant shouts from Khusrau's camp were soon lost in the abusive din of Prince Salim's supporters.

Giranbar, maddened with pain and opium, stepped back before charging head on into the milder Apurva. The force of Giranbar's charge was such that Apurva seemed to totter on his legs. Screaming in rage, and blinded by fury, Giranbar charged again to smash Apurva with his monstrous head. Intimidated by the rushing Giranbar, Apurva turned sideways to avoid a collision, as a result of which Giranbar slammed broadside into Apurva's unprotected flank, goring him deeply with his sharpened tusks. The second mahout, seated behind, was thrown from his station on impact, and was immediately crushed by the massive hind paws of his own elephant.

Giranbar found the twitching, disembowelled form of the trampled mahout an irritating impediment to his chase, and, sweeping up the mahout with his open entrails, threw him high and wide into the air.

There was a collective gasp of horror from the spectators, as Giranbar continued to pursue a shrieking, terrified Apurva towards the Jumna. At a signal from the emperor, the *Tapancha* rushed forward to help the loser.

Immediately, there were furious shouts of disapproval from Prince Salim's camp, as they objected to the participation of Ranthamban on the loser's side. They wanted to see the absolute rout of the upstart Khusrau and the burial of his dreams in a rapidly flowing Jumna. A sea of white turbans moved threateningly towards the *Tapancha*.

Prince Khusrau, enraged by the misdemeanour of his father and his insolent supporters in the presence of the emperor, kicked his horse into a gallop.

Meanwhile Apurva, shrieking and bellowing, and bleeding from several deep wounds from the continuous gorings of a crazed Giranbar, was slowly being pushed into the deep waters of Jumna.

Akbar watched in dismay and horror the spectacle below him. He stood and leaned over the balcony to get a better view, and saw Prince Khusrau surrounded by his Rajput warriors having a heated discussion with his father, Prince Salim.

'Father, in your inebriated state, you have forgotten the rules of decorum in the emperor's presence?' Pointing towards the raucous, boorish brigade, he spluttered, 'This... this lot of imbeciles, these louts, have the temerity to raise their fists and voices in the emperor's presence? They are worse than street dogs...'

'Enough,' shouted Prince Salim, as his hand went for his sword. 'Get out of my sight, you ungrateful wretch, before I displace your head.'

Suddenly there was a massive shout of displeasure, as Ghiyas Beg, a minor noble of Prince Salim from his Illahabas days, picked up a small boulder and threw it at Ranthamban's mahout. The mahout, intent on reaching the warring elephants, did not see the missile coming until it was too late. The emperor's mahout reeled from the impact, as blood gushed from his forehead. Veteran of many such wounds in the imperial wars of conquest, he rallied, urging Ranthamban into a lumbering run.

The emperor, incensed at this violation of royal decorum and aggression against the imperial elephant, turned angrily to Khurram and growled, 'Khurram, run and tell your father to stop this hostility right now, or I will have him and his uncivilized retainers clapped in irons. Hurry!'

'Yes, Shah Baba.'

Down below, a fair boy stood rooted to the spot as he watched the emperor instruct a young prince with utmost urgency. There was something so achingly familiar about him. It brought back memories of his dead mother and an era of childhood bliss.

In shallow waters, Giranbar was aggressively fighting Ranthamban and Apurva on his own, and with opium-induced strength and courage, he was more than a match for them.

Humiliated and defeated, Prince Khusrau thundered across to the balcony where the emperor was dismally sitting. Guided by his rage and acute humiliation, Khusrau had strong words to convey.

'Your Majesty! The rules of conduct and engagement were brazenly destroyed, and you let it happen! Prince Salim, evil as always, and surrounded by his group of traitors and criminals, violates every rule and because of your weakness, lords it over others, who suffer because of your lapses.'

The emperor's face was suffused with anger, and he hissed, 'Guard your tongue, Khusrau! You are not to come in our presence till you have learned your manners. *Takhliya*!'

A flotilla of small boats had surrounded the warring elephants, and the beasts were eventually separated by bursting fire crackers tied on long poles near their eyes, ears, and heads.

Mounted *ahadis* had to ride amongst the rioting supporters to drive them away.

Returning home, a bemused Abdur Rehman listened in affected silence to the story of his young retainer's memories of the past. Allah only knew what lay in store ahead, but he would abide by the promise made to his late father, Sheikh Abu'l Fazl Allami.

There was a cold darkness in the emperor's heart as the day's venom settled over him.

The behemoths had spoken.

*

(CHAPTER 24)

HUKUMAT-E-CHUGATAI

(Rule, Chugatais)

Kothi in Rawatpura

Close to Agra Fort

11th October, 1605

11:25 p.m.

She pulled him closer to her breasts and, running her fingers through the greying hairs on his chest, said with concern, 'You are not your usual robust self today, my lord. Are you not feeling well, or should I use the special oil?'

Zia Ul Mulk forced a smile to his lips, as he let her expert fingers run over his chest and abdomen. 'There is much restlessness in my mind tonight, Anjuman Bai. Maybe one more glass of wine will do me good.'

He watched her supple form as she bent down to pour a silver tumbler full of red rich wine from a long-necked silver pitcher. In spite of her glorious body and sensual ministrations he had failed to achieve an erection today, not that it worried him unduly. He had more serious causes to worry about.

Settling herself once again close to him, she encouraged him. 'My lord, if it may please you so, you could share your worries with me. I have been your mistress for almost two years now, and I hope that I have given you pleasure and solace, as I have derived from your presence in my life.'

Zia slipped his hands under her arms and softly cupped her breasts. The wine and her heady fragrance was invigorating and the words came tumbling out. 'There is much confusion and disarray in the royal court, Anjuman. With the emperor's continuing ill health, may Allah cure him soon, there is utter chaos and devilry within the fort walls. While earlier, the fort was a bastion of grace and magnificence, it now seems to be a shrunken mass of old stones and hideous shadows. At times, when I walk through the arched corridors and vaulted halls of the *Shahi Chowki* and the royal stables and garrisons, a shiver runs down my spine as if there are dead, but seeing eyes watching our every move. And, let me tell you, Anjuman, I am not the only one. The whole court talks in whispers now.'

'As if the walls have ears,' completed Anjuman.

'Exactly. Within the fort, I fear my own shadow.' Zia casually straightened a strand of hair that was falling across her face.

'We have heard as much, sire. There is talk in the city that ever since the elephant fight, the emperor has been struck with some strange affliction.' She playfully caressed his limp penis, and mournfully said, 'Alas, the same affliction seems to have struck my lord also. Wait, I know the cure for this condition.'

Zia Ul Mulk ran his fingers through her hair, spread out over his abdomen, as she set herself to reviving his member with small, sensual flicks of her tongue and soft manipulations of her fingers.

He settled on his back comfortably as he recognized the familiar sensations of blood rushing to his groin. Anjuman looked up with a smile and then again engaged herself with her ministrations.

Looking at her bobbing head, he reflected on the future. There were daggers drawn from both the aspiring heirs; the rightful claimant, Prince Salim as the eldest and only surviving son of the emperor, and the brash upstart, Khusrau.

'Anjuman, you *are* a miracle worker! My ardour seems to have returned.'

Anjuman admired his rigid, throbbing penis and mischievously mumbled through her busy lips, 'Your ardour had not gone anywhere, sire, it was just lurking around the bushes.'

Zia Ul Mulk Qazwini laughed uproariously. For him, Anjuman was a delightful bundle of sensuous mysticism and ribald wit, and made his lonely life tolerable.

'You would not find it all so funny, Anjuman, if you had to spend one full day in the court nowadays. The old retainers and faithful of the emperor have been sent away, and the old fox, Mirza Aziz Koka, who acts as the vice regent, has arrayed the imperial staff with his own trustees. Raja Man Singh, normally such a doyen of correctness and imperial loyalty, has also fallen into the same warped frame.'

Her head came up again. 'And what exactly is a "warped frame" my learned lord?'

'The crooked idea of installing Prince Khusrau on the emperor's demise is what I am referring to. Prince Salim as the eldest and surviving son has the first right to the throne.'

Anjuman sat up. 'Then this will interest you, sire. There is a chance that Prince Salim might be arrested tomorrow. I have...'

Zia's voice hardened as he pushed her away. 'How do you know? Who told you?'

'A eunuch from the royal harem overheard Raja Man Singh and Khan e Azam as they were passing by the *Daftarkhana*. He is very friendly with my younger maid, Kamini, and spends several afternoons regaling her with ridiculous stories of the harem. Selectively, she passes them on to me.' She gave a hard tug on his erect penis. 'Next time you push me away, I shall take a part of your manhood with me!'

'Why did you not tell me earlier, woman?' There was annoyance in his voice.

'Oh, lord! I hear gossip every day, and if I were to relate each one of those far-fetched yarns, then the few hours that I get with you would be lost in these silly tales.'

'What did they say?' Zia's voice was gruff.

'They were talking about arresting Prince Salim when he comes to visit the emperor tomorrow. They mentioned the name of some Rajput nobles, too.'

There was a faraway look in Zia Ul Mulk's eyes, as he tried to envision the drama set to unfold. He turned back to Anjuman.

'Any other information that you believe pertinent to this, Anjuman? It is vital to the empire.'

'Not that I can think of anything, sire. But, may I make a suggestion, *Huzoor*?'

'Speak, woman.'

'The arrest of Prince Salim could not have been planned without the active connivance of the royal harem, possibly even one of the queens. I am told the harem is full of strong and vicious Tatar and Uzbeg guards, and their fighting skills are comparable to the fearsome *ahadis*.'

'Even more so, Anjuman,' replied Zia, 'because these Tatar and Uzbeg women have no other ties in this world except their warrior's role in protecting the royal family. They have nothing to lose, hence, nothing to fear. And your presumption is correct, my love. The high and the mighty from the imperial seraglio are involved.'

Anjuman snuggled closer to him and put her legs over his torso. Her fingers once again became active.

Zia Qazwini relaxed. There were many hours to daybreak and the prince's safety could be ensured later. The urgent need was for him to make love to this beautiful and intelligent woman, here and now.

*

Lee of the fort walls

Khijri Gate side

12th October, 1605

10:20 a.m.

Zia Ul Mulk Qazwini sat on a mossy rock and glared gloomily upriver. He had been waiting here in the guise of a simple peasant since early morning, waiting for Prince Salim to come as usual in his river barge for his daily obeisance to the emperor. A herd of buffaloes had joined him a few hours ago, and were peacefully grazing on the tall sharp grass which grew near the riverbank.

The early morning haze had not lifted until about a few hours ago, and he was confident that the prince would not venture out in the winter fog. A small boy in tatters was busy cleaning his teeth with a *neem* twig. Every once in a while he would spit out the crushed remnants and glance enquiringly at Zia Ul Mulk, as if inviting a rebuke.

Squinting against the sun, Zia saw a crimson sail in the far distance. He immediately knew it was the royal barge for no one else could fly the royal crimson. As it drew near he could easily make out the triangle of the three main sails, and the twelve oarsmen on each side. He kept sitting quietly, not wanting to draw attention to himself. Many eyes, with criminal intent, would be watching the arrival of Prince Salim today. He could see the royal archers stationed behind the arrow loops in the fort walls.

He waited for the barge to draw closer to the jetty, and then sauntered towards it, unfastening his dirty pyjamas on the way. When the jetty was hardly fifty yards away, he lowered his pyjamas and sat close to a clump of thick grass to defecate.

The royal barge made a large curve to starboard and slid to the side of the pier, its protective ring of rag-filled sacks bumping against the wooden planks. A few young sailors jumped down trailing long cords of rope and moored the barge safely.

Zia waited until the gangplank was lowered and a few of the personal bodyguards of Prince Salim had secured the pier. He quickly jumped up, and fastening his pyjamas ran towards the jetty as he saw a knot of men gather at the head of the gangplank.

Pulling himself up on the wooden jetty he was confronted by a group of soldiers with drawn swords.

'I need to see the prince,' Zia shouted deliberately.

One of the soldiers smote him on the head with his shield. 'What are you shouting for? Are you drunk, or are you mad?'

'None. I just want to speak to Sheikhu,' Zia Ul Mulk shouted again.

This time, a hand with an iron guard on the forearm hit him behind his neck, sending him sprawling into the dust.

'Who is there?' commanded a voice from the deck.

'It is a mad man, Your Majesty.'

Zia scrambled to his feet, and, still reeling from the blow, took off his dirty turban. 'It is me, Your Majesty, Zia Ul Mulk Qazwini. It is dangerous here for you, Majesty.'

Prince Salim looked intently at him, and then with a flicker of recognition called out, 'It is all right. Get him aboard.'

Qazwini ran up the gangplank and explained in a rush, 'You must leave right now, Highness. There are plans to arrest and imprison you today. You must leave. Now!'

The fear in Zia's eyes convinced Prince Salim. A peremptory command was given. 'Cast off now! Man your stations.'

The gangplank was hurriedly drawn up and knots loosened on the moorings.

Zia pointed towards Khijri Gate, which had opened, and a squad of armed soldiers were running in the boat's direction. The sailors had cast off the moorings and were attempting to move the barge by pushing the oars against the jetty planks. The oarsmen on the other side of the barge were furiously deep paddling to bring the barge around in an arc. As the soldiers reached the pier, the barge had moved a good fifteen feet, and was rapidly drawing away.

The master oarsman standing on a small drum started orchestrating the oars with a song-like cadence. 'Heave and pull, heave and pull.'

Zia, sighing with relief, turned and performed the *kornish*. 'Please accept my thousand pardons, Majesty! I had no other way to draw your immediate attention than by shouting your name cherished by His Imperial Majesty.'

Salim laughed. 'For a moment, Qazwani, I really thought that we had a mad man in our midst. And my guards have become lax. They had ample time to remove your head from your shoulders, but they failed.' Seeing the troubled look in Zia's eyes, Salim turned away with a smile.

As the barge sailed downriver to the prince's temporary abode, several pairs of disappointed eyes watched their quarry get away. Kohl-rimmed eyes, being common to Rajputs and Moslems alike, made it difficult to ascertain the conspiratorial crew. A stained glass window from the royal harem slammed shut in disgust as the river barge pulled itself away with frenzied haste.

On the riverbank, the buffaloes continued to graze peacefully, oblivious to the close calls of an alternative history.

*

The three Jesuit fathers walked slowly from the monarch's bedchamber. They had gone with high hopes of convincing the dying 'Emperor Achebar' to embrace Christianity and attain salvation, but the emperor had met them in distinctly high spirits.

Their persuasion was to no avail, as Akbar cheerfully but firmly reminded them that he had equal regard for all religions, and was already a *Mureed* of his Chosen God. Hakim Ali Gillani, the emperor's physician, had them turned out politely after only a few minutes of pointless persuasion.

*

As twilight set in and the palace lamp lighters went about their business of lighting the several hundreds of small and large lamps, two luminaries of the emperor's court furtively exchanged whispers.

'Raja Saheb, now that he is forewarned, it will be very difficult to contain him without bloodshed.'

'Or maybe a civil war, Khan e Azam,' agreed Raja Man Singh.

They stopped near the rear corridor of the *Daftarkhana*, as Mirza Koka opined, 'We must stay alert, and keep Khusrau away from the court for a few days. We need to work out a consensus on this issue. Tomorrow afternoon, the abode of Rai Singh Kachhawa?'

Raja Man Singh nodded and then turned left to descend the steps to the *Diwan e Aam*.

In the royal harem, Salima Sultan Begum threw a glass decanter against a pillar, shattering it.

*

Raja Man Singh had reached the house of Rai Singh Kachhawa at about noon, on the pretext of blessing his newborn son, for whom the sixth day ceremony was being held today. Several nobles were sitting in the special tent raised for them, and Raja Man Singh could count the presence of at least half a dozen nobles who could be expected to side with Prince Khusrau.

Khan e Azam Mirza Aziz Koka arrived, and, as per prior arrangements, was ushered next to Raja Man Singh. The lesser nobles gave a wide berth to these two court grandees as they conferred alone.

'It is imperative, Khan e Azam, that a council be called at the earliest opportunity to put this proposal forward. Even though the majority of *mansabdars* belong to the Rajputs, their allegiance to our cause cannot be predicted.'

'You are absolutely right, Raja. There are many amongst us who shall fight in the name of religious law, and the inviolability of the eldest son's claim. Also, the close association of the Kachhawas to Prince Khusrau might not be quite acceptable to the staunch Mohammedans.'

Raja Man Singh smiled. 'Well, it is their bad luck then. Both Prince Salim and Prince Khusrau have Rajputs for mothers – and from *my* clan, the Kachhawas. One is my aunt, the other my dear sister, now residing in heaven.' The irony was not lost on Khan e Azam Mirza Koka.

'Such are the antics of Destiny, my friend! Let us call a council one week from now. It shall give us ample time to sound out and convince many of the nobles who could prove decisive if it comes to a show of force. I hope you are comfortable with this arrangement, Raja?' The anxiety in Mirza's voice was evident.

Raja Man Singh tweaked his moustache as he glared at the minor noble who was impertinent enough to stare at him for a moment longer than was polite, or political. The lesser noble immediately looked away.

Raja Man Singh spoke softly. 'A week is good enough. I am taking Khusrau under my protection from today.'

Khan e Azam nodded his approval.

*

Bhairon Ka Sthan

Irchha, near Lahore

18th October, 1605

Sunset

Chooza Mastan was busy preparing a small bonfire of dead branches and twigs, and swinging his head to the celestial music which only he could hear. Many years ago, the temple priest Ramadeen and his family had welcomed this funny, mystical man with his long hair and beard, who sported a massive turban on his head. With time, Chooza Mastan blended perfectly into the family and became a permanent part of the shrine. He seemed to live in his own world, and, like a true Sufi, could spend hours together muttering and gesticulating to his unseen God. When asked about his residing in a Hindu temple, his answer would put even the most hard-core Hindus and Moslems to shame. On one such occasion he replied, as always, 'Tell me, *Janab e Auliya*, the address to my Allah's abode, and I shall go and sit there.'

When there was no response, then he continued, 'Allah resides in each one of us, and in all the living things which He created. He resides where there is peace, He resides where there is love and He resides where there is care and respect of fellow men. That is where He resides. And that is why, my *Koh-e-ilm*, I stay here.'

Ramadeen and a few other people sat around, waiting for Chooza Mastan to light the bonfire. In a corner sat a few ladies cooking some vegetable broth with garlic and mustard oil in a copper vessel. The priest's daughters had kneaded a small mountain of dough and were now covering it with a damp cloth to keep it moist and fresh. *Teevradand*, the huge black temple dog, lay passively near the shrine. These many years had been hard for him and he was not as ferocious as he once was, much to the visitor's relief.

As darkness approached and the bonfire cackled into life, the conversation veered towards the news received from Agra today of the emperor's health.

'The emperor has driven himself too hard these past five years. It has taken its toll on his health.' The stated opinion of Mir Ghulam, a disciple of Chooza Mastan, brought forth a flood of views.

Ramadeen looked at Mastan, and, seeing no special interest of his in the ongoing discussion, spoke forth. 'Emperors are born to rule, and that in itself begets pleasure and toil in equal measure. Our emperor has a robust constitution, and has ruled for more years than the number of summers seen by many of you. When the mind surrenders, then the body follows.'

Another of the regulars spoke up. 'You are right, Priest. The market is abuzz with descriptions of the ill-fated fight between Prince Khusrau and Prince Salim's elephants. It is being said that Prince Khusrau's insolent and profane behaviour that day against his father in the emperor's presence has precipitated this crisis.'

A lady who was quietly stirring the broth suddenly stopped. Then she started stirring again.

Chooza Mastan signalled Mir Ghulam to fill his *chillum* as he danced a small jig in the dog's direction. *Teevradand*, used to his strange antics, closed his weary eyes and, sighing, settled his massive head comfortably on his paws. Chooza smiled and sat back on his haunches.

There was silence in the compound as the sweet smell of *chillum* mingled with the smoky aroma of the broth. Most of those assembled stared into the fire and mulled over the future.

Soon, *Teevradand* pricked up his ears, as hooves galloped over the country path to the temple. As they neared the shrine precincts, the riders dismounted and tied their horses at the gate.

Baqar Khan, along with Ibrahim Khan and half a dozen other riders, entered with their coarse shawls wrapped around their faces. As they neared the bonfire, a woman detached herself from the group and went towards Ratna Devi and her companion, and with a small *taslim* sat a few feet away. As she removed her shawl, the wheat-coloured, aged face of a woman past her prime was revealed. Her black eyes searched frantically for her beloved Firdaus.

Ratna Devi, as if understanding her anguish and unspoken question, put her hand on her arm and gently consoled her. 'You know he is no more, Jaffer Biwi. Take heart and have faith in Allah's mercy. Allah has taken him to a better place, away from the filth of riches, royalty, and deceit. He sleeps in Allah'sarms.'

Great, heaving sobs wracked her body as she looked forlornly into the spitting fire.

Baqar Khan and the new arrivals smiled, as Chooza Mastan pulled on his *chillum* and, gazing towards the dark sky, proclaimed, 'Our time has come.'

*

Diwan e Aam

Agra Fort

20th October, 1605

9:40 a.m.

Khan e Azam Mirza Aziz Koka was the wrong man in the wrong place. And this was certainly not the right time to create new equations, with the dogmatic and intolerant beliefs of the fanatical Sayyeds of Barha. But he had little choice left, considering the emperor's deteriorating condition over the last few days.

He waited for the Barhas to stop arguing, before continuing,

‘The accusation of favouring my son-in-law, Prince Khusrau, is not true and you know that very well, Sayyed Ahmed Khan. Deep in your heart you know the truth very well. So do all of us.’

Qulij Khan Andijani who had been a silent spectator until now, spoke up. ‘The rebellion of Prince Salim that you refer to was an erroneous and misjudged act and is in the past. The prince sought forgiveness, and the emperor forgave him in full court. You were also present that day, were you not Mirza Kokultash?’ The reference to the Persian term for ‘foster brother’ was a well-aimed reminder to Khan e Azam about his loyalties.

‘The forgiveness was an act of compromise. With Prince Murad and Prince Daniyal dead, the emperor really had no choice. For continuance of the dynasty, and preservation of the realm, he had to compromise.’ Mirza Koka was trying hard to keep his voice normal.

‘Let us not forget that Prince Salim is the eldest son, hence, he has the first right to the throne,’ Faridun Berla interposed.

‘You are right, Berla, but is it our fate to be ruled by a king who remains intoxicated on wine and opium, and leads a life of wanton debauchery?’ The sombre words of Raja Man Singh cut through the hostility.

After a few seconds’ thought, the Berla noble replied. ‘Prince Khusrau, by raising the banner of revolt against his father, has done no better. In fact, he is so belligerent as to raise his voice at his father in public. Prince Salim, with all the accusations directed at him, can never be accused of shameful behaviour or belligerence in front of the emperor.’

‘Yes.’ Murtaza Khan Barha joined the fray. ‘Prince Salim is just, noble in word and speech, and suffers his militant son in forgiving silence.’

‘As his father suffers him,’ muttered Jagannath Kachhawa, close kin of Raja Man Singh.

Raja Man Singh could see the futility of pursuing their proposal in such a hostile environment, and started thinking of ways to save himself and Prince Khusrau from the impending imperial wrath. It would be a good idea to sail immediately for Bengal, he mused.

Ram Das Narwari, a minor noble from Mewat, with his opium-eclipsed mind, announced, 'Prince Salim has also promised to protect Islam!' Immediately, there were frowns of disgust from the assembled Rajput nobles, irrespective of their allegiance.

The mercurial and acerbic Mirza Azim Koka could tolerate the toothless arguments no more. His voice rose. 'What does Islam mean to you, you idol worshipper? You are just a parasite waiting to live off your flattery and false loyalty to the throne. Do not preach to me about protecting Islam. We are all born to protect Islam. Which also means that the emperor has to be youthful, vigorous, determined, and not a slothful rebel with grandiose dreams of—'

'Enough!' shouted Sayyed Khan Barha. 'Enough. There shall be no discussion on this matter now.'

'The truth cannot be denied, Mirza Azim Kokultash. We are Chagatais, and our traditions will prevail. The son cannot supersede his father to become king, and there it rests. Your whims, fancies, and desires have no place in our books. If the father is alive, he will be crowned king. That is what our *Shi'ar-o-ture-yi-Chagatai* lays down, and that is what we will follow.' The solemn words of Saeed Khan Chagatai, a high *mansabdar* of five thousand *Zat* in Akbar's court, stilled the conflict.

'*Rule, Chagatais*,' shouted a jubilant Sayyed Khan Barha as he led his followers from the *Diwan e Aam*.

*

By evening, almost all the nobles, including Khan e Azam, had turned up at Prince Salim's palace ready to offer their allegiance to the new emperor. The exception was Raja Man Singh, who, fearing retribution from the new emperor, was preparing to flee by boat to Bengal, taking Prince Khusrau along with him.

The news arrived that the emperor had died.

The impetuous and uncouth Barhas wanted the *naqqara-i-shadiyana* to be beaten. Prince Salim forbade the beating of celebratory drums in honour of his late father, the emperor.

In the royal fort, Emperor Akbar was alive.

(CHAPTER 25)

ZAHAR-E-PADSHAHAT

(The Poisoned Realm)

Akbar's royal chambers

Agra Fort

21st October, 1605

11:00 a.m.

Raja Man Singh waited nervously outside the emperor's chamber. Yesterday, a royal emissary had delivered the emperor's message late in the night, summoning the Raja at his earliest convenience. For the last two hours, *hakims* and *vaids* had been moving in and out of the main bedchamber with small vessels and goblets of potions and herbal pastes. Begum Salima Sultana had joined Ruqaiah Begum at the emperor's bedside an hour ago.

Raja Man Singh winced as a deep groan was heard inside. He could not stop his tears from forming, as he recollected his more than four decades of loyal service in the shadow of this great king, who now lay vanquished by the ravages of a treacherous son and the poisoned love of his own queens.

The Ayurvedic *Vaid* Bhima hurried out of the monarch's chamber and in a hushed whisper asked Man Singh to go inside.

Raja Man Singh softly entered the room and with bowed head stood to one side. The emperor was propped on bolsters, and lay with his eyes closed. Mariam Uz Zamani, along with Ruqaiah Begum and Salima Sultana Begum, sat on either side of the emperor. Hakim Gillani, deep shades of perplexity etched on his face, stood near the silver chest of drawers, using a gold pestle to mix some herbs for a recuperative potion.

Prince Khurram, with deep sadness in those long brown eyes, sat quietly on a silver stool by the emperor's head. His hand lay against the emperor's cheek.

One of the two attendants of Hakim Gillani touched him on the shoulder and indicated Raja Man Singh. The hakim glanced at him from under his furrowed brows, and nodded almost imperceptibly as he continued to grind his potion.

The Raja remained still, yet Akbar, with some cognitive sense, opened his eyes and looked directly at Raja Man Singh, who immediately performed the *kornish*. Fixing his eyes on the Raja, the emperor indicated with his fingers for all to leave. The Begums looked at one another, but Akbar again gestured for them to leave. The Begums withdrew with deep bows.

Akbar feebly called out, 'Begum, send me some rose-flavoured *pethas*, please.'

Begum Salima replied with a *taslim*,'Immediately, Your Majesty.'

Hakim Gillani had stopped his work, and indicated for his assistants to leave. 'You cannot have *pethas*, Your Majesty. It will bring back the stomach ache again.'

'Hakim Ali, my old friend, let me have now whatever I want to have. Even a condemned man has his last wishes fulfilled, and who can stop me? I am the emperor, correct?'

'Yes, Your Majesty. But your stomach needs rest, and all these potions must get a chance to work, Your Majesty,' the exasperated hakim replied.

'See, my dear friend, I do not wish to meet Death on an empty stomach. I shall journey like a true emperor. Let Death also know that its decisive blow could not lessen my majesty.' Akbar's voice was getting stronger with each word.

'*Lahaul vila qu bat*! What kind of words are these, *Shahenshah*? May you live a hundred years!' Hakim Ali quickly touched his cheeks in penance.

'Now, leave us for a while, Hakim Ali. I need to see Raja Man Singh in private.' The hakim put his pestle on the silver chest and withdrew. Akbar turned towards Khurram, and said, 'Khurram, my prince, run along for a while and come back when the *pethas* are here. We can demolish them together. Love you, my child.' Akbar caressed Prince Khurram's cheek, and he withdrew with a quick bow.

At a signal Man Singh approached the reclining emperor, and as his downcast eyes fell on the golden threaded slippers of the emperor, a great sob escaped his lips. The emperor gestured for him to come closer, and suddenly Akbar stretched out his long hands to grab the front of Man Singh's *qaba*, and with an effort pulled himself up.

Unbalanced by the sudden pull, Man Singh almost fell on the bed as the emperor's face, suffused with anger, stared at him. Twisting his hands into a fist, Akbar tried to raise himself.

Just inches away from Man Singh's face, he hissed, 'Raja! How could you even think of betraying my trust?'

'I have done nothing wrong, Your Majesty.' The voice of Man Singh quivered with fright.

'Ashamed you should be, Raja, ashamed! You tried to arrest Prince Salim, my son and heir to the throne, and you say you have *done nothing*! Yesterday, you and that mentally retarded foster brother of mine, Azim Kokultash, again tried to instigate my knights against the empire.' He shook Raja Man Singh roughly and tried to drag himself up.

'Your Majesty! Please relax, Your Highness. I have served you faithfully all my life...'

'Enough!' roared the emperor. 'I brought you to my court as an eleven-year-old, and I treated you as my own son. I called you *Farzand*, and not without reason. And this is how you repay me?'

The flood of words would not stop. 'I gave you the highest *mansab*, and more importantly, I gave you my trust!' The furious emperor's will and voice broke down, as he wept. 'What have you done, Man Singh, what have you done?'

Raja Man Singh, with tears streaming down his cheeks, gently laid the weeping emperor on the bed, and in a voice choked with emotion, said, 'Your Majesty, never have I ever even dreamt of bringing grief to you, my lord, never. I could not bear to see you grieving at Prince Salim's wilful treason, and his ways of sedition. My loyalty lies with you, Your Majesty, and no one else. I was honoured when you called me *Farzand* and I made every effort to honour your words as a son should. I travelled, and fought, across the length and breadth of the empire under your flag, and my blood flowed for Your Majesty.'

Raja Man Singh bowed near the emperor, and, weeping like a wronged child, held his monarch's hand. 'My only fault, Your Majesty, is that I could not bear to see you reviled by treacherous royals, and I acted to protect your honour and your empire. I am sorry that I have grieved you so, and having lost your trust, I have no wish to remain in this poisoned realm. Please permit me to leave your empire for ever, Majesty.'

Body wracked with great heaving sobs, Raja Man Singh bent and softly kissed the emperor's hand. 'Farewell, my sovereign. May Krishna bestow a long life to you.'

He left his weeping emperor, grieving the loss of his empire and its future.

They would never see each other again.

*

A few minutes later, Hakim Ali Gillani entered with a small golden dish of *pethas* covered with rose petals and silver foil.

'As desired, Begum Salima sends these with her compliments, Majesty.'

Akbar indicated his bedside. 'Please leave it here, Hakim Ali, and wait outside. If Prince Khurram comes, tell him that I am resting, and he can come again later.'

'As you wish, Majesty.' He quietly placed the dish by Akbar's bedside and withdrew.

With great effort, Akbar leaned to his left and took out the blue stoneware plate referred by *hakims* as the *Zeher Parakh Rakabi*. In the *Mir Saman*'s list, it was described as the emperor's poison testing plate.

He transferred the *pethas* onto the blue plate, and waited. The colour slowly turned pink.

His cheeks quivering with unseen pain and fresh tears streaming from his eyes, the emperor stuffed his mouth with the sweets. After a few minutes, another handful went into his mouth.

As the sun reached its zenith, the emperor flung the remnants of the sweetmeat out of his window to fall in the courtyard below.

Immediately, a flock of crows descended on the fragments and devoured all signs of them in a few minutes of frenzied pecking.

After half an hour, Hakim Ali cautiously came inside the room to find the emperor staring at the frescoed ceiling. The hakim looked at the now empty golden dish and wondered at the sudden appetite of the emperor. He bent to remove the dish from the bedside when his eyes fell on the *Zeher Parakh Rakabi* lying near. The colour seemed like pale lavender to him. As he bent for a closer look, his eyes met the emperors'.

A single tear formed and then rolled down the corner of Akbar's eyes. That evening there were many dead crows in the fort's vicinity.

The realm of the Grand Mughals had clearly been poisoned, never to recover.

*

(CHAPTER 26)

JANNATE HAMESHGI

(The Eternal Eden)

Begum Ruqaiah's Chamber

The harem, Agra Fort

25th October, 1605

9:20 a.m.

Begum Ruqaiah's personal astrologer, Pundit Govinda of Kashi, was ushered into her chamber by the harem eunuchs. Old and weak now, Pundit Govinda shuffled into the room and with folded hands bowed deeply to the queen.

'Welcome, Learned Priest! We are honoured by your presence today.' Begum Ruqaiah's voice, normally so soft and gentle, was hoarse and uncultured today, as she bade the astrologer to sit on a cushioned silver stool provided for him.

'May I first present my apologies, Your Highness, for the delay in coming here? I was at Kashi when your epistle reached me through the royal couriers. It took me a while to reach here, as much as I hastened.' The astrologer's voice had become weak with age, but the shine in his eyes remained.

The queen nodded her acceptance, and Pundit Govinda continued. 'I am extremely sorry to learn of the emperor's ill health, Your Highness. But, you need not worry, my child. I drew the emperor's horoscope with my own hand, and I remember that he is destined to live to the age of eighty-four, so why do you worry?'

'You have a phenomenal memory, Learned Sage. I have the emperor's horoscope with me,' the Begum answered quietly.

Pundit Govinda snapped a toothless smile. 'How could I forget, Your Majesty? It is not every day that someone gets to draw an emperor's horoscope.'

Begum Ruqaiah sighed as she proffered another rolled parchment to Govinda. Her voice was low as she said, 'Learned Sage, this parchment here contains the actual birth details of His Majesty. It was drawn by the chief astrologers of our most revered Emperor Humayun, *Jannat Ashiyani*, in his presence.'

The astrologer spread the several native charts in front of him and studied the additional parchment, bearing what seemed like Persian script clumsily sewn onto the first chart.

Ruqaiah Begum spoke softly. 'I had forgotten about this set of papers, Learned Sage, as it was given to me many, many years ago by Jiji Anaga, one of the emperor's foster mothers, and the mother of our Khan e Azam Mirza Azim Kokultash. She asked me to preserve it safely.'

The sage looked up from his intensive study of the Persian script, and stated, 'I can see that, now. This attachment to the chart mentions that the emperor's native chart was drawn by *Jannat Ashiyani's*, may peace be upon him, court astrologer Mulla Chand, using a Greek astrolabe and Ulugh Beg's *Zig-i-Sultani*. Another set of horoscopes was drawn by Emperor Humayun's trusted vedic astrologer, Jotik Rai, as also a third set was drawn by the famous Safavid polymath, Mir Fathullah Shirazi, using Iranian techniques and Ptolemy's *Almagest*.They are all appended here.'

'Is this accurate, sire?' the Begum asked, worried.

'It certainly is, child. It clearly mentions here that these native charts were prepared in Emperor Humayun's presence, and under his guidance. It remained in the custody of Jauhar Khan, the emperor's personal servant, who looked after our current emperor in his infancy. Jauhar Khan, having fallen severely ill in 1560, gave it to our emperor's *Atagha*, Khan-e-Kalan Shamsuddin Muhammed Atgah Khan and his wife, Jiji Anaga, for safekeeping. It also explicitly mentions here that Jauhar Khan did not wish Maham Anaga to know of its existence.'

'Sire, is there any cause for worry?' Begum Ruqaiah was sweating with worry on a cold October morning.

'Please allow me some time to study the charts, Your Highness.' Pundit Govinda hunched over the charts.

After just a few minutes of perusal, he was shaking his head every few seconds and rubbing his eyes.

Shortly, he pushed away the charts, and looked at Ruqaiah Begum with disbelieving eyes. There was anguish in his voice, as he exclaimed, 'All our predictions were wrong. Emperor Akbar was not born on the fifteenth of October, 1542. He was born on the twenty-third of November, 1542. Our horoscopes are a hoax! A hoax!'

Pundit Govinda covered his eyes in shame, as the bewildered Begum slid on the floor and grasped his hands. 'Please explain yourself, sire. What are you suggesting?' There was desperation in her voice.

Govinda took a few deep breaths to steady himself and, with tormented eyes, stared between the charts and the Begum's face. At last he said in a broken voice, 'Our emperor was born on twenty-third of November, 1542, which was a full moon night, and he was therefore named *Badruddin Mohammed Akbar*. Since the natal charts were not so favourable, Emperor Humayun ordered his astrologers to shift the date to a more propitious date. Hence, the fifteenth of October, 1542 was selected. And, since it was not a full moon night, the name *Badruddin* was replaced with *Jalal Ud Din,* implying strength.' He looked down again at the charts spread before him.

'And what do the original charts predict, sire?'

There was panic in Govinda's voice. 'They all concur on the same date, Highness. It is *the second of Aban, 1014 Hijri. The twelfth Jumaidi-Ulakhir*. Which corresponds to this day, the twenty-fifth of October, third day of Kartika, 1527 Vikram Samvat!'

High wails rose from the royal suite of Ruqaiah Begum as Pundit Govinda was almost thrown out by hefty eunuchs.

He still clutched the genuine documents of Fate.

*

Emperor's Bedchamber

Khwabgah, Agra Fort

Friday, 25th October, 1605

8:00 p.m.

Emperor Akbar lay on his back with his breath coming in short gasps. The *hakims* and *vaids* had been constantly moving in and out of the emperor's chambers over the last several days bearing miniature pots and vessels of pastes, lotions, and astringents to cure the strange malaise of the emperor, who was unable to pass bodily fluids.

Hakim Ali Gillani had first controlled the prolonged dysentery which had virtually sapped the emperor of his legendary strength. This, over the last four days, had somehow aggravated into strangury, with the monarch's body bloating with retained body fluids.

Hakim Ali clearly remembered the day when he had treated the emperor with the accursed medicine to quell the dysentery, and its fatal side effects:

'What good are your potions and medicines, Hakim Ali, if you cannot even cure your emperor of common dysentery, which any hakim worth two dams can also cure?'

Hakim Ali busied himself with preparing a fresh pot of mint and bel leaf potion mixed with jaggery and cardamom. 'I am trying my best, Your Majesty,' he replied quietly.

'Your best is not good enough, you old fool! You have been sitting on your pompous behind these past many years and just living off my largesse, you ungrateful wretch! You could have cured me right at the beginning, but you waited for eight days without giving me a single drop of medicine. You want me to die. You are also a conspirator in this nest of vipers around me. I will give you lessons in treachery!'

Infuriated beyond reason, Akbar snatched an arrow from his quiver, which hung near his head, and rushed at Hakim Gillani, hitting him several times across his arms and chest with the shaft of the arrow.

Hurt to the core, the veteran hakim picked up a basin full of water. As the water slushed inside the basin, Hakim Gillani picked up the small silver vessel in which the astringent was kept. He poured the astringent into the basin, and immediately the water stopped rippling.

'See!' cried Hakim Gillani, 'my science is not at fault. It is your constitution which fails you, Majesty.'

'Shut up, fool!' roared Akbar. He put the basin to his lips and drained its contents.

In a few hours, acute strangury had set in.

Hakim Ali, in desperation, had called for the services of Ayurvedic practitioners Mahadeo, Bhima, and Narayan to try their potions for relief. He had watched in silent alliance as liniments of *till* oil, rue, chamomile, white lilies, and dead scorpions had been rubbed into the area just above the emperor's groin. He had watched in dismay as bed bugs were introduced through the urethral opening to irritate and activate the bladder functions. On the advice of an *Aghori*, fruits bitten by venomous snakes and furious cobras had been fed to the ailing monarch. Hakim Sajeebo had made tablets out of the ashed genitals of ferrets mixed with tenfold sugar. The only recognizable result of such medications was a further deterioration in the emperor's condition.

The palace hung heavy with a sense of foreboding and impending doom. The royal attendants whispered in the corridors, wondering at the mysterious silence of the roosting pigeons, mynahs, and sparrows in the fort walls and crevices. Normally, they would set up a raucous chatter as they settled in for the night.

Mansur Khan, the emperor's personal valet, was walking around with a stick to chase away the two crows which were time and again squawking outside the *khwabgah* windows.

It was six hours past sunset when Shahzade Salim entered the fort with a large contingent of nobles loyal to him. Prince Salim smiled inwardly as he found the bows deeper, and salutations more energetic than on his previous visits. Just behind him rode the Sayyeds of Barha with their clansmen, and Rukn Uddin Rohilla with his large body of followers. In deference to the emperor's critical condition, the fanfare from the *naubatkhana* was short and low.

Moving rapidly from the forecourt into the Akbari Mahal, the prince quickly ascended the steps to be met by Ehteram Beg, who had taken it upon himself to spend the maximum of his hours outside the emperor's chamber. With a deep bow, he was escorted to the marbled threshold where several of the court grandees stood.

The chief eunuch, Saeed Alam, held the silver doors open, as Prince Salim entered and saw his father lying propped up on bolsters, eyes closed. Around the bed stood his closest friends and nobles in silent farewell. His foster brother, Khan e Azam Mirza Aziz Koka's lips were moving in fervent prayers, as the emperor's friend and mate of innumerable hunts, Sadr Jahan Khan was wiping streams of tears from his aged, weathered face.

Prince Khurram, eyes red from weeping and fatigue, sat on Akbar's left with his hand on the emperor's arm, and frequently passed his hand over the emperor's chest, as if coaxing the heart to sustain.

Hakim Ali Gillani had aged considerably over the last fifteen days. His fair, aristocratic face with its long silvery beard and sparkling eyes had shrivelled, and a veil of melancholy hung over him. In almost sixty years of service in the emperor's reign, he had vanquished battle wounds, festers, suspected poisoning, and epileptic fits. But, even in his vast repertoire of medicinal skills, he had no cure for an emperor who eagerly courted Death with poisoned sweets.

He knew that in the regime to come, and in the whispered corridors of the realm, in pages of history and in discussions amongst his peers, his perceived incompetence would be reviled time and again. Strangury, in poison, now had a very powerful ally, and it worked with insidious hostility to hasten the monarch's end.

Prince Salim, eyes red with unshed tears, came forward and stooped to touch the emperor's feet with his forehead.

Akbar, sensing the presence of *Shehzade*, opened his eyes. A small smile curled the tips of his moustache as he gazed affectionately at his only surviving son and heir. Prince Salim knelt by his father's side and kissed his hand as tears ran down his cheeks. There was an ocean of unclaimed affection and love in Akbar's eyes as he spent his last moments in the clasp of the son whom he had loved and cherished like none other.

Prince Salim, small sobs affecting his efforts to speak, remained kneeling with his lips on the emperor's hand. His tears, warm with the spirit of remorse and a son's final farewell, washed the sins of his inglorious acts.

Khurram, drawn by the ancient binds of the Timurids, came and stood behind Prince Salim, gently putting his hand on his father's shoulder. For one brief moment in history, three generations of Mughal emperors were conjoined in mutual harmony.

The attending nobles captured this scene in their eyes forever, as Hakim Ali Gillani, in his flawless Persian and momentarily imbued with the spirit of Sheikh Abu'l Fazl Allami, exclaimed 'The sins of all times, when touched by the emperor, flee to the farthest climes, for such is the majesty of His Majesty!'

'*Ameen*,' whispered the grandees.

With an effort, Akbar gestured to Mirza Aziz Koka to bring his imperial turban and place it on Prince Salim's head. As he settled the turban, Akbar gestured for Salim to girdle the imperial sword *Fath Ul Mulk* around his waist.

Prince Salim knelt again to kiss the emperor's ring, and the grandees thus assembled, performed the *kornish* for the new sovereign.

Tranquillity settling on his face, Akbar turned towards his loyal friends of six decades, and smiled a last farewell. Slowly, his eyes closed for the last time, carrying a picture of the grieving Prince Khurram.

The two crows that had waited patiently since early evening flew off their perch from near the *khwabgah*'s window into the stillness of the night beyond.

The sizzling arrow, sent by an exhausted Saeed Alam, failed to discern between the blackness of the night and the crows, and fell harmlessly into the river weeds.

It was a few minutes to midnight on the night of the twenty-fifth of October, 1605.

*

The twenty-sixth of October, 1605 was the Hindu festival of Deepawali, and it dawned with the lamentations of a sorrowing empire.

A Sufi mystic counting beads in the deserted mosque of Fatehpur Sikri cast a solemn glance towards Agra Fort, and whispered, 'Never again for the next five hundred years will Hindustan be illumined with the radiance of a mighty emperor.'

*

Emperor Akbar, ever the gracious host and, as the reigning monarch of Bihishtabad, invited posterity to come and share the joys of eternal bliss.

On the small, red stone arch directly in front of his tomb's entrance, his invitation was engraved for generations to come:

'These are the Gardens of Eden. Enter them, to live forever!'

*

(CHAPTER 27)

MAZAH-E-TARIKH

(History is but a Mockery)

The Royal Chambers

Akbari Mahal, Agra Fort

26th October, 1605

5:10 p.m.

Prince Khurram stood silently as *Shehzade* Salim walked slowly into the suite of rooms which until a few hours ago had served as the emperor's bedchamber. There was a strange stillness in the fort today as if its very own life had ebbed. The gold-embroidered curtains of rich silk and polished cotton, the gleaming chandeliers, the chests and assorted furniture of silver and gold, the weapons of shining steel with rubies and emeralds in the hilts and scabbards, the gold inlaid frescoes on the walls and ceilings had all lost their lustre and remained in silent repose.

Prince Salim wearily sat on a silver chair in his father's chamber. His time with the royal ladies in the harem had not been easy. Nothing again would ever be easy, he thought, as he looked at the now empty bed of gigantic proportions. It had always seemed normal when Akbar reclined on it, but today it seemed huge in its emptiness. Prince Salim wiped an errant tear as he thought of the colossal personality of his father, who stood only slightly short of seventeen hands, but could fill up an entire war tent with his persona.

In a few minutes it would be time for him to ride back to his own palace, and attend to pressing matters which required his immediate attention. He glanced at Prince Khurram standing silently in the shadows, and beckoned him. Wrapping his arms around his heartbroken son, he said, 'You did well to serve the emperor until his last breath, Khurram. Your mother Taj Bibi and I, as well as your

grandmother, Mariam Uz Zamani, are very proud of you, child.'

'I loved him, Your Majesty. He was my Shah Baba.'

'And he loved you the most, Khurram.' There was a catch in Prince Salim's voice.

Khurram silently proffered a rolled parchment.

Salim looked at him enquiringly. 'What is this, child?'

'Shah Baba asked me to give it to you after his burial at Bihishtabad.'

There was concern in Salim's eyes as he asked, 'When was this given to you, Khurram?'

'Two nights ago, Majesty. He sent everybody out, including Hakim Ali Gillani, and made me write it in Turqi. He also said that this letter must remain within the three of us.' Khurram's voice was heavy with grief.

'Thank you, my son. Now, you must retire and take some rest. You must be very tired.'

Khurram bowed and withdrew.

Prince Salim spread the first page of the parchment on the gold inlaid table, as an attendant lit another lamp and swiftly withdrew.

'My dearest Sheikhu,

I know this must have been a tiring day for you, having made the burial arrangements and walking with my bier to Bihishtabad. At least this is what I presume!

I once heard you complaining to Begume-khas-Mallikaye Begum about Khurram's dislike for our ancestral language Turqi, hence, I have "commanded" Prince Khurram to write in the language of our ancestors. Before I leave on my long journey, I have tried to remove this small measure of discontent also between you and Khurram. Do look after Khurram, Sheikhu, as he is a lovable, affectionate child and worships us. In his moments of interplay with the court nobles, I have, at times, found his haughty demeanour intimidating, but then that is his legacy as a Timurid prince!

I carry many unkind cuts as I embark on this honorific journey, borne on the shoulders of some of the strongest and most faithful generals in Hindustan, but I have tried to mitigate the pain and sufferance of my own soul. After my demise, I do not wish for you to see me as a cruel, war-loving emperor or as an insensitive, power hungry father unwilling to relinquish his throne.

Sheikhu, when you poisoned me fourteen years ago, it was imprudent of you. You were hasty, you were unprepared, and you did not enjoy the support of the nobles as you do now. Twenty-one years is not an age to dream of an empire!

I, on the other hand, was in the prime of my life and health, glorious after my conquests of Rajputana, Kashmere, Sindh-Balochistan and Odisha, with the full support of my Grandees and the glitter of a golden road ahead of me.

You did choose the wrong time, then!

It was only after the Barahsingha *gored me in my left testicle, four years after Khurram's birth, that my health started deteriorating. The ministrations of Hakim Ali and Sheikh Abu'l Fazl did provide me intermittent relief, but did not cure the infection completely.*

Similarly, of Salima Sultana Begum, I have never said anything but kind words. But, what is there to lose now, except the veil of chicanery and deceit.

I was always aware of her hatred for me, so well concealed but burning inside her. She held me responsible for the murder of Bairam Khan and making her a widow at the young age of twenty-one. Though I married her and gave the full protection and love of my imperial persona, she simmered in the embers of a deed done many decades ago. I suffered the anxiety of spending my nights in the arms of a woman with revenge and treachery on her mind, for close to four decades. I smiled, and I made small talk, I played with the shadows and I played with Death every time I ventured into the royal seraglio.

I was aware of your plot to poison me this time, with the active connivance of your stepmother, Salima. I ate the poisoned pethas *like a hungry beggar – for now I was begging for release from my regal bondage.*

My body and mind, even my will to live, could not suffer the multiple attacks of a perfidious son coveting the throne, and a wife nurturing a pathological hatred for one who had decorated her life with the love and majesty of a mighty empire.

This time your timing was right!

Much of history and its bizarre accoutrements will unfold upon you as the years will go by. But, remember this, my son, I have only wished you well in my life.

History, tainted by the half sought knowledge of chroniclers or travellers, will remember me as the cruel emperor who had Anarkali walled in, and a princely romance buried. But, know this, son, cruelty was not my speciality. I always nurtured love, never buried it.

Believe what you may... Only time will tell!

The hourglass of my life now runneth low... Take care of your sisters, and mothers. Let them feel the protective umbrella of a mighty emperor once again. Treat them well who have served us well – let their woes become your own. Seek the guidance of your elders – some of them had marched and fought with my grandfather, Emperor Babur. Let your hand be so loving and forgiving that they never pine for our ancestral lands left behind.

The candle is burning out; so is the wick of my life.

Goodbye, my son! I leave sans pain!

Allah Hafiz!

*

BHAIRON KA STHAN, ICHHRA, LAHORE.
IN EXISTENCE. THE STORY RESTS HERE.

(CHAPTER 28)

EKHTITAM-E-WAQYA

Epilogue – The Story Rests Here

Allahabad

30th November, 2014

11:32 p.m.

I close the folder holding the translated pages of the black-covered manuscript and wait for my eyes to clear of the accumulated tears.

I can feel the pain and remorse of the grieving Prince Salim at his heinous attempts to poison his own father – one successful. I sit with him in the darkened chambers of the deceased emperor and relive the asphyxiating agony of a dying emperor being poisoned by his own wife and son. I can smell the presence of Akbar, carrying the essence of musk, astringents, and herbal potions, as he lies waiting for Death to come and liberate him.

It is a thick manuscript and just the first section has been translated and returned. There are several more sections ready for translation.

I flick back to the last page which carries the scan of a sketch, and study the lines carefully. The walled precincts enclose a tall conical temple, constructed on an octagonal platform with four or five broad steps leading up to it. There is a long barracks-like structure with a low roof, which must have been the *langar khana*, as it carries a broad veranda across its breadth. To the right and back are a cluster of small dwellings and an old well, which must have been the priest Ramadeen's dwelling.

I search for the trees under which Chooza Mastan must have sat and can espy a few gnarled trunks in the extreme left corner of the sketch. And, oh yes, there is a small pile of firewood ready to be kindled. Hazrat Chooza Mastan may dance any moment!

I look at the translator's scrawled text below the Persian script. It reads '*Bhairon ka Sthan*, Ichhra, 1 kos west of Walled City, Lahore.'

And the next line reads 'The story rests here.'

I mull over the ramifications, and wonder what secrets are hidden in the old walls of the Hindu temple.

Will they ever talk?

I need to go to Lahore… The words of Shakespeare come unbidden:

There is a tide in the affairs of men, which, taken at the flood, leads on to fortune; Omitted, all the voyage of their life, is bound in shallows and in miseries.

I must go.

History calls. The walls shall speak.

To be continued..............

*

HISTORICAL NOTES

Chapter 00 : PROLOGUE

Chunar Fort has been in existence over the last two thousand years or more, changing shape and form, imbibing history and hiding many secrets and lores within its underground chambers and silent walls.

As per chronicled history, the fort has passed through seventeen rulers- 3 Hindu, 2 British and 12 Mughals. The British Indian Invalid Battalion *was* stationed there as part of its light duties.

There is a British cemetery on the left, at the base of the fort approach road. It is a protected site of The Archaelogical Survey of India, and the blue board does tell you so. British as well as Mughal soldiers are buried there.

There ***is*** a village of Ahraura about 3 Kos from Chunar Fort.

The fort holds an enormous secret in its belly, which shall be unfolded in Volume 4.

*

Chapter 01 : Birth Of A Million Splendid Suns

The birth of Prince Khurram at Shahi Qila, Lahore, was a matter of much rejoicing for Emperor Akbar. Begum Ruqaiah Sultana did have a Hindu astrologer named Gobinda, whom she trusted implicitly.

Akbar did name the infant prince as 'Khurram' and he was the ' Millennial Child Of Munificence' as he *was* born exactly 1000 years from the birth of Islam, which is recorded as the date on which Prophet Muhammed, Peace Be Upon Him, received his calling as the 'Holy Prophet' and moved from Mecca to Medina with his followers. The Muslim calendar, *Hijra,* commences from the year 622 AD *Julian* and after conversion to the Gregorian Calendar in 1582-83, the 'Millennial Year' is 1592 (1000 AH).

The horoscope of Prince Khurram was cast by Pundit Gobinda and a copy of it remains in the personal collection of astrologer Debi Prasad at Bikaner, and is now probably in the Rajasthan State Archives at Bikaner.

Fatima Banu Begum was the first child of Emperor Akbar born from Begum Ruqaiah Sultana in 1561. She died just seven months later. After her, twin sons Hassan and Hussain, were born to Begum Ruqaiah and Akbar, and died within a month.

Old mughal chronicles do list the fact that after the death of his first three children, Agra Fort was considered haunted by their spirits and several unexplained 'ghostly' encounters and paranormal activities were reported, especially in the royal harem. Eventually, Akbar decided to shift his capital to Fatehpur Sikri.

The imperial harem of the Mughals had more than 3000 inmates, including royal queens, concubines, attendants, slave girls and entertainers. The *Padshah* could bed anyone if his heart so desired. Fatal killings of male offsprings through refined methods of poisoning to the more brutal forms of incapacitation and 'flinging' from the fort walls, were regular features.

*

Chapter 02 - *WE*

It is a matter of historical record that the Mughals, especially from the period beginning with Akbar's reign, did not refer to themselves in the singular 'I' but always resorted to the plural 'We'! In their psychological makeup, they transcended the singular entity and seemed to encompass their Realm... Such was the majesty of their claim on the minds of their subjects!

Prince Aurangzeb had the fairest complexion amongst the Mughals and was referred to as 'The White Serpent' by a disaffected father, after a wandering *faqir* had warned Prince Khurram Shahjahan that his third son, Aurangzeb, would bring about the ruin of the Mughal dynasty. It is evidenced in the handwritten diary of Princess Jahanara : Diary of a Mughal Princess - Jahanara Begum - Daughter of Emperor Shahjahan.

A published copy of this is available in the personal library of the author.

Chapter 03 - The Warrant Of Exile :

The mysterious and tragic tryst of Prince Salim and Anarkali is not a figment of imagination, conjured up by some idle minds and gossiping travelers of the sixteenth/seventeenth century, but retains some threads of historical content. Quite plausible, in fact.

Stories have ranged from Anarkali being Akbar's favourite dancer to being the mother of Prince Daniyal ; from being a Kashmiri slave girl to being a Persian courtesan ; from being Prince Salim's tangled lover in exile to being a tragic lover enwalled in an ancient Lahore wall.

None could be farther or closer to the truth .

The undisputed fact is that Anarkali was very much a part of Prince Salim's sojourn at Lahore, and her tomb is very much a part of Lahore history. Till recently, it was being used as a Records Office of the Panjab Government in Pakistan.

She was indisputably beautiful, too.

The court historians, in compliance of '*Shahi Firmans*' and royal expediency, throttled this story of unrepentant love and buried her voice for ever.

Her exile is undeniably possible. So is her enwalling. So is her survival.

*

Chapter 04 - The Prayers for Revenge :

Kalanaur is located about twenty eight *kos* from Lahore.

There ***is*** a Three Domed Mosque there, which still survives. On Emperor Akbar's coronation in 1556 at kalanaur, the imperial *khutba* was read in this very mosque for the first time.

Akbari Takht, the square raised platform for Akbar's rushed coronation, still survives at Kalanaur, a short distance from the Three Domed Mosque.

There is an Anarkali Bazaar at Kalanaur, which survives till this day.

*

Chapter 05 - The Rivers of Molten Gold :

It is recorded in history, albeit as a one liner, that there was a massive fire in the Shahi Qila at Lahore in March 1597, during the *Nav roz* preparations.

The worst affected were the royal palaces and the *Toshakhana,* which sustained enormous damage. The silver and gold vessels and ornamentations on the walls, ceilings and fixtures were in such huge quantities and so severely burnt, that they flowed in small rivulets of gold and silver.

The ordinary citizens did get an opportunity to scrape the streets of gold !

And, the hindu temple of Lord Bhairava, Bhairon Ka Sthan at Ichhra near Lahore, is not an imaginary structure built out of the author's deep devotion to Lord Bhairava, but still stands 'intact' in the busy markets of Ichhra, which is now a suburb of the sprawling city of Lahore.

*

Chapter 06 – This Is Your Home, Birbal :

Akbar did proceed from Lahore to Kashmere just four days after the devastating fire at Shahi Qila. His royal court remained at Kashmere for seven months, to return in November 1597.

Though Prince Salim accompanied the Emperor to Kashmere, the royal harem was left behind at Lahore.

In Kashmere, Akbar spent a major part of his time in the pursuit of hunts and other leisure activities.

Yakub Shah Chak, the son of defeated Sultan of Kashmere did submit himself to Akbar.

Raja Birbal *was* killed by the Yusufzai's in the Swat valley, and the Shah Chak's were primarily responsible for ambushing the Mughal troops in Burliyas Pass, leading to Raja Birbal's slaying.

The teenaged sons of Raja Birbal, Lala and Hiram Rai, never could perform the last rites of their father, as his body was never found.

The *Qamargah* was the preferred type of hunt for the Mughals.

Haji Jamal Baluch *was* the Best Huntsman Of The Realm.

The gnarled *neem* tree by the side of Kashmeri Darwaza which leant to brush the royals goodbye on their Kashmere journey, still stands, and still leans to the right !

*

Chapter 07 – The Tunnels Of Tryst :

The possibility of such trysts happening is very much alive, as Morchi Darwaza was linked to the Shahi Qila by a tunnel. The *Laal Haveli and Laal Khoo* still exist close to the Morchi Darwaza, as does *Mohalla Shia and Mohalla Teer Garran.*

Morchi Darwaza, one of the ancient thirteen gates of Lahore, still stands in testimony to all that might have happened as Prince Salim scoured the tunnels for his romantic trysts with Anarkali. The vast sections of rooms, steps and recessed alcoves are now encroached by petty sellers of bangles and plastic toys. It is now a major bazaar for dry fruits, kites and fireworks.

Fireworks ? Indeed !

Present day Lahore is a maze of underground tunnels in the ancient Walled City, and for this reason, it is also known as *'Androoni Sheher'.* There are several tunnels running from the Shahi Qila, including one from near the royal bath.

*

Chapter 08 – The Prince And His Shadow :

Emperor Akbar permitted the first ever Church to be built in Lahore as a special favour to the Jesuit priests. Over the centuries it has been destroyed and rebuilt many times.

The *Maidan Diwan e Aam (Garden Of Public Audience)* inside the Shahi Qila is a humongous forecourt measuring almost three and a half lacs square feet (730 sq ft *460 sq ft). Special '*durbars*' were held there.

Mirza Kamran's Baradari on the west bank of Ravi does exist, and the royal pavilion still survives with lush gardens flowing in to the river.

*

Chapter 09 – The Royal Interlude :

Raja Mirza Man Singh was the Governor for Suba of Bengal, with his capital at Akbarnagar. The Hadeefa Mosque *was* built by him along with several other buildings.

Popular History and common perception do allude to Akbar's directives for the extermination of Anarkali *urf* Nadira.

*

Chapter 10 – Death, Come Not Near :

The village of Gulyana is more than 900 years old, and is the largest village/council in the District of Gujar Khan, near Rawalpindi. It was an important market during mughal period.

Anarkali is believed buried in an ancient wall over which Emperor Jahangir (Prince Salim) built a mausoleum during his visit to Lahore in 1608. It now serves as the official Archives of the Panjab Civil Secretariat.

*

Chapter 11 – The Silent Voice of God :

Prince Murad died just a few hours before the arrival of Sheikh Abu'l Fazl Ibn Mubarak at the Royal Shikargah in Dihari, as a result of acute alcoholism. He is buried at Humayun's mausoleum complex in New Delhi.

Samand Manik and Chitt Ranjan were decorated cheetahs of Akbar, and were entitled to all the ranks and privileges mentioned. Emperor Akbar had more than 1000 hunting cheetahs .

Similarly, *Mahuwa* was a decorated hound in the imperial kennels, and *Fenni, Kallua and Bachawa* were Akbar's favourite dogs.

Akbar did have Debi Brahmin and Sufi Taj Uddin hauled up outside the fort walls, suspended in mid air outside his bed chamber's window, nestled on a bed of blankets for night long discussions. The reason for such trapeze acts are not clear. Maybe the saints declined to enter the harem precincts. Or, it could be just one of Akbar's singular peculiarities.

In ancient scrolls, the name of Mukund Brahmachari comes up as a Hindu ascetic who took rebirth as the emperor Akbar. In the ancient Indian text of *Bhavishya Maha Purana,* this story is encapsulated in the section *'Akbar Badshah Varnan'* spread over 97 verses in Sanskrit.

*

Chapter 12 - Coins In The Well :

Prince Khurram (later Emperor Shahjahan) survived an attack of small pox at the age of seven while travelling to Deccan on a war campaign. He carried the shallow pock marks all through his life. The royal historians and royal artists never depicted this for obvious reasons.

Turqi, the ancestral language of the Mughals was never a favourite of Prince Khurram, and Ruqaiah Begum made special efforts to converse with him in pure Turqi only. He was of keen intellect and excelled in martial activities.

The huge well between the dimunitive Akbari mosque and the splendid *Diwan e Aam* does have a tunnel leading out of Agra Fort. Most of the ancient and medieval forts had tunnels to be used as a means of escape in case of siege or defeat, and were large enough to accommodate horse riders.

*

Chapter 13 – The Seeds Of Rebellion :

The July of 1600 did see a rebellious Prince Salim marching on to Agra as Emperor Akbar was busy in the Malwa campaign. It is a fact that he was denied entry into the fort, and Mir Qulich Khan, the Garrison Commander and trusted general of Akbar met him outside the city limits and diplomatically ensured Salim's withdrawal towards Illahabas.

It is also a fact that Salim, scared and ashamed of meeting his grandmother, Dowager Empress Hamida Banu Begum, escaped by boat towards Illahabas with a few trusted generals and sycophants. His army followed over land.

*

Chapter 14 – The Tower Of Skulls :

The villagers of Khanwa do report the sounds of battle and cries of wounded dying men, on certain nights. Residents of Fatehpur Sikri also endorse this.

The Battle of Khanwa did take place as depicted, and brave Rajputs did stuff themselves into the mouths of cannons to stem their destructive prowess.

*

Chapter 15 – The Tears Will Not Stop :

The Ashoka Pillar at Illahabas (Allahabad) Fort does stand till this day, and the script in Brahmi carries the same six edicts as in other pillars. Further, it has the *schism edict* of Emperor Ashoka for the senior officials (*mahamatras*) at Kaushambi, directing them to stay united and eschew dissension.

The Pillar also records the charitable deeds of his Queen, Karuvaki.

A later inscription of 4th century CE is ascribed to Emperor Samudragupta, in the Gupta script which followed the Brahmi script.

Jahangir, the fourth Mughal Emperor, while occupying the fort during his rebellion and as the Subedar, had the names of his ancestors deliberately inscribed.

The visit of Raja Birbal of 1575 is also recorded there.

Prince Salim did proceed as far as Etawah in late February / early March of 1602 at the head of a seventy thousand strong army to challenge the emperor. A stern warning from Akbar orchestrated with war preparations, sent prince Salim scurrying back to Allahabad .

*

Chapter 16 – The Persian Curse :

Hastening back to the royal court at Agra from the Deccan campaign on Akbar's orders, Sheikh Abu'l Fazl did stop at Sironj with Gopal Das Nakta. His chief officer, Asad Beg was actually ordered back to Burhanpur by the Sheikh himself, as he proceeded onwards with a very light escort.

On 11th August,1602, Sheikh Abu'l Fazl was warned by a roving mendicant of impending death. He chose to ignore the warning.

The sequence of his ambush and slaying closely follows the historical chain.

Emperor Akbar was driven to extreme anguish at the news of the Sheikh's treacherous murder and did not attend the court for several days. He did order the extermination of the murderous Bir Singh Bundela's clan.

*

Chapter 17 – The Satanic Court :

Prince Salim during his rebel years at Illahabas Fort changed the name to Allahabad, which continues till date.

Prince Daniyal did die in a hunting lodge near Burhanpur of acute alcoholism, and Murshid Quli Khan was charged and punished for supplying hard liquor concealed in the rusty barrel of a flint gun, which hastened the prince's end.

*

Chapter 18 – The Scent Of Apples :

Emperor Shahjahan (Prince Khurram) was supposed to carry the scent of apples on his hands, the result of a *faqir's* blessings. As per historical notes, this scent left him on the day of his death.

Princess Jahanara, who stayed with the imprisoned Shahjahan till his death, has also recorded this fact in her personal diary, ' *The Life Of A Mogul Princess – Jahanara Begum – Daughter of Shahjahan'.* I have a copy of this in my personal collection on the Mughals.

*

Chapter 19 – Shallow Flows The Jumna :

Emperor Akbar did mount a war campaign against the rebellious Prince Salim in August 1604, but had to turn back due to recurrent news of Mariam Makani's critical condition.

The famous temple of a recumbent Lord Hanuman is located in the lee of the great fort of Akbar, near Sangam, Allahabad, and is konown as ' Bade Hanumanjee Ka Mandir.' Every year, the river Ganges comes up to the temple precincts, and after washing Lord Hanuman's feet, recedes to its former point. This phenomenon is avidly recorded by all the newspapers.

Several attempts have been made in the past by Mughals and the British (including the use of cranes) to raise the statue of Hanumanjee to an upright position, but none have succeeded.

*

Chapter 20 – Bayaan-i-Asad Beg :

The chief officer of the slain Sheikh Abu'l Fazl Allami, Asad Beg, was entrusted by Emperor Akbar to investigate the true course of events leading to Bir Singh Bundela's murderous assault on the *Vizier.*

The report is chronicled as *Wakiat-i-Asad Beg* in Mughal records.

*

Chapter 21 – The Shattered Pillar :

The Dowager Empress, Mariam Makani – Hamida Bano Begum passed away in the early hours of 10th September, 1604.

Emperor Akbar, along with one thousand four hundred nobles had their heads shorn of hair, as a mark of respect to the departed soul.

*

Chapter 22 – Thou Art A Coward :

Prince Salim did submit unconditionally to Akbar in November, 1604. The emperor did raise his hand on Salim for his revolt and transgressions of the past.

On the emperor's orders, Prince Salim was confined to a chamber for ten days, under Raja Sallavihan, and the two attendants, Arjun and Rup Khwass.

*

Chapter 23 - The Behemoth's Prophesy :

The elephant fight is a historical fact.

The war tuskers, *Giranbar, Apurva and Ranthamban* would have moved in the manner depicted.

The unsavoury exchange between Prince Salim and his ambitious son, Khusrau, did happen in the emperor's presence.

Immediately after this prophetic fight, Akbar slid into a state of health decline, from which he was never to recover. The end was just thirty five days away.

*

Chapter 24 - Rule, Chugatai's :

There was a conspiracy to arrest Prince Salim, and Zia Ul Mulk Qazwini did warn him as he was about to disembark, thus shaping Mughal history as we know it.

There was a conference of the higher nobles regarding succession, and the Sayyids of Barha prevailed in cementing Prince Salim's claim as the rightful successor.

The *Shiar-o-ture-yi-Chugatai* reigned supreme.

*

Chapter 25 - The Poisoned Realm :

Emperor Akbar was suspected of being poisoned in 1591.

The strange case of Akbar's last illness also indicates some form of poisoning, but court historians in the new dispensation under prince Salim, crowned Jahangir, obfuscated the facts. Obviously so.

Raja Man Singh did flee from Agra with prince Khusrau. His destination was Bengal, but he was cajoled back into Emperor

Jahangir's court by his younger brother, Madho Singh, who assured him of a royal pardon offered by Emperor Jahangir.

Emperor Akbar's most loyal general and *Farzand*, Mirza Raja Man Singh was not present at his side when he passed away.

*

Chapter 26 – The Eternal Eden :

The personal ewer bearer of *Jannat Ashiyani* Emperor Humayun, Jauhar Khan, has mentioned the full details of Akbar's birth on 23rd November, 1542, and his initial naming as *Badruddin Mohammed Akbar.* The later promulgation to record the birth on 15th October, 1542, and change of name to *Jalauddin Mohammed Akbar* is also mentioned.

The relevant records in '*The Tezkereh Al Vakiat'* by Jauhar , is available in my personal collection on the Mughals.

The acrimonious outbursts of an ailing emperor against his old friend and most trusted physician, Hakim Ali Gillani is a matter of hidden mughal records.

Emperor Akbar passed away peacefully having ensured a peaceful transition by gesturing his final directives to place the imperial turban and to gird the imperial sword *Fath Ul Mulk* around Prince Salim's waist.

Prince Khurram, later Emperor Shahjahan, was with his beloved ' Shah Baba' till the last breath.

He was buried at Bihishtabad, the present day Sikandra.

The Emperor was dead !

Long live the Emperor !

*

Chapter 27 – History Is But A Mockery :

Emperor Akbar had always suspected prince Salim of trying to poison him. As early as 1591, Akbar had harboured secret suspicions about prince Salim's unreasonable haste to ascend the throne, using means foul or fair !

Salim's revolt and his act of getting Sheikh Abu'l Fazl assassinated was further evidence of his haste and avarice.

With both his favoured sons Murad and Daniyal dead, due to acute alcoholism, Emperor Akbar really had no choice but to embrace his recalcitrant son, Prince Salim. For, the empire must live !

Salima Sultana Begum, though often depicted as Akbar's favourite wife, could have nurtured a secret hatred against Akbar for making her a very young widow, when he had her husband, Bairam Khan murdered.

Facts truly are stranger than fiction !

*

Chapter 28 – Epilogue – The story rests here:

The momentous reign of Mohammed Jalaluddin Mohammed Akbar had come to an end, and the New Order under Emperor Nuruddin Jahangir was about to commence. Prince Khurram would be initiated into his early brush with the administration of an empire, suffused with violent wars, clandestine love and murderous intrigue.

And, the spirit of Anarkali would haunt the Realm forever....

*

GLOSSARY

1. Aalim – Learned Moslem priests
2. Aameen – Amen
3. Aasi – Criminal
4. Aghori – Hindu ascetic
5. Ahadis – Royal guards
6. Alampanah – Refuge of the Universe
7. Allahu Akbar – Allah is great!
8. Androoni Sheher – Walled City of Lahore
9. Argajah – Fragrance favoured by Mughals
10. Arrack – Opiate
11. Arsh Ashiyani – Residing in Heaven
12. Asir Namaaz – Late afternoon namaaz

13. Atagha – Guardian

14. Ba-adab Ba – Mulaizah, Hoshiar – the call to be respectful

15. Bagicha – Garden

16. Bandooqchis – Matchlock men

17. Baradari – Building open on all sides

18. Barangars – Right wing of army

19. Barasingha – twelve horned deer

20. Barchis – Spears

21. Behroopiya – Indian folk artists who impersonate in different forms

22. Bewafai – Treachery

23. Bishtis – Water bearers

24. Burj – Tower

25. Chaar Taslim – Form of obeisance

26. Charbagh – Four square gardens

27. Charpoy – String bed

28. Cheetah – Indian leopard

29. Chogah – Male outer wear, loosely worn

30. Dadu- endearment term for elders

31. Daftarkhana – Office

32. Dak – Post

33. Dak Chowki – Mail/post/also for relay horses

34. Dams – Monetary units (forty dams made one rupee)

35. Darbar – Open Court with King presiding

36. Daroghas – Inspectors
37. Dastarkhwan – Feast
38. Dharma – Religion
39. Diwanb-e-Khas – Hall of Private Audience
40. Diwan e Aam – Hall of Public Audience
41. Diyas – Small earthern lamps
42. Djinns – Ghosts, spirits
43. Emperor Echebar – Emperor Akbar
44. Faateha e Janaza – Funeral prayers
45. Fakir – Moslem ascetic
46. Farman-i-Sabtis – a form of imperial order
47. Farzand – Son
48. Fath Ul Mulk – Humayun's sword: Victor of the Realm
49. Faujdar – Head of a garrison
50. Firangis – Foreigners
51. Firmaan – Imperial request
52. Gurj – Mace
53. Hakim – Physician
54. Hamam – Royal Bath
55. Harkaras – Drum beaters during hunting
56. Hathi Paer – Elephant's Walk (Path in Shahi Qila, Lahore)
57. Haveli – Mansion
58. Hijri – Moslem Year

59. Howdahs – Seat on an elephant's back
60. Hulqa – Inferior elephant
61. Huzoor – Sire
62. Illahi – Year set by Akbar
63. Jahanpanah – Refuge Of The World
64. Janab e Auliya – A form of respectful address
65. Jaranghars – Left wing of army
66. Jharokhas – Protruding balconies
67. Jharshahi – Five coloured flag, also known as 'Panchrangi'
68. Jinsi Muamalaat – Matters of sex
69. Kabristan–graveyard
70. Khadims – Servants, attendants
71. Khalifa – Successor; leader of Caliphate
72. Khamagami – Greetings in rajasthani
73. Khasa cadre – Elite cadre
74. Khidmatgaars – attendants
75. Khutba – the prayers read proclaiming Emperor's rule
76. Khwajasera – Chief eunuch
77. Koh-e-Ilm – Mountain of Knowledge
78. Kornish – Form of obeisance
79. Kos – 3.66 kilometres
80. Kutub Khana – Library
81. Langurs – Indian monkeys

82. Madar – Calotropis Gigantea- shrubs native to India
83. Magreeb Namaz – Evening prayers
84. Mahouts – Elephant drivers
85. Makhdum-ul-Mulk – High priest
86. Malechh – Unclean person
87. Mansabdars – Nobles
88. Markhor Goat – Goat of enormous size; now extinct
89. Masha Allah – Praise to Allah
90. Mastan – Moslem ascetic; steeped in Sufi love
91. Mir Arz – Chief of plaints
92. Mir Bahri – Admiral of the fleet
93. Mir Bakarwal – Head of the kitchen
94. Mir Bakshi – Head of army and war material
95. Mir Kutub – Chief librarian
96. Mir Manzil – Master of road journeys
97. Mir Saman – Chief of imperial furniture and estate
98. Mir Tozak – Chief of protocol
99. Mohurs – Gold coins
100. MuhrUzek – the Royal Seal
101. Muns – 1 Mun = forty kilos
102. Mureed – Disciple
103. Mushrif – Clerk
104. Naggara-i-Shadiyana – Drums of celebrations

105. Naggaras – War drums

106. Nagphani – Prickly pears

107. NaubatKhana – Portal above the main gate for musicians

108. Nilgai – Blue Bull; Indian antelope

109. Nishaan – Imperial letter/Royal order

110. Padshah Ghazi – Emperor

111. Panchrangi – Five coloured

112. Panjari – Sailor

113. Parvanahs – Royal orders

114. Peregrims Cave' – Traveller beware!

115. Pethas – Famous sugary sweets of Agra

116. Phuphi – Paternal aunt; Father's sister

117. Poshtu – Drink made of opium

118. Qaba – Cloak like attire for men

119. Qamargah – Form of hunting

120. Qarawal Baigi – Chief of hunt

121. Qarawals – Skirmishers

122. Qol – Centre of the army

123. Qorchis – Royal attendants normally of Persian origin

124. Qubbedar – Persian conical head wear

125. Rotis – Indian flatbread cooked over fire.

126. Sadr i Sudur – Head of religion

127. Sahiban i Ihtemam – Mace bearers tasked with path clearance

128. Salat-al-Janaza – Funeral prayers

129. Sarpat – Indian wild grass, razor sharp.

130. Sehr – Dawn

131. Serpench – Aigrette

132. Shahajida – Male outer wear

133. ShahiFirmaans – Royal orders

134. ShahiKotwal – Chief of police

135. ShahiQur – Emperor's personal arms bearer

136. Shankh – Conch shell

137. Shama i Kafuri – Lamps almost three yards high and with multiple wicks

138. ShastKhatt – Male outer attire

139. Shehnai – Indian musical instrument, like Oboe

140. Shi' ar-o-ture-yi-Chugatai – Code of Chugatais

141. Shikargah – Hunting lodge

142. Shikaris – Hunters

143. Sowars – Horse riders, cavalry

144. Suba – Province

145. Subedar – Governor of a province (Suba)

146. SultanatMughaliya-Padshah Ghazi, Zillu' Illah, Imam i Adil – Empire of the Mughals, Emperor, Shadow of God, and Chief Justice

147. Syce – Horse attendant

148. Takhliya – Dismiss

149. Tapancha – Reserve elephant

150. Tarahs – Reserves of the troop

151. Taslim – Form of obeisance

152. Tasliq-i-Qar – Guard of honour

153. Tir-Andaz – Archers

154. Topchis – Cannoneers

155. Toshkhana – Treasury

156. Tribeni – Confluence of three rivers: Ganga, Jumna and mythical Saraswati at Allahabad (Illahabas)

157. Tufangchis – Matchlockmen

158. Ulemas – Moslem priests

159. Umeras / Umrahs – Nobles

160. Ustaad – Master, expert

161. Vakil – Senior representative

162. Waqia Navees – writer; recorder of facts

163. Zamindoz – form of obeisance by the upturned palms on the floor

164. Zat – Rank

165. Zenankhana – Harem

166. Zig-i-Sultani – Ephemeris constituted by Olgh Bek

167. Zille' Illahi – Shadow of God

168. Zuhr Namaz – Namaz at noon

BIBLIOGRAPHY DAGGERS OF TREASON

1. The Emperor Akbar – Ferdinand Augustus, Count de Noir
2. The Relics of the Lesser Mughals – P.K. Dutta
3. Ain-i-Akbari – Abu'l Fazl Allami; translated by Blochman
4. History of Jahangir – Beni Prasad
5. The Mughal Throne – Abraham Eraly
6. Nobility under Akbar and Jahangir – Afzal Husain
7. Tabakat-i-Akbari – Nizamuddin Ahmad Bakhshi
8. The Great Mughals and their India – Dirk Colliers
9. The Mughal Empire – J.F. Richards
10. History of Mughal India – Satish Chandra
11. The Central Structure of the Mughal India – Ibn Hasan
12. The Great Mughals – Bamber Gascoigne

13. Muntakhab Ut Tawarikh – Al' Badauni; Vol. 1,2 and 3

14. Jahangir's India – Paelseart

15. Akbar – Rahul Sanskritayan

16. Maathir-Ul-Umara – Vol. 1 and 2 – Nawab Shams Ud Daula Shah Nawaz Khan

17. Mughal Darbar ke Sarkar – in 5 volumes – originally written by Abdur Razzak Khwafi.

18. The History Of Jahangir – Francis Gladwin

19. Tezkereh Al Vakiat – by Jouhar Khan, ewer bearer of Emperor Humayun

20. The Jahangirnama – By Thackston

21. Shahjahanama – Munshi Devi Prasad

22. Muntakhab Al Lubab – Mohammed Hashim Khafi Khan

23. Diary of a Moghul Princess – Jahanara Begum – Daughter of Emperor Shahjahan

The above list is not exhaustive.

COMING SOON

THE JHELUM BETRAYAL

The second book unravels the dark secrets of Jahangir's reign, dominated by the guile of Empress Nurjahan; the rise, fall and resurrection of prince Khurram and the spectre of a disguised Anarkali haunting emperor Jahangir's reign.

This historical fiction brings alive the royals, courtiers, battlefields and the sighing forts as we travel with Khurram Shahjahan 'Bi-daulat', in his quest to regain the royal affection of his father, manipulated and sedated by Empress Nurjahan and the treacherous Court. The Jhelum Betrayal explodes with an uncanny insight into the steaming cauldron of sex, greed, fratricide and opulence of The Great Mughals.